Catherine Ryan Howard's debut novel *Distress Signals* was published by Corvus in 2016 while she was studying English literature at Trinity College Dublin. It went on to be shortlisted for both the Irish Crime Novel of the Year and the CWA John Creasey/New Blood Dagger. Her second novel, *The Liar's Girl*, was published to critical acclaim in 2018 and was a finalist for the Mystery Writers of America Edgar Award for Best Novel 2019. That same year, *Rewind* was shortlisted for the Irish Crime Novel of the Year and was an *Irish Times* bestseller. In 2020, *The Nothing Man* was shortlisted for the Irish Book awards. She is currently based in Dublin.

56
DAYS

56 DAYS

CATHERINE RYAN HOWARD

CORVUS

To Iain Harris,

because I couldn't think of what to get you for your

fortieth and also, just because

First published in Great Britain in 2021 by Corvus, an imprint of
Atlantic Books Ltd.

10 9 8 7 6 5

A CIP catalogue record for this book is available from the British Library.

Hardback ISBN: 978 1 83895 162 7
Trade paperback ISBN: 978 1 83895 163 4
E-book ISBN: 978 1 83895 164 1

Corvus
An imprint of Atlantic Books Ltd
Ormond House
26–27 Boswell Street
London
WC1N 3JZ

www.corvus-books.co.uk

Printed and bound in Great Britain by Clays Ltd, Elcograf S.p.A.

TODAY

It's like one of those viral videos taken inside some swanky apartment complex, where all the slim and fit thirty-something residents are doing star jumps behind the glass railings of their balconies while the world burns. But these ones stand still, only moving to look down or at each other from across the courtyard, or to lift a hand to their mouth or chest. Their faces are pale, their hair askew, their feet bare. Dawn has barely broken; they've just been roused from their sleep. No one wants to film this.

The residents look like they could've all been in school together except for one. Number Four is older than her neighbours by a couple of decades. She owns while the others rent. The patio of her ground-floor apartment has a bistro-style table and chairs surrounded by carefully arranged potted plants; most everyone else's is used to store bikes or not at all. Last Saturday night, she threatened to report Number Seventeen's house party to the Gardaí for breaching restrictions unless it ended *right now*, and when it didn't she stayed true to her word. She is a glamorous woman, usually well dressed and still well preserved, but this morning she is unkempt and barefaced, dressed in a pair of baby-pink cotton pyjama bottoms and a padded winter jacket that swings open as she strides across the courtyard.

She is also the only one who knows the code that silences the fire alarm. It went off five minutes ago – that's what has woken them – and the residents assume they have her to thank for taking care of it.

There has never been a fire here but, in the last few weeks, three fire alarms – four if you count this one. The residents have complained repeatedly to the management company that the system is just *too* sensitive, that it must be reacting to burnt toast and people who smoke cigarettes without cracking a window, but in turn the management blame *them* for triggering it. The noise no longer signals danger but interruption, and when it went off a few minutes ago they all did what they usually do: went outside, on to their balconies and terraces, to see what they could see, to check for flames or smoke, not expecting any and finding none.

But this time there *was* something unexpected, something interesting: two uniformed Gardaí standing in the middle of the courtyard, looking around.

So they stayed out there, watching and wondering.

The woman from number four stands with the Gardaí while remaining the regulation six feet away. She's pointing at one of the ground-floor apartments – the one right in the corner, at one end of the complex's U-shape. They have little patios instead of balconies, marked off with open railings instead of solid glass perimeters. No one is on that patio. Its sliding door is closed. But from some vantage points, the glowing orb of the living-room's ceiling light is visible through the thin grey curtains.

What's going on?

Whose apartment is that?

Nobody knows. The Crossings is a relatively new complex and interactions are mostly limited to pleasantries exchanged at the letterboxes, the bins, the car park. Sheepish smiles during that window on Friday and Saturday evenings when it seems like everyone is going down to the main entrance to meet their food-delivery guy at the same time. The residents are used to living above and below and beside other people's entire lives while pretending to be utterly unaware of them; hearing each other's TVs and smelling each other's cooking but never learning each other's names.

Even in these last few weeks, when they've all been at home all day every day, they've studiously avoided acknowledging each other when they take to the outside spaces – the balconies, the terraces, the shared courtyard – in an effort to maintain some pretence of privacy, to preserve it. The crisis-induced camaraderie they've been watching in unsteady, narrowly framed short videos online – someone calling bingo numbers through a megaphone at a block of flats; a film projected on to the side of a house so a cul-de-sac of homes can have a collective movie-night from their driveways; nightly rituals of hopeful, enthusiastic hand-clapping – never really took hold here. They have kept their distance in more ways than one. No one wants to have to deal with a familiarity hangover when normal life returns, which they are all still under the impression will happen soon. A government announcement is due later today.

One of the guards twists his head around and looks up at them, these nosy neighbours. He pulls his face mask down with a blue-gloved hand, revealing pudgy cheeks at odds with a weedy body. They say that the Gardaí looking young is a sure sign you're getting older, but this one actually *is* young, mid-twenties at the most, with a sheen of sweat glistening beneath his hairline.

'False alarm,' he calls out, waving. 'You can go on back inside.'

As if any of them are standing there waiting to see a fire.

When nobody moves he shouts, 'Go on,' louder and firmer.

One by one, the residents slowly retreat into their apartments because none of them want to be pegged as rubberneckers, even though that's exactly what they are. This is the only interesting thing that has happened here in weeks – if you discount the fire alarms, it's the *only* thing that's happened.

Are they really expected not to look?

Most of them leave their sliding doors open and elect to drink their morning coffees just on the other side, so they can see without being seen. The couples mutter to each other that, really, they have a *right* to know what's going on. They live here, after all. The solo occupants wonder if there's been a burglary or maybe even something worse, like an attack, and if something happened to them now, with things the way they are, how long would it be before anyone noticed, before anyone found them?

This apartment complex is not far from Dublin's city centre. Before all this started it was buttressed by a near-constant soundtrack of engine noise, squealing brakes and car horns coming from the busy road that runs alongside. But in these last few weeks the city has slowed down, emptied out and shut down, in that order, and, occasional false fire alarms aside, the loudest noise lately has been the birdsong.

Now, the sound of approaching sirens feels like a violence.

56 DAYS AGO

'Go ahead,' are the first words he ever says to her.

They are both on the cusp of joining the queue for the self-service checkouts in Tesco. It's Friday lunchtime and her fifth time this week coming in for yet another unimaginative meal deal: a colourless sandwich, a plastic bag of apple slices and a bottle of water, which she's just noticed is the type with the sickly-sweet fruit flavour added. This realisation has stopped her in her tracks, paused by a stack of Easter eggs (Easter? *Already?*) and wondering if she can be bothered to go back and change it when she almost certainly won't drink it anyway.

That's when she looks up and sees him, politely waiting for her to make her move, leaving a space for her to join the queue ahead of him.

He's taller than her by some margin. Looks about the same age. Neither muscular nor soft, but solid. His dark hair is thick and messy, but she has no doubt it took forever to pomade into submission, to perfect. He wears a blue suit with a navy tie and a light blue shirt underneath, but the sleeves of the jacket are creased with strain, the shoulders bunched, and the back of the tie hangs longer than the front. The top button of his shirt is open, the collar slightly askew, the tie pulled off-centre. He looks a little red in the face, his cheeks pink above patchy stubble.

And he's so attractive that she knows instantly the world he lives in is not the same one in which she does, that he can't possibly experience it the same way. A face like that affords a different kind of existence, one in which you arrive into every situation with some degree of pre-approval. But you don't know it, don't realise that you're being ushered into the Priority lane of life every single day.

She wonders what that does to a person.

There's an intensity to him, too, something simmering just beneath the surface. She imagines for him a whole life. He's a man who works hard and plays harder. Who has a circle of friends he calls exclusively by inexplicable nicknames while they sit around a table in the pub necking pints and watching The Match. Who runs purely to run off bad calories. Who has someone somewhere that knows a completely different version of him, someone he is unexpectedly and devotedly tender to, who he only ever looks at with kind eyes.

'It's okay,' she says, waving the bottle of water, starting to move away. 'I've just realised I've got the wrong one.' She turns and heads back towards the fridges, feeling his eyes on her as she walks away.

And the beat of her own heart, pulsing with promise.

———

The second thing he says to her is, 'Nice bag.'

She has just come out of the supermarket, on to the street, and doesn't know who's talking or if they're talking to her.

When she turns towards the voice she sees him standing in the next doorway, looking right at her. The sandwich he's just bought is tucked under his arm, getting squished by the pressure. There's the hint of a grin on his face, tinged with something else she can't readily identify.

She stops. 'My ...?'

'Your bag,' he says, pointing.

He means the little canvas tote she's put her purchases in. He must do because her handbag is across her body and resting on her other hip, the one he can't see from where he's standing.

The tote is blue and has a Space Shuttle on it, piggybacking on an aeroplane as it flies over the skyscrapers of Manhattan.

She lifts and looks at it, then back at him.

'Thanks,' she says. 'It's from the Intrepid. It's a museum in—'

'New York,' he finishes. 'The one on the aircraft carrier, right?' He says this not with smug knowingness but endearing enthusiasm. 'Have you been?'

'Yeah.' She doesn't want to sound like she's too impressed with herself, so she adds, 'Once.'

'Was it good?'

She hesitates, because this is it. This is where she makes her choice.

People think the decisions you make that change the

course of your life are the big ones. Marriage proposals. House moves. Job applications. But she knows it's the little ones, the tiny moments, that really plot the course. Moments like *this*.

Her options:

Say something short and flippant, move on, end this now.

Or say something that prolongs this, stay longer, invite more, open a door.

She keeps a screenshot on her phone of a quote by, supposedly, Abraham Lincoln: *Discipline is choosing between what you want now and what you want the most*. Maybe that's true, but discipline has never been her problem. It's *fear* she struggles with. She thinks *courage* might be choosing between what you want now and what you want the most, because what she wants now is to walk away, to shut this down, to close the doors. To retreat. To stay in the place where she feels safe and secure.

But what she wants the most is to be able to live a full life, even if the expansion comes with pain and risk and fear, even if it means crossing a minefield first.

This one, maybe.

Ciara grips the handles of the tote and imagines her future self standing behind her, pressing her hands into her back, pushing, whispering, *Do it. Go for it. Make this happen.* She ignores the heat rising inside her, her body's alarm. She reminds herself that this isn't a big deal, that this is just a conversation, that men and women do this all day, every day, all over the world—

'Yeah,' she says. 'But not as good as Kennedy Space Center.'

He blinks in surprise.

He straightens up and steps closer.

Moving aside so a woman pushing a double-buggy can get past, she takes a step closer to him, too.

'You know,' he says, 'I've never met someone who can name all five Space Shuttles.'

'And I *still* haven't met someone who knows there are six.'

She bites her lip as every blood cell in her body makes a mad dash for her cheeks. What the hell did she have to go and say *that* for? What was she thinking?

'*Six?*' he says.

She's already ruined it.

So she might as well make *sure* she has.

'There was *Challenger*,' she says to the crack in the pavement by her right foot, 'lost 28 January 1986 during launch. *Columbia*, lost 1 February 2003 during re-entry. *Atlantis*, *Endeavour* and *Discovery* are all on display – *Atlantis* is the one in Kennedy Space Center. But there was also *Enterprise*, the test vehicle. It flew, although never in space. It didn't have a heat shield or engines, but it *was* the first Orbiter. Technically. Which is actually what people mean when they say, "Space Shuttle", usually. They mean the orbiter itself. The rest is just rockets. And *Enterprise* is the one that's at the Intrepid.'

A beat of excruciating silence passes.

She forces herself to lift her head and meet his eye, lips parting to mumble some lie about needing to get back to work, foot lifting in readiness for scurrying away from this absolute disaster, but then he says—

'I was going to go get a coffee. Can I buy you one too?'

There are numerous coffee options on this street and the vast majority of them come served with a side of serious notions. There's the café that roasts its own beans and makes you wait five minutes for a simple filter coffee that only comes in one size served lukewarm. It's right next to the place that has spelled its name wrong and, inexplicably, with a forward slash: KAPH/A. The most popular spot seems to be a little vintage van in the service-station forecourt, the one with a hatch whose chalk-drawn menu lists not coffee blends but levels of depleted wakefulness: Fading, Sleepy, Snoring.

Ciara is relieved when he directs her past all of them and into the soulless outlet of a bland coffee chain instead.

'Is this okay?' he asks as he holds the door open for her.

'This is great.' She steps inside, turning to talk to him over her shoulder. 'I like my coffee served in a bucket at a reasonable price, so ...'

'I've passed the first test, is what you're saying.'

He winks at her and she laughs, hoping it didn't come out sounding like a nervous one, although she *is* nervous.

Because of the implication in the word *first*.

Because *she* has to pass this test too.

Because this is already the weight of one whole foot on the edge of the minefield and she has no idea how wide it is, how long it will take her to get all the way across, how long it will be before she feels safe and comfortable and secure.

In the minute it took to walk here, he has told her his name is Oliver and that he works for a firm of architects who have the top floor of the large office building across the street. He is not an architect, though, but something called an architectural technologist. He explained it by saying that architects design the buildings and then architectural technologists figure out how they're going to actually build them. He tried to dissuade her of the idea that it's any bit as interesting as it sounds, promising that, in reality, it's mostly spreadsheets and emails. When she asked him if it's what he always wanted to do, he said yes, once he'd come to terms with the fact that he was never going to be astronaut.

Then he asked her what she does.

She explained that after *her* astronaut dreams fell by the wayside, she ended up working for a tech company who just happen to have one of their European hubs in a sprawling complex of glittering glass-and-steel office buildings a few minutes' away from where they stand. She held up her bright blue lanyard and he read her name off it and said, 'Nice to meet you, Ciara,' and she said, 'Nice to meet you, too.'

Now, at the counter in the coffee shop, she says she'll have a cappuccino. He orders two of them, both large.

'To go?' he suggests. 'We might snag a seat by the canal.'

'Sounds good to me.'

She tries not to look too pleased that he wants to prolong this, whatever *this* is, into drinking the coffees as well.

She goes to wait at the end of the counter and watches him

pay at the till with a crisp ten-euro note. She sees the barista — a teenager; she can't be more than seventeen or eighteen — steal glances at him whenever she thinks he's looking at something else. She wonders if he's aware of that and, if he is, what it feels like. (Approval or scrutiny?) She traces the lines of his body as suggested by his clothes and wonders what it would feel like to know the skin underneath, *if* she will know it, if this really is the start of something or just an anomaly.

She imagines those arms around her, the strength in them, how it would feel to be held by him.

Then she tries not to.

She doesn't put sugar in her cappuccino, even though she normally does, and she thinks to herself, *If this becomes something, I'll never be able to put sugar in my coffee now.*

The sun has been appearing and disappearing all day; when they go back outside, they're met with mostly blue sky. The canal bank is busy with lunching office workers, but they find a spot on the wall by the service station, near the lock.

They settle down.

He prises the lid off his cappuccino to take a sip. She resists the urge to tell him that this will make it go cold faster but lets him know when he's managed to collect a crescent of foam on his upper lip.

'So,' he says, 'Kennedy Space Center.'

'What about it?'

'Tell me things that will make me very jealous that you've been there.'

She describes the bus tour that takes you around the launch pads, the Vehicle Assembly Building and the famous blue clock that you see counting down to launch on TV. Tells him about the IMAX cinema and the Rocket Garden. The 'ride' where they make you feel like you're on a launching Space Shuttle, how they tilt it straight up so you're lying on your back and then forward a bit too much so you start to slide out of your seat in a clever approximation of zero-G. The Apollo Center where you get to see an actual Saturn V rocket, lying on its side at ceiling-height above the floor. The shuttle *Atlantis*, a spaceship that has actually *been in space*, on magnificent display.

'It's revealed to you,' she says. 'Unexpectedly. A surprise. You're herded into this big, dark room to watch a video about the Shuttle programme and then, at the end, the screen slides up and reveals the Shuttle just ... Just *there*, in all its glory, right in front of you. With the cargo bay doors open and at an angle so it actually looks like it's flying through space. It's amazing. People actually gasped. After I'd walked around it and taken all my pictures and read all the exhibits and stuff, I went back to where I'd come in and I waited for the screen to go up so I could watch *other* people's faces, so I could see their reactions, and it was ...' She sees what looks to her like his bemused expression and panics. 'It's just that I wanted to go for so long – since I was a child, really – so it was a bit like, I don't know ... Walking around a dream.'

A long moment passes.

Then he says, 'I *really* want to go.'

Relief.

'You should,' she says.

'Thing is, I hate the heat.'

'Don't let that stop you. It's all ice-cold air-conditioning and misting machines. Plus, it's not always hot and steamy in Florida. I went in March and it was actually quite nice.'

'Was this a girls' trip or ...?'

She pretends not to have noticed that he is fishing for information and he pretends not to have noticed her noticing but pretending not to.

'Work, primarily,' she says. 'A tech conference in Orlando. So I was able to slip away and go geek-out without an audience, thankfully.'

Ciara turns to look out at the canal. It is beautiful up close, she'll give it that. The water is still, the reflections in it defined. The weather is pleasant enough for people to sit on the benches in their coats but not to show skin or plonk down on the grass. A steady stream of office workers and lunchtime runners crosses back and forth on the narrow planks of the lock right by a sign that warns of DEEP WATER. Watching them makes her nervous, and she looks down at her coffee instead.

She can feel his eyes on her.

'Cork, right?' he says.

'Originally. We moved to the Isle of Man when I was seven.'

'The Isle of Man? I don't think I've met anyone who lived there before.'

She smiles. 'Well, I can assure you, thousands of people do. My dad grew up there and thought I'd want to, too.'

'Did you?'

'Not at the time, no. But it was all right in the end. What about you?'

'Kilkenny,' he says, 'but we moved around a lot.'

'How long have you been in Dublin?'

'What's it now' – he makes a show of thinking about it – 'six weeks?'

'*Six weeks?*'

'Well, six and a half. I arrived on a Tuesday.'

'Where were you seven weeks ago?'

'London,' he says. 'And you?'

'How long am I in Dublin?' She pretends to think, mimicking him from a moment ago. 'Well, next Monday it'll be, ah … seven days.'

'Seven *days*? And here was I thinking *I* was the newbie.'

She laughs. 'Nope, I win that game.'

'Where were you before?'

'Cork, since I finished college. I went to Swansea. Not-at-all-notable member of the Class of 2017, here.'

His face can't hide the fact that he's trying to do the maths. She almost offers, 'I'm twenty-five,' but that's not how this game is played.

She doesn't know much but she knows *that*.

'What about you?' she asks. 'Where did you go?'

'Newcastle,' he says flatly.

Ciara senses that something has changed, that she's lost

him somewhere along the line. What was it that did it? She has no clue, but knows she can look forward to lying awake in the dark and wondering for days to come, forensically analysing everything she said and then re-analysing it, trying to find the wrong thing, the mistake, the regret.

'I'm going to be late back.' He says this a fraction of a second *before* he shakes his wrist and looks at his watch.

He stands up then and, not knowing quite what to do, she does as well.

'Yeah, I better go, too,' she lies. 'Well … Thanks for the coffee.'

He chews on his bottom lip, as if trying to decide something.

'Look,' he starts, 'I was going to go see that new Apollo documentary. On Monday. Night. They're showing it at this tiny cinema in town. Maybe – if you wanted to – we could, um, we could go see it together?'

She opens her mouth to respond but is so taken aback by this invite that she delays while her brain tries to catch up with this change of course, and into this pause he jumps with an embarrassed, 'God, I'm so shit at this.'

This.

She wants to tell him that no, he's not, and she doesn't believe for a second that he thinks he is, but mostly she doesn't want to have to respond to him referring to this as a *this* because what if he didn't mean what she hopes he did?

'That sounds great.' She flashes her most reassuring smile. 'Sure. Yeah.'

He says he will book the tickets. They arrange to meet outside the building where he works at half-five on Monday evening. He gives her his phone number in case there's any last-minute problems and she sends him a text message so he has hers. They walk back together as far as his office, then wave each other goodbye. She doesn't take a deep breath until she's turned her back to him.

And so it begins.

TODAY

Technically speaking it's Friday-morning rush-hour, but Lee has the roads to herself. She makes it to Kimmage in no time at all and lucks into a parking space right outside the house. The street is still, its residents robbed of all their reasons to get up early, to start their days somewhere further away than another room of their home. There's been no commutes for weeks now, no school runs, no tourists arriving in or heading off. Even the plague of early-morning joggers from the start of lockdown seems to have tapered off.

The nation's collective motivation to make the most of this is waning, that much is obvious. She wonders how many sourdough starters have been, by now, unceremoniously fecked in the bin.

Lee rolls down the driver's-side window and settles in to drink her coffee. The coffee that she had to watch someone make with gloved hands and theatrical caution as if it wasn't a cappuccino they were making but a bomb, whose cost included the forced sanitising of her already dry and chapped hands before and *after* collecting, that only has two sugars instead of her preferred three because now the barista has to put them in for you and she was too embarrassed to ask for that many, the coffee that she'd literally risked life and limb to get.

She refuses to let it go cold after all *that*.

With her free hand, Lee pulls down the visor and inspects the wedge of her own face she can see in the little mirror there. She seriously needed her roots done *before* they shut down the salons; the brunette is practically down to her ears and in this natural light, appears to end in a blunt line. Like every other morning she's left home in a hurry, hair still wet, and now it's drying into her trademark helmet of electrified frizz. She thought she had thrown some make-up on but it has evidently managed to clean itself off in the last half-hour. The smudge of tan foundation on the collar of her white shirt is the only evidence it was ever there at all.

She *really* needs to get her shit together.

There's a part of her that wishes she had a different job, the kind that's normally done from a stationary desk in an office and can now be – now *must* be – done from home. She's found herself fantasising about being one of those women who live alone, temporarily free from all exhausting social expectations, finally able to establish a skincare routine and a yoga *practice* with that one on YouTube that everyone raves about; to crack the spine on the healthy-food cookbooks her family have been pointedly gifting her for years; to go for long walks along beaches and clifftops and through woodland, the kind of treks that leave you pink-cheeked and aching with smug self-satisfaction and reconnected with nature (although Lee would have to connect with it first); emerging from the other end of this lockdown a shinier, smoother, brighter version of herself, Lee 2.0.

And honestly, she'd settle for painting her living room and losing half a stone.

But there's no beaches or clifftops or woodland within a two-kilometre radius of her front door, the hardware shops are closed and there is no lockdown for her. She's still at bloody work.

On the passenger seat, her phone beeps with a new text message.

She knows damn well who it is before a glance at the phone's screen confirms it: KARLY.

Detective Sergeant Karl Connolly. She'd added the 'Y' to annoy him and it had worked a treat.

The message says: *BTA?*

Lee doesn't pick up the phone. She takes another long, slow sip of her coffee. But when her phone beeps for a second time, she curses, shoves the coffee into the cup holder between the front seats and climbs out of the car.

The house looks exactly as it did the only other time she was here. A narrow, two-storey red-brick terrace that, were it in mint condition, would easily sell for half a million around these parts. But this one is crumbling. The bricks need cleaning and the roof tiles repairing. The window frames are wooden and rotting in the corners. Paint is enthusiastically peeling off the front door. A skip is parked in the driveway, half-full with seventies furniture and broken things.

It was there the last time, too. Lee distinctly remembers seeing the cracked salmon-coloured bathroom sink because her parents had one just like it. This house was a work-in-progress without much progress, and now, like everything else, its renovation is on pause.

She should ring the doorbell, announce her presence. *Should*. But she isn't in a charitable mood this morning. Instead, she goes to the front window and touches her fingers to the underside of its cement sill, feeling for the hollow she's been told is there. She quickly finds it – and the pointy end of the key that's inside.

Stealthily, she lets herself in through the front door.

The house is still, the air a little musty, stale. There are no carpets on the ground floor – only bare, dusty floorboards – but a heinous swirl of shit-brown and bright orange clings to the staircase. She starts up it, moving slowly and carefully, testing her weight on each step so as to avoid a telltale creak.

There's no noise in the house, no sounds from upstairs, but the quiet has a deliberateness to it.

Someone is *maintaining* it.

He's not asleep, then, but awake and waiting for her.

Maybe he even heard her come in.

Lee reaches the landing. Four doors lead off it. One is open on to a room filled with building materials: a workbench, some sort of sanding machine with its electrical cord wrapped around itself, boxes marked CRACKLED WHITE 7.5 x 4. Another is showing her a bathroom that appears to be in mid-update. A third looks like it can only be hiding a boiler. The fourth then, to the front of the house, is the master bedroom.

That door has been pulled closed but isn't fully shut.

She pauses outside, then kicks it open with such force that it opens all the way, hitting the wall behind it with a thunder clap.

The first thing she sees is the wallpaper. It must have been bought on the same shopping trip that found the diarrhoea-after-carrots-carpet on the stairs. It's an acid trip of bright blue paisley, and it hurts her eyes.

Then the smell hits: sweat and sex and alcohol, trapped and cooking in the room's warm air.

She should've worn a mask, she thinks now. God only *knows* what's floating around in here.

'Well,' she says, 'what seems to be the problem?'

Karl is lying on the bed, presumably naked under the fitted sheet that he's somehow managed to lift off the bottom corners of the mattress and drape across his lower half.

This must have taken some doing seeing as both his arms are outstretched, hands higher than his shoulders, like Christ on the cross.

Only Karl's wrists aren't nailed to the headboard, but handcuffed to it.

'*Two* sets?' Lee frowns. 'Where'd you get the second lot?'

'Go on,' Karl groans. 'Lap it up.'

'Oh, I fully intend to.'

'You know, I could've sworn I heard you pull up outside five minutes ago.'

23

'How long have you been like this?' Lee asks.

'All bloody night.'

'Did you sleep?'

Karl attempts a shrug, then winces at the pain this move causes him. 'Dozed. Hey, do you think you could free me before this interrogation continues? I'd get better treatment in the cells.'

'How did you text me if—'

'Siri.'

Karl nods towards his phone, lying on the bedside table.

'She got a letter wrong in the last one,' Lee says.

'You take your time.'

'Look, you're lucky I came at all. And I'm just dying to find out what Plan B was.'

'I know this is the best thing that's ever happened to you, Lee, but I can't actually feel my hands here.'

She indulges in an eye-roll before relenting, fishing her keys from her trouser pocket and moving towards the bed.

'Whatever you do,' she says, 'hang on to that fitted sheet.'

Karl scoffs. 'Like you wouldn't love a look.'

'I've *had* a look, remember? Although I barely do. Wasn't particularly memorable.' She pulls Karl's right wrist towards her – he yelps in pain – and bends to work the small key into the cuff's lock. 'So where is she, then? *Who* is she?'

'Fuck knows. On both counts.'

'Ever the romantic, eh, Karl?'

'I've *seen* you open cuffs. What the hell is taking so long this—'

The key clicks in the lock and Lee ratchets the cuff open enough to slide it off Karl's wrist.

His arm drops on to the bed like a dead weight that's been cleanly detached from his body. Gingerly, he tries to bend it but only manages a few degrees before spitting out a string of curse words, closing his eyes and giving up.

'Are the keys even here?' Lee asks, moving to the other side of the bed to work on the other set.

'Took them with her. Told me she was going to flush them down the toilet. Well, joke's on her because it isn't even connected.'

Lee makes a face. 'Where are you ...?'

'Porta Potti. Out by the shed.'

'Did she know that before she came back here?'

'No, and she came *over*.' He grins. '*And* she came—'

'If you finish that sentence, I swear to God, I'm locking you back up.'

When the second set is removed, Karl lurches forward, wincing as he tries to bring his arms closer to his body, increasing both the vehemence and the range of his muttered swears with every inch.

'Christ. My arms feel like they're on *fire*.'

'Well, let that be a lesson to you.' Lee steps back from the bed. 'And she lives less than 2K away, I suppose, this mysterious, angry woman?'

'Don't know.' He shrugs. 'Didn't ask.'

'Karl, for feck's sake. You *will* end up on Snapchat at the rate you're going and even *I* won't be able to save your arse then.'

A relatively new phenomenon: members of the Gardaí ending up named and shamed on social media. The last one that got the attention of the higher-ups was a video clip from a house party hosted by a known drug-dealer, at which a Garda currently stationed in the district was a seemingly enthusiastic and friendly guest.

'I didn't tell her I was a *guard*,' Karl says, as if such a thing was preposterous even though he'd managed to get locked in two sets of handcuffs during a sex game with a stranger whose visit to his house also constituted a breach of the country's current COVID-19 restrictions.

'Where did you tell her you got the handcuffs from, then?'

'I didn't. We weren't doing much *talking*, Lee, if you know what I—'

'Do even less of it now.'

Lee looks down at the second set of cuffs, which she's still holding, and sees a mark in blue paint near the lock and two initials scratched into the metal by the hinge: *E.M.*

She shakes her head. 'Seriously, Karl?'

'What?'

He looks up at her, at the cuffs in her hand, back at her face. He's managed to bring his arms into his lap but is rigid in that position, like his entire upper body is encased in an invisible plaster cast.

'Don't you "What?" me. You *know* what. These are Eddie's. Blue paint, initials. That's what it said on the report the poor guy had to file because he thought he'd lost them.'

'He did lose them. He forgot to take them off that coked-up eejit we hauled out of the house party in Trinity Hall a few weeks back.'

'You *know* he's already on thin ice,' Lee says.

'And *you* know why: he's shit.'

'It wouldn't occur to you to help the guy out a little bit?'

'I *am* helping him out,' Karl says. 'Out of the force, because he doesn't belong in it.'

Lee's phone starts to ring.

The number on the screen belongs to the station on Sundrive Road, which instantly piques her interest.

Why would someone at the station be calling, when she and Karl aren't due on shift for another half an hour?

And why not just hail them on the radio?

'Lee,' a male voice says when she answers. 'We've got a problem.' She recognises it as belonging to Stephen, one of the lads on the unit. 'Can you talk?'

'Yeah,' she says. 'Go on.'

'A call came in at the crack of dawn from our friend over at The Crossings, the one-woman residents' association. We assumed it was just going to be another waste of everyone's time, so we, ah ...' He clears his throat. 'Well, we sent Ant and Dec.'

'You did *what*?'

Since the unit's two newest members look like Confirmation boys and one of them is called Declan, they'd instantly earned a nickname inspired by the eternally youthful duo of TV presenters.

'We didn't think it was going to be anything,' Stephen

says. 'Same one has been calling every other day to tell us her neighbours have friends over.'

'And what was it this time?'

'There's a body in one of the ground-floor apartments. And not a pyjamas-in-their-own-bed kind.'

'Fuck,' Lee says.

'Lucky for us, she called an ambulance too and Paul Philips was driving it. As soon as he arrived on scene, he realised what it was and told Ant and Dec that they'd better call Mummy and Daddy.'

Two green bananas, alone together at a crime scene, with no senior officer to tell them which is their ass and which is their elbow. The first members on scene in a potential murder investigation. Lee knows nothing more than this, but she can already see any hope of a successful prosecution getting further away with each passing, inexperienced second.

She pinches the bridge of her nose, closes her eyes.

When she opens them again, she sees Karl looking at her questioningly.

'I know this is bad,' Stephen says in her ear, 'but we didn't think—'

'We'll talk about the not-thinking later. I'm with Karl, we'll go straight there now. Text me the full address. Send me a few cars. Tech Bureau and pathologist, too. If anyone else gets there before us, tell them to set up the cordon. No one leaves. Then call Ant and Dec back and tell them one of them needs to stand outside the apartment door and the other one needs to meet me outside the building and they are not to so much as *breathe* until I get there. Keep this off the air until you hear from me again. And start praying that this gets un-fucked up before the Super gets wind of it. Got all that?'

'Got it.'

After she ends the call, Lee throws Eddie's cuffs on to the bed in a high arc, hitting Karl square between the legs with their full weight and then some, sending him into a spasm of new pain.

She doesn't wait for him to recover.

'Get dressed,' she says. 'We need to go. *Now.*'

53 DAYS AGO

Him not being there, not waiting for her outside his office building as arranged, is not the worst-case scenario. The worse-case scenario is him not being there but somewhere else that offers a view of that spot, from where he can watch her waiting for him like a fool. To avoid this, Ciara arrives twenty minutes early and buys a coffee in the Starbucks just around the corner, which she sips at one of their outdoor tables with her eye on the time. When it gets to the half-hour, she waits a minute more before leaving, crunching on a chalky mint to ward off coffee-breath.

He is the first thing she sees when she turns on to the main street. There, where he said he'd be, waiting for her.

Relief floods her veins.

He turns and waves. She waves back, doing her best to look like she's dashed here straight from the office.

He is dressed as he was on Friday; men's suits are indistinguishable to her, for the most part, but it could be a different one. The tie is a different colour, anyway. The thick strap of a beat-up leather messenger bag rests across his body. He has no coat or jacket, even though she is glad of hers already and there's a whole night to get through yet. She has gone for standard work clothes, but on a day when she is making an effort: a black shirt dress over black boots and tights, her trusty green winter coat, black handbag.

It's odd to see him now, smiling and coming towards her, when they have so recently been strangers and he looks the way he does. She has managed to forget, in the seventy-odd hours since she last saw him, how striking he is.

What it feels like to look into those eyes.

To have them be looking back at you.

He is stretching out an arm to greet her with a hug before she has a chance to worry about *how* they will greet each other and what acute awkwardness might ensue if it turns out they have different expectations. The hug is loose and polite, one-armed on either side, not at all intimate. But she gets a whiff of whatever scent he's sprayed on himself – in the last five minutes, going by its potency – and to be so close to him, to touch him and be touched by him, even momentarily, is heady and disorientating. Her body's reaction takes her aback and she doesn't hear what he says immediately after they break away and turn to walk side by side in the direction of town, so distracted is she by the fading heat of the contact.

'Hmm?' she says.

'I said maybe we shouldn't have done that. You know, hugged.' He sticks his hands in his pockets. 'You heard they cancelled the parade? Although it's probably for the best.

It's all tourists at that thing anyway. The only time I've ever done anything for it was when I was abroad.'

They've cancelled the St Patrick's Day parade. That's what he's talking about.

As they walk side by side up the street, she sees women walking in the opposite direction steal glances at him as they pass. This makes her feel both completely invisible and superior to them at the same time.

These women haven't even noticed she's there too, but she's the one walking with him. It's a weird brand of pride.

'Same here,' she says.

He tells her that when he was in London, Patrick's Day was one of the biggest nights of the year. A ticketed event at an Irish pub packed to the rafters, leprechaun outfits, drinking green beer – all things they wouldn't be caught dead doing at home. One of his top ten hangovers ever. His brother had been visiting, which didn't help.

He asks her if she has siblings.

'No, I'm that rare specimen,' she says, 'the Irish only child.'

'In the same realm as a unicorn sighting.'

'Leprechaun, surely?' She smiles. 'But yeah. Is it just you and your brother or ...?'

'Just us.'

'Is he here?'

'He lives in Perth now. Has done for a while. Got the whole set-up out there: mortgage, kids, pensionable job.' A pause. 'I can't see him ever coming back. He loves the weather.'

They cross the road to Baggot Street Bridge.

'Favourite movie?' she asks.

'I think his is the second *Godfather*.'

She laughs. 'And yours?'

'*Jurassic Park*.'

'I don't have one,' she says, 'before you ask. I just don't know how people can narrow it down.'

'I feel that way about food.'

'Well, there, I can do categories. Favourite cocktail, favourite pizza, favourite sandwich – but that's as far as I go.'

'Go on then.'

'Sandwich is toasted cheese,' she says. 'Toasted with mayonnaise on the outside. *Has* to be mayonnaise. Not butter. That's the best way to get it golden. Pizza is roast chicken strips and red onion. Can't beat it if the ratio is right. Cocktail ... Well, I'm not a big drinker, really, but I do like a French 75.'

'What's that?'

'Gin and lemon juice, little bit of sugar syrup, topped with prosecco. Or champagne, depending on how much it costs. It's basically adult lemonade.'

'Where does a good one?'

'Oh,' she says, 'I'm nowhere *near* discerning enough to know that. If it comes in a flute and tastes a bit fizzy, it'll do me. And to be honest, the flute isn't a deal-breaker.'

'And you've only been here a week ...'

'*And* I've only been here a week.'

'Well,' he says, stopping to bow slightly and roll his hand towards her like the maître d' of a posh restaurant, 'I've been here *six* weeks so I'm practically a Dubliner now—'

'Certifiable, surely.'

'—and so I know where we can get a nice cocktail. It's even near the cinema.' He holds out an elbow so she can curl her arm around his. 'Shall we?'

They talk about work and TV shows and whether or not more things will be cancelled because of this faraway flu, and stroll through a city that feels quiet even for a Monday night. He tells her that a lot of the multinationals have their people working from home already. She says she knows and then he rolls his eyes at his forgetting that she works for one of them. She says she'll be shocked if she's still in the office at the end of the week, that they're all just waiting for an official announcement. A few departments have already made the move. She thinks she can do her job just as well at home. She explains that the problem is they have thousands of workers sitting within feet of one another in a confined space, breathing recirculated air and using the same bathrooms, teaspoons, etc., and every day of the week dozens of them are coming into work fresh from trips to other facilities and offices abroad, having travelled through airports and squeezed themselves into crowded aeroplanes. It's the potential threat they're acting on, not the reality. At least for now. Someone got the measles last year and it was the same sort of thing – not because the overlords are humanitarians, but because workers being home sick affects the bottom line. Better to have them home working for a while, even if it ends up being a total overreaction.

'Here we are,' he announces.

While she was nattering on, he's steered her off Grafton Street and now they are standing in front of a fancy hotel. The smooth, dark gloss of its first-floor bay windows promise low, warm light inside. Lush green foliage drips from the portico. Through gold-edged double glass doors she can see an imposing staircase covered in plush carpeting. A uniformed doorman in gloves and a hat stands sentry just outside. International flags blow gently in the breeze above polished gold lettering that spells out the hotel's name: THE WESTBURY.

She's heard of it but didn't know it was here, didn't know it was down this street, in this building that's only ever been in her peripheral vision as she walked past.

'The bar does amazing cocktails,' he says.

'Great.'

She tries to sound like she means it, like this *is* great, but her eyes are on the doorman. He's just a bouncer in better shoes. She is hyper-aware of the scuffed toes of her fake leather boots, the thin fabric of her dress and the bobbles of wool on the sleeves of her winter coat. The coat that was sold at a price that suggested you should be happy to get a month of wear out of it, the same one she's wearing for the third winter in a row. If she had known this was where they'd be going, she would've worn something else. She might have even tried to stretch to buying something new.

She should have known. Of *course* Oliver is a man who goes to places like this, who assumes he is welcome in them

— because he is. The face, the suit, the cool confidence. He strides right up to the door as if the doorman isn't even there and this is, apparently, the way to do it. The doorman not only opens the door for them but greets them both with a wide smile.

Having disentangled their linked arms to walk inside, Oliver puts a hand against the small of her back as they ascend the stairs. He's not steering her or claiming her, but reassuring her. She wonders if he can sense how uncomfortable she is.

Another staff member, a glossy brunette, greets them at a hostess stand and directs them into the bar. When she says, 'Right this way,' she says it to him from beneath a fluttering of long, dark eyelashes.

The bar is a feast of mirrored things and shiny edges, of crystal chandeliers and glasses, of plush leather upholstery and marbled surfaces. Hundreds of different coloured bottles line the wall behind the counter. The lighting, like the rest of the hotel, is low and warm. A real fire burns at one end. More uniformed staff stand waiting to tend to them.

It's like a movie set and, for a moment, Ciara feels a little mesmerised.

The place is practically empty, with only a handful of patrons, who all sit around one table at one end, by the roaring fire. They are directed away from them to a cosy, circular booth at the other.

When prompted, she hands over her coat to be disappeared to some plush cloakroom and tries not to think about the hostess seeing the PRIMARK printed on its tag. Then she chastises herself for thinking about that at all. Oliver gives the hostess his suit jacket without even looking at her.

They sit down.

He unbuttons his cuffs and starts to roll up his sleeves. His forearms are pale and covered in coarse, dark hair. He wears a silver watch that looks heavy.

'So what do you think?' he asks. He waves a hand to indicate that he's asking about her thoughts on the bar.

'Bit grubby, if I'm honest. They could *really* do with sprucing the place up a bit, couldn't they?'

He grins. 'You should see the bathrooms, they're absolutely disgusting.'

'Better or worse than those holes in the ground they have in France?'

'You'll *wish* you were in one of them.'

Their banter feels like rapid gun-fire and after each successful exchange, she feels a bit dizzy with relief, like she's gone over the top in the trenches and made it to cover without taking a hit.

A waiter approaches them with two cocktail menus.

'Ah, we'll have two' – Oliver looks to her – 'what are they called?'

'French 75s. Please.'

'Excellent choice,' the waiter says. 'Will I leave the menus?'

'Please do.' She reaches to take one from him. 'Thank you.' And then, to Oliver, 'Let's see what else they've got in here …'

But what she's really looking for is the price of the drinks they've just ordered. She flicks through, pretending to muse with deep interest over the other cocktail options. She tries not to react when she turns a page and sees it: the cocktails are €24. *Each.*

'Speaking of bathrooms,' Oliver says, sliding to move out of the booth. 'I've drunk about a litre of coffee today, so …'

'Don't fall in the hole.'

'If I'm not back in five minutes—'

'Wait longer, I know.'

She watches his back disappear through the bar's doors. Then she pulls her handbag on to her lap and starts fishing around in it for her wallet. She does a rough calculation of the creased notes inside: enough to cover the cost of two rounds of these drinks plus a cab home, just about.

He'll probably pay. He'll *likely* pay.

But still.

She slides two fingers into the little pocket attached to the bag's lining and relaxes slightly when she feels the thin hardness of her debit card, the raised text on it against her fingers.

She'd rather not have to use it, but she can if need be.

She'll figure something out.

They have just ordered a third round when he says, 'You're not going to believe this.'

Her cheeks feel warm, her limbs languid, her tongue loose.

She's not yet drunk but drunker than she expected she'd get, than she knows she should be. It's because she didn't have any lunch. *Couldn't* have any; nerves had stolen her appetite. She pulls her glass of water closer and silently resolves to drink it all before she takes even one more sip of alcohol.

She says, 'Try me.'

He shows her a flash of something on his phone. 'The film started ten minutes ago.'

'You're joking.'

'We could make a run for it. They're probably still on trailers and it's only a couple of minutes away.'

'Would it be terrible—' she starts at the exact same time *he* says, 'Or we could just stay here.'

They both laugh.

'I hate rushing,' he says.

'Me too.'

'And I like drinking.'

'Me too.'

'And I like you.'

'Well, I *am* very likeable.'

He laughs. He's impressed with her.

After that quip, she's a little impressed with herself.

'So,' she says, clearing her throat. She needs to change the subject, to give herself some time to come back from the tipsy cliff-edge. 'Do you come here often?'

'Oh, come *on*.'

'I genuinely want to know.'

'This is actually only my second time here,' he admits.

'And the other time was with work. I just …' He pinches the stem of his glass and slides it back and forth a little until the liquid starts to slosh around inside. 'I wanted to come back here with … *Not* work.'

'Not work. Wow. I bet you say that to *all* the girls.'

'Do you like it?'

Their eyes meet as he asks this and it occurs to her that up until now, practically sitting side by side, she hasn't been making much eye contact with him at all.

It's just as well because the way he's looking at her now …

She never really understood the phrase *piercing* when applied to eyes, but that's what his are. He's not just looking at her but *in* her, it feels like, right through the thin veneer of this pretending. It's as if he has X-ray vision that can effortlessly penetrate all the way to the real Ciara, the one who's curled up and careful and desperately trying to protect herself from what it might feel like if this evening goes horribly wrong.

She looks away, back to her glass.

'I do,' she says. 'I do like it. I mean … Look, it's not really where I'd usually be, let's put it that way.' The alcohol fizzes in her bloodstream, disintegrating walls his gaze has been weakening all night. She can't let them fall away completely, not on this, their very first date, but she can put her face to one of the gaps and speak to him across clear air without having to risk a step outside the boundary. 'I can't really afford to come to places like this, to be honest. Not on the regular, anyway. And if I'd known this is where we'd end up,

I would've dressed differently. I was afraid the doorman was going to stop me and say, "Sorry, love. No Penneys apparel allowed inside."'

'He calls you love *and* says *apparel*? Who *is* this guy?'

She slaps him playfully on the forearm.

'You know what I mean.'

'For the record,' he says, 'I think you look lovely.'

She mumbles, 'Thank you,' to her glass.

'It's just a bit special, isn't it?'

He could mean the bar. Or the drinks.

Or this night, with her in it.

'Here's what I like about this place.' She's careful to speak her words more slowly than she's thinking them, distinctly pronouncing each one. Or so she hopes. 'It's hidden. It's not a secret, but it's not on show. You can't know this is here when you walk past this building on the street, but come inside and turn a corner and it's revealed to you, this beauty that's been here all the time. Waiting. And I love that. I love discovering places like this because it makes me wonder about what *else* is inside all these buildings I walk past everyday. What else is just waiting to be discovered? There's a whole hidden city. *Several* hidden cities. All hiding in plain sight in this one.'

'So you like secrets,' Oliver says.

'No.' It comes out too quickly, sounding too harsh. She says it again, slower and softer. 'No. It's … There's a place in New York, a bar, that you have absolutely no way of knowing is there unless you're told about it by someone else who has been told about it because no part of it faces the street and there's no sign, and the only way to get in is through a secret door in *another* bar.'

'That sounds exhausting,' he says.

'And so *unnecessary*. Like, just serve good drinks and be nice to people and stop with all the shite. But that kinda thing – *that's* a secret. And secrets are about denying people things. The truth, yes, but also the experience, the knowledge … You're just trying to keep them out of the cool gang. You're trying to decide who gets to be in the cool gang, and that's just …' Ciara stops, having lost her train of thought. Where had she been going with that? The warmth of the alcohol is spreading unbidden throughout her body. 'It's not secrets I like. It's discovering things that are new to me but actually were always there. Secrets are a different thing. They're destructive.'

Silence.

She dares to turn and look at him and finds that his eyes are on her. For a second she thinks he might be about to move to kiss her, and she hopes not because she's not ready, she's not prepared, and she's definitely a little bit drunk and she'd rather not be, not for *that*, but instead he nods and says, 'I know what you mean,' and then that he has to go to the bathroom again.

'Three times in one night?'

'I've broken the seal,' he says gravely.

'I actually have to go, too. I'll go when you get back.'

'I can wait?'

'I can wait longer.' She waves a hand. 'Go on.'

This time, when he's gone, she forces herself to finish her water in three long gulps. Then she takes one of the clean cocktail napkins from the table, folds it neatly and tucks it inside her bag. When she looks up the waiter is standing there, smirking at her conspiratorially, and she flashes him a guilty smile and says, 'A souvenir.'

'It's going well, then,' he says.

'I think so.'

'I think so too.'

He sets down their fresh drinks, winks at her and leaves.

When they've both drained their glasses, he suggests they make a move. She's surprised by how late it is – almost ten, how did *that* happen? – and she says so. She finds out that he paid the bill while she was in the bathroom and she protests but not too hard, and thanks him.

His hand is on the small of her back again as they descend the stairs, but it's pressed firmly against her body now. She's carrying her coat over her arm and can feel the heat of his skin through the thin material of her dress. She hopes *he* can't feel the band of her tights sticking into her flesh. She wonders what he *can* feel.

They face their own reflections in the dark glass of the doors, and she is struck by how good they look, him and her, coupled together.

And then, how quickly this has happened, how fast they've gone from strangers in a supermarket queue to him here beside her, touching her, telling her things about himself.

Maybe this *can* be easy.

But what comes next?

She assumes they will go somewhere else, have one for the road, and maybe grab some late-night fast-food somewhere – God knows she could do with it – or maybe—

'Can we get a cab?' Oliver says to the doorman, a different one from before.

This throws her but she doesn't outwardly react. She wants to know where they're getting this cab to but she also doesn't want to threaten the delicate equilibrium of these next few moments. She feels like a time-traveller exercising extreme caution in the present, which is actually the past, because she knows how good the future is and doesn't want it to change one bit.

It's harder not to react when the cab pulls up and Oliver opens a door and motions for her to get in, but then after she does stays there, standing outside the car.

He's not getting in, she realises.

He leans down, one hand on the roof, until his face is level with hers.

'I'm gonna walk home,' he says.

'Oh.' Disappointment washes over her in a wave. 'Sure. Right.'

'Are you around Thursday evening? We could actually go see the film this time.'

She nods. Smiles briefly. 'Yeah.'

'I'll text you.'

'Okay. Great.'

'Goodnight.'

'Goodnight.'

He closes her door for her and moves to the front passenger side, where the window is rolled down. He bends to drop something into the seat – enough money to cover the fare, she'll figure out in a second – and waves at the driver.

He gives her another wave as the car pulls off.

She doesn't quite understand what just took place. He wants to see her again, okay, but not any more tonight? Not now?

'Where to, love?' the driver asks over his shoulder.

Any confidence she had in her ability to navigate these waters dissipates. She doesn't have a clue what she's doing. She should just give up now.

'Home,' she says absently, before realising that he's asking for an address.

TODAY

Lee noses the vehicle in behind a squad car parked on double-yellows outside a curved apartment complex of smooth grey brick, glass and exposed steel off Harold's Cross Road. Karl finishes his breakfast – a can of Red Bull – just as she cuts the engine.

She can see a uniform waiting for them outside what looks like the main entrance: a pair of glass doors under a sign that says THE CROSSINGS in polished gold lettering. His thumbs are hooked into his ballistics vest and he's shifting his weight from foot to foot. Lee can't tell from this distance whether it's Ant or Dec but she's not sure she could from up close either. Same with their namesakes. She settles on Presumed Dec for the time being.

There's no sign of their reinforcements yet, but it's barely been ten minutes since she hung up on Stephen.

She checks her phone for the message she'd asked him to send: the body is in apartment number one. She hopes there's only a handful of units on each floor. The closer the scene is to the main entrance, the fewer people will see them arrive, thus the more chance they have of fixing this before things go any more wrong.

She turns to Karl.

'Are you clear on what you're doing?'

'Cleaning up the massive soft shit this pair just took?'

'This isn't their fault, Karl. It's whatever eejit sent them out here, alone. And we don't know *what* they did yet, so try not to go in there all, you know, being *you.*'

'Funny *and* attractive?'

'An absolute dickhead.'

Karl clamps a hand on his chest as if he's just been shot in the heart.

'They've only been on the job five minutes,' Lee says. 'Cut them some slack, is all I'm saying.'

'You know, you should really put something on that bleeding heart of yours.' He opens the passenger-side door. 'I think I might have seen a first-aid box in the back ...'

Once they're outside, the uniform hurries towards them. They meet on the path.

'Detective Inspector Leah Riordan,' she says to him, 'and Detective Sergeant Karl Connolly. What have we got here ...?'

'Michael,' the young guard finishes. He pulls down his mask. 'Garda Michael Creedon.'

'What's going on here, Michael? In brief.'

Lee is encouraged by the fact that he flips open his notebook before answering.

'Well, we, ah, got here around half seven,' he says, scanning his notes. 'Seven twenty-six. One of—'

'Seven twenty-six?' Karl asks. 'Are you sure?'

'Yeah. I wrote it—'

'Not seven twenty-seven?'

The young guard's cheeks start to colour, and Lee digs Karl in the ribs before motioning for Michael to continue.

'Ah, yeah, so ...' He clears his throat. 'One of the residents was here waiting for us – Gillian Fannin. She lives in number four. She's the one who called it in.'

'What did she call in,' Lee asks, 'exactly?'

'A smell in the hall that she thought was coming from her neighbour's apartment. Number one. Three doors away from hers but in the same corridor. She presumed it was just rotting food waste or something at first, but it was getting worse so ... This morning she goes to knock on the door – but the door is open.'

'Open how?'

'She described it as pulled closed but not fully shut. The lock wasn't engaged. She pushed it open a couple of inches – she was going to call out, see if anyone was home – but the smell was much worse then and she retreated, went back to her own apartment and made the call. Well, two calls – one to the station, one to 999 for an ambulance.'

'So she didn't actually go inside?'

'She says she didn't, no.'

'What was the door like when you first saw it?'

'As she'd described,' Michael says. 'Like she found it. It doesn't seem to lock unless you pull it shut.'

'Does she know who lives there?'

'She thinks it's a young guy, in his twenties or thirties, but that's it. She hasn't seen him in a while, maybe a couple of weeks. I checked the letterboxes but they only have numbers on them. No names.'

'Good thinking,' Lee says, throwing the guy a bone. She can practically feel Karl roll his eyes at this beside her. 'The paramedics – they went in?'

'One of them' – he looks down at his notes again – 'Paul Philips, he went in briefly. Came back out, said this wasn't anything they could help with and advised us to call the station and tell them what was going on. Said he hadn't touched the body, that it was clearly in an advanced state of decomposition. And that if he had to make a guess, he'd say whatever happened in there happened a couple of weeks ago.'

'Did they leave?'

'I think they're parked around the back, by the vehicle entrance. He said something about pronouncing death for you if you didn't want to wait for the pathologist ...?'

'Yeah, they're able to do that now. But let's wait and see. Did *you* go in?'

'No, Declan did. Again, very briefly. The body is in the bathroom, the first door off the hall, so he didn't have to go in very far. And from there he said he could see into the living room and the bigger bedroom. Seems to be empty apart from ...' He clears his throat again. 'He was only in there a few seconds.'

Still plenty of time to destroy critical evidence, but maybe the blast zone won't be as big as Lee had feared.

'Is the front door the only access?'

Michael shakes his head, *no*. 'The ground-floor apartments have railed-in terraces. You could easily hop over. The sliding door that leads out of number one looks closed from the outside, but I didn't check if it was locked. I was trying to touch as little as possible.' He points over his left shoulder. 'There's also a side gate and two fire exits, all alarmed according to Ms Fannin, plus you have the underground car park. The entrance to it is round the back.'

'Anyone coming or going?'

'Not in or out this way. I think the time of the day is on our side there. One guy did try to leave for a run but he went back without much hassle. But we don't know about vehicles.'

'Fire exits – is there one at the far end of the corridor?'

Michael nods.

'So there's nothing between that exit and the door to apartment one? No other apartments?'

'There's a door to the stairwell,' he says, 'but that's it.'

Lee nods at Karl, who understands: the fire exit will be their main access through the cordon. They'll have to get the alarm system disabled first.

'Okay, good. Michael, I'm going to leave you with DS Connolly here to help him get things organised while I go inside and see what we're dealing with. We should have a few more hands on deck any second now and once we do, I want to get that car park blocked off and this place secured. Hopefully Number Four is just an early riser and all her neighbours are still asleep.'

Michael winces. 'No such luck there, I'm afraid, Inspector. When we arrived, we thought we could go in via the side entrance. But when we pushed it open, well, it turns out it was an emergency exit. The fire alarm went off throughout the building, woke everybody up. So by the time we located Ms Fannin – she met us in the courtyard – we, ah, we had an audience. The residents were all out on their balconies, watching.'

'Oh, *great*,' Karl mutters.

'The main thing now,' Lee says to Michael, 'is making sure everyone stays put.' To Karl, 'I'm going to take a look inside. You're good to go out here?'

'Yes, boss.'

Lee says a silent prayer for Garda Michael Creedon as she turns and heads inside.

One of the glass doors has been propped open with a fire extinguisher; a keypad and electronic sensor suggest it'd be locked otherwise, accessible only by residents.

As soon as she crosses the threshold, the smell hits.

A sign on the wall directs her to the right for apartment number one, but the corridor curves so she can't tell how many feet away from its door she is right now. Judging by the shape and size of the building, she must have somewhere between thirty and forty feet to go yet, and a door is open directly behind her and the air this morning is fresh and cool, and yet ...

She can already smell it: the cloying, pungent aroma of rotting human flesh.

Like a cheap perfume years past its use-by date mixed with

meat that's been left to turn in the sun, spores multiplying and warming and spreading until they've replaced every last molecule of unscented air. It's not that bad in the lobby, but it's bad enough in the lobby to know that that's how bad it's going to get.

She thinks about poor Declan, standing outside the apartment's door all this time. This will definitely be a story he trots out over pints with the lads in the years to come. She just hopes he won't be ending it with *and that's the day I decided to quit.*

Lee has a rummage in the pockets of her blazer, triumphant to find the very end of a packet of forgotten Silvermints just about still wrapped in their foil. There are benefits to forever failing to be organised and making clothing choices based purely on what looks the most clean.

Two clean mints, one fuzzy with lint. She puts them back in her pocket, then takes a face mask from another one and snaps the bands around her ears.

The lobby is small but bright, benefiting from a second pair of glass doors directly opposite the ones she's just come through. They lead to a central courtyard. Lee doesn't go out there but scans it through the glass: a pleasant area landscaped to within an inch of its life, with vibrant green trees, wooden benches and a trickling water feature that she knows will make her want to pee as soon as she hears it. The building bends around the space in a gently curved U-shape, with a pair of large, wrought-iron gates filling in the open end. Emergency vehicle access, she guesses.

She counts three floors of apartments, about thirty in all if each one has one balcony. The ground-floor units have little tracts of private space outside patio doors, maybe about a narrow parking spot's worth, demarcated by a metal railing. But the railings are low and open between their horizontal lengths, so easily climbed over, just as Michael said. There's no one in the courtyard that she can see and from this angle, it's hard to tell if there's anyone watching from a balcony.

She turns back around.

Next to the main doors is a small and clearly brand-new hand-sanitiser dispenser. She looks for a lever before realising it has an electronic sensor, and sniffs the air as she rubs the clear liquid into her hands.

Lemongrass. Fancy.

The steel holder where the fire extinguisher should be is attached to the wall below a row of framed notices. The first is headlined HOUSE RULES above a bulleted list of – Lee squints – twenty-three separate instructions the residents of The Crossings apparently have to abide by.

Sounds like school, she thinks. Or prison.

The second is one of the government-issued, bright yellow COVID-19 information sheets. One of the early ones, going by the fact that it only contains three recommendations: wash your hands, practise good coughing etiquette and maintain a distance of two metres away from other people.

The third framed notice is what to do in case of an emergency. Lee takes out her phone and dials the number for the management company printed in red across the top.

It's immediately picked up by an answering machine that instructs her to call a different number outside of office hours.

She checks the time on screen: eight forty-five.

She dials the second number from memory. It rings twice before bringing her to the very same voicemail.

'Fan-fucking-tastic,' she says out loud. She leaves a message with her name, rank and number and a demand that someone call her back immediately.

Then she turns to the letterboxes. Four neat rows of slim boxes with stainless-steel doors fixed low to the rear wall. She pulls a pair of blue latex gloves from her trouser pocket and puts them on, snapping them over the cuffs of her blazer to form a seal. She uses an index finger to open the narrow flap of the box marked '1', bending down to see if she can see what's inside.

There's a slim, white envelope, but she can't see any text on it from this angle.

She starts down the corridor, passing a set of lifts. It's lit by strips of overhead fluorescents, motion-activated; they flick on as she goes. The corridor curves to the left, revealing three more doors and Garda Declan ... *Casey? Is that his last name?* Standing with his arms folded outside the door marked '1'.

He has two masks on: an inch of the blue, papery material of a disposable one is just visible behind the black cloth that covers his face from the bridge of his nose to his jawline. Not a bad idea, Lee thinks. A thin sheen of sweat glistens by his hairline and what she can see of his face seems to have a bit of a grey-ish tinge to it.

'You can go wait outside,' she says. 'Get some fresh air.'

The young officer doesn't need to be told twice; he's moving away before she's even finished talking.

The apartment door is about an inch from being completely shut – closed, but without the locking mechanism lined up. No visible marks or stains on the door, the frame or the handle. Looks like there's a light on on the other side.

Lee takes out the two clean Silvermints, lifts her mask with a finger and pops them into her mouth. She lets them sit on her tongue, waiting until she can detect the sting of their menthol. Then she exhales hard, filling the mask with the smell of peppermint. It won't last long – the mints are already softening, chalky edges crumbling – but it's better than nothing.

She pushes open the apartment door – lock looks intact, nothing stuffed in the mechanism – revealing a narrow hallway. Hardwood floor, white wall, a silver-framed mirror hanging on the wall to the left just above a console table. The light is coming from a fixture on the ceiling but it looks like there're other lights on elsewhere in the apartment too.

On the right is a door that opens outward, open about halfway, blocking most of her line of sight into the rest of the apartment.

Hitting her is what feels like a solid wall of smell.

Smell isn't even the word for what's in the air. A smell is something you have to breathe in to detect. What's emitted by a decomposing body does all the work for you, leaving you no choice in the matter. It floods your nostrils and rushes into your mouth and claws at the back of your throat. It clings to every skin cell and clothing fibre and strand of hair. It makes your eyes water. It's less of a smell and more of an invasion. An all-out assault.

So much for her bright idea with the mints – every last molecule of menthol is immediately vaporised.

Lee steels herself and steps inside.

50 DAYS AGO

Leo is about to make a statement, live from Washington, DC. The apartment doesn't have a TV so Ciara finds a livestream online and watches it horizontal on the couch with her laptop balanced on her stomach.

It's not even light over there yet. He walks to an artificially lit podium set up outside a grand-looking building shrouded in pre-dawn darkness, his face solemn and serious.

She wonders what he's thinking. He's a medical doctor as well as the leader of the country. He must understand more than most.

He begins to speak, slowly and deliberately, reading easily from some unseen teleprompter, but looking as if he's talking directly to the lens.

The virus is all over the world.

We have not witnessed a pandemic of this nature in living memory.

We will prevail.

As soon as the programme cuts back to the talking heads in the news studio, Ciara shuts the laptop and then surprises herself by bursting into hard, hot tears.

She's not scared, at least not physically; the virus may be in the country but it still feels very far away from her. It's mostly a benign flu, from what they say. She trusts that the people who are supposed to know how to protect her from this will, that they already are. But all this is still …

Well, *scary*.

Some of the things the Taoiseach said she'd heard before, many times, but in sci-fi virus thrillers and post-apocalyptic zombie movies, not from the mouth of the leader of her country in a press conference so pressing he had to do it in the pre-dawn dark on the other side of an ocean.

And this is real-world.

Hers.

Her mother once told her that the scariest thing she saw on TV on 9/11 was a live shot of the southern tip of Manhattan when thick, dusty smoke was billowing into the sky from between the injured buildings. It was a familiar shot of a city her mother felt she knew even though she'd never been, because she'd seen it destroyed and invaded and exploded countless times across decades' worth of TV shows and Hollywood movies. But this scene was rendered utterly alien by the fact that it was happening for real. The mundane and the incomprehensible, smashed violently together – it caused cognitive dissonance, her mother had said. She'd read about it somewhere, probably in one of her self-help books.

What if *she* gets this thing?

Ciara can't deal with that particularly worry right now, so she replaces it with another one: why hasn't Oliver called her?

They're supposed to meet again in a few hours, but she hasn't heard from him since he put her in that cab outside The Westbury three days ago. It's exhausting to be worried *and* actively trying to keep yourself from not being that. The very fact that plans are already in place might well be *why* he hasn't called or messaged her. Everything is set except for the exact time and actual location of their meeting, and maybe he's presuming they'll meet outside his office after work just like they did last time, because this is the thing they were *supposed* to do last time but didn't, so maybe in his mind this promised text is just a formality, firmly in the *just checking we're still on for ...* category of communication, and that's why he's leaving it until the last minute.

Or maybe he's changed his mind.

The radio silence since Monday night can be bent to support both hypotheses, that's the problem.

And can they even still *go* to the cinema, after Leo's speech?

Ciara opens up her laptop again and surfs national news sites until she finds a bulleted list of what's happening, published ten minutes ago and updated in the last two. She scrolls down. Schools, colleges and childcare facilities will close. Museums, theatres and other cultural institutions will close, too. No mass gatherings of more than one hundred people indoors or five hundred out, which still sounds like an awful lot to her. Shops, restaurants and bars to remain open but with the immediate implementation of social-distancing measures. Everyone must aim to limit their social interaction.

It sounds straightforward but nothing is, not now. Cinemas aren't mentioned by name – do they qualify as a cultural institution? Or are they like shops or bars, somewhere that can remain open so long as they limit the number of people allowed inside? Oliver said this one is small, so it might not even have that many seats and, really, how many people are going to go see a space documentary of a Thursday night? Especially now, after *that*. And what exactly does 'limit social interaction' mean? If he is her only interaction, does that qualify as limiting?

What happens if he decides *not* to include her in his?

She closes her eyes and rubs at them in frustration.

Of course this would happen now. Of *course* it would. After all this time, she's somehow managed to cultivate a seed …

And here comes a bloody once-in-a-lifetime, global pandemic to kill it off.

You couldn't make it up.

Her phones rings, startling her. It's wedged down the side of one of the couch cushions; in reaching for it, she accidentally answers the call. There's no time to prepare for talking to the name she sees as she puts the device to her ear: OLIVER.

'Hello?' She's immediately convinced that her attempt at sounding casual has failed spectacularly.

'Ciara?'

'Oliver.' She feels the urge to stand up. 'How are you?'

'Good – apart from the whole, you know, end-times-plague thing. You?'

'Same.'

'Did you watch Leo's speech just now?'

'Yeah.'

She starts pacing back and forth in front of the window.

'It's all a bit surreal, isn't it?' he says.

'Very.'

'Are you limiting yourself to one-word responses on purpose, or …?'

'No.'

He laughs at that.

'So,' he says. 'Tonight. I don't know if the cinema is even still open … And I'm not sure if I really *want* to go there. Have you ever seen *Outbreak*?'

'Is that the one where a monkey bites the doctor from *Grey's Anatomy*?'

'Odd angle, but factually correct.'

'Then yes. But years ago.'

'Well, there's a scene in a cinema where you can actually *see* the germs coming out of people's mouths. I thought it was funny at the time but now …' He sighs. 'I don't know. I could just be overreacting.'

She says, 'Hmm,' because she doesn't know where he's going with this and doesn't want to show her cards before he does.

This is so bloody exhausting. She wishes she could just press a button and skip ahead, past this part.

'We could do something else?' he suggests. 'We could—'

'Yeah.'

'—go get a drink or something. Are you still in the office?'

Her mortification at reacting too eagerly is quickly replaced by terror that he might be about to suggest coming *here*.

'It's just that I was going to say we could meet in the same spot,' he says. 'Outside my office? But if—'

'No, no. That'd be great. Actually, I *am* working from home now but I live, like, five minutes away from there, so …'

'We could meet somewhere else if it's better?'

'No, no. That's good. Let's do that.'

'Five thirty?'

'See you then.'

He ends the call and she falls back, spent, on to the couch, where she allows herself half a minute of sweet relief.

So she *hasn't* fucked this up.

Yet.

Apart from how busy Tesco's is and the disproportionate number of people rushing from its doors clutching jumbo-sized packs of paper products, nothing about Baggot Street seems to suggest that anything is wrong. All the shops are open, including the florist. So too are the cafés, pubs and restaurants. Ciara thinks a few too many people are wearing winter gloves for this kind of weather, but that could just be because she's looking for signs that the world has changed, evidence that these people are the kind who watch the news too. When she pulls the cuff of her coat down to avoid touching the button at the pedestrian crossing with her bare skin, it feels like overkill. A part of her hopes that no one has seen her do it, that *he* hasn't.

But he couldn't have, because he's late today.

While she waits she tries to distract herself from overreacting to this by focusing on the two men standing outside Tesco in the plain black uniform of store security guards. One of them is sucking on a cigarette he's keeping hidden in his palm, listening while the other one talks animatedly and points into the shop. A third person, a woman in a skirt-suit, comes out and joins the conversation. She keeps glancing nervously behind her, back inside. Ciara thinks maybe they're flustered about how many people are in-store.

This distraction works a little too well and Oliver is suddenly *there*, beside her, apologising as he bends to kiss her on the cheek – an upgrade from their last greeting, sending a little electric shock through her skin. She feels the same flutter of nerves in the pit of her stomach that she did when she saw him the last time, and she wonders if this is what people mean when they talk about butterflies.

He blames his minor delay on a meeting that ran over. The partners had been hoping for the best and been uninterested in planning for the worst, so now the office is abruptly closing from tomorrow and no one quite knows how that's going to work.

There's a lot to figure out, he says.

'How about you? How are you getting on?'

'Grand,' she answers. 'Honestly, it's not even that different. My job is like ninety-nine per cent silently staring at my computer anyway. Okay, I have to pay for my own VitaminWater now but, apart from that ... My couch *is* a lot comfier than those horrible ergonomic chairs they make us sit on.'

'So are you, like, coding all day or ...?'

She smiles. '"Coding"?'

'Oh yes, I know *all* the lingo.'

'Do you now?'

'What can I say? I read a *lot* of Wikipedia.'

She laughs. 'I don't code. I'm in web services. It's like technical customer service. I'm basically the IT guy who asks if you've tried turning it off and on, but with cloud-computing clients so it's a *little* bit more complicated than that.'

'I thought you lot made apps or something.'

'That's just what we want you to think. The actual money is in server farms, cloud computing, slowly but surely moving towards a place where the entire internet will run on our equipment so our maleficent leader will effectively control the world ... That kind of thing.'

'Should I be scared?'

'It won't change anything.'

'Let's go get a drink, then.'

He suggests a pub on Haddington Road, around the corner. They walk towards it side by side, without touching.

'You're not thinking of going to Cork?' he asks. 'To your parents?'

She's confused and not just by the *parents*, plural. 'For what?'

'It's just that, one of the guys in the office, that's his plan. Legging it to Galway tomorrow. His dad is a GP and he's telling them that we'll all be confined to our localities soon. There'll be no going anywhere. Although personally I think he's just looking for an excuse to make his mother do his washing. He's a bit younger than us, so ...'

'How do you know that?'

'What?'

'That he's younger than *us*.'

Oliver raises an eyebrow. 'Should I be bracing myself for a bombshell?'

She lets a beat pass, enjoying this. 'I'm twenty-five.'

'Phew.' He mock-wipes at his brow. 'Although I figured. You said you were Class of 2017. I did the maths.'

'Well done.'

'On a calculator.'

They cross Baggot Street by the bridge, passing a man just about carrying two boxes of beer, one stacked on top of the other, hurrying in the opposite direction.

Priorities, she thinks.

'This is the bit where you tell me how old *you* are,' she says.

He grins. 'Is it?'

They reach the pub, which is actually more of a sports

bar. One elderly man sits in the far corner of an enclosed smoking area at the front of the building, a box of cigarettes and a lighter neatly aligned on the table next to his pint.

As Oliver pulls the door open he says to her, 'I'm twenty-nine. Just.'

Inside, a long, narrow room with a bar on the left stretches away from them. It's full of nooks and crannies, of snugs and booths, and all of them are empty. Suspended screens are tuned to Sky Sports. There's no music to compete with the commentators. If it hadn't been for the man with the pint outside, she might think they've accidentally walked into a place that's not open for business yet.

She tells Oliver he has quite the eclectic taste in drinking establishments.

'Yeah, well ...' Again the hand on the small of her back, gently directing her to a booth just inside the door, protected from the rest of the bar by a stained-glass partition. 'I've chosen tonight's location purely based on its potential infection rate.'

'Lovely.' She slides into the booth. 'But how about we not to talk about that? I'm in the mood to stick my head in the sand for an hour.'

'Fair enough. What can I get you?'

'A glass of white wine, please.'

'Any particular kind?'

'So long as it's cold and not Chardonnay ...'

'God, you're *so* demanding.'

He winks at her before turning away.

She angles her body towards the window so half a minute later she hears rather than sees the barman approach Oliver at the bar. He must have been in the back. After their order is placed, it becomes apparent that he *was*, and why: he explains that they're rearranging the interior so they are in line with the government's new social-distancing guidelines ahead of St Patrick's Day.

Ciara can't imagine how a bunch of drunk people on the country's drunkest day of the year will figure out how to stay two metres apart, in a *pub*, but the barman seems confident. She supposes he has to be.

'Here you go.'

Oliver carefully places her glass of white wine and his pint of something on the table and then slides into the booth until he's sitting next to her, but still a polite foot away.

'They're rearranging the tables,' he says, lifting his chin to indicate the back of the bar.

'I heard.'

'Some of the booths are already taped off.'

'Taped off with what?'

'Hazard tape,' he says. 'Black and yellow stripes.'

'That's … slightly terrifying.'

'I would say "And surreal", but I think I've already maxed out my allowance of that word for the week. See also: *unprecedented*. Anyway …' He puts a hand on her forearm, lightly squeezes it. 'Let's talk about something else. Or attempt to. Why did you move to Dublin?'

She has told him this already, she thinks.

She says, 'Because of my job.'

'But you knew the job was here before you applied for it. So why did you apply?'

'Oh, you know.' She looks into her wine glass, picks it up, takes a sip. 'The usual. I fancied a change. A new adventure. Fresh start.'

'Was going on a date with a rando you met in the supermarket part of that plan?'

Date.

'It might help achieve its objectives,' she says without looking at him, feeling her cheeks warm under his gaze. 'We'll see.'

The long silence that follows this is so excruciating for her that she fears she will spontaneously combust.

'I know what you mean,' he says then. 'That's why I'm here. Why I left London.'

When she turns to him she sees that his gaze is fixed now on something that isn't there, some memory in the middle distance, and although she wants to ask him what he's thinking about, wants to know more about whatever it was that went on in London, she has a very real sense that now isn't the time, that it's too soon.

'Cheers,' he says, picking up his glass. 'To fresh starts.'

Two more rounds later, the barman comes to tell them that he's closing up early. He apologises profusely but they tell him they understand. They are the only patrons, they have been since the man outside left more than an hour ago, and it's obvious the staff need them out of the way to get ready for opening under very different conditions tomorrow. The hazard tape has crept as far as the booth directly across from theirs.

The barman has kindly brought one more round, on the house, to soften the blow, but it's not even nine o'clock when they've finished it.

'We could go to mine,' Oliver suggests casually.

She agrees to this plan with as much nonchalance as her tipsy self allows and then slides out of the booth with as much grace as she can muster. The amount in each case, she suspects, is nowhere near as much as she hopes. But Oliver's eyes are looking a little unfocused and it takes him longer than it should to put his suit jacket back on, so she has to conclude that they're both a little drunk or at least well on their way there.

She hopes his place has food in it, for both their sakes.

They arrive at his apartment complex arm in arm; she doesn't quite remember when that happened, or who initiated it, but she's happy with this turn of events. They've walked along the canal for a bit, back towards hers – although she didn't mention that because she doesn't want him suggesting they go to her place, not yet – and then turned left, and there might have been a park on the right at some point ... Now they are outside a modern building shaped like a 'U', standing at its glass doors while Oliver roots for his keys.

Gold lettering above the doors says it's called THE CROSSINGS.

She reads this aloud, adding a question mark at the end. This many drinks in on an empty stomach, it seems like a silly name.

'Harold's Cross,' Oliver says, by way of explanation.

'Whose what now?'

He laughs. 'That's where we *are*. Harold's Cross. It's the name of the area.'

'Oh.'

He touches a plastic fob to a sensor and one of the doors obediently clicks open. They enter a lobby made of glass; a light comes on overhead, making Ciara blink.

Through another set of doors opposite, she glimpses a central courtyard with a little tinkling water feature in its centre, surrounded by wooden benches and carefully planted trees and flowerbeds. The apartments rise up around them on three sides, each of their balconies empty, soft lights on behind wispy curtains.

'Do you have roommates?' she asks.

'It's just me. It's a work thing. Came with the job. Only temporarily, though. I get it rent-free for three months.'

'And then what?'

'And then we'll see.'

He grins in a way that makes her think he wants her to think she'll have some part to play in that.

Christ, she *really* needs to eat something.

She follows him past the lifts and down a long corridor of spaced-apart doors from whose other sides there comes no sound. She keeps a couple of steps behind because there is no way after this much time and that many glasses of wine that her make-up still looks the way it did when she left the house, and the bright white spotlights clicking on directly overhead will only make it worse.

She's relieved when he pushes open his own door – 1 – to reveal a dim, softly lit space beyond.

'Come on in,' he says, waving a hand theatrically.

She smiles and accepts the invite, the heels of her boots making a hollow noise as they connect with the hardwood floor.

He takes her coat and says he'll give her the tour, which consists of him walking her into the living room while pointing at things – the closed doors of two bedrooms and a third, partially open one which leads to a wet-room-style bathroom with a monsoon shower and subway tiles.

The living space is open-plan, with a glossy kitchen area to the rear. The walls are white and decorated with arty, abstract prints. ('They came with the place.') A rich brown leather L-shaped sofa faces a faux fire that 'burns' inside a black glass box recessed into the wall once Oliver hits a switch. Above it hangs a flat-screen TV bigger than Ciara's dining table. He pulls the curtains closed across the big windows – no, sliding doors – that face into the courtyard.

There are no things, no possessions. Nothing personalising the space except for a lone magazine lying open on the couch. But it's not a clinical neatness that's going on here – more like a barely lived-in vibe, as if this is a holiday home he's just checked into for the night.

The kitchen has the same odd, cold, bareness: the countertops are empty except for a bottle of supermarket own-brand olive oil and a roll of kitchen paper.

'I could fit my entire place into this room,' she says.

He walks back to her. 'I realise this is very much hashtag-first-world-problems, but it's actually a bit *too* big. I feel like I've been rattling around in here, all by myself.' A pause. 'Alone.'

Their eyes meet, a spark of electricity connecting the air between them, a fork of lightning in an otherwise dark sky.

'Well,' Ciara says, hoping she can get the next three words out before her entire face is aflame, betraying her, showing her for the nervous wreck she actually is. 'I'm here now.'

'And I'm glad you are.'

He has said this softly, and now he reaches for her.

She lets him.

He slides his arms around her waist and pulls her close until their faces are touching, cheek to cheek. She can feel the heat of his breath, smell the beer on it. The acute intimacy of this, coming so suddenly, is disorientating, and that mixed with the wine makes her feel loose and fluid.

Less anxious. A braver version of herself.

Maybe even a different person altogether.

He presses his lips against her temple and murmurs, 'I don't want to infect you.'

She can hear – and then feel – him smile. She slides one hand around his waist until it's resting on the small of his back. His skin feels hot beneath his shirt. She runs her other hand up his arm and across his shoulder, until she is touching the skin on his neck, cupping his jaw, pulling him towards her.

'I'm willing to risk it,' she says to his lips.

By her estimation, they have now spent around ten hours together, just talking. But when his mouth finds hers, they tell each something neither of them could possibly say: that they are two very lonely people hungry for touch, needing it, *starving* for it. Tenderness quickly turns to desperation, as if they're both trying to cross the barrier of their own skins.

She unbuttons his shirt. His chest is covered in a blanket of fine, dark hair. She presses her palms into it and then up towards his collarbone and on to his shoulders, lifting the material from his skin. It's when he steps back to do the rest himself that she first glimpses it: a thick cord of scar tissue, snaking nearly all the way down his side.

Seeing her looking, he angles his body to give her a view of the whole thing.

'I know,' he says. 'Impressive, right?'

The silvery thread of smooth, newer skin is about half an inch wide and curves from just underneath his left shoulder blade down to his waist. Pairs of pale dots appear at neat intervals, one on either side: the skin's memories of the staples that must have held it in place while it healed.

She traces it lightly with her fingertips. 'What happened?'

'It's not a nice story.' He sighs then, as if resigned to the telling. 'I got in a fight. On a night out. When I was seventeen. Drank too much, got too brave, looked at some guy the wrong way. Looked at the *wrong* guy the wrong way. He waited for me outside, broke a bottle off the wall. I know I'm lucky it wasn't worse, but ...' He turns back to face her.

'I feel like I paid a high price for one moment of madness. Not even madness, just stupidity. And now I have this thing on my body forever that isn't anything to do with who I am.'

'I'm so sorry,' she says.

'It's not your fault.'

'It's not yours either.'

He looks away. 'I don't know about that.'

She touches his cheek, pulling his face – and eyes – back towards her.

There are no nerves now, no overthinking.

She feels a strange peace; the voice in her head has, miraculously, gone away.

These last few days have felt like a door being opened very, very slowly. Now, finally, Ciara is ready to step through.

I can do this, she thinks.

It was easier than she'd thought it would be, but there is no solid ground on the other side.

She doesn't care. She lifts her face to his and kisses him.

She steps over the threshold and throws herself into the fall.

56 DAYS AGO

'Go ahead,' are the first words he ever says to her.

They are both on the cusp of joining the queue for the self-service checkouts in Tesco. It's Friday lunchtime and his fifth time this week stopping in for a sandwich, because he comes in here every weekday round about now and has done, almost without fail, since he started working at the firm across the street.

It's also his fifth time this week seeing *her* in here, doing the same thing.

Seemingly.

He might not have noticed her at all if it weren't for the bag: a little swingy canvas thing with a picture of a Space Shuttle on it. It was the bag that initially caught his eye, on Monday. Come Tuesday, he saw it again. When he saw it on Wednesday, he wondered if it was odd that he would see it – her – three days in a row and, on Thursday, he concluded that it definitely was.

That's when he noted the way she carried the bag: by its handles, swinging by her side, even though it was clearly empty and would be until she made her way through the checkouts. Why not just keep it folded in her hand, or tucked under her arm, or put away in the little bag with a strap she wore over one shoulder until she was in need of it?

It was almost like she *wanted* people to see her carrying it.

Or, perhaps, just for him to.

That's what had started the wheels turning. He wondered: why had he never seen any other blue-lanyard-wearing employees in these aisles? Like all good tech companies, they probably had free food in their building, *good* free food, like fresh sushi and an in-house barista, so why would one of their employees queue up for a bland, soggy, plastic-wrapped supermarket sandwich that they had to pay for?

Maybe he just hadn't noticed it before.

But then how was it that even though he took his lunch at a slightly different time every day, leaving his desk only when there was a natural break in his work, she always happened to be in here at the exact same time as him?

Five days in a *row*?

Today, he'd spotted her standing by the drinks fridge just inside the entrance, waiting patiently for a twenty-something guy in a spray-on blue shirt to make his selection so she could step in and make hers.

He saw the bag first, swinging empty as it always was, and then the green winter coat she seems to be in every day.

All this week, he's been logging details.

Just in case.

She's shorter than him by a foot, about the same age,

slim but not skinny; there's a softness to her cheeks and the line of her jaw. Attractive in a quiet way. Her hair is light brown and cut bluntly at the ends, so the two sides swish like curtains against her shoulders as she moves. Her lanyard hangs from a bright blue ribbon and displays a barcode, a small passport photo and the logo of a tech company with a cloud-computing arm whose European HQ occupies an entire building just a couple of minutes' walk from here. There's a couple of lines of text on it he hasn't got close enough to read.

He's never caught her looking at him, but that's neither here nor there. She could be not looking at him on purpose, or just really good at doing it surreptitiously.

Or this could all be pure paranoia on his part.

He'd walked past her and made his way to the very back of the store, where he'd waited his turn at the deli counter to order his usual: chicken, stuffing and mayo on rye, no butter. To stop himself from scanning the aisles for emerald-green wool, he'd taken out his phone and focused intently on the latest headlines in a news app. Then he made his way to the checkouts where he saw that she was just about to join the queue – perfect timing, but whose? – and he'd hung back so she'd have to do it in front of him, and that's when she'd stopped and looked up and their eyes had met.

A flash of something – surprise? Recognition? – crosses her face just as he thinks to himself, *I've seen her somewhere before*.

Somewhere else, in different circumstances.

But where?

When?

'It's okay,' she mumbles, waving the bottle of water she's holding in her right hand. She takes a step back. 'I've just realised I've got the wrong one.'

She turns on her heel and hurries off in the opposite direction.

And now he thinks, *Gotcha.*

He knew coming back to Ireland would be a risk, but he had presumed that enough time had passed for him to be yesterday's news. Besides, anyone interested in exposing him would have to find him first. He goes by his mother's maiden name now. He's severed all contact with anyone he knew or had known on the day he left London, save for two people: his brother, who can be trusted, and Dan, who is professionally obligated to be. Oliver has a better cover story now and is more practised in sticking to it. He doesn't take risks. He *won't* take them.

There can't be a repeat of what happened in London.

But now he's seen this vaguely familiar woman swinging her little Space Shuttle bag in the supermarket across from his office every day for five days in a row, at a slightly different time each day, and it's got him paranoid.

Who is she, really?

What is she?

When Oliver gets outside, he ducks into the nearest doorway and takes out his phone again. Opens the browser and types his name into the search bar. His actual, given one. Nothing comes up except the same old stuff. He checks Twitter by using twitter.com/ireland as a URL. It loads the @ireland page and, crucially, a search bar; he doesn't have an account himself but this lets him search while also bypassing signing in. The laws that govern reporters and the publications they work for don't seem to apply to this apparent cesspool of a site, but he finds nothing there either. Maybe he *is* just being paranoid.

That's when it happens.

He looks up and sees her, just about to walk past him, swinging that damn bag.

He isn't planning to do it. There's no premeditation at all on his part – and that, right there, is the problem, the same thing that got him into trouble the last time, in London, and the first time, all those years ago.

He doesn't think, he just *does*.

He opens his mouth and the words, 'Nice bag,' come out.

She stops dead, blanches. 'My ...?'

He's already regretting it. He shouldn't speak to her. He knows that, he's not stupid. But the only thing worse than her being a journalist is her thinking he's too stupid to see that she is.

And he's done it now.

'Your bag,' he says, pointing.

She looks down at it, then back up at him.

'Thanks,' she says. 'It's from the Intrepid. It's a museum in—'

'New York,' he finishes. This one must really have done

her homework. 'The one on the aircraft carrier, right?' *Let's see how much of it she's done.* 'Have you been?'

'Yeah. Once.'

That's smart of her. It won't take much detail to make that story sound convincing because, hey, she was only there the one time.

'Was it good?' he asks.

'Ah …'

And it's this, her hesitation, that does it. That's what convinces him that his suspicions are correct.

In this moment, the fear of what that might mean for his future is dwarfed by the high of the win, by the smugness of having smoked her out. But he can't *say* that he has, can't tell her that he knows. If he confronted her, that would only give her the confirmation she seeks and the fodder whatever rag she works for desperately wants.

So he opts for the next best thing: playing dumb and watching her squirm.

Because why should he suffer?

Why the hell can't they just leave him alone?

Yeah, okay, the Space Shuttle thing was clever – the T-shirt with the NASA logo was one of the most reported-on pieces of evidence all those years ago – but there's no way she's as prepared as she thinks she is. She can't be. This is all just a thin layer of cover and he's sure he won't have to dig too deep to find the bottom of it, to expose her for who – and what – she really is.

'Yeah,' she answers finally. 'But not as good as Kennedy

Space Center.'

Oliver blinks in surprise. This one has come to *play*.

He steps closer to her, watching for the telltale flinch or ripple of unease across her face. But not only does she fail to react, she actually *takes a step closer* to him.

'You know,' he says, 'I've never met someone who can name all five Space Shuttles.'

'And I *still* haven't met someone who knows there are six.'

Her tone is somewhere between challenge and condescension, and it throws him. If she *is* a journalist, shouldn't she be doing her best to butter him up? Isn't insulting him the last thing she would do if her goal was to get him to talk?

Or is this a double-bluff, an attempt to throw him off her scent?

'*Six?*'

She starts naming them.

But not *just* naming them. She also tells him where each one ended up. She has dates. She even includes the *Enterprise*. She calls it an *Orbiter*. And she says all this to the footpath, which goes to strengthen his suspicions that she's prepared this in advance and is now reciting it from memory.

But ...

It also gives him a chance to see her lanyard up close. The passport-style photo on it is definitely her, just with longer hair and standing in an unflattering, bleached-out light. The text says her name is CIARA W and that she is something called a TECH CS CONCIERGE.

It looks legit.

It swings him back to unsure.

Maybe she *isn't* a journalist. Maybe she really does work for the tech company around the corner and likes Space Shuttles enough to carry around a bag with one on it and where he's seen her before this week is *here*, on this street, because she works nearby.

But that doesn't account for why, five days in a row, she's been here at the same time he has when he's been here at a slightly different time each day. Not by much, granted – he always leaves within the same twenty- or thirty-minute timeframe – but *still*.

This fact is a stone in his shoe: something small, but incredibly bothersome.

He needs to find out more, to know enough to get rid of it.

'I was going to go get a coffee,' he says to her. 'Can I buy you one too?'

He leads her to the branch of Insomnia a little further up the street, because he knows that, being a chain, the counter will be laid out a certain way. He's not sure he has enough cash on him to pay for the drinks, and he won't take his debit card out in front of her. If she is what he suspects she is, she could know his mother's maiden name, and seeing it printed on something official after his first name would be confirmation for her that she's found her man.

She says she'll have a cappuccino so he orders two, and suggests they get them to go so they can drink them outside, maybe by the canal if they can get a spot. She seems eager to accept this invitation and inordinately pleased that he has offered.

He swings back to suspicious.

But then she goes to wait at the end of the counter while he stays by the till to pay. It doesn't matter anyway because he finds a ten-euro note in his pocket, but if she *was* trying to confirm his identity, wouldn't she have stayed close and tried to get a glimpse inside his wallet?

Back to unsure.

This is so bloody exhausting.

The weather has been changing its mind all day but when they go back outside, the sun is shining. They find an empty spot on the low wall by the service station that offers them a view of the canal, and once they've settled down he asks her to tell him about Kennedy Space Center.

He has never been, but he has seen things about it online and on TV. They never went anywhere but France on holiday when he was young and now, travel to the United States is out.

Have you ever been arrested or convicted for a crime that resulted in serious damage to property, or serious harm to another person?

Ciara doesn't seem fazed by the question. If anything, she seems eager to talk about the place. She tells him about a bus tour that takes you around the launch pads, the 'VAB – the Vehicle Assembly Building' and the famous blue countdown clock. About the IMAX cinema and the Rocket Garden, which seems to be exactly what it sounds like. The 'ride' that simulates a Space Shuttle launch and which, she says, makes your neck hurt. The Apollo Center where you get to see a Saturn V rocket and the shuttle *Atlantis* on display.

'It's revealed to you,' she says. 'Unexpectedly. A surprise. You're herded into this big, dark room to watch a video about the Shuttle programme and then, at the end, the screen slides up and reveals the Shuttle just … Just *there*, in all its glory, right in front of you. With the cargo bay doors open and at an angle so it actually looks like it's flying through space. It's amazing. People actually gasped. After I'd walked around it and taken all my pictures and read all the exhibits and stuff, I went back to where I'd come in and I waited for the screen to go up so I could watch *other* people's faces, so I could see their reactions, and it was …'

She is really laying this on thick, if it is an act. *Too* thick.

His face must be saying as much because she looks at him then and seems to realise the same thing.

'It's just that I wanted to go for so long,' she says quickly. 'Since I was a child, really. So it was a bit like, I don't know … Walking around in a dream.'

He says, 'I really want to go.'

This isn't a lie.

She looks relieved. 'You should.'

'Yeah … Thing is, I hate the heat.'

That *is* one.

'God, don't let that stop you. It's all ice-cold air-conditioning and misting machines. Plus, it's not always hot and steamy in Florida. I went in March and it was actually quite nice.'

'Was this a girls' trip or …?'

She pretends not to have noticed that he is fishing for information and he pretends not to have noticed her noticing but pretending not to.

'Work, primarily. A tech conference in Orlando …'

One of the guys he shared a flat with back in London attended a conference there last year – something to do with sustainable travel, ironically – so Oliver happens to know that there *is* a big convention centre in the city. And because he'd been surprised to hear this, thinking it was all rollercoasters and human-sized rodents in red shorts, he'd said, 'Orlando? Really?' and his flatmate had told him that the city actually has the most convention space by square metre of any US city and only Las Vegas has more hotel rooms. So her story fits, but does it do that because it's the truth, or because she's done her research?

She's looking towards the canal now, sipping her coffee silently, and he uses the opportunity to study her.

'Cork, right?' he asks.

He's not especially good with accents but he thinks he can hear traces of the city's in hers.

'Originally,' she says. 'We moved to the Isle of Man when I was seven.'

He doesn't think he's ever met anybody who actually lives there. All he knows about it is that it's in the Irish Sea and they have motorcycling races.

When she asks him where he's from, he says Kilkenny.

No one remembers where he was from originally, only where it happened, so this is a relatively safe share of some truth. When she asks him how long he's been in Dublin, he offers a little more of it by admitting it's been six weeks.

'And where were you seven weeks ago?'

'London,' he says. 'And you?'

'How long am I in Dublin?' She makes a show of thinking about this. 'Well, next Monday it'll be, ah ... seven days.'

'Seven *days*?' And on five of them, he's seen her? 'And here was I thinking *I* was the newbie.'

She laughs. 'Nope. I win that game.'

'Where were you before?'

'Cork. Since I finished college. I went to Swansea. Not-at-all-notable member of the Class of 2017, here.'

He does the maths in his head.

Class of 2017. Presuming she went to university when she was seventeen or eighteen, that'd make her ... Twenty-five or -six. She said they moved to the Isle of Man when she was seven, which would be ... Around 2002.

A year before it happened. Two years before the trial.

'What about you?' she asks. 'Where did you go?'

'Newcastle,' he says absently.

He's thinking about her being out of the country back then and which column to put this information in. The timeline is pretty tight – tight enough to make him wonder if it wasn't designed to be that way. And even if it's true, who's to say that Irish news headlines didn't reach the Isle of Man?

He feels tired suddenly, spent by the effort of playing this game. Of *having* to play some version of it, always. Even now, years after the fact.

And not being able to get a reading on this woman, at least not one he can hold on to for very long.

There has to be a more efficient way to find out who she really is.

'I'm going to be late back.' He looks at his watch – he still has a good twenty minutes left on his lunch hour – and stands up.

She stands up as well. 'Yeah, I better go, too. Well … Thanks for the coffee.'

And then he has an idea.

'Look,' he says, 'I was going to go see that new Apollo documentary. On Monday. Night. They're showing it at this tiny cinema in town. Maybe – if you wanted to – we could, um, we could go see it together?'

He can't read her expression.

Is that shock? Unease? *Panic?*

Maybe he's pushed her too far. If she's been tasked with getting close to him then this should be welcome, but if that's the case she also knows who he is, *what* he is, and this would explain her hesitation at the prospect of spending more time with him.

'God,' he says, looking away. 'I'm so shit at this.'

But then she appears to recover and tells him that sounds great. He offers to book the tickets and suggests they meet at 5.30 p.m. outside his office. She asks where that is and he explains.

'I'll give you my phone number,' he says then. 'Just in

case there's any last-minute problems.'

'Sure, yeah.'

He calls out the digits and she taps them into her phone – and just as he'd hoped, she sends him a text message so he has hers.

'I'll add you to my contacts as Space Shuttle Girl,' he says.

She smiles. 'I like it.'

'Better put in your actual name as well.' He keeps his eyes on his phone as he says this, tapping away at the screen, tone as casual as he can make it. 'Ciara …?'

'Wyse,' she finishes. 'W-Y-S-E.'

Mission accomplished.

They walk back together as far as his office, then wave each other goodbye.

As he turns to enter the building, he realises that she never asked *him* his last name.

Oliver takes the lift up to the fourth floor and turns left into the offices of KB Studios. Friday is always busy with off-site client meetings and this combined with the time of the day has most of the desks deserted. He goes to his and tilts his computer screen so that even if someone were to come and sit down right next to him, they'd have a hard time seeing what he was at.

He opens the internet browser and types *Ciara Wyse* into Google. When he presses ENTER, the screen fills with results.

A Ciara Wyse recently retired as the principal of a local school. Another has a professional bio on the website of a firm of Donegal accountants. There's a smattering of social accounts belonging to teenage girls with the same name and a Pinterest board linked to that name filled with ideas for tattoos.

None of them seem to be her.

But there are also a number of LinkedIn profiles. He logs on to the site and double-checks his privacy settings; as ever, they are set to hide his identity when browsing other users' pages. When he searches for her within the site, he finds her straight away; she's the top result.

The photo is a professional headshot of her with longer, darker hair. Under Education, it lists a secondary school in the Isle of Man and a BSc in Business Management from the University of Swansea. Class of 2017, just as she'd said. Experience includes three different positions in something called Operation and Supply Chain at Apple's plant in Cork – she went back there after Swansea, then – and her current role: Technical Customer Service Concierge for Cirrus Web Services, Dublin office. The start date is listed as February 2020. There's very little else on the profile and she only has a couple of dozen connections, but everything on it fits with what she said.

Still, it's just a page on a website where the user enters the text. He could make one right now that says he went to Harvard and works as a NASA astronaut.

What he needs is independent confirmation.

He searches on Twitter, Instagram and Facebook, but finds nothing – at least, nothing set to public – that looks like it could be her.

He drums his fingers on his desk, thinking. Then he goes back to Google and puts *Cirrus Web Services Dublin* into the search box.

There's a local phone number listed for the building on Burlington Road. He doubts it's anything more than a connection to a faraway call centre where Ciara won't be, but it's worth a try.

He punches the number into the phone on his desk and puts the receiver to his ear.

It rings just once before a recorded voice says, 'Thank you for calling Cirrus Ireland. If you know the extension number, please enter it now. Otherwise press zero for reception. Please note that—'

He presses zero. There's a click and one ring, and then a male sing-song voice says, 'Good afternoon, Cirrus. How can I help you?'

'Ah, hi. I'm not sure I have the right number – is this the building on the Burlington Road?'

'Who are trying to reach, sir?'

'Ciara Wyse. She's a' – he flips back to the other window on his computer screen and reads from her LinkedIn profile – 'Technical Customer Service Concierge.' He can hear a distant clacking of keys on the other end of the line as he speaks.

'I can't connect you,' the guy says, 'but I can give you her extension number?'

'That'd be great.'

'It's 5-4-1-0.'

He scribbles the number on a pad of Post-its by his keyboard, even though he doesn't intend to actually call her. That would be taking his paranoia to unprecedented heights.

'Thank you,' he says.

'Thanks for calling Cirrus Ireland.' *Click*.

Oliver is even more confused than before. Either this is, by far, the most elaborate scheme he's ever been up against or Ciara really is who she says she is.

A nice girl with no agenda other than the age-old one. The *normal* one. Liking someone, wanting to get to know them, hoping that things will eventually turn ...

Romantic.

The word seems foreign to him, borrowed from another language.

And what if she *is* that? It doesn't mean the threat is neutralised. It merely swaps one danger for another.

Isn't this just how the mess in London began?

He should delete her number. Forget all about her and start bringing a packed lunch. Because nothing can happen. Even if – *if* – he managed to feign normality for a while, the truth would eventually come out. It's too big to hide.

Everything is so much easier when he stays away from other people. The only way you can lose your own shadow is to stand in the dark.

The problem is, Oliver hates the dark.

He takes out his phone and finds the text message she sent him for the purposes of giving him her number. *For future ref: Enterprise, Columbia, Challenger, Discovery, Atlantis,*

Endeavour. Rocketship emoji, winking face emoji.

His thumb hovers over it, ready to swipe to delete.

That's what he *should* do.

But he doesn't.

TODAY

Lee pushes the bathroom door back just enough to get past it, ignoring the horror that lies on the other side of it for now.

She knows that *that's* there. What she needs is to check if anything else is too, first.

If any*one* else is.

She tells herself to ignore the smell that is tickling her gag reflex, to focus on the scene, to log the details – and to move fast because she isn't going to be able to do that for very long.

Three more doors lead off the hall, each one standing open.

On her right, after the bathroom: a small, sparse bedroom. The narrow wardrobes are built-in – and empty – and the only furniture is a bare box-spring pushed up against the far wall and what looks like a dining table that has been commandeered as a desk.

Sitting on it is a closed laptop, some loose papers and pens. The laptop wears a sticker that says KB STUDIOS. A printer sits on the floor underneath the desk, plugged out.

The roller-blinds on the room's single window are all the way up, offering a view of the courtyard.

At the end of the hall, facing the front door: the master bedroom. The double bed is unmade, the charcoal-grey sheets thrown back from the side closest to the door but left undisturbed on the other. She opens the drawer in the bedside table and finds it empty except for dust. Inside the wardrobe sit two suitcases, one large and one small, empty going by the weight of them; a small pile of folded jeans; a row of hanging suits and shirts; a drawer of socks and underwear.

All men's, all a similar size. Someone in their twenties or thirties, she'd guess, going by the style. There's also some running gear and a washbag with deodorant, men's moisturiser and a blue bottle of Acqua di Parma.

She estimates that only about a third of the wardrobe space is being used.

There is another window to the courtyard in here, a larger one, with its blinds pulled all the way down. A lamp by the bed is turned on.

Through the door off the left of the hall: an open-plan living space. At one end is the kind of kitchen Lee is used to seeing in Instagram ads for new developments in Dublin but never actually in anyone's home: smooth, white and clinically glossy.

It has an empty, unused look. She figures there must be fourteen feet of counterspace in its L-shape, but there's nothing sitting out except for one of those George Clooney coffee machines, a lone oven glove and a set of keys with a plastic fob attached.

The keys are on a ring printed with a Viva Property logo.

A breakfast bar marks the end of the kitchen and the start of the living room, which is furnished only with a large, brown leather couch and a small coffee table. A flat-screen TV hangs on the wall above a faux fire. The walls are painted white and hung with the kind of meaningless abstract prints that chain hotels buy in volume, the type that achieve an exact balance of not drawing the eye but also sufficiently breaking up bare-wall blankness.

The thin privacy curtains are pulled across the sliding doors that lead to the little terrace outside; when she makes a gap in them with a single finger, she sees a table and two chairs out there, and the remains of a citronella candle. The door is closed but when she pulls on it, it opens easily.

One of the living room's two ceiling lights is on.

This survey has taken her about forty seconds and she figures she can do another twenty or so before the coffee she drank for breakfast threatens a reappearance.

Lee goes back out into the hall and opens the bathroom door all the way so that it folds back against the hall wall, but doesn't actually touch it, just in case there's something of evidentiary value on the handle that they'll need to collect in due course.

As she does this, she glimpses what awaits her and feels something flex right at the back of her throat.

She breathes in through her nose, trying to find any

remnant of the mints, trying to convince her brain that menthol is all she can smell. Upchucking inside a face mask in the middle of a scene *really* wouldn't be a good look.

Let's just get this over with.

Lee looks down.

The bathroom has no windows and the ceiling light is on. The body is kneeling on the floor. Face pressed against the tiles, arms by the sides, directly beneath the shower head. Clothed in what looks like jeans and a T-shirt. Barefoot. Short, light brown hair. Facing away from her. A male, she thinks, but she couldn't swear to it: she doesn't have a great view and won't get one without disturbing the scene, and parts of the body are oddly misshapen. Bloated in some areas, sunk in others. An advanced stage of decomposition. No obvious wounds or blood, at least from her vantage point. A putrid sludge of fluid surrounds the body and connects it to the plughole like a speech bubble. The skin—

She swallows hard, forcing back bile, and steadies herself.

She can only see the skin on the soles of the feet, the back of the neck and the nearest arm – the deceased's right one – from the elbow on down, but that much is bad enough. It's puckered on the feet and a deep purple colour, and the arm is showing evidence of skin slippage: the top layer has become separated, like peeling after a particularly bad sunburn.

At least there's no flies, she tells herself. If that sliding door had been left open … She'd already be back outside, trying to find a not-terrible place to throw up.

The bathroom is wet-room style, with an even floor of

marbled black tiles throughout. A glass shower panel stands in a black metal frame next to the former site of a matching glass door, now in a thousand little diamond-like nuggets that lie strewn all over the floor. She can see a few pieces glinting in the deceased's hair.

She turns to look behind her.

There's a mirrored medicine cabinet on the wall. She opens it, scans the contents. It doesn't take long; like the rest of the apartment, it's mostly empty.

Some disposable face masks, loosely stacked on a shelf. A bottle of thickening shampoo. A box of plasters and a blister pack of small, green pills.

Careful where she steps, she moves closer to see if she can make out what's stamped on them. *542*, she thinks it says, confirming that they are what they look like: Rohypnol, the date-rape drug.

She closes the cabinet and turns to the sink.

There's a small shelf above it but otherwise no storage, so it doesn't take long to determine that there's nothing else in the bathroom except toothbrushing supplies (one toothbrush), a few rolls of toilet paper and a bottle of hand-soap. Plus one bath towel, hanging on a hook by the door.

The smell is steadily drawing the coffee up into her oesophagus.

Lee turns back to the body. Moving any closer to it will disturb the glass on the floor and God knows what else, but she does her best to lean over to see if she can get a better look at the head and—

She gags when this new angle reveals a fist-sized cluster of maggots wriggling in and around what looks like a head wound near the left temple.

She wants to run.

She wants to throw up.

She wants to run out of here right now *while* throwing up, but she tells her brain to remain calm, just a few more seconds, that's all she needs ...

She fixes her gaze on the wall tiles directly across from the wound and starts moving it upwards in a straight line—

There.

At about chest-height, above the head: a smudge of brown. Dried blood.

Contact.

35 DAYS AGO

Ciara does another circuit of the flat, counting her steps as she goes. She starts in the little kitchen, standing at the counter with her palms flat on the only surface that isn't stovetop or sink: a thick off-white slab of Formica whose smooth gloss has long been scrubbed away. Take three steps and she's in the living room, which is also the dining room, which is also the bedroom, which is only separated from the kitchen by what she's seen people on property programmes call *a breakfast bar*.

Five steps to cross the floor to the couch. Seven from the couch to the door. Two from that door to the front door. She turns back around and counts out the four steps it takes her to enter the bathroom.

Oliver's a foot taller than her. He'll be able to do it in even fewer.

She stands before the mirror above the sink and inspects the glass for smudges. She opens the medicine cabinet and tries to see the contents as a stranger would. She did this very thing already, not even half an hour ago, but on second thoughts the blister plasters might make him think of red-raw skin and seeping wounds, specifically *her* red-raw skin and seeping wounds, so she slides them behind a pack of soothing eye-gels until they disappear from sight.

Then, as an afterthought, she hides the hair removal cream too.

She once spent a summer in college working as a housekeeper in a seaside hotel and something from her training drifts back to her now.

Sit where the guest will sit. Lie where the guest will lie. See what the guest will see.

She puts the toilet lid down and perches on it, looks around.

The bathroom is like the rest of the flat: tiny and from the seventies. It has an avocado suite, rippled linoleum on the floor and a shower curtain attached to a precariously positioned tension rod. It's already come down on her twice in the short time she's lived here, once hitting her square on the forehead and leaving a red mark. At least the caulking has been redone recently, but its brightness only serves to highlight how much the wall tiles have yellowed over the years.

She scans the floor for dust, wayward hairs, a dropped cotton bud sullied with wax.

All clear.

The bathroom has no window and the fan doesn't work, only a narrow vent in the wall above the bath that she's already excised the dust from. She's bought a little canister of non-offensive air freshener – *Soft Cotton*, it claims to smell like, although how you can *smell* something is soft is beyond her – but now she wonders if its current placement, sitting on top of the cistern, seems a bit passive-aggressive … Does it look like a demand? She puts it on the little shelf below the sink instead, turning the label out so it's easy to find.

Four steps back into the everything room, seven steps back to the couch.

She sits down carefully so as not to disturb the placement of the throws or the plumped-up cushions, and systematically scans the room for dust, cobwebs or any other offences.

She finds none. She doesn't think the flat was *this* clean on the day she moved in.

She wonders, yet again, what he'll make of it. She tries to see it as he will, as she did before she got a little used to it. For a studio in a crumbling tower block, it's actually not that bad. A large window offers clear-sky views because she is on the top floor of the complex's tallest red-brick block in a city where almost everything else is much shorter. Right now, the evening sun is filling the room with natural light and the room's bare white walls are reflecting it, amplifying it. There's a small, square dining table with two chairs and a battered, sunken couch currently hiding beneath a deep purple throw she bought in Penneys – or *three* purple throws, because they were small and that's how many of them it took to mostly cover it. A desk doubles as a dressing table. Most of one wall is taken up with what looks like a built-in wardrobe in beech effect but is actually a Murphy bed that folds down, its sheets and pillows kept in place by Velcro straps. A faded canvas print of a sunrise over Dublin hangs by the door to the kitchen, but it's too big for the space and has been hung slightly askew and half-a-foot too high. Nothing matches and there are few personal items, save for the NASA mug that's been demoted to a pen pot and the small stack of well-thumbed books lined up neatly beside it.

She's already carefully considered each spine and how it might make her look. The collection promises stories about the Apollo moonwalkers, a tech start-up that failed spectacularly and the crisis aboard the space station *Mir* back in the nineties, as well as a pulpy thriller, a millennial literary novel that's been on the bestseller charts for what feels like years and a copy of *Pride and Prejudice*, brittle and yellowed from years of rereading.

She's hidden the book she's actually reading – a historical romance – in one of the desk drawers.

She's also cut the anthers out of the pink lilies arranged in a vase on the dining table just in case he doesn't know not to touch them, just in case he arrives in one of his knit jumpers with the little polo-player emblem embroidered on the left breast and leans down to breathe in their scent.

She scans again but can't find anything out of place. This should give her confidence but it has the opposite effect: the perfection feels exceptionally delicate, impossible to maintain, even just for these last few minutes.

Her eyes flick to the digital clock on the TV.

Almost eight. He'll be here any second.

Five steps back into the kitchen. She opens a cupboard and checks again that her two wine glasses are clear, no smudges or residue. That there's ice in the freezer. That when you open the oven door you aren't met with a chemical whiff of oven cleaner you might suspect will somehow taint the taste of cooked food, or the sight of a long-forgotten chip burned to a black ash.

'Do you think he put this much effort into prepping *his* place for *you*?' she asks the empty kitchen.

Of course he didn't. But his place is brand new. And enormous.

She has to work to impress.

The buzzer goes.

She rushes to the intercom and says, 'Hello?' into the microphone as if anyone at all might respond, as if the buzzer-presser is a mystery man, as if it would be anybody but him.

Then she takes a deep breath and tells herself to *calm the hell down.*

'Hey,' he says, his voice sounding tinny through the speaker. 'It's me.'

She presses the button that releases the door lock downstairs and hears the corresponding mechanical *click* through the speaker.

'Sixth floor,' she reminds him, even though she's already told him this twice by text. The only response is the sound of a heavy door left to slam closed.

She releases the button and goes back into the main room. One last check of it. One last check of herself, in the mirror.

But by the time she's done she still hasn't heard the *ding* of the elevator or the *clunk* of the fire door swinging shut at the end of the hall, so she has time to check again. She finds a smudge of mascara beneath her left eye now. How did that happen? *When* did it?

She licks a finger and carefully rubs it off.

Ding.

Clunk.

Showtime.

She opens her front door and sticks her head out into the hall. He's in jeans, a T-shirt and a black leather jacket. Carrying a brown paper bag by its handles and a bottle of wine by its neck. When he sees her, he smiles.

Every time she sees him like this – up close, coming towards her, coming *to* her – she can't quite believe that it's really happening.

That it *still* is, three weeks in.

She smiles back. 'You found me.'

'This time.' He looks sheepish. 'I *may* have gone to the wrong block first ...'

She laughs because this is exactly what she warned him would happen if he didn't follow her instructions to the letter. There's several identical-looking blocks in the complex, no decent signs and multiple entrances and exits.

When he reaches her, she steps back inside so he can come in.

He stops to bend down and meet her lips with his, lifting the wine as he does, absently pressing its cold glass against her side. The chill of it through the thin material of her shirt startles her momentarily, as does the reality of this tall, strong, male body being in the smallest, tightest space of her flat.

In the same moment, the lock turns in the door directly across the hall.

Shit.

The door opens a crack, no more than two or three inches, its rusting safety chain not even pulled taut. An elderly woman – her eyes narrowed, her white hair pulled into a tight bun, one blue-white hand of swollen knuckles and yellow fingernails holding a surgical mask over her mouth – appears in the gap with only gloom visible beyond.

Maura, the sixth floor's self-appointed Chief Enforcement Officer.

'No visitors!' she barks.

Ciara pushes Oliver inside. 'I think that's just from midnight tonight, Maura.'

'Oh, so he'll be leaving before then, will he?'

'Well, actually … He's, ah, moving in. So we'll be one household now. It's fine.' Ciara fixes a smile to her face. 'You don't need to worry.'

Maura's eyes narrow further still. 'He's got nothing with him.'

'His stuff is coming later. Tomorrow.'

'There isn't room enough in there for two.'

'We'll manage.'

'And I suppose Niall knows about all this, does he?'

'He does indeed.' Ciara raises a hand to wave and starts to pull her door closed with the other one. 'Have a good evening now, Maura. Let me know if you need anything.' She shuts the door.

When she turns, she sees him standing in the middle of the living room – the everything room – looking around with great interest, and she silently curses Maura for interfering, for messing up her carefully choreographed plans.

She wanted to *see* him see this place for the first time. She wanted to be able to gauge his reaction.

'So I live here now?' he asks, grinning.

'That was my delightful neighbour, Maura. If we were in East Germany, she'd have the Stasi on speed dial.'

'And Niall?'

'That's my landlord.'

Oliver pretends to wipe this brow. 'Phew.'

'I mean, he *is* also my ex-husband—'

'Right, right.'

'—and the father of my secret child.'

'Oh, I assumed.'

'That I had a child or that he was the father?'

'Both, I think.'

'But he lets me live here rent-free so long as I keep sleeping with him, so …'

'Good deal.'

'You know,' Ciara says, 'this joke isn't that funny when you know what Niall looks like.'

'And what does Niall look like?'

'His age. Which is about eighty-five, I'd say.'

Oliver laughs.

They've already had the exes talk. She told him that she only has one even worth mentioning: Jack. Met in college, started off friends, stayed together for eighteen months after graduation. When things went south, he told her the problem was that she didn't want a nice guy but the actual problem was that he wasn't one.

Oliver said there'd been a girl that he'd met at university. For a long time, he thought she was *the* girl. But then she'd gone to work abroad for a year. They'd carried on long-distance, or so she'd led him to believe – but the day she came back she told him she'd met someone else and that was that.

If you discount short-lived flings with flatmates (and they both do), neither of them have ever officially lived with anybody. Neither of them have any faith in dating apps; they've already traded their best horror stories. Both also claim to be crap at flirting – at everything, really, associated with convincing other people to be with you above anyone else – but yet it's been three weeks and here they are.

'So,' she says. 'Would you like a tour? I should warn you it could take as long as ten whole seconds.'

'I like it,' he says, looking around. 'It's …'

'Claustrophobic?'

She doesn't find it claustrophobic. Not really. Or at least she hasn't until now. But this is the first time she's ever had a visitor in here, and it's *him*, all six foot of him, and all she can think about is how claustrophobic it must be making *him* feel and how different it must look to where he lives, and she wants him to know that she knows that, that she isn't naïve, that she isn't stupid.

And that bed. That bloody bed. She's almost certain he's too long for it. She could nearly plot this whole evening out with certainty now: it'll be nice, and he'll stay, but from now on they'll resume their routine of staying at his bigger and better place.

And she won't object.

'I was going to say *compact*,' he says. 'And it's well designed, really. You don't see windows this size on other blocks this age.' He sets the bag and bottle on the dining table and lifts his hands. 'The, ah, bathroom?'

She points. 'Just in there.'

He goes, and she takes the bag and the bottle and carries them into the kitchen.

The bathroom is on the other side of the wall behind her now. As she unpacks the food she listens to the gush of water from the tap. It goes on for ages: he's doing it properly. When he returns, he brings the lemony scent of her antibacterial handwash with him.

'Where do you sleep?' he asks.

She points. 'That's the bed, there.'

'It comes down from the *wall*?' He looks childishly excited about this fact.

'Trust me, the novelty wears off in about five minutes.'

'Everything's so neat. Where's all your, you know, *stuff*?'

She explains she came to Dublin from Cork with one large

suitcase and her laptop bag. One of her friends was supposed to come up in his father's van with the rest, but … *Essential travel only*. There were a few bits and pieces already here – pots and pans, an iron and ironing board, that kind of thing – and whatever she needed that she didn't have she picked up in Penneys before they closed. Until things go back to normal her *stuff* will be sitting in boxes in the garage of her parents' house.

'But actually, I kinda like it this way,' she says. 'I might not even bother bringing up that much of it.'

He's stopped at some fancy deli near his place and got them a ready-made meal for two that only needs to be heated up in the oven. The foil tray looks like it's filled with lasagne but the label says *bobotie*. Ciara has no idea what that is. The price is on there too and she can't help but think about how much more food the same amount of money could buy in a supermarket if you were just willing to cook it yourself. There's also a plastic bowl of *bistro salad* and two individual *tartes au citron*. The wine has won a gold sticker from somebody.

She steals a glance at him.

He's bent at the waist, head to the side, reading the spines of her books.

She sets the oven to the temperature the bobotie's label dictates. It'll take ages to heat up; maybe she should've done this before he arrived. She puts the wine bottle on the counter and wipes it with an antibacterial wipe. She does the same with the food cartons. She throws the wipe in the bin and washes her hands. She takes the wine glasses out and pours two glasses before putting the bottle in the fridge.

Then she washes her hands again.

The new normal, which is in absolutely no way normal at all.

She doesn't actually believe that the bottle or cartons present a danger, but *he* believes it. He told her he heard something about it on the radio during the week and she's since read a couple of articles online. The shops are so busy now that all the stuff on the shelves was probably just put there, and customers pick stuff up and put it back, and one of them might well have coughed on it …

Better to be safe than sorry, Oliver says. He has asthma. That's an *underlying condition*. He doesn't want to risk getting this thing, and she certainly doesn't want to be the one to give it to him.

She carries the two glasses (five steps) to him and says, 'Here,' handing his over. As he takes it, he slips his free arm around her waist and gently pulls her close.

'Are you okay?' he asks.

She breathes him in. 'Better now.'

'Were you watching?'

She nods.

The announcement came less than two hours ago. The Taoiseach has said he doesn't want to use the word *lockdown* but that's effectively what it is. For the next two weeks, starting at midnight tonight, everyone is to stay at home. You can leave to buy food or to 'briefly' exercise within a

2km radius of your residence, but unless you're an essential worker, that's it. No visits to other homes, no arranging to meet people you don't live with – even *outside*.

Ciara knows she should be processing the bubbling panic in the pit of her stomach that something really, really bad is happening, but she's too busy with the tight worry in her chest over what this will mean for *them*, for her and Oliver.

She senses that he has the same question she does but isn't asking it.

She lets a beat pass, then another.

Then she decides that she just can't stand to wait any more and asks, 'What are we going to do?'

When he shrugs, her stomach drops.

Are they not on the same page here? Has she been reading this all wrong?

Panicked, she begins to backtrack, to downplay, words tumbling out of her mouth before she can think about them.

'I mean, it's less than two kilometres from here to your place, so ... We could go for socially distanced walks ...? Maybe? I know we're not technically supposed to but that should be okay, right?' He's frowning; she rushes on. 'And is it really that bad if I go to yours and you come to mine? Neither of us are going into work. Neither of us are seeing anyone else.' She instantly regrets this choice of words and the fact that they've sent a flash of heat to her cheeks. She's only *assuming* he's not seeing anyone else. 'If we're only in contact with each other, we can't spread it. Or catch it, even … Right?' She desperately wishes she hadn't ended that sounding so nakedly dripping with hope.

Here is her worst fear realised: despite how well all this has been going, she's only ever one stupid move away from ruining absolutely everything.

He backs away from her and for one horrible moment she thinks that now *he* thinks she might be contagious, that she's just inadvertently revealed to him that she's a careless person, that her handwashing and social-distancing aren't medical grade.

But then he takes her hand and leads them both to the couch.

They sit down and she takes a gulp of her wine to stop herself from vomiting out any more words.

'The thing is …' He's still holding her hand; he squeezes it. 'The thing is, Ciara …'

God, just come out with it.

Is he dumping her? Is that what this is?

Can he dump her, when they're barely together?

'I don't really *want* to break the rules. They're there for a reason.'

Her limbs feel suddenly heavy with resignation. It's as if she's deflating on the inside, like the burst balloon inside a hardened shell of papier mâché. All she wants to do now is kick off her shoes and fall back against the couch and drink the rest of the wine all by herself.

She wants him to leave.

She wants him to stay.

The truth is, however well this may seem like it's going, they don't know each other, not really. This situation is revealing that, up close and in harsh lighting.

They don't know what the other one does in times like this. Are they the kind of person who wears a mask before it's mandatory and disinfects their phones and wipes their groceries down, or are they drinking cans in the park with friends on a sunny Saturday and sneering at anyone who tut-tuts as they pass?

In between favourite movies and what they studied in college and where they hope to go this summer, they forgot to ask each other *what kind of person are you in a global pandemic?*

'What if ...?' he starts.

She turns to him, seized by the hope that all is not lost but trying not to show it. But he's looking unsure, or maybe too embarrassed to say whatever's on his mind.

'What?' she prompts.

'I don't know if ...' He inhales deeply, slowly, and then everything after that comes out in a tumbling rush. 'Well, I have two bedrooms, don't I? We'd be okay if we were in the same household. We wouldn't have to worry about the rules. And as it is, when I'm not working, I'm with you, so it wouldn't really be that big of a change, would it?' He swallows. 'And it doesn't have to be like, an actual *thing*. It's just a temporary arrangement. Two weeks. And we can play it by ear. Just take one day at a time. And if it doesn't work out, you still have *here*, so ...'

He stops and looks at her hopefully.

She wants to smile and say yes but first, she wants to make sure.

'What are you saying, exactly?'

'What I'm saying is ...' He squeezes her hand again. 'Ciara, why don't you move in with me?'

53 DAYS AGO

'And so *unnecessary*,' Ciara says. 'Like, just serve good drinks and be nice to people and stop with all the shite. But that kinda thing – *that's* a secret. And secrets are about denying people things. The truth, yes, but also the experience, the knowledge … You're just trying to keep them out of the cool gang. You're trying to decide who gets in the cool gang, and that's just …' She stops, apparently having lost her train of thought. 'It's not secrets I like. It's discovering things that are new to me but actually were always there. Secrets are a different thing. They're destructive.'

Secrets are destructive.

The words flip a switch.

Oliver had been happily riding a wave of warm, fizzy drunk thanks to those things Ciara had recommended, but now he feels that shift into an uncomfortable heat.

A sheen of cold sweat at his temples, a flush on his cheeks.

The sudden surety that he's made a terrible mistake.

He chose this bar because it was deep inside the hotel and unlikely to be frequented by passers-by; the clientele was mostly travellers from other places who would soon go back there. But now its distance from the outside, its lack of fresh air, makes his chest constrict with panic.

He can feel her eyes on him.

A single bead of sweat is threatening to depart from his right temple, the one she can see.

'I know what you mean,' he says absently.

This was supposed to be a fact-finding mission. He'd decided to meet up with her, glean as much information as he could and then use it to determine once and for all whether she was something he needed to worry about.

That's what he'd told himself he was doing, anyway. He'd refused to dwell on how much he'd been *looking forward* to doing it.

To begin with, everything had gone to plan. He hadn't bothered booking tickets to that documentary; there was no point risking this kind of contact just to sit beside her silently in the dark for the night. They needed to talk. He was intending to 'realise' he'd got the start time of the film wrong and suggest they go for a drink while they were waiting, but then she'd brought up cocktails and given him an easy in.

She evidently wasn't time-conscious and didn't notice they were drinking themselves late and, better yet, didn't care when she discovered this. It had all been working out.

So much so that he'd forgotten what *it* was supposed to be.

Getting to be normal always did that to him. The pretending could be potent. And he *liked* her, liked being around her, liked the way she made him feel.

Which was bad, because he couldn't afford to feel good.

That was always when bad things started to happen.

'Sorry,' he says, shifting his body away from her and out of the booth. 'I need another bathroom break.'

She frowns a little. 'Three times in one night?'

'I've broken the seal.'

'I actually have to go, too. I'll go when you get back.'

'I can wait?'

He can't. He feels shivery and feverish and a little bit sick. He has let this evening get away from him.

'I can wait longer,' she says, waving a hand. 'Go on.'

He hurries down the carpeted stairs, keeping one hand on the gold railing. The steps feel soft and unsteady beneath his feet, like they're unmoored and floating. The main doors are directly opposite the last one, but so is the doorman and a couple pulling suitcases out of a cab. Oliver makes an abrupt left turn into a tunnel of polished marble and heads for the automatic sliding glass doors at the far end, slipping down a couple of the marble steps, willing the electronic sensor to hurry up, to let him out—

The doors separate with an excruciating slowness and he turns sideways to push through them and out on to a dark, deserted street.

It has the look of a place mostly made up of the worst sides of other places: loading bays, back doors, rubbish bins. Directly opposite is a tanning salon squeezed in between a gym and a medical supply shop, the kinds of stores that cover up their windows instead of using them for display. The only person he can see anywhere nearby is a Deliveroo cyclist stopped at a distant corner, her face lit by the blue light of her phone.

The night air feels cold and sharp as he leans against a wall and gulps it down.

He's so sick of all this, of *being* this. He wishes he could just settle for his lot in life, make some kind of peace with it. Because every time he's tried to build a sarcophagus over the past, it's cracked before he's even finished it.

So why does he keep torturing himself by trying?

He freezes at the *whoosh* of the automatic doors sliding open for a second time, thinking Ciara has followed him outside, but it's a different woman who emerges into the dark.

She's older, and skinny in that tight, severe way, with a long blonde ponytail swishing halfway down her back. She's wearing very thin, very high heels and carrying a leather purse like a large envelope under one arm.

It occurs to him that he is a six-foot sweaty man standing in the shadows on a dark deserted street at the exact same moment she turns and sees him and her features jerk with fright.

'Sorry,' he says, holding up a hand, stepping forward into what he hopes is the light from inside. 'Sorry.'

She stands stock-still, blinking at him.

The deep V of her dress and the bright light above the door conspire to showcase a thin, pale, three-inch scar at the base of her throat, neat enough to suggest she got it during some long-ago surgery.

It makes him think of his own scar and the various lies he's told to explain it.

'I didn't mean to frighten you,' he says.

The woman's features soften and she makes a noise somewhere between a laugh and an exhale.

'Jesus,' she says, 'I think I just actually had a heart attack.' She pulls the bag from underneath her arm and begins to root in it. 'Okay, I get it, Universe. Smoking is bad for my health.'

'Sorry,' Oliver says again.

She takes a box of cigarettes from the bag. It's had a time of it: the lid has been ripped off and the remaining cardboard is creased and misshapen. She takes two limp cigarettes from it and holds them up, offering him one.

'I don't really smoke,' he says, eyeing it.

She shrugs. 'Neither do I.'

He takes the cigarette and lights it with the matches she offers: a small black matchbook branded with the name of the hotel.

The actual act of smoking is never anywhere near as good as the anticipation of doing it but even so, the first drag makes him feel better. So much better that he decides not to worry about Ciara smelling it on him when he goes back upstairs. He'll make something up, say he got a phone call and went outside to take it, and some guy came and stood right next to him and smoked.

'Having a good night?' the woman asks.

He can't even begin to establish the real answer to that question. He exhales, blowing the smoke away from her, into the night.

He says, 'It's all right.'

'Drinking or dining?'

'Drinking.' He takes another drag. 'Too much, maybe. You?'

'Dining.'

'How is it?'

'The food is great,' she says, 'but the company is awful.'

'Bad date?'

She laughs sharply, as if the idea of her being on a date is utterly preposterous.

'Bad boss. Bad job. It's a work thing.'

'What do you do?'

She takes a short, light drag. 'I'm a kind of head-hunter.' Releases a thick cloud of smoke. 'Recruitment. Finance. All that boring stuff.' She holds the cigarette close to her face and watches the orange glow of its tip burning through the paper. 'Anyway, it's free food and a night out. With the way things are going we might not get to have many more of those this side of Easter, so ...'

She takes another pull and winces.

'You really *don't* smoke,' Oliver says, 'do you?'

'Am I that obvious? No. Not regularly. I just like the smell – and how they're a cast-iron excuse to get away from people when the need arises and you've already used up a socially acceptable number of bathroom breaks. They're my very expensive, very bad-for-you escape hatch.' She stubs her cigarette out on the wall and nods towards what remains of his. 'If that tastes like the sticky strip on an envelope, it's because they've probably been in my bag since Christmastime – at least.'

'It tastes fine,' he says. 'Thank you.'

'Are *you* on a date?'

The look she gives him as she asks this suggests more than an idle curiosity.

'The truth is,' he says, 'I don't really know.'

But he silently adds *I hope so*, which surprises him.

And then worries him.

'Well ...' She gives him a little wave as she turns towards the doors. 'Either way, enjoy the rest of your night.'

He goes back upstairs with the aim of bringing this evening to a close at the earliest opportunity. He pays the bill while Ciara's in the bathroom so having to pay it later won't delay their leaving. He gets the waiter to take away what's left of his cocktail and drinks determinedly from his water glass, trying to dilute the dominance alcohol currently has in his bloodstream. He's resolved to remain alert for however long it is until there's a natural moment to suggest they go, sitting rigidly, his physical discomfort a reminder that this isn't a situation into which he should relax.

If Ciara notices a change in him, she doesn't let on. She's at least a little drunk, too. Her eyes look different now, her pupils larger than before, and here and there she trips a little over words or stutters once or twice before she gets them out.

Maybe she's just not that observant. She didn't question why he was gone so long or seem to detect the smell of smoke off his clothes or breath. He didn't even have to bother coming up with a lie to explain them.

Another one.

She jokes about the cult-like nature of her company's orientation programme while he watches the levels in her glass. As she lifts it to her lips to drain the last mouthful, he suggests they go.

She nods enthusiastically. 'Sure. Let's.'

She seems a little unsteady on her feet so he gently steers her to and then down the stairs with a hand on her back. She's carrying her coat over her arm and he can feel the heat of her skin through the thin material of her dress.

He wonders what *she* can feel.

They face their own reflections in the dark glass of the doors, and he is struck by how good they look, coupled together.

And then, how quickly this has happened.

Three days ago they didn't know each other. Now she is beside him, letting him touch her, telling him things about herself. The speed of it feels dangerous, like a race car approaching a tight corner without any working brakes.

They leave the warm glow of the hotel and push their way through the revolving doors into the night.

'Can we get a cab?' he asks the doorman, a different one from before.

He steals a glance at Ciara's face but there seems to be no reaction to this at all.

The doorman steps into the street and waves at something unseen around the corner. A beam of headlights lights up his lower half, and then a cab backs up to the door. Before the doorman can do it, Oliver steps forward and opens the back door, motioning for Ciara to get in.

She gives him a little smile of gratitude as she does, but her face falls when he closes the door and makes no move to walk around to the other side.

He leans down, one hand on the roof, until his face is level with hers.

'I'm gonna walk home,' he lies.

'Oh.' She seems to deflate with disappointment. 'Sure. Right.'

'Are you around Thursday evening?' he asks. 'We could actually go see the film this time.'

He has no intention of seeing her ever again. But the invitation will make *this* moment more comfortable and that's all he can think about right now: extricating himself from this with as little friction as possible.

She nods, smiles briefly. 'Yeah.'

'I'll text you.'

'Okay. Great.'

'Goodnight.'

'Goodnight.'

He closes the door and moves to the driver's open window. He pulls a twenty from his pocket and drops it through, on to the seat. The driver frowns at it, then looks up at him in question. He waves a hand to signal to him that he's not getting in. The driver shrugs and moves to release the handbrake.

Oliver gives Ciara a wave as the car moves off.

He thinks he's been lucky, in a way. Her saying that thing about secrets pulled him out of … Whatever he was in earlier in the evening. A false sense of security. Complacency. Under some kind of spell.

He'd been enjoying himself, that was the problem. Enjoying *her*.

He starts for Grafton Street; he'll get his own cab. They could've shared one, really, but he's not sure where she lives and he couldn't risk revealing his address to her.

There's losing the run of himself for half an hour and then there's doing something so monumentally stupid it might force him to start all over again.

Again.

TODAY

The street outside the main entrance to The Crossings has begun to buzz with activity. Lee's reinforcements have arrived, along with the Technical Bureau – she can see a scenes-of-crime officer unloading equipment from the back of the van, and Tom Searson, one of the deputy state pathologists, suiting up nearby. She waves at him; he waves back. Strips of blue and white Garda tape flap in the breeze, the ends knotted around railings and lamp-posts and traffic cones. Uniforms mill about in shirtsleeves, despite the fresh chill of this early-morning sun. There's a couple of rubberneckers standing with their arms folded across the road, but no press yet. Although with all this out here and nothing else going on anywhere in the country except for the nightly roll-call of death from the Department of Health, it's surely just a matter of time before they arrive.

She's surprised to find that Garda Michael Creedon has been appointed chief clipboard-wielder of the outer cordon – a nice, clean gig with a mirage of authority – and she feels a warm ripple of pride at the idea that Karl might have done something nice and that it happened because he'd actually listened to her.

Or her prayer worked.

Michael is talking to another uniform; when Lee gets close, she recognises him. It's Declan, mask hanging around his neck now, looking considerably less grey than the last time they met. She nods at him as she ducks under the tape and then, just as she turns her head away, catches the two of them exchanging looks. Blink and you'd miss it – literally – but its content may as well be written on their faces.

Michael: *Tell her.*

Declan: *Fuck that, shut up.*

She stops a few feet away and beckons Declan with a jerk of her head. There's another silent conversation before he obeys.

Oh great. Thanks for landing me in it.

Don't make things even worse.

'How did you get on in there?' she asks him.

A shrug, no eye contact. 'Fine.'

'Did you touch anything?'

'I had gloves on.'

There it is.

'That doesn't answer my question,' Lee says. 'Gloves leave marks too. And they can smudge prints or even destroy other forensically valuable evidence. But look, we all make mistakes. And you might be lucky here because if I had to call this right now, my guess would be that this guy drugged himself for shits and giggles and then fell through his shower door and hit his head. So maybe it won't even matter. But *you* don't get to decide what matters. That's my job. So, tell me: what did you touch?'

A beat passes before whatever bravado was there falls clean away.

'I think maybe I made a mistake.' Declan clears his throat. 'I know I did.'

'Well, don't make another one now.' Lee looks at him expectantly, waiting.

'The showerhead was dripping,' he says. 'I didn't think, it was like a reflex action—'

'You turned it off.'

'Yes,' he says miserably.

She tries to picture the shower controls: a flat, silver lever that you'd push down to stop the flow of water.

'Show me how.'

He makes a fist and bumps it lightly against an invisible surface. In all likelihood, it was just the side of his hand that made contact.

'I'm sorry, Inspector.'

'Don't worry about it for now. I could have done the same thing myself.' She wouldn't have, but she might have done back when she was as green as him. 'If things weren't as ripe in there, you could have had paramedics going in, turning him over and what not, so we'd have a lot more disturbance to deal with than that. It's the kind of thing you won't do twice, so next time, when it really matters, you won't make the same mistake.' She hopes it won't really matter this time, for both their sakes. 'Just be more careful in future. And well done for not upchucking your guts. Things were pretty grim in there.'

Over his shoulder, she sees Karl approaching. She dismisses Declan and steps away so she and Karl can talk without being overheard.

'What was all that about?' is Karl's opening line.

'Nothing important. Where were you?'

'Car park. Basement level.'

'Anything interesting?'

'You need a fob to get in but the sensors let you out. Each space is assigned and there's no vehicle in number one. But it's not empty – the local Lidl is missing a trolley and that trolley is missing a wheel. Which makes me think—'

'It's been empty a while,' Lee finishes.

'So either someone else took the car or there wasn't one to begin with. We'll have to wait for the CCTV to confirm. Any word from the management company?'

'Not yet. And if I don't hear from them in the next five minutes I'm going to send a bloody car to the office. Emergency number my arse.'

'Are they' – Karl makes air quotes – '*essential workers*? Because if they're not, there won't be anyone there.'

'You know, I don't think apartment one is a permanent residence. There's hardly anything in there, no personal items, place barely decorated ... I'm thinking it's like an Airbnb. Which would tie with there being no vehicle, right? And no one noticing that this guy has been missing for the last two weeks. Maybe he wasn't even supposed to be here. Maybe he got caught out when the lockdown came in.'

'Two *weeks*?' Karl makes a face. 'Did you vom?'

'Looks about that long. Smells it, too. And your concern is touching, but no. *You* definitely would have, though.'

'This hungover, yeah. Probably. So what have we got?'

'Body of a male,' Lee says. 'I think. Lying face-down in the shower. Kneeling, really. Glass door completely shattered – safety glass, so pebbles of it are all over the show. Head wound, currently a maggot buffet breakfast. Consistent with him falling through the shower door and hitting his head on the bathroom wall.'

'So an accident?'

'Maybe.'

'Was the shower on?'

'No,' Lee says after a beat. Technically true. The *drip-drip-drip* of a not-quite-turned-off shower does not a shower make. 'And guess what he has in his medicine cabinet? You'll love this: Rohypnol.'

Karl raises his eyebrows. 'What the hell is he doing with that?'

'Falling through shower doors is my guess.'

'But why would you roofie *yourself*?'

'I don't know,' she says. 'Lockdown boredom? Maybe he doesn't like banana bread. What's bothering me is that the door to the apartment was unlocked, open an inch or so.'

'So?' Karl shrugs. 'He could've just let the door close behind him whenever he last entered the apartment and didn't realise it wasn't locked.'

'And he was dressed. In the shower.'

'The shower he fell *in* to, probably.'

'Maybe.'

'There's always something that doesn't fit,' Karl says.

'Either way, we have an officially declared crime scene. I've already called the Super. I think *he's* thinking accident too, but also that it's better to be safe than sorry.'

'Did you tell him about Tweedledum and Tweedledee?'

Lee shakes her head, *no*. 'It didn't come up.'

'It will. Shite always floats to the surface eventually.'

'That doesn't mean I need to reach in and pick it up with my bare hand in the meantime, does it? What about the door-to-doors?'

'Just started,' Karl says. 'Everyone's home, so they'll be a while.'

'What are we asking?'

'Do they know who occupies apartment one, when did they last see them if so, anything suspicious or out of the ordinary in the last few weeks, yada, yada, yada. Your standard fare. I think it's five questions, total.'

'How many have we got on it?'

'Three pairs. One per floor.'

'Did you remind them to stay outside? To talk to them from the corridor? To wear their masks?'

'What am I, their mammy?' Karl's gaze fixes on something over Lee's shoulder. 'Hold up. Who's this Instagram account come to life?'

Lee has no idea what that means, but when she turns she sees a man approaching Michael at the cordon. Late twenties, suit and tie. Chunky silver watch. A glimpse of novelty socks. Everything he's wearing is fit so snugly that she fears she could be committing a sex crime just by looking at him. How does he sit down without ripping the seams? How does he get *into* them in the first place?

'If that's not an estate agent,' Karl says, 'then I'm a teetotaller. Why do they always dress like they've a much better job?'

'To promote feelings of wealth and trust. Property is the most expensive purchase you'll ever make. And I just had to go into a closed space during a pandemic to look at a putrefying corpse that's been cooking for a couple of weeks, so maybe leave the estate agents alone, eh?'

Michael is pointing at her and Karl, sending the too-tight-suited man hurrying over to them.

'Kevin O'Sullivan,' he says. 'Viva Property Management.' He goes to extend his hand, then catches himself and aborts the move, then takes a step back again for good measure. 'Sorry, I keep doing that.' He looks around. 'What's going on? What's happened?'

'You've got a decomposing body in there,' Karl says flatly.

'Mr O'Sullivan.' Lee takes a half-step forward, planting herself firmly between the two men before Karl can say any more. 'I'm Detective Inspector Leah Riordan and this is my colleague, Detective Sergeant Karl Connolly. We received a call this morning about an odour coming from apartment number one, whose front door was also unlocked. When we arrived, I'm sorry to say that we discovered a deceased individual inside. They appear to have been there for some time.'

Kevin manages to look both horrified *and* transfixed.

'Shit,' he says, putting a hand to his mouth. *Stop touching your face*, Lee thinks. 'What happened?'

'We don't know yet.'

'But is it, like, a *crime*?'

'We'll soon find out. Can you tell us who lives there? ID-ing the deceased and notifying their family is our top priority at this point.'

'Ah, yeah ...' Kevin roots inside his suit jacket, pulls out some folded pages: a spreadsheet of names. He scans them. 'Ah. Actually, no, I can't tell you – I don't have an individual name for that one. It's a corporate let, rented by KB Studios on Baggot Street. I think they're architects ...? They'd know who's in there. Who, um, *was* in there.'

Lee looks at Karl, who nods and steps away.

'Meaning what?' she says to Kevin. 'They just rented it for a few weeks, a month?'

'No, they've had it ages. From the start, I'd say. That's almost two years ago now. They have two. It's a twelve-month lease but they use them themselves for shorter stays.' As he talks to her, his eyes keep straying over her shoulder, to where she knows the Tech Bureau van is parked. 'Just to have at their disposal, you know? Relocations, visiting clients, that sort of thing. Someone could stay three months or they could stay a night.'

'What about cleaning? In between stays?'

'Yeah, they'd have that,' Kevin says. 'Organised through us. But not at the moment. Not since lockdown began.'

'Talk to me about CCTV.'

'We have it, yeah.'

Lee resists the urge to point out that she knows that, that she can see with her own eyes the fish-eye cameras mounted around the complex.

'I'll need to see it,' she clarifies. 'The footage.'

He hesitates. 'Am I, like, supposed to show it to you? Don't you need, like, a warrant or—'

'That's just on TV, Kevin.'

'Oh.' He blushes. 'Right. I'd, uh, have to go get the footage for you. It's monitored off-site.'

'And how long would that take?'

'They're out by the airport so maybe an hour for me to get there and back? But I don't know how long it'll take to download. How much do you need?'

'How far back does it go?'

Kevin frowns, thinking. 'Seven days, maybe?'

'I'll take as far back as you've got, all cameras. If anyone stops you, tell them the truth and give them my name, okay? Here.' She fishes a somewhat battered, standard-issue business card from inside her blazer and hands it over. 'Show them that. Is there an on-site maintenance person, someone who'd have access to any locked doors, know how to disable the fire alarm, that kind of thing?'

'We have a guy,' Kevin says. 'He'd be on call.'

'Can he come here right now? We'll need his assistance.'

'I'll tell him to.'

'As quick as he can, okay?'

Kevin nods firmly like he's just been tasked with a life-saving mission, and turns sharply on his heel.

When he's gone, Karl rejoins her, sticking his phone back into his pocket.

'So KB Studios is indeed a firm of architects,' he says. 'The office number is redirecting to the mobile phone of a receptionist who's at home. She doesn't know anything and she says that kind of info is with the office manager. She's going to get him to ring me back.'

'We've got a problem.'

Karl snorts. 'Just the one?'

'The CCTV only goes back seven days.'

'Well, if it's an accident, we won't need it. And that's still, what? Nearly a hundred and seventy hours of video we'll have to watch? I can hardly wait.'

Lee sighs. 'And here I was thinking I might treat myself to a takeaway and veg out on the couch tonight ...'

'Why? Because you're overdue a break from your hectic social life? You know, I was thinking about this morning, Lee – have you even noticed we're in lockdown? Like, how has your life changed, actually?'

'When were you thinking this? Was it before or after I had to get your naked arse out of two sets of handcuffs?'

'We'd both be a *lot* more emotionally scarred if they'd been anywhere near my arse.'

'Thank God for small mercies.'

'So, wait, we've no ID? Was there no wallet or—'

'There's an envelope in the letterbox,' Lee says, remembering. 'But if it's not a permanent residence, it's probably not even for him. Could just be junk.' She nods towards the building. 'Let's go check.'

Karl motions towards the cordon. 'After you, boss.'

34 DAYS AGO

Early the next morning, Ciara wakes up in the warmth of Oliver's bed.

After dinner, they'd finished the wine, and after that she'd expressed regret that they didn't have more of it. Oliver had suggested a walk to the off-licence and then, gently, that they should carry on to his place after that. She'd spent the whole day cleaning the flat from top to bottom and money on things she didn't actually need – like three god-awful purple throws – because he'd never been to her place but had been pushing to see it for at least the last ten days. It was getting mildly annoying, so she'd given in. Now, two hours after he'd arrived there, he was suggesting they leave.

'You can have a look at your new room,' he'd joked.

She'd already seen it, actually, but she couldn't tell him that. A few days before, when he was in the shower, she'd taken a peek behind the only door in his apartment that always seemed to be closed. On the other side was nothing more exciting than a spare bedroom.

A single box-spring with no headboard was pushed up

against one wall, opposite some built-in wardrobes. The mattress was pristine and there was a protector still neatly folded in plastic packaging lying at one end. The roller-blinds on the window were pulled all the way down and the air in the room smelled faintly of new paint, as if no one had ever stayed in there for any length of time.

'You just don't want to sleep in my bed-that-comes-down-from-the-wall,' she'd said to him. 'That's it, isn't it?'

He'd grinned. 'Oh, I'd have no problem *sleeping* in it ...'

And she'd laughed and looked away so he wouldn't see the sudden flare of heat on her face.

Their sex isn't as awkward and fumbling as it had been the first two or three times, back when it came like full-stops at the end of evenings where Ciara, knowing what was coming, had made sure to drink enough to make it possible, to silence the parts of her that screamed she shouldn't be doing this, that reacted as if Oliver's touch was something her skin was allergic to. She'd taken to closing her eyes and trying to shut down her brain, telling herself that this, too, was another excruciating beginning that, if she managed to get past it, would lead to better things, better feelings, a better *life*. And it did get a little easier with each go, like a dance she was gradually learning the steps to, the moves slowly becoming muscle memory. But still, she found herself occasionally shocked by the cold bareness of Oliver's skin, the restriction of his weight on top of her, parts of his body in hers like some kind of foreign invasion.

She rolls on to her side now and looks at him.

He's still sleeping, his bare back to her, as far away as he can be while remaining on the bed. His breaths are deep and regular. This is how they always end up when she stays over: repelled, even though they begin the night in each other's arms, her head resting on his chest.

She can see the top of the scar just above the sheets.

She rolls on to her back and stares at the smooth white ceiling. She hates this bit, the morning after the night before. Daylight is no one's friend and, she's convinced, her active enemy. Above the blankets she knows there's only what's left of yesterday's make-up on her puffy face, and beneath them there's nothing at all.

She feels vulnerable and exposed.

She wishes she could just put on underwear and a T-shirt before she goes to sleep and tell him that that's how it needs to be for her, but she hasn't managed to find a voice to say it in yet. She imagines she can feel a dampness between her thighs that she worries might transfer to his sheets. She absolutely hates not knowing what time it is.

From the moment she wakes up like this she's waiting for the moment she can return to her own place and start putting herself back together in her own time. Shower. Fresh make-up. Clean clothes.

Building herself back up, reassembling the woman who will be ready to meet him again later in the day for lunch or dinner, to sip a glass of wine they both know is the first stepping stone in a row of several that will lead her right back here again.

Putting things on she knows he will be taking off, that she *hopes* he will, because if he is that means that they are still moving forward, that this is still happening, that this is working.

But from tomorrow, all that will have to happen here, in this apartment. There will be no other place. She's not ready for it, but it's a go. She's agreed to it.

Because she wants to keep seeing him and this, right now, is the only way.

Over the course of three Saturdays, she's watched the life drain out of Dublin city.

On the first – the day after Oliver spoke to her outside Tesco's – the pubs were still open even if the parade had been cancelled and the tourists who'd flocked into what should've been ground zero for Patrick's Day festivities hadn't yet fled. They'd milled around Stephen's Green with their outstretched iPhones and *Carrolls Irish Gifts* bags, wearing too many layers for the mild spring weather, feeding the pigeons on purpose and the seagulls inadvertently. They'd all seemed to Ciara to be inexplicably carefree, carrying on as if everything was normal, as if they hadn't noticed that the only non-tourists around were loners scurrying nervously past, clutching grocery bags and giving them sidelong glances, doing their best to avoid getting close. Even the Italians, who, by then, must have known all too well what was coming, seemed utterly untroubled. The only anomaly was a guy in his late teens wearing a mask, holding his phone in front of his face while he spun around to offer the lens a three-sixty view of the streets behind him. In what sounded like a German accent he was narrating the scene, pointing out that he was the only one wearing a face-covering. At the time, he'd struck Ciara as a bit of an alarmist.

A week later, the tourists were gone and the vast majority of businesses had pre-emptively closed. The people left on the streets were few but from both ends of the caution spectrum. She'd seen two women in their twenties sitting outside one of the few remaining open cafés exchange glances as a man hurried past wearing latex gloves and a mask that, by then, Ciara could identify as *respiratory* as opposed to *surgical*. The women had had stiff, waxed bags bearing the logo of a high-end clothing store by their feet and were drinking coffees in seats nowhere near two metres apart.

It was as if some people thought the end was nigh while others hadn't even seen the papers.

A strange phenomenon of all this, she'd discovered since, was that you yourself were capable of being both types of people. One afternoon, Ciara had put on a nice dress and waves in her hair and set off in chilly sun to Oliver's place. The sky was blue, the birds were chirping and she felt good. She was also making this walk a little earlier than she usually did, during the *Six One* news bulletin instead of just after it, so she'd missed her nightly ritual of waiting on the couch for the four numerical horsemen of the apocalypse: new deaths, new cases, total deaths, total cases.

She'd *forgotten*, just for a few minutes.

But directly across the canal was a construction site surrounded by blue hoarding and, overnight, new signs had been stuck to it. Multiple copies of the same one, their surfaces bubbling and creased from a hasty application. The only words large enough for her to read at that distance were in the headline: YOU CAN HELP STOP THE SPREAD OF COVID-19! It was like walking out of real life and on to the set of a Hollywood virus thriller, only the poles were reversed. *This* was what was real, and that was terrifying.

This morning, the first of this de facto lockdown, it's as if some awful event has come in the night. There's nowhere near enough vehicles on the road to justify calling it *traffic*. The loudest sound is that of her own footsteps, the hollow heel of her boots hitting the path as she walks alongside the canal. She passes a pharmacy with a handwritten sign in the window screaming, HAND SANITISER 50ML IN STOCK €4.99 MAX 3 PER CUSTOMER! But if you want it, you'll have to wait for it because the lights are off inside and a metal grate is in place across the door. Above the rooftops stands an array of motionless cranes, stopped clocks in the sky.

By the time Ciara reaches her building she has only passed one other pedestrian, an older man walking a small dog who'd stepped out into the bus lane to give her the requisite two-metre berth, and she sees only one other neighbour as she goes inside, a Lycra-clad gym-bro doing planks on the dewy grass.

An information sheet about COVID-19, government issued, has appeared in the lobby, taped up next to the list of emergency numbers, and an industrial-sized bottle of hand sanitiser is sitting in a little pool of clear liquid on a stool by the main door.

As she slides her key into the lock, she thinks about all the units in this building and all the hands that have touched the same door she is touching right now. She takes the fact that there are fewer units at Oliver's place and, so, fewer people, and mentally adds it to her collection of reasons why this might not be a terrible idea, actually.

Inside her flat, she kicks its door closed behind her and goes straight to the bathroom sink to wash her hands – in the dark, because she won't touch the light switch until *after* the handwashing.

That's what Oliver says you should do and now that they're riding out this thing together, she feels obligated to follow his lead.

She also finds these cleansing rituals oddly calming. Anything simple with a series of steps will probably have that effect, even when it's in an attempt to minimise the risk of catching a deadly virus.

She strips her clothes from her skin and stands in the scalding stream of the shower until the bathroom grows thick with steam. (His shower is better, too – there's another reason.) Then she wraps herself in a towel and trails water droplets through the living room and into the kitchen, where she makes herself a cup of tea and a slice of buttered toast and wonders what should she pack?

What exactly does a girl need to move in with a guy

she barely knows because there's a global emergency, the country is going into lockdown and her apartment is about the size of matchbox?

She lands on: everything. She has so little stuff that it all fits into her one suitcase.

Even now, transferring her underwear from a drawer to the case, she still can't quite believe that she's doing this, that she's *moving in with him*. But here's another reason to add to her collection: she's not. Not really.

She's just *staying with him* for a couple of weeks. She's not letting this place go. Nothing about this is permanent or irreparable.

Not yet, anyway.

And there's a lot about this that is incredibly lucky or at least could prove to be, in time. These strange, *unprecedented* circumstances – when all this is over, she vows to never use that word ever again – they might just conspire to take her via express train to everything she's ever wanted when there might not even have been a route there otherwise.

Only time will tell.

When Oliver opens the door he holds out a hand, presenting her with the set of keys that lies in his palm: one standard silver one that will open the door to the apartment and one small black plastic fob that will open the main door to the building.

'I would've put them in a gift box or tied them with ribbon or something,' he says, 'if I had any.'

She smiles and reaches for them, and for him with her other arm – but he suddenly snatches his hand away and steps back.

A shadow of something unreadable crosses his face and then something more readily identifiable begins to fill it: embarrassment.

'Your hands,' he says to the floor. 'Sorry.'

'Of course, yeah. I just forgot.'

She's already turning towards the bathroom.

'I'm not trying to be a dick, it's just with the asthma—'

'No, I'm glad you reminded me,' she says. 'Really.'

She doesn't quite understand why he tried to *hand her something* before he did it, but fine, whatever.

Before any resentment can bloom, she catches herself. *He has asthma. That's an underlying condition. Handwashing is something she should be doing anyway, whether he's there to nag her about it or not.*

She pushes the bathroom door open with an elbow and goes to the sink.

As she sluices water over her hands, she feels something that wasn't there before: a ridge of hard, dried skin on the outer edges of her little fingers. After she dries off with a hand towel, she rotates her wrists so she can get a better look. The skin there is peeling, red and sore. Protesting. She makes a mental note to buy some hand lotion. This makes her think of going to a pharmacy, which makes her think of what else she might buy while she's there, seeing as any sort of retail experience is a major operation now.

They're talking about this thing being a dry cough, fever, aches and pains. Apparently some people get upset stomachs, too. She tries not to think about the nightmare of having too much coming up or too much coming out *here*, in the only bathroom in Oliver's apartment, with him right outside the door, and focuses instead on what might help if that happened.

Paracetamol, cough syrup and some Imodium wouldn't go astray ... Maybe some of those dissolvable packet things you drink to replace your electrolytes, whatever electrolytes are. Antibacterial handwash, if they can get it – which she doubts. The shelves in her local Tesco have been empty of it for going on two weeks now.

She looks up, into the mirror, and notices another mirror on the wall behind her: the door to the medicine cabinet. She's already had a snoop inside it – she did that the first night she was here – but now she opens it to take an inventory.

There are only two shelves and they seem to be mostly filled with personal products. A thickening shampoo. Razors. Shaving oil. Two boxes of condoms, one of which is open at one end and lying flat, so she can see there's only a couple left inside.

A blister pack of sea-green pills with the number *542* stamped on to them, mostly gone; she thinks they might be antihistamines. All that counts for medical supplies is a packet of supermarket plasters and a tube of Deep Freeze.

A thought crosses her mind, unbidden, as she closes the cabinet door.

No inhalers.

———

She finds Oliver in the spare room, lifting her suitcase on to the bare bed. The air smells of furniture polish; he must have been cleaning while she was gone.

'I promise you I'm not paranoid,' he says when he sees her in the doorway. 'Despite all evidence to the contrary.'

She waves a hand. 'It's fine. Really.'

The blind is all the way up, offering a view of the courtyard through the leaves of a tree, and the window has been opened a crack. She goes to it to get a better look and sees that a crack is as far as it'll go; it's a safety feature.

Oliver comes up behind her, puts his arms around her waist and speaks into the fall of her hair.

'I just want us to be safe,' he says. 'For *you* to be.'

'I know. Honestly, it's fine. I want us to be safe too.' She twists around to face him and lifts her lips to his.

He kisses her once, briefly, and then pulls back to say, 'Speaking of – you haven't been kissing anyone *else*, have you? Is that why you wouldn't let me come with you this morning?'

'I haven't, no. But I *did* lick all the buttons at pedestrian crossings between here and my place, so …'

He laughs and kisses her again, longer and deeper.

Then he pulls her close until they are pressed together, her head turned so she can rest a cheek against his chest.

She puts her arms around him, sighing contentedly as she relaxes into his hold.

'What's it like out there, anyway?' he asks.

'Weird. You'd really notice the difference since yesterday.'

'I suppose that's good? Shows people are taking this seriously.'

'I don't know if everyone *is*, though.'

She pulls away and goes to her suitcase, starts to unzip its lid. He's opened the doors of the built-in wardrobes for her and even put some empty hangers on the rail. There's no question that she'll be sleeping in his room, but she likes that he's offered this one for her belongings, what few of them she has.

She starts lifting items out.

'What do you mean?' he asks.

'Well, I called my mother while I was at my place. Ended up spending most of the conversation having to explain to her that, yes, the two-kilometre restriction applies to her too. And *why* it does.' Ciara rolls her eyes. 'She thinks everyone is overreacting.'

A beat passes before Oliver asks, 'Did you tell her?'

'Tell her what?'

'About me. About *this*.'

'Clearly,' Ciara says, as she takes a black dress from the case and shakes it out, 'you haven't met my mother. That'd be a *no* and another, louder, more emphatic *no*. She didn't even want me to move to Dublin. If she heard about this, she'd probably drive up here and drag me back to Cork by my hair. Actually ...' Having hung the dress in the wardrobe, she turns to look at him. 'I haven't told anyone. Have you?'

'I *was* going to tell my brother, but I don't have to.'

'Do, if you want. It's not classified information, it's just—'

'—when you think about it—'

'—it'd be easier this way, right?'

Oliver nods. 'That's what I was thinking.'

'Not just this bit, the moving-in-together-for-lockdown stuff, but—'

'Everything else, too,' he finishes.

'I just hate all this stuff, you know? As soon as you tell anyone you're in a relationship, you have to, like, *define* everything. And then comes the bloody Spanish Inquisition.' When Oliver frowns at this, she says, 'Okay, so, maybe that's just *my* family. But this is kind of perfect, isn't it? We have, what, two weeks? To just be us. To see what happens without having to explain it or label it or justify anything to anyone else. I mean, we literally *can't* see anyone else. No one can come visit – not that I even know anyone here yet. And no one knows I'm here. Who's going to know I'm not still in my own place?'

Oliver is grinning. 'So we're in a relationship now, are we?'

'Did you hear anything after that bit or …? And technically any connection between two people is a relationship, so.'

'Good save.'

'I thought so.'

'We are, though.'

She meets his gaze. '*Are* we?'

'Do you want to be?'

'Do *you*?'

'I asked you first,' he says.

'So we're playing *that* game …'

'Well, we've literally nothing else to do.'

She laughs at this.

'I would like it,' he says then, 'if we were.'

'Me too.'

'So let's be.'

They look at each other, expectant and awkward and embarrassed, until they both break and laugh. Then Ciara turns back to her open suitcase, her cheeks warm, to pull out more clothes.

Oliver moves to help her.

Her NASA mug is sitting on top of some jeans. He lifts it out.

'So you're a meatball girl then,' he says.

She has no idea what this means. Her first reaction is that he has insulted her somehow, that she should be offended, but then when she considers that he's never even come close to saying anything like that before, her second reaction is total confusion.

'A *what* girl?'

Oliver points to the insignia on the mug, the blue circle littered with tiny white stars and slashed with a red vector.

'That's what that's called,' he says. 'The meatball. The logo they had in the eighties, the one with just the letters – that's the worm.' He pauses. 'You've never heard that before?'

'Don't think so.' She turns to pull more clothing from the suitcase and takes it to the wardrobe. 'But in that case, I am *definitely* a meatball girl. I hate that other one. It's awful.'

It takes her at least fifteen seconds to hang a dress and refold two T-shirts so she can add them to a stack and in all that time, Oliver says nothing. When she turns back to him, she finds him still holding the mug, looking down at it.

'Hey,' she says.

He lifts his head.

'You okay? You're staring at that thing like you're in some kind of daze.'

'I was just thinking,' he says, 'what's the red slash about?' He points to it on the mug – the sideways V-shape that bisects the blue disc. 'What's that supposed to be?'

'Isn't it a wing?'

He raises his eyebrows.

'The blue disc is a planet,' she says, 'the stars are space, the little white orbital line thingy represents space travel and the red thing is a wing, for aeronautics.'

She wants to add *I think* to that but she knows she's right, so she forces herself to swallow it.

Oliver smiles.

'Well,' he says, 'I guess you learn something new every day.'

50 DAYS AGO

Mid-morning, word spreads around the office: Taoiseach Leo Varadkar is about to make a statement, live from Washington, DC.

The only screen that plays TV channels is the one in the conference room. They pile in there, bringing coffees and sticky pastries so that watching this terrible, unprecedented news can double as their elevenses.

Oliver is the last one in. Jonas, a Swede who started on the same day as him, is standing just inside the door.

They exchange nods.

'Here we go,' Jonas whispers, his eyes flashing with excitement.

Over the course of the last month or so, Jonas has spent at least twice as much time scouring the internet for coronavirus stories than he has doing any actual work, as far as Oliver can tell. In the last fortnight, the guy has become completely obsessed with northern Italy. Oliver knows this because the *other* thing Jonas spends an indecent amount of time doing is telling Oliver, in ever increasing detail, about the stuff he finds online.

Earlier, he'd been reading something on the *New York Times* website, intermittently shaking his head and muttering things like, 'Oh my God,' and 'What the *fuck*?' Oliver had refused to take the bait but it was pointless, because Jonas eventually leaned into the space between their computer screens and told him all about it anyway. Italy is two days into a draconian national lockdown, he said, shutting everything except pharmacies and grocery stores outside which, of course, huge queues have formed. With not enough ventilators to go around, doctors are having to decide who lives and who dies, literally, and who dies is invariably the elderly.

'And Ireland is just two weeks behind,' Jonas said gravely. '*Two weeks.*'

Oliver didn't think the *New York Times* was publishing fake news, but still, these facts felt like they had that kind of quality. They were so outlandish, insane.

Things couldn't be *that* bad a couple of countries away, surely?

He hadn't been too worried about it, up until now. He'd just assumed that whatever was going on over there would be stopped long before it arrived *here*. This would just be like all the other news stories: it would go from so much coverage you'd wonder what the hell they filled the column inches and airtime with before they had this to talk about, to realising, one day, that you hadn't heard anything about it in a while.

Just like Oliver's own story, once upon a time.

But now here they are, gathered on a weekday morning to

listen to the country's leader say something about the virus's arrival in Ireland that is so serious, he can't wait until he gets back to Ireland to say it.

A hush falls on the room as the TV screen changes from an anchorman sitting behind a desk in a TV studio to a live shot of the Taoiseach walking to a podium set up outside some grand building. It's still dark over there. His expression is one of utter seriousness. Over his shoulder, a tricolour billows in the breeze.

'Lockdown,' Jonas whispers. 'Has to be.'

But it's not.

Varadkar begins to speak, slowly and deliberately, presumably reading from some unseen teleprompter but looking as if he's talking directly to the lens, as if he's addressing each person individually and the nation collectively at the same time.

The virus is all over the world. It will continue to spread but it can be slowed.

We said we would take the right actions at the right time. We have to move now to have the greatest impact.

You should continue to go to work if you can but where possible should work from home. In order to reduce unnecessary face-to-face interaction in the workplace, break times and working times should be staggered and meetings done remotely or by phone.

The air in the room is suddenly charged with tension.

Bodies shift, pairings separate. A few guys exchange nervous smiles, tittering laughter. Oliver counts thirteen of them, standing shoulder to shoulder in this poorly ventilated room, and takes a step backwards, out of it.

He really doesn't want to end up catching this thing.

He can't afford to. Going to a GP, getting tested, being admitted to hospital – anything like that, anything *official*, anything that involves IDs and paperwork and *history* ...

The virus is especially dangerous for him, but not for any medical reason. He's worried about a different kind of exposure.

As Oliver starts back across the office, he hears the TV fall mute behind him and Kenneth, the managing director, say, 'Okay, okay, okay,' in a tone that suggests he wants everyone's attention. 'Go to your desks for now. Alistair is on his way back from a site-visit and he and I will sit down this afternoon, work this out. But I think it's safe to assume we'll all be working from home for the next couple of weeks, so you can start to plan accordingly ...'

Oliver reaches his desk, sits down and tunes out.

His phone is lying by the keyboard; he taps the screen to wake it up.

No new text.

He thought she might have sent a *Still on for tonight?* message; maybe she hasn't seen the news yet.

He has to admit, though, that, ever since Monday night, he keeps catching himself thinking about her – or maybe what he's doing is thinking about Monday night.

To just sit in a bar and have a drink and enjoy a conversation was a lightness he hasn't felt in a long, long time. It was like someone had built him a bridge across the dark, turbulent water so, for once, he could take a break from trying to claw himself up from its tangled, muddy depths.

And he liked it.

He liked just being able to *be*.

Before he can think too much about it, he picks up his phone and calls her.

He's surprised by how much he welcomes the sound of her voice, how much better he feels knowing that they are still on for tonight.

But after he hangs up, he feels a prickling sensation at the base of his skull – almost always a sign that he's doing something he shouldn't be, that he's working against whatever primordial survival instinct has carried him this far.

He'll be careful, he tells himself.

He *is* being careful. He's already decided this will be the last time. After tonight, he won't see her again – and he probably won't be *able* to see her, so he won't even have to make the decision.

It's just that he liked the feeling of being with her, of being *Oliver* with her.

And he wants to feel it one more time.

33 DAYS AGO

Early on Sunday morning, they drive to the largest Tesco they could find on Google Maps, which is a long eight kilometres outside the two-kilometre radius they're supposed to remain within. Oliver has rented a GoCar for the occasion and is sitting tensed in its driver's seat, two hands wrapped tightly around the wheel, eyes never leaving the road ahead. She has told him repeatedly that the two-kilometres thing is just for exercise, that you can travel further to shop for essential items, but he's unconvinced.

'God, you *really* don't like breaking rules, do you?' she asks him ten minutes into the journey. 'Look, if we get stopped, we get stopped. It's not a big deal. No one's going to arrest us. They won't even make us turn around because this is within the rules. And even if they *do*, so what? We'll just turn around and come back.'

There's one last point on her tongue – *and anyway we're only doing this because of you* – but she bites it back.

They are on the hunt not just for a week's groceries, but for a printer as well. Oliver has realised he's going to need one, twenty-four hours after every retail location that would typically sell such a thing has been ordered to close. Ordering it online might mean waiting a week or more for it to be delivered, so they are chancing their arm and driving outside their inclusion zone to a supermarket-megastore in the hope that among the porridge oats and toilet rolls, they will find electrical equipment too.

A couple of weeks back, when he first started working from home, Oliver went and bought one of those eye-wateringly expensive coffee machines that will only make coffee from just as eye-wateringly expensive coffee capsules. Ciara can't help but think *that* would've been the time to get whatever he needed to do his job, but she's keeping quiet on that front as well.

'It's not that,' he says. 'I'm just not used to driving.' He flicks on an indicator at a T-junction even though they're the only car on the road. 'But I don't like breaking rules, you're right.' He throws her a quick smile. 'It's mostly the driving thing, though. I never drove when I was in London.'

'Should I be worried?'

'Not when the roads are like this.'

Traffic is so sparse that almost every time they come to a red light, they are the only vehicle to stop at it. Their route is taking them through empty suburbs; cars sit parked in driveways with the gates closed behind them and curtains remain drawn.

It's as if, Ciara thinks, Dublin has decided that since there's nowhere to go and nothing to do, the only thing for it is to have a citywide lie-in.

But she's wrong. As they approach the entrance to the Tesco Extra near Liffey Valley, it becomes clear that in actual fact the entire city has had the exact same idea as them.

A long tailback of cars waits just to gain entry to the car park. It takes nearly twenty minutes to make it to the entrance where a bored-looking teenager in a reflective vest directs them to follow the car in front, as if they couldn't have figured that out without his waving arm. It takes another ten minutes to find an empty space and their reward for that is to join the queue of what must be fifty or sixty people, all spaced two metres apart, that snakes out of the store's main entrance and down the full length of its façade before twisting back around on itself. Nearly another hour passes before they get to the top of the queue, where a stone-faced security guard tells them it's strictly one-customer-per-trolley today.

Ciara thinks he's telling them that they'll each need to collect a trolley before they go inside – why on earth would *that* be a rule? – until Oliver turns to her and says, 'It's okay. I'll go do it,' and she puts it together: the rule is that they have to shop *alone*. They can't both go inside.

Oliver is already moving away from her, towards the doors.

She starts to say, 'But ...' then stops because she doesn't know what the rest of the sentence is.

Somewhere behind them, a woman sighs theatrically.

Someone else mutters something sweary under their breath.

'Email me the list, will you?' Oliver calls over his shoulder.

And then he is gone, disappeared into the store, and Ciara is left standing outside by herself, wondering what the hell she's supposed to do now.

She can't even go sit in the car. He has the keys.

'You can go in, too,' the guard says, 'but you have to shop separately.' He holds up a hand in a *stop* gesture to let her know that she can't do this just yet, that she'll have to wait until another person comes out. Her face must communicate some kind of reaction to this because he adds, 'It's to keep the aisles as clear as possible so everyone can stay well away from each other.'

When she hears tut-tutting from behind her, Ciara feels compelled to say, 'Of course, yeah. I understand,' more loudly than she might have otherwise.

'It'll just be a minute,' the guard says.

She pulls out her phone and looks for the grocery list they made that she's recorded in her Notes app. Oliver is an okay cook while she's mostly a microwaver, so the bulk of the meal-planning was his. She doesn't know what he's going to do with things like lamb cutlets, a fresh mint plant, garam masala (?) and tahini (??) but he's promised she won't starve. They've also made what Oliver nicknamed their Doomsday Prepper List. They're saying if you get this thing you'll have to isolate yourself from everyone else for up to two weeks, so they both tried to think of non-perishable things they could stock up on – extras, to have just in case.

It was, in a weird way, fun. A challenge. They came up with dried pasta and ready-made sauces, the kind that don't

go off for years. Bread mixes that can be baked as needed —
but only the brown or soda ones, because they need water
adding, not milk. Porridge oats. Sweet snacks so full of
preservatives they'll last until the *next* global crisis. Tinned
fruit. Tinned fish. Tinned beans. Maybe some multivitamins,
just in case. Instant coffee, the fancy kind with supposedly
fresh grounds mixed in. Cartons of oat milk because it doesn't
require refrigeration and won't completely ruin the coffee.
Bottled water, although when the shops open again Oliver
says he's going to buy one of those filter jugs. Toothpaste and
shower gel. Toilet paper, toilet paper, toilet paper, because
who wants to be trapped in a confined space with someone
they don't know very well, who may be suffering from
intestinal issues, without an ample supply of *that*?

There is no part of Ciara that believes for one moment that
either of them will ever need to survive on a diet of dried
pasta and tinned grapefruit segments, but the idea of having
them is reassuring nonetheless.

She emails the list to Oliver and waits to hear the *whoosh*
that confirms its safe departure.

Another three or four minutes pass before a man in his
forties emerges from the doors pushing a trolley overflowing
with crates of beer, and the guard gives Ciara the okay to
go inside.

Running to catch up with Oliver seems like a childish
contravention of the rules, and not one he'd approve of. And
anyway, he can manage the shopping by himself. They've
already agreed she'll reimburse him for half the total in cash;

she can just give it to him afterwards. But she might as well have a browse rather than stand outside, bored and waiting for him.

As soon as the sliding doors close behind her, she's struck by how eerily quiet it is inside. She's never taken any notice of how much sound there normally is in a vast supermarket – chatter, she supposes, and trolley wheels on the floor and rubber soles squeaking – but she's sure this is the first time she's ever been able to hear distant music being played from some concealed speaker system. The one-person-one-trolley system is evidently working; the only other person she can see is the uniformed staff member directing her to follow the large red arrows stuck to the floor.

Ciara grabs a basket to keep up pretences and goes where she's told.

The flower bays and magazine racks are empty. An own-brand clothing area has been roped off with a sign that says: THIS SECTION IS TEMPORARILY CLOSED. WE APOLOGISE FOR ANY INCONVENIENCE. Even as Ciara advances into the food aisles, she meets no other customers, only staff members hurrying to empty the contents from stacks of blue bins and transfer them to the shelves.

Milk fridges and bakery baskets are stuffed to overflowing, but elsewhere there are huge, yawning gaps where product should be. There *is* toilet paper, but signs warn one packet per customer; Ciara puts one in her basket because it seems silly not to. The pasta section has been picked clean and she doesn't see any of those bread mixes in the aisle where she knows they should be; apparently they weren't the only ones with *that* bright idea.

It's a weird feeling to know that whatever you need, you must get it *here*, right now. There's nowhere else to go except shops just like this one and smaller versions of it with more limited product ranges.

What if this thing lasts longer than two weeks?

She grabs a packet of ballpoint pens in the Stationery aisle, and some razors and a bottle of hair conditioner in Beauty. When she finds a small selection of paperbacks with discount-price stickers on them, she picks up a few in turn, inspecting the text on their back covers until she remembers that she shouldn't be touching things unnecessarily. She chooses two at random and throws them into her basket, mentally updating its total cost.

She doesn't find Oliver until she reaches the last red arrow on the trail and emerges at the row of checkout desks. He's three tills away, stuffing things into his backpack. There's no one waiting behind him and the cashier is protected behind a Perspex screen, so she hurries to join him.

The last item on the belt is a large box containing a Canon printer. She hastily dumps the contents of her basket behind it.

'You got one, then?'

Oliver swings around, surprised to see her. 'Oh. Yeah. Thankfully.'

The cashier sees Ciara's toilet paper and does a little eye-roll, evidently unimpressed by her rule-bending.

'No pasta, though,' Oliver adds.

'I saw. Whoever thought there'd be a *pasta* shortage in Ireland?'

'Hey, at least we've moved on from potatoes.'

He hands her a scrunched-up plastic bag, one of the ones she saw him stuff into his backpack before they left the apartment.

The question is, what's in the backpack now?

She could swear that, just before he turned around, she saw him hastily zip it closed in a way that makes her think he's put something in there he doesn't want her to see.

Operation Grocery Shop takes up most of the day. Between the queueing to park and the queuing to get in, it's gone two by the time they're driving back to Harold's Cross. Unloading the car takes two trips up to the apartment, and then wiping everything down and finding somewhere to put it takes an age. Oliver seems to visibly relax when they reach the collection point for the GoCar – to which they're returning it now – without having encountered any Garda checkpoints. His shoulders and spine lose a tension that they'd been carrying for much of the day. He may claim it's about his driving, but on the walk back they passed two squad cars in the process of setting up a roadblock and Ciara would swear she felt the hand holding hers grow clammy with a cold sweat at the sight.

But she didn't ask him about it.

She's still caught on the backpack.

She'd watched for it when they'd returned to the apartment the first time: he'd hurried off into the bedroom with it before coming back to the kitchen without it, so whatever was in there, it wasn't food.

What would he have bought in that place that he didn't want her to see? What *could* he have?

And why hide anything from her at all?

She'd casually asked him for the receipt in the car on the way home, under the pretence of figuring how much she owed him. But he'd told her he didn't know where he'd put it, even though she'd watched him slip it inside his jacket at the checkout.

Had he genuinely forgotten that?

Or just outright lied?

When they return to the apartment a second time, Oliver starts tearing at the printer box and Ciara announces that she's going to have a shower.

She takes a towel into the bathroom, locks the door behind her and strips. She turns the monsoon shower head up full, the temperature to just below scalding and stands under its pressurised rainfall for thirty seconds, making sure to get the ends of her hair dripping wet. Then she steps out of it, wraps the towel around her and sinks down until she is sitting cross-legged on the tiled floor, back against the door.

She needs a minute alone.

To think.

The backpack isn't a big deal. People are entitled to privacy and there's plenty of things you can buy in a supermarket that you might not want to announce to the woman you've just started a relationship with. Like …

The best she can up with is haemorrhoid cream, which she's not even sure they sell in supermarkets, but there must be lots of things.

A thick steam starts to swirl in the air above her.

The problem is that it's reminded her that there could be a set of kitchen knives in there. Or a naggin of vodka he'll drink before noon from a water bottle. Or something from the Health section that he needs because of some undisclosed medical condition.

The problem is she doesn't know *what* could be in there, because she doesn't know *him*.

Not well enough to feel certain she's safe here, living with him in this place where no one else knows she is.

She *wants* to be here. She does.

But *should* she be?

A hard knock on the bathroom door startles her.

'You alive in there?' Oliver's voice, muffled by the door.

Ciara jumps up, out of the towel, and back into the shower stream before answering so that her, 'Yeah?' sounds like it's coming from the right place.

'I've put dinner on,' he says. 'Ready in ten minutes or so.'

'Okay,' she calls out. 'Great.'

She hears a clicking noise then – is that the door handle? Is he trying to get in?

Or is he just checking to see if she's locked it?

She waits.

'Is everything all right?' he asks after a beat.

'Yeah. Fine. Why?'

She waits for an answer but none comes, and a few seconds later she thinks she hears the door to the living room *clunk* closed.

She stays in the bathroom for another few minutes to keep up appearances, then gathers up her things and unlocks the door.

The steam spills out behind her into the colder air of the hall – directly opposite, the door to the living room is indeed closed.

She pauses next to it, head turned, listening. There's no sound at all coming from the other side.

What's he doing in there?

She moves closer until her left ear is almost touching the wood.

Nothing. But then—

She thinks she might have just heard a scrape of metal on cement.

Which would mean he's outside, on the terrace.

There's a *drip-drip* sound then, much closer, and after a beat she realises it's her, shedding droplets on to the hall floor, marking the spot where she's been earwigging, the sodden ends of her own hair giving her away.

She ducks into the master bedroom, clutching the towel she's wrapped around her, closing the door behind her with a soft *click*.

And then locking it, too.

The key has always sat in the lock but she's never heard it turn, and she winces now at how loud it is. Hopefully he's still outside. Why would she be locking this door right now? She can't think of any plausible reason and she certainly can't share the real one: because she's going to look for the backpack.

She puts her clothes back on first – her trusty jeans and a plain black T-shirt, creased from its time as a ball on the bathroom floor – and then scans the room.

There's really only two places it could be: in the wardrobe or under the bed. She checks them both, in that order, careful to leave no obvious sign that she's been rifling through Oliver's things.

But there's no sign of the backpack.

Did he come in here and take it while she was in the shower? Why would he do that? What the hell is in there that he doesn't want her to see?

She checks again to make sure she hasn't missed anything, but the backpack definitely isn't there. It's quick to search; Oliver doesn't have much stuff. Clothes and shoes and toiletries just about covers the lot.

But then he did say this was a temporary home. Maybe he only left London with whatever he could bring on the flight.

'Ciara?'

She freezes.

Oliver's voice sounds like it's coming from the living room. She quickly turns the key, opens the bedroom door wide and then hurries to the full-length mirror hung on the wall by the wardrobe, where she still has a line-of-sight to the door to the living room.

The shower has steamed all the make-up off her skin but not her eyes, leaving her lashes smudged and messy with wayward mascara. She wets a finger and drags it underneath each eye in turn, trying to repair the damage and trying to look like that's what she's been doing in here all along.

The living-room door opens with a flourish and Oliver appears.

When he spots her in the bedroom, he grins at her mischievously. 'You ready?'

'Ah ...' Her hair, she notices now, looks plastered to her head. 'Yeah.' She pushes her hands up into it, massaging her scalp, in a futile attempt to rescue it.

'You look lovely,' he says.

'Now *that's* a boldfaced lie.'

'Lovely to *me*.'

Ciara rolls her eyes at him.

'Come on then.' He holds out his hand, beckoning her. 'Let's go.'

'Go where?'

'Just come with me.'

'What's going on?'

'For God's sake, woman. I'm trying to surprise you here. Help me out.'

She takes his hand and lets him lead her through the living room, through the open patio doors and out on to the terrace—

The terrace has been transformed.

Strings of miniature LED lights have been wrapped around the railing; they glow warmly in the light of a setting sun. The table is now wearing a red-and-white checked tablecloth and is set for dinner for two, complete with flickering candles and champagne flutes. She laughs when she sees that a chair from the kitchen has been commandeered as a platform for a plastic yellow bucket, the kind children play with at the beach, only filled with ice and holding a sweating bottle of prosecco inside. Oliver's phone is lying on the tabletop, softly playing something folksy and sweet.

She turns to him.

'I was confined to Tesco for supplies,' he says, 'so I had to improvise. Don't look too closely at those lights – they're actually little unicorns. And the tablecloth is made of paper and the flutes are plastic. And those candles are the ones you light to keep bugs away. But I think I did good, right?'

She doesn't know quite what to say. She manages, 'What's this all for?'

'Well, *you*.' He puts a hand on the back of his neck and rubs it absently, which she's started to notice he always does when he's embarrassed or afraid that he's about to be. 'You moving in, I mean. Even if it's just temporary and because of an unprecedented global emergency – I'm electing not to take that part personally, just so you know. I just thought we should, you know, mark the occasion. And since we can't go anywhere ...' He grins. 'I should warn you, though, I didn't put quite the same effort into dinner. Or any effort. It's a pizza and garlic bread. From frozen.'

'Thank you,' she says, finding her voice finally. 'This is … It's lovely.'

She means it.

He reaches for her and she lets him.

'So are you,' he whispers into her ear.

That's when she sees it. Over his shoulder, through the open door. In the brightly lit living room.

Deflated and empty now, lying on the floor by the couch.

The backpack.

48 DAYS AGO

Saturday morning, they wander around town for a while searching for somewhere to have breakfast. She points out a bustling café at the top of Dawson Street with seats outside, but he doesn't really want to give hundreds of people the opportunity to take a good long look at his face as they stroll past, and he doesn't like feeling as if someone unseen could be watching him. When he suggests a small, basement-level restaurant a few doors down, she makes a face and says that maybe somewhere bigger and more open would be a safer option – you know, global-pandemic-wise? In the end they settle on Bewley's on Grafton Street, partly because they're both vaguely aware that it's supposed to be somewhere special and partly because there's already a queue of people waiting to get in, a good sign.

As soon as they get through the doors themselves, Oliver sees that it's the perfect choice. Inside it has the same airy, high-ceiling design as grand continental cafés and, better yet, the host leads them all the way to the back and around the corner to a little table where there'll be no passing traffic.

He offers Ciara the seat that faces into the café so he can sit with his back to it.

He doesn't care about the food or the coffee. He just wants to make sure that he won't have to regret this any more than he already does.

He picks up the menu and pretends to read.

'I am *starving*,' she says, picking up hers.

Thursday night was supposed to be the end of this. He was going to meet her for a drink and then disappear. That's what he'd needed to do and he *was* going to do it.

And it would've been easy to, what with everything that's going on now. She probably wouldn't even have thought twice about it, and she certainly wouldn't have suspected him of anything.

Instead, they'd ended up back at his place. Undressing each other. Somehow. Now she not only knows where he's living but she's slept in his bed and seen his scar.

Caught out unexpectedly, he'd told her the same story he'd told Lucy back in London. He hopes this isn't a sign of things to come.

Part of him can't believe that it's happened, but a larger part knows it did because he'd *wanted* it to.

Because he likes her.

He likes her and it's going to ruin everything.

Again.

'What are you having?' she asks. 'I think I might get the baked eggs.'

He knows he's standing with his hand in the fire. He can

see the flames tickling his skin. And past experience tells him that any moment now, the heat will burn through the outer layer to his nerve endings and drop him into a world of screaming pain.

There's no other possible outcome, he knows this.

But he just can't pull his hand away.

He likes the heat.

'Sounds good,' he says. 'I think I'll have that too.'

They set their menus down. He can't see any waiter in this section of the café, but presumably one will appear.

'Don't look,' Ciara whispers. 'But in the corner, to your right.'

Then she lifts her chin to indicate that he *should* look.

One of their fellow patrons is standing, balanced precariously, on her own chair, pointing a camera the size of a small dog at the tableful of artfully arranged food and drink below them. After she inspects the results of the latest shot on the camera's screen, the photographer bends down to slide a coffee cup a couple of inches to the left, wobbling a bit as the wooden chair rocks unsteadily beneath her feet.

Behaving in public in a way that attracts so much attention without seemingly caring who sees is such an alien behaviour to Oliver that he classes it as a kind of psychopathy.

'Anything for the 'Gram,' Ciara mutters.

They woke up in the same bed this morning but they haven't stayed together since; after he suggested they walk into town for breakfast, she'd told him she'd meet him there instead, that she needed to 'get ready' at her place. Change clothes, put on make-up, whatever else women do. It gave him an hour at home alone, which he used to search for her on social media, more thoroughly this time, using all the information he'd gleaned – but, again, to no avail.

He hasn't been able to find anything even resembling a corresponding profile on Twitter, Facebook *or* Instagram, despite forensically searching for every possibility he could think of. Her full name. Her first name plus 'Dublin'. Her first name plus 'Cork'.

All those with her last name and first initial.

All recent posts tagged with things like #thesidecarbar, #cocktails and #French75 in case her username was a string of random numbers or some other name altogether.

Nothing.

Not even an account set to private that *might* be her. No old posts belonging to other accounts in which she'd been tagged.

She just wasn't there.

And not just on social media, but online in general.

Apart from the LinkedIn profile he'd found for her on the day they'd met, there wasn't a single Google search result about her. She was *so* not there, it was suspicious.

A person would have to work at keeping the internet so clean of their name.

Or would they?

Maybe if you were a normal person, it wasn't that hard.

And Ciara might just *not use* social media. It wasn't unheard of. After all, weren't digital detoxes all the rage?

And in the hours they've spent together, he's never seen her take a single picture with her phone. Any time he's caught a glimpse of her screen, she seems to be checking her email or scrolling through news headlines.

And now that she's brought up the subject, it's an opportunity he can't waste.

'You're not on the 'Gram, then?' he asks.

She shakes her head. 'Nope.'

'Not now or you never were?'

'I think I had an account for about five minutes a few years back, but I never posted anything to it. Why? Are *you*?'

'Oh, so you're going with pretending you haven't already had a look for me on there, are you?' He grins.

'I haven't! I swear ... Honestly, it wouldn't even have occurred to me.'

'Really?'

'Really.'

'So you're not down with all the cool kids, then?'

'I think,' Ciara says, 'that using the phrase "down with all the cool kids" might preclude you from being that ...?'

'Fair. And I'm not, to answer your question. On the 'Gram.'

'What a shame. You'd be *such* a hit on there.'

'Would I?'

'With *that* face?' she says. 'Of course you would. And you're an architect, for God's sake—'

'Not quite.'

'You would be on there. Social media is no place for nuance. You need to milk all that building buildings shit.'

'That's actually what my degree course was called: Bachelor of Building Buildings Shit.'

She laughs. Then says, 'So why *aren't* you on there?'

'Honestly …?' He exhales, buying time. He needs to do a better job of this than he did with the scar. *Keep it simple.* 'I just don't, you know, *get* it. I'm not against it or anything, I just wouldn't know what to do with it.' He pauses. 'Why aren't *you* on there?'

'Because I've seen behind the curtain.'

'That sounds ominous.'

'I meant for it to.' She leans forward, elbows on the table. 'Look, nothing is free, right? We pay for these apps with our data. That's what all those user agreements that no one ever reads actually say. But the fact that all these tech giants are collecting information about us is not what everyone should be worried about – it's what they're *doing* with it that's terrifying. I can make a list of documentaries for you to watch – horror movies, really – but the too-long-didn't-read is that they're feeding the data to AIs that are working to erode the very idea of free will. I can't stop it – I don't think anyone can, it's too late – but I don't need to actively help either. So I'm down to just LinkedIn because in our industry if you're not on there it's like you don't exist at all, but that's it. Our robot overlords are coming regardless, but I'm not going to hold the door open for them.'

He allows himself a moment of believing all this, of contemplating what it would mean for him if this were actually true, if Ciara really didn't use social media. He tries to imagine it. What if there was no danger that, through her, his name and face would make their way online, sending some vigilante Twitter mob into the street bearing torches and pitchforks, catching the attention of the tabloid media?

He could keep seeing her. For a little while longer, anyway.

So long as she keeps believing *him*.

TODAY

The smell in the lobby is worse than before.

Through the glass doors opposite, Lee can see that the occupants of the apartments in the corridor between here and the scene have wisely taken to their terraces. For the time being, they can't leave unless they have what counts as an emergency reason, and a global pandemic has put paid to most of those. Normally they might relocate them to a hotel, but in the current circumstances that's not the easy option it might have previously been. Once the forensics guys have done their business and the pathologist has been and gone, the body can be removed and the apartment can be cleaned. Until then, she hopes the weather stays fine for them.

Masked up and trying to breathe through her mouth, Lee opens the box assigned to apartment one with a key that one of the uniforms has borrowed from the woman in apartment four. Apparently all the letterbox keys are the same here; she wonders if the residents know and, if so, how they feel about that. She retrieves the contents with a gloved hand. While the uniform hurries off to return the key, Lee takes her bounty back outside – and herself away from The Smell.

Karl is waiting by their car, looking inordinately pleased with himself for somehow managing to rustle up two takeaway coffees.

They sit into the front seats, leaving the doors open so they can keep one ear on the scene and respond if anyone needs them.

He sets the cups on the dash and pulls a clear evidence bag from the glove compartment, holding it open so Lee can drop the envelope inside.

It's slim and cream, smooth and stiff. Premium paper. Like something a wedding invite might come in.

There's nothing on the front except a name handwritten in blue ink.

Oliver St Ledger.

The name tugs on something at the back of Lee's mind, but she doesn't know why it should. It doesn't mean anything to her. She can't think where she might have heard it before, or in what context.

'What's that?' Karl asks, pointing.

Lee flips the bag around and sees more handwritten words on the back of the envelope, just above the flap.

This isn't what you're worried it is.

'I bet it *is* what he's worried it is,' Karl says.

They can't open it; scenes-of-crime will have to do that, just in case. For now, Lee sets it on the dash, name-side up.

They both sit back and stare at it while they sip their coffees.

Lee frowns. 'Did you put sugar in this?'

'Three,' Karl says. 'And don't you dare tell me you can't taste it.' He shakes his head. 'You'd *really* want to get your bloods checked.'

'I'm not the one having a can of Red Bull and two Marlboros for breakfast.'

'What did *you* have then? An egg-white omelette and a wheatgrass shot?'

'I didn't have anything,' she says. 'I'm fasting.'

'Sure you are.'

'Does that name mean anything to you?' Lee jerks her chin towards the envelope on the dash. 'Oliver St Ledger?'

'Should it?'

'Don't know. It sounds familiar to me, and St Ledger is a fairly uncommon name here. I don't think I've ever actually met anyone called that, though.'

'Maybe you're thinking of an actor or something.'

Lee pulls her phone from a pocket and, one-handed and somewhat awkwardly, opens up the browser on it and enters *Oliver St Ledger* into the Google search bar. The results are your typical internet soup: social media profiles, obituaries, a staff listing on a university website.

But there are very few exact-name matches, hardly anything for Dublin and nothing at all that would explain why that name would mean something to her.

'No stamp,' Karl says. 'Hand-delivered.'

'I'm impressed you noticed.'

'The caffeine is kicking in, what can I say?'

Lee reaches for the plastic bag and flips it over, so they're now looking at the message on the back.

'"This isn't what you're worried it is," Karl reads aloud. 'What does *that* mean?'

'Your guess is as good as mine.'

'My guess is bad break-up,' he says. 'Or custody battle. Or a bunny-boiling psycho-stalker bitch.'

'I take it back. Remind me to sign you up for Sensitivity Training, will you, Karl?'

'Is that the role-playing thing? I did that already.'

'I'm not sure it took.'

'What do you think it means, then?'

'Well ...' Lee sighs. 'I think we've probably been biased by the fact that we found it in the letterbox for an apartment where someone's been decomposing for a fortnight. It could be something innocuous. Positive. *Nice*, even. Like ... an invitation.'

'All right, Pollyanna.'

'Did that architect crowd ring you back yet?'

'Nah. I'll try them again.' Karl takes out his phone and unlocks it with a thumb, spilling a few drops of coffee on the leg of his jeans in the process. 'Let's ask them if they're missing an Ollie.'

Ollie.

Ollie St Ledger.

The name and everything it means comes speeding from the back of Lee's brain to its front and centre.

Suddenly she knows exactly where she knows it from

and this knowledge lodges a cold stone of dread right in the centre of her chest.

'Back in a sec,' she says to Karl, who already has his phone to his ear.

Lee climbs out of the car, setting her coffee on the roof. She walks a few steps away, dials the reception at Sundrive Road and asks if anyone there has a mobile number for Detective Inspector Bill O'Leary, retired. Someone has a number of someone who might, and she waits while they make a call.

Ollie St Ledger.

Christ, if it's *him* in there …

She'll be lucky to get that takeaway *next* Friday night.

Still on hold, Lee returns to collect her coffee and sips it while pacing back and forth just outside the outer cordon of Garda tape.

Through the rear windscreen of the car she can see that Karl has finished his call and is now looking at her questioningly in the rear-view mirror's reflection.

She turns her back to him.

She won't say anything until she's sure.

Ollie St Ledger. He'd hardly be using that name. He *wouldn't* be, surely? He'd have changed it. To his mother's maiden name, usually, in cases like this. That's what tends to happen.

Not that there's a lot of cases like his one.

A voice comes on the end of the line and says they've got Bill's number, that they'll text it to her.

Lee stops pacing and looks down at the phone, waiting for the message to come in, willing the sender to type faster.

If he's not using that name – and he almost certainly isn't – that means that whoever put that envelope in his letterbox knows who he really is.

Or *thinks* they do, which if that envelope is related to the fact that he's lying dead on the floor of his bathroom now and they're wrong about it is much, much worse.

Ding.

Lee taps the number in the text, initiating a call.

It rings an excruciating number of times before the voice of an older man answers with a gruff, 'Yeah?'

'Bill, it's Lee Riordan. How are you?'

A beat passes before he says, 'Concerned that this isn't a social call.'

Straight to business – just how he was back when they worked together, fifteen years ago. She was still in uniform then, fresh out of Templemore, and Bill was already the wizened elder statesman, famous even outside the force for his involvement in several high-profile cases.

'It's not,' Lee says. 'Unfortunately.' She takes another step away from the car, the cordon, everyone else, and lowers her voice. 'Bill, I'm at a scene in Harold's Cross and I've got something sensitive to ask you. I have a name. I just want to know if it means anything to you. That's *all* I'm asking, at this point, for both our sakes. A yes or no is all I'm looking for. Okay?'

'Okay ...'

Lee takes a deep breath. 'Ollie St Ledger.'

The pause that follows is so long, she pulls the phone from her ear to check the call is still connected.

Bill says, 'It means something to me, yes.'

'Thank you. I thought it would, but I wanted to make sure.'

'If you need me—'

'I might. Is this the best number for you?'

'So long as I hear the phone ringing. Hearing isn't what it used to be. But the wife will if I don't.'

Lee hesitates. She should leave it there, but ...

She feels obligated to give him something in exchange for this.

She says, 'I think maybe he's dead.'

Another long pause. Then:

'Good.'

Click.

Lee goes back to the car, sits back in.

'KB Studios do have an Oliver,' Karl says, 'but his last name is Kennedy. Guy I spoke to says the firm has an apartment here, yeah, and he thinks Kennedy could've been staying in it, but he's not sure. Seems to be the company motto.' He mimics a television-commercial-voiceover. '*KB Studios: Where We're Never Sure.* Remind me never to hire them to, you know, design a building, would you? And no pictures on the website or any social that I can find, but the guy described Kennedy as late twenties, six foot, light brown hair, good-looking. But also said he had big ears and an angular jaw so … I know he was pretty ripe *and* face-down, but could that be what's in there?'

'What's in there,' Lee says, 'is a complete and utter shit storm. Potentially.'

'Oh?' Karl frowns. 'Who were you talking to?'

'We'll need to keep this very close to our chests, for now.'

'Loving the suspense, Lee, but—'

'At least until we're sure.' She sighs. 'I really *was* looking forward to that takeaway, you know.'

'For fuck's sake, what's—'

She turns to look at him. 'Do you remember the Mill River case?'

32 DAYS AGO

After the warm glow of Sunday night, Monday feels like the cold, sharp shock of the real start.

Ciara opens her eyes to darkness but, after a few seconds, finds the weak grey light forcing its way around the edges of the window blind. Oliver is, as ever, turned away from her on the other side of the bed. He's still deeply asleep, snoring lightly. Last night, she made sure to leave clothes folded on the floor right by what is apparently her side of the bed now: a pair of polka-dot pyjama bottoms and an old, bleach-splattered T-shirt that has been relegated to sleepwear. She picks them up and tiptoes out of the room, closing the door softly behind her, and pulls them on in the gloom of the living room.

The snazzy coffee machine is about as quiet as a tractor engine, so Ciara boils the kettle instead, flipping the switch to OFF before the bubbling and hissing really gets going, and stirs in a spoon of instant coffee granules swiped from their Doomsday Prepper stock.

She doesn't really care what it tastes like; it's mostly the smell she finds she needs in the morning.

The door that leads to the little railed-in terrace unlocks with a gentle *click*, but makes a louder *whooshing* noise when she slides it back. The table still has the checked tablecloth on it from last night and the lights are still twisted around the railing; she feels silly when she recalls her suspicions that he had something more sinister hidden in the backpack.

What did she seriously think was in there?

She pictures Oliver's face just after the reveal, when he was apologising for having to scavenge his romantic-meal materials from Tesco. The hint of heat on his cheeks, the nervous smile, the way he dips his head when he's embarrassed so it's as if he's looking up at you, despite his height...

Ciara smiles at the memory.

She chooses the chair that gives her a better view of the courtyard and, around it, the other apartments, and holds her coffee with two hands.

The sky is growing brighter by the minute. It is striking how quiet it is. But it's a *dis*quiet. The city has been winding down for, what? Two weeks now? But over the weekend, it's come to a stop. The absence of traffic noise — of engines and horns and tyres on tarmac — is the biggest change, and the most disconcerting one of all. She is a ten-minute walk from the heart of the half of the city that sits on the southside of the river, and there is no sound at all save for distant birds and the rustle of a light breeze through the courtyard's trees.

She thinks, I could be the last person on earth and not know it.

And then that she could be the last person on earth and no one would ever have even known she was here.

Movement.

Ciara sees the bright pink thighs first and for a split second is confused about how the legs they belong to seem to disappear at the knee, but then she blinks and realises what she's looking at: not a woman levitating in the air but one wearing leggings that are grey from the knee down, doing yoga stretches on her balcony.

Oliver told her there's a gym in the building, but it pre-emptively closed last week and now, under this de facto lockdown, it'll have to stay that way for the foreseeable future. He'd said he was going to start running again; she'd said, 'Off with you,' and told him about her rule of only running if she was being chased, if it was running *away*. She likes the idea of going for walks, though. It's nice around here – it's leafy, and there's the canal – and some of the city is still within their 2K. It'll be interesting to see it as it must be now, all emptied out. And walking will give her a chance to think.

She takes another sip of her coffee.

Yoga Woman is lunging now. She's blonde and lithe. Even from this distance – the woman is on the other side of the complex and one floor up – Ciara can see how the material clings to the woman's skin and how that skin clings to her body. She supposes that's why this woman has the confidence to do this *on her balcony*, to a potential audience of all her neighbours. She wonders if the woman wants people to watch, if it's the yoga that makes this woman feel good in the mornings, or the attention.

As if she can hear Ciara's thoughts, the woman straightens up, comes to the glass railing and rests her hands on top of it.

And turns her head to look directly Ciara's way.

That's what it feels like, anyway. It's hard to tell from so far away and there's the leaves of a courtyard tree equidistant between them, but Ciara feels her skin prickle with the sense of being watched.

She looks down into her coffee cup, exaggerating the movement, so the woman gets the message that *she* isn't staring back at her.

'Oh, for God's sake.'

Ciara jumps at the sound of Oliver's voice right behind her, inadvertently sloshing coffee over the rim of her cup and splashing a few drops on to her thighs. She turns to see him standing in the open door, holding two cups, one of them out to her.

'Give me that,' he says. 'And take this.'

'What is it?'

'Coffee,' he says. 'Which I know is *not* what you're drinking, I saw the jar on the counter. That's for, like, when we get to *The Road* stage of the apocalypse. No need to punish yourself with it until then.'

Ciara rolls her eyes good-naturedly, dutifully puts the cup she has down on the table and reaches for its replacement.

'Why didn't you use the machine?'

'I forgot how,' she lies. She takes a sip of her new, proper coffee. It does taste better. That machine must be quieter than she thought.

'Thank you,' she says. 'And good morning.'

'Good morning to you, too.' He steps outside now, bare feet on the cement, and bends down to kiss the top of her head. Then he sits into the other chair, a careful action designed to keep all his coffee in his cup. 'So, do you always get up this early on a school day?'

'*Is* it early?'

'Just gone seven.'

'Well, then … yeah. I suppose. This is about my normal time.'

Oliver looks around the courtyard. 'God,' he says, 'it's so quiet.'

'No traffic. I think that's the big change today.'

'No anything. So – what's the plan?'

'Well, I need to log into our system by nine,' Ciara says. 'Do you mind if I take the spare bedroom after lunch? I have to take a couple of calls then, so …' Over the weekend, they dragged the dining table into the spare bedroom to serve as a desk. The deal is that one of them will take the makeshift office in the morning, the other in the afternoon. Whoever doesn't have it gets to lie on the couch, use the coffee table or sit at the breakfast bar – or even work from bed, if they like. 'I'm just going to tackle emails this morning. I can do that from the couch.'

'Fine by me.'

'And I think I'll go for a walk around noon. I might even try to do that every day and I'm telling you this so I actually *do* do it. Accountability, and all that jazz.'

'Then here's what we'll do,' Oliver says, leaning forward. 'I'll take the bedroom for the first half of the day, you have the couch. When you go for your walk, I'll make lunch. Then, if you don't mind, I'll go for a run around five, and you can do dinner?'

She makes a face.

'Okay,' he says. '*Start* dinner. Like, preheat the oven.'

'I can do that. Although you might have to show me how to work the oven.'

'And then tonight, I thought we could start on *From the Earth to the Moon*?'

It's some show about the moon landings he's been on about.

She smiles. 'Sounds like a plan.'

Oliver settles back into his chair, satisfied.

She's noticed this about him: he needs a plan in place and will build it if there isn't one already. He has to know what's happening now and next and after that, and what's happening has to have some kind of structure to it. She saw the logic in this for their empty Saturdays or lazy Sundays, but it seems like overkill for a weekday that's mostly going to be spent on work.

Still, she supposes having some structure to their days in lockdown can't be a bad thing.

Ciara risks a look at Yoga Woman's balcony.

It's empty.

She's gone.

When Ciara reaches the end of Harcourt Street, she sees that the gates at the corner of Stephen's Green opposite are closed. She isn't able to read the text on the neon-yellow signs cabled-tied to the railings until she's crossed the road and is standing in front of them, but the branding is familiar by now and she's already guessed what they say: due to COVID-19, they've closed the park.

This doesn't make any sense – it's a *park*? – but there's no one to complain to. She starts off around the perimeter railing instead, catching glimpses here and there of the perfectly empty green, leafy spaces beyond. It looks peaceful but doesn't sound it; there's a cacophony of incessant squawking coming from inside. Apparently the seagulls that usually terrorise Grafton Street shoppers have already commandeered the park for themselves.

A Luas tram slinks past carrying just three passengers. Two uniformed Gardaí pass on bicycles, barely going faster than her own two feet, weaving figure-of-eights on the road and chatting casually to each other like they're out for a Sunday spin. She's one of only a handful of pedestrians.

There's also an ominous buzzing noise she can't quite place – quiet at first, then steadily growing louder. She thinks an alarm has been set off somewhere until she sees the man standing twenty feet away, manipulating a set of handheld controls, looking upward. She follows his gaze and spies the drone, a tiny black object moving steadily across the midday sky, just above the rooftops, capturing bird's-eye footage of a near-empty city.

Ciara had imagined getting a coffee and drinking it on a bench by the duck pond in the park, but now she sees how naïve such a plan was: the park is locked and there is nowhere to get a coffee. Even the little convenience store at the top of Grafton Street, while still open as an essential business, has an OUT OF ORDER sign on its self-serve coffee machine.

She will have to think of something else to do each day, somewhere else to sit and think. Because she knows she needs it, the processing time. She's not used to being with another person twenty-four hours a day, and everything has happened so fast.

Life has suddenly exploded on her, that's what it feels like. She came to Dublin. She found Oliver. An unprecedented global emergency began. She and Oliver have moved in together.

And that's just all in the last month.

Last night, after Oliver had fallen asleep and rolled away from her, she'd lain awake in the dark for a little while, unable to quieten her mind as her thoughts raced. It's not that she doesn't want to be where she is – on the contrary, she's *exactly* where she wants to be. Things are working out for her here better than she'd even hoped – and quickly.

But the speed is the very problem. It feels as if some

unseen force has a hold of both her elbows and is pulling her along, like those protestors you see on the news being dragged away by police in riot gear with their toes barely touching the ground. It's not that she's being pulled towards a place she doesn't want to go, it's just that ...

Everything is happening so, so fast.

She thinks if she can just have some time to herself, outside, each day, those hours will act as speed bumps and slow it all down.

Just enough to make her feel like she's in control again.

For today, though, this will have to do.

Ciara does one loop around the railings of Stephen's Green and then starts back towards the apartment.

She hears the voice even before she's put her key in the front door.

It's male and angry and has the amplified, disembodied quality of coming from a speaker. She can't make out any words but she can instantly identify the emotion: frustration.

Anger, even. Maybe.

Ciara shakes the keys and closes the door behind her with a *thump* in an attempt to signal her presence, but the voice continues, uninterrupted.

Oliver must be on a video-call in the spare bedroom, whose door she can see is standing open. He probably wasn't expecting her back this soon. The other voice is older, and as she advances down the hall she hears it say, 'I thought we'd agreed you wouldn't hide things from me.'

She goes to the door of the room to pull it closed, to afford Oliver and this man some semblance of privacy. But Oliver is seemingly still unaware that she's even come in. He's sitting at their makeshift desk with his back to her. She can see that the screen of his laptop is filled with the face of a man with white-grey hair and a tanned, lined face, his webcam positioned at that awkward and always unflattering angle of just below the chin and straight up the nose.

The man is shaking his head as if in disbelief, and Oliver's posture – shoulders slumped, head down – seems to be communicating some kind of shame or defeat.

'You can't—' the man onscreen starts, then stops to frown at something over Oliver's shoulder.

Her, Ciara realises on a delay.

Oliver whips around, his face a question.

Sorry, she mouths at him, and swiftly pulls the door closed.

She doesn't hear any more.

Oliver doesn't come out for another fifteen minutes.

By then Ciara has made an executive decision and started lunch, which, in keeping with her cooking ability, is chicken-and-cheese toasties ready to be shoved under the grill, served with the limp remains of a ready-made salad bowl that's been sitting in the fridge since Friday. She has made an effort elsewhere, though, setting two places at the breakfast bar, complete with neatly folded squares of kitchen paper and glasses of iced water sitting on mismatched coasters she found in a drawer.

'Sorry about that,' Oliver says when he emerges. He looks sheepish.

'Is everything okay?'

'Not really, no.' He sees the layout on the breakfast bar. 'What's all this?'

'Day-one enthusiasm.'

He smiles weakly. 'How long before we're standing at the counter absently eating fistfuls of dry cornflakes straight from the box, do you think?'

'I'd guess Friday.'

She lifts the sandwiches on to a baking tray and slips them under the grill.

'How was your walk?'

'For some reason they've locked up Stephen's Green, which is annoying.' She turns to face him, folds her arms. 'What was all that about? Who was that guy?'

Oliver runs a hand through his hair.

'That was my boss,' he tells the kitchen floor. 'And that was about ...'

If Ciara had to guess what Oliver was about to say, it'd be something about a fuck-up at work. He doesn't talk much about it, but he has alluded once or twice to some big project near the Silicon Docks, which she thinks is all those modern glass buildings between the river and the entrance to the port tunnel where the more ostentatious American tech companies have their European HQs, all standing empty now because they've sent their thousands of workers home to work from there.

But what he says is, 'Because of *you*.'

She can't imagine what this means.

'*Me?*'

'Remember how I told you this place came with the job? Well, it's employee accommodation. Not my own.' Slowly he raises his gaze, meets her eye. 'So technically I'm the only one who's supposed to be staying here.'

It takes her a beat to understand.

'And your boss just saw me,' she says, thinking aloud. 'Here, during lockdown. So he knows I'm not just visiting.'

'He didn't actually see you, but he knew someone was there. He asked and, well, I didn't lie. I didn't think I had to, but ...' Oliver shifts his weight from one foot to the other. 'He said that kind of thing wasn't allowed, not even now. And then he made a point of telling me that this isn't the only apartment the firm is renting in the complex. Turns out it's one of two. And the other one has, apparently, one of the senior partners in it. And Kenneth made a point of telling me that wherever that one is, it has a view of my terrace. I'm so sorry, Ciara, but ...'

She has two thoughts then.

The first is that he very rarely says her name and actually, come to think of it, how often does she say his? There's something soothing about hearing it come out of his mouth, in his voice. It sends a bead of warmth rising up from deep within her chest.

Which is surprising.

The second is that she has to leave.

She has to leave.

And that thought floods her entire body with heat, the kind of heat that accompanies blind panic.

From somewhere behind her, a faint smell of bread burning begins to waft through the air.

'Should I go right now?' she says.

Oliver frowns.

'God, no. No. I didn't mean …' He comes to her, takes both her hands in his. 'You're not going anywhere. They're just being ridiculous. Totally ridiculous. All I'm saying is that I don't think we can sit outside any more, because whichever apartment that asshole is in, he has a clear view of our terrace. And I've told Kenneth you'll go back to your own place today.'

'Oh.' Ciara's shoulders drop, the tension dissipating, and now she's embarrassed that she got it so wrong. She starts laughing. '*Oh.*'

Oliver laughs too. 'You really went *straight* to doomsday scenario there, didn't you?' He pulls her close, kisses her gently. 'You're not going anywhere. But you might be about to set the fire alarm off.'

'Shit!'

The sandwiches are beyond saving, their tops burned to a crisp. Oliver thinks it's hilarious and reminds her that he was supposed to make lunch today, and says that perhaps he *should*. After some half-hearted protesting, she lets him.

It's only afterwards, when she carries her laptop into the 'office' for the afternoon stretch, that the thought occurs to her: the timeline doesn't fit.

Oliver said that when she went to close the bedroom door, her boss saw that someone else was there and asked him if there was. That's when the talk of employee accommodation and a senior partner in another apartment began.

But before Ciara had even advanced down the hall, before she'd got anywhere near the doorway, she'd heard the other man raise his voice.

I thought we'd agreed you wouldn't hide things from me.

You can't—

So what had that been about? What had Oliver been hiding from him?

And what was he hiding now, from *her*?

35 DAYS AGO

Fresh out of the shower, Oliver sits on the couch in a towel to watch the Taoiseach's speech live.

With effect from midnight tonight, Leo's steady, even voice blares from the TV – probably from *all* the TVs, everywhere, throughout the country, *for a two-week period until Easter Sunday, April 12, everybody must stay at home in all circumstances except for the following situations. To travel to and from work, for the purposes of work, only where the work is an essential health, social care or other essential service that cannot be done from home. To shop for food or household goods, or to collect a meal. To attend medical appointments or to collect medicines and other health products. For vital family reasons such as providing care to children, elderly or vulnerable people. To take brief, individual exercise within two kilometres of your home. All public and private gatherings of any number of people, outside a single household or living unit, are prohibited. All public transport will be restricted to essential workers. Outside of the activities I've listed, there should be no travel outside of a two-kilometre radius of your home for any reason.*

The Taoiseach doesn't use the word *lockdown*, but it's clear that that's exactly what it is. Basically: everyone has to stay at home for the next two weeks.

In their *own* home.

They can't meet anyone, indoors or out, who doesn't live with them.

Oliver stares at the TV screen, shaking his head in disbelief.

This is so perfect for him, it's bordering on ridiculous. If he had had the opportunity to *design* a set of circumstances, he couldn't have come up with anything better than this.

He'll ask Ciara to move in with him.

Or to come stay with him for the next couple of weeks. Let's put it like that, he tells himself, so as not to scare her off.

According to the rules, that's the only way they'll be able to keep seeing each other. If they remain as they are now, living separately as two individual households, they won't be able to see each other at all.

It's unclear to him if this is a legal stance or just advice, but Oliver has no intention of breaking any rules. He wouldn't do anything that would prompt a member of An Garda Síochána to so much as look his way, but there are other, worse punishments. He's already seen plenty of pictures and videos shared online of people who *other* people suspected of contravening restrictions, and in many of them the people were clearly identifiable. He can't risk that.

He'll tell her he can't risk it because of his – non-existent – asthma; that the rules are there for a reason and he wants to abide by them.

He doesn't know why she'd say no when she's effectively living in his apartment anyway; she only goes back to her place to work. He hasn't been there yet, but he's going tonight. Based on what she's told him about it and what he found when he Googled current rental listings for the complex, his place is twice the size – and he doesn't think she has any balcony or private outside space.

Unless, of course, she doesn't *want* to come stay with him. There's always the possibility that he's read her all wrong, that whatever he thinks is happening here actually isn't, that she doesn't feel at all the way her actions imply she does.

But he doubts it.

So theoretically, for the next two weeks, they could be together all the time.

Alone together.

Not seeing anyone else. No colleagues, no friends, no family. Because they *can't* see any of them. He's felt relatively safe since she's *just* moved to Dublin and, as she'd said herself, didn't even get a chance to get to know any of her co-workers before they were all told to go and work from home, but this would be an entirely different level of security.

Not only can she not introduce him to anybody, but she can't expect *him* to introduce *her* to anybody either. It won't be at all suspicious that she's not meeting his friends, or colleagues, or family, or anyone else who knows him.

And he's already established that she doesn't use social media, so there's no threat of her Geotagging pictures taken in his apartment or anything like that.

Maybe there's even an opportunity here to encourage her not to tell anyone about this, to keep it a secret. Because it's a bit crazy to move in with a guy you've only just met, isn't it?

And, really, she's just coming to stay for a couple of weeks, to ride out the lockdown. No need to say anything to anybody, when you think about it.

This could be his chance. The one he's been waiting for.

We are not prisoners of fate, Varadkar booms from the TV screen. *There is no fate but what we make for ourselves.*

He thinks the leader of the country might have just quoted a line from the *Terminator* movies while announcing grave new measures needed to stop the spread of a deadly virus – is that wise? – but that aside, Oliver finds himself agreeing with this sentiment for the first time in his entire life.

He might not have to be a prisoner of his fate any more. A global emergency might just be about to release him from it.

What happens next is up to each and every one of us.

Two weeks, Oliver thinks. If he can convince Ciara that this is a good idea, he has two whole weeks.

When no one else can contradict anything he says.

When he can be with her all the time and be anyone he wants to be while he does it. Be the man *she* wants to be with, the Oliver she thinks she knows.

He can become him, fully, finally, and leave all his other selves – with their other names, their dark mistakes – far, far behind.

29 DAYS AGO

In one moment Ciara is deep in a dreamless sleep and in the next she is wide awake and the world is on fire.

A siren is wailing.

So loud that the peak of each iteration feels like something has reached into her ear canal and pinched whatever's at the very end of it, deep inside the centre of her skull.

And it's *here*, this ceaseless noise.

With her, in this pitch-black room.

But when she turns she sees that Oliver, for some reason, is not.

It takes a moment for Ciara's brain to absorb the shock and put the pieces together: the building's fire alarm has gone off in the middle of the night and Oliver isn't in bed beside her. His half of the duvet is folded back on to her and when she touches a hand to the exposed sheet, she feels no warmth in it.

But the siren is louder than her thoughts, so she can't think about that now. She can't think about anything. She has only one objective and it's to get to a place where she can't hear this torturous noise.

She throws back the covers just as the door to the bedroom opens, the warm glow of the light in the hallway swiftly banishing the majority of the dark. Oliver stands in the doorway in silhouette, rendered a shadowman by the hall light.

She can see enough to see that he's dressed. Sweatpants and a T-shirt – what he puts on when he gets up in the morning but before he gets actually dressed. He only wears his boxers to bed, so wherever he was, it was more than a sleepy trip to the bathroom.

What was he doing?

The open bedroom door has made the siren even louder; the alarms themselves must be in the hall. She reaches for the jeans she wore yesterday and hung from the back of the chair last night, and jams her bare feet into the trainers she had neatly set on the floor.

She is dimly aware of Oliver not moving as she does this. He remains in the doorway, still, his facial expression blurred by the dark, seemingly unaffected by this brain-piercing noise.

He holds this position even when she reaches him, making no effort to move out of her way.

She calls out his name but he doesn't react. It crosses her mind that he could be sleepwalking, but now that her eyes have adjusted there's enough light to see that he's very much awake and alert.

Awake and alert and blocking her way out of the bedroom.

'Oliver,' she says again.

And then, as if coming out of a daze, he nods and steps aside.

She pushes past him into the hall and grabs her coat from the hook by the door. Her keys are on the hall table; she slips them into a pocket. *My phone*, she thinks then. This could be an actual fire and God knows how long they'll be out there if it is. She should take that, too. *Where is it?* She doesn't usually bring it into the bedroom with her, so she dashes into the living room – the lights are on in there – and scans for it.

It's on the coffee table, next to Oliver's phone.

Which just at that moment lights up with a notification.

She barely glances at it as she picks up her own phone, but she thinks it was a text message.

Touching the screen of *her* phone makes it light up too – with the time: 4:01 a.m.

Why would someone be texting Oliver at four in the morning?

She turns back around.

'Where are you going?' Oliver shouts over the din.

She points at the door. 'Out!'

The entire world is starting to feel as if it's made of noise and Ciara can't take much more of it. Whoever designed this alarm did their job extremely well. She needs to get away, to get outside. But as she starts down the hallway she feels a tug on her arm and then a pull, a force strong enough to spin her right around.

Oliver pulls her into the bathroom and shuts the door.

The siren, mercifully, drops a few decibels. She can hear

him when he speaks, but there's a distant buzzing sound that feels as if it's coming from inside her own ears.

'It'll go off in a second,' he says, putting his hands on her shoulders. 'It's a false alarm. Happens all the time. Every time someone burns their dinner. Relax.'

But his touch doesn't match this sentiment. It feels different.

Not reassuring, but holding in place.

She says, 'Who's making dinner at four a.m.?'

'Or someone comes home drunk and lights up in the lift.'

'Comes home from where? There's a lockdown.'

His response to this is a shrug. He's standing with his back against the door.

'Oliver,' she says evenly, 'there could be a fire. I want to go outside.'

'But there's no *need*.'

'Oliver,' she says again, this time in the exhale of a nervous laugh, because this situation is at once completely absurd and increasingly unsettling.

What the hell is he doing?

Her mind runs towards dark places. He's a foot taller than her, stronger than her, and he's preventing her from leaving a small room in the middle of the night during a potential fire. Physically holding her in place. She has her phone but ...

She can see him snatching it from her hand, throwing it against the tiled wall. They're in the smallest space of the apartment, at the end of the hall, while a deafening siren wails. Even if she screamed—

She pulls herself back. *No.* She's just overreacting.

To *his* overreacting.

'I need to not hear this noise,' she says, breaking away from him and reaching an arm around his side to get to the door handle.

'It'll stop in a second.' He repositions his body, blocking her path again.

'You don't know that.'

'I do. Happens all the time.'

'You just moved here.'

'And since I did, it's been happening all the time.'

'Well, until then …'

She reaches again, ducking a little, and grabs hold of the handle.

Oliver grabs her wrist.

She looks down at his fingers pinched around her own skin and then up, very slowly, into his face.

'What are you doing?'

A tense beat passes.

Then he lets go.

'The senior partner,' he says. 'At KB Studios. He'll be out there too.' His tone is desperate and his eyes glisten as if he's on the verge of tears. 'And it's four in the morning. You can't be visiting if you're here at four in the morning.'

Responses to this rush up Ciara's throat – it'll be dark, we can stay away from him; we can separate, he won't recognise her anyway; who the hell cares when the alternative is either going insane from this noise or *burning to death in a fire?* –

but instead of saying any of them, she yanks her arm free and turns around, to the medicine cabinet.

She opens it and pulls out the packet of masks Oliver came home with a couple of days ago, carelessly enough that other things come out too (a can of shaving gel, a box of plasters), which she lets fall to the floor.

Along with all the masks as they spill out of the packaging, except for the one she holds in her hand. She snaps the elastic bands over her ears, roughly pulls on the material until it feels like it's sitting comfortably on her face and then slams the cabinet closed again for good measure.

Her hands, she realises, are shaking.

'Good idea,' Oliver says, 'but you really *don't* need to go out—'

'Let me go.'

It sounds like what a prisoner might plead of her captor and she fully intends it to.

The words have an immediate effect on Oliver. Something melts away from him. He hangs his head.

And he steps aside so Ciara has a clear path to the door.

She doesn't waste any time. She pulls it open. With the siren back at full tilt, it feels like the inside of her brain is burned by each wail. She runs down the hall, towards the front door.

She doesn't look to see if he's following her.

She doesn't care if he is.

On the other side of the apartment door the noise is even worse, with siren wails from every individual unit joining the assault from the speakers installed in the corridor. It's a tunnel of aural torture and Ciara can't get outside fast enough. When she reaches the double doors that lead into the courtyard, she jabs the PRESS TO EXIT button and pushes her way out into the night.

A small crowd of residents has gathered in the courtyard. They stand at varying distances from each other, shifting their weight from foot to foot, arms crossed against their chests. Everyone has the pale, puffy face of the deep sleeper suddenly disturbed, is wearing some combination of pyjamas and outerwear, and is stealing surreptitious looks at their fellow neighbours. They've all been locked up together for a while now but have never seen each other quite like this, together in a group, up close. Other residents stand on their balconies, shivering in shirtsleeves and looking annoyed.

No one else is wearing a mask. Ciara quickly pulls hers off and stuffs it into her coat pocket. She'd only be *more* conspicuous with it on.

The siren wails out here too, but at a much more manageable level. There is no sign of any flames or smoke. She can see there are red bell-like units outside everyone's balcony doors; a little blue light on each one flashes on and off. She feels very sorry for anyone who lives in the vicinity.

One woman paces up and down by one of the courtyard's benches, barking into her mobile phone about *this happening yet again* and how *this disruption is utterly unacceptable* and why *every false alarm makes us less likely to be alarmed when there's an actual fire.*

The other residents are mostly silent, not even talking to each other. Some rub at their eyes, others roll them. One lights a cigarette.

She can't see anyone who might be the partner at the architect firm that Oliver is apparently living in fear of and no one seems to be paying her an unusual level of attention.

The woman on the phone drops the device to her neck and says to no one in particular, 'They're saying I can't turn it off. They're telling me to wait for the fire brigade.'

A ripple of scoffs and sighs spreads through the residents.

'We'll be here *ages*,' someone groans.

A thumping has started in Ciara's right temple, a pulse out of time with the wail of the siren. As she stands in the cold, she feels it spreading out across her forehead and down over her right eye, but she doesn't know if it's actually getting worse or if thinking it is is what's making her feel that way.

She wants to be in bed in the dark with a Solpadeine tablet. She wants to not be hearing this bloody noise. She'd settle for one out of two for the moment.

Ciara goes back through the double doors that lead to the lobby, and then out the second set directly opposite them, on to the street.

On this side of the building, the night holds everything still. The roads are bare, the sky is a dark mass of starless cloud. There's a row of terraced houses opposite, just beyond the narrow strip of unlit park; she counts eight whose windows she can see from here and zero signs of life. Surely it would be like this at this time of night anyway, but there's a deeper level to this stillness, a concentrated quality that she hasn't experienced anywhere before. It's as if the city has been reduced to its inanimate parts, the brick and the steel and the glass. The flow of human life that would otherwise be passing through it has slowed to such a trickle that it no longer leaves an afterburn in the night.

It's *empty*, that's what it is.

While she can still hear the siren, it's nowhere near as loud.

And then a voice says, 'God, it's so much better out here, isn't it?' and Ciara turns and finds herself face to face with Yoga Woman.

She thinks that's who it is, anyway. What she looks like up close matches what the woman on the balcony looked like from far away. Blonde, late thirties/early forties, with a body only a gym could maintain. Unlike Ciara, she's properly dressed – jeans, socks and trainers, an oversized cardigan – and there's no trace of sleep on her face.

She's smiling at first but then the smile starts to fade and Ciara realises she hasn't reacted to this woman's presence at all, hasn't said a single thing yet, just looked at her blankly, and now might be the time—

'Sorry,' Ciara blurts. 'Miles away there. I think I'm still half-asleep. And yeah. It was so loud in there, I couldn't think.'

'I'm Laura.'

'Ciara.'

'I would shake your hand, but ... We can bump elbows.'

Ciara thinks the other woman is joking until she raises an arm and proffers it for a bump.

'Have you just moved in?' Laura asks then.

'Oh, I don't— I don't live here. I'm just staying with a friend. For now. During … all this.'

'Kind of like a lockdown buddy?'

Ciara isn't confident that this isn't a euphemism, and Laura's knowing smile suggests that it *is*. So she mumbles, 'Something like that.'

'I should've got one of those. I'm on my own and going a bit stir-crazy.' Laura looks back at the building, turning her body directly towards the nearest streetlight. It illuminates her features, including a thin, white scar across the base of her throat. She frowns a little. 'He must be a very deep sleeper, this buddy of yours.'

Ciara feels a ripple of dread at the prospect of having to talk to him, of having to go back in there, with *him*, after *that*.

He pulled her into that bathroom and then physically prevented her from leaving.

Or did he just do a very bad job of trying to get his point across?

And who was texting him at four in the morning?

Over Laura's shoulders, Ciara catches a glint of light: a reflection on one of the glass doors as it swings open.

Oliver steps on to the street, looking around, scanning.

For her.

But when he turns and sees her, he abruptly turns on his heel and goes back inside.

What the ...?

Laura turns around to follow Ciara's gaze.

'Everything all right?' she asks.

'Fine,' Ciara says absently.

'I wanted to—' Laura starts, at the precise moment the siren wail stops. 'Oh.' She smiles. 'Well, there we go. Hallelujah.'

'Finally.' Ciara takes a step towards the doors. 'I'm getting such a bad headache. Honestly, I wouldn't have been able to take much more of it.'

'I have some paracetamol if that's any—'

'Oh no. Thank you.' Ciara turns back, smiles gratefully. 'I have something.'

'Are you sure? I've got the good stuff.'

'No, no. Really. Thank you, though.'

'Is it Oliver?'

Ciara stops.

She's sure she's misheard.

'Sorry?'

'It is Ollie?' Laura asks. 'That you're staying with?'

Both women have moved from their original positions. Laura is now shrouded in shadow, while Ciara is excruciatingly aware that she is fully illuminated by the street light.

She tries to keep her expression totally neutral while also trying to figure out what the hell she should say.

Who *is* this woman?

And how does she know Oliver?

'If you ever need help,' Laura says then, 'I'm in number fourteen. Any time, day or night, just knock. Or buzz. Okay?'

Ciara blinks at the other woman, confused.

'If you ever need anything.' Laura is staring at her intently, as if trying to silently communicate something she can't say out loud. 'Anything at all.'

Their exchange ends then on two odd notes.

Instead of walking back inside with her, Laura stays exactly where she is, on the street, and bids her goodnight.

And as Ciara walks away, she feels the other woman's eyes on her back and then another feeling, a *sense*, that something isn't quite right.

There's a different alarm buzzing now, a silent one, but she doesn't know what set it off or how to make it stop.

In the moments before the fire alarm went off, Oliver was sitting on the couch in the living room, swiping absently through the pages of an e-book on his phone. He kept finding himself lost in the text, having to go back and reread the previous paragraph or page, only to find himself lost again a few lines later.

He couldn't spare it any attention.

His mind was on other things.

And then the phone vibrated in his hand and the text message he'd been waiting for flashed up on screen – but it said the opposite of what he'd been hoping it would.

From: RICH

Don't see another way for now. Too dangerous. Get out of there.

Oliver was blinking at the words when a deafening wail started up from all directions: the fire alarm.

Which meant—

Panicked, he dropped the phone on to the table and hurried into the hall. Through the open bedroom door he could see that Ciara was already awake and getting out of bed, pulling on clothes and sticking her bare feet into her trainers.

He didn't move, didn't know what to do, couldn't think.

It was as if Rich's words had had some kind of immobilising effect on him, a verbal stun gun.

Don't see another way for now. Too dangerous. Get out of there.

He was sure Rich was wrong.

But Oliver was equally sure that Rich could never be persuaded of that.

Ciara pushes past him and hurries into the living room. The touch of her body against him wakes him from his stupor, switching him into action mode, and he follows her. She seems frantic, wild-eyed, searching—

For her phone, it turns out, which is sitting on the coffee table not far from his.

Just as she bends to pick it up, the unthinkable happens: *his* phone lights up with Rich's text message. He never actually opened it, so his phone is alerting him to it for a second time.

Oliver thinks his heart actually skips a beat.

But Ciara just picks up her phone and starts back towards him, towards the door. It seems like she didn't even see it.

'Where are you going?' he shouts over the din of the alarm.

She points behind him. 'Out!'

And then she pushes past him for a second time, out into the hallway.

This is his third fire alarm since he moved in, and his second middle-of-the-night one. The first time he did what he was supposed to do: he went outside. So did everyone else; the courtyard was soon filled with residents. He'd hung back in the shadows, head down, pretending to be enthralled by his phone. He'd avoided invitations to politely chitchat and ignored the opportunity to engage with any of his neighbours. He didn't want to get to know any of them and he certainly didn't want any of them to get to know *him*.

Forty-five minutes passed. It turned out to be a false alarm.

The second time it had gone off during the day, so he'd hesitated to leave. The door next to his own was a fire exit that opened on to the street; unless the fire was in his own apartment, he wasn't in any danger. He figured the chances were there wasn't even one, and he was right. Another false alarm. He watched the courtyard through the curtains until the residents who could stand the noise started drifting back inside and the others rolled their eyes and folded their arms and put their phones to their ears, presumably ringing the absentee management company. Then he'd gone into the bathroom, where the siren wasn't as loud, put on his headphones and waited it out.

There'd been no need to take another chance.

But Ciara doesn't have the same motivation to protect her privacy, to hide her face. If they go out there now, together, she could end up chatting to anybody. To *every*body. Saying something careless. Pointing at him, calling him over, introducing him.

He can't let that happen.

After Ciara leaves, Oliver waits four minutes. Five. Six.

The siren continues to wail.

He pulls back the curtains in the living room, but can't see anything in the courtyard except the other residents gathered there. He slides open the door and ducks his head out, but there's no smell of smoke and no sign of fire. He studies the faces close enough for him to see but detects nothing on them except annoyance.

Another false alarm, then. Just like he thought.

He goes back inside.

His phone is still lying on the table. He deletes the message from Rich, double-checking that he's not only got rid of the message itself but the entire thread of their recent exchanges. He'd thought he was safe at this hour of the night, but he didn't count on the fire alarm.

He doesn't think she saw the message, but he can't be sure. What if she comes back in and asks him about it?

Don't see another way for now. Too dangerous. Get out of there.

How can he possibly explain away *that*?

That's when he realises that he didn't see Ciara outside, in the courtyard. He goes back out on to the terrace, this time going as far as the railing, to scan for her, but there's no sign.

Where is she?

He ducks back inside. The alarm continues to wail. He knows it's purely psychological, but it does sound even louder now than it did when it first went off.

Where did she go, if not out there?

Maybe she's just being careful and standing away from everyone else, in a corner somewhere.

Or maybe she's struck up a conversation and is telling one of the neighbours all about him.

He paces in the hallway, willing the bloody alarm to go off. If it just went off now, she'd come back inside and he could set about repairing this absolute shitshow of a night ...

But the wail of the alarm continues, unabated.

Eventually he grabs a mask from the bathroom floor and his keys from the hall table, and goes out into the corridor. The siren wail kicks it up a notch. Oliver hurries to the lobby where, through the glass doors, he sees the residents huddled outside in little groups. They stand at varying distances from each other, shifting their weight from foot to foot, arms crossed against their chests. Everyone has the pale, puffy face of the deep sleeper suddenly disturbed and is wearing some combination of pyjamas and winter coat.

What no one is wearing, however, is a mask.

He quickly pulls off his own and stuffs it into a pocket before anyone can turn and look – wearing one when no one else is would only draw attention, would only make him stand out when what he needs to do is blend in.

Ciara isn't among them.

He turns and looks at the main doors, the ones that lead out on to the street. Would she have gone out there? Maybe she would if she had actually listened to him, if she thought that the fictional senior partner at his firm posed a threat.

He pushes through the doors and—

Sees her, standing a little way up the street.

Relief, first of all.

But then he sees the *other* figure in the shadows, the featureless silhouette. A woman. The woman that Ciara is talking to. She's dressed in day clothes, but she must be another resident, trying to escape the siren's relentless wail.

Over this woman's shoulder, Ciara's eyes find him.

But at the same time, the woman turns to see what Ciara is looking at, a movement which illuminates her face with streetlamp light and—

Oliver abruptly ducks backs into the shadows of the doorway, out of sight.

What the—

It can't be.

That would be an astronomical coincidence.

And it's dark, it's the middle of the night, he's under stress and he only saw her for a fraction of a second …

But in bright light. And he's been awake for a couple of hours already. And perhaps it's no coincidence at all.

The woman with the scar and the cigarettes. Who Oliver had scared half to death, unintentionally, outside the rear doors of The Westbury. Three weeks ago, when he'd taken Ciara there for cocktails.

Outside his apartment building at just gone four in the morning, that's who Ciara is talking to.

TODAY

'Mill River,' Karl repeats. 'Shit. You think he's one of *them*?'

Lee holds up a hand in a *stop* gesture.

'Roll it back a bit there, Karly boy. We've no ID. All I am saying is that the name on that envelope is a match for one of those boys, and their names were never released to the public. They're legally protected. Still are. And this was back in, what? 2003? Pre-Twitter and Facebook. Before people started violating court orders while sitting on their arses at home thumbing their phones. So apart from friends and family, the school and probably a few people in the locality, the general public didn't actually know this name. *I* only know it because I was on traffic at the funeral. I'm not *supposed* to know it. I don't, officially.'

'Who did you call?'

'The senior detective from back then.'

'And he confirmed?'

'Yup.'

'Shit,' Karl says again. 'Could it be a coincidence?'

'Course it could. But I wouldn't say that's a very common

name to find on an Irish twenty-something, would you?'

Karl shakes his head, disbelieving.

'So what do we do with this information?'

'We be very, *very* careful with it,' Lee says. 'The more people we tell, the more chance there is of it getting out. And we're not just trying to keep it on the QT that it might be him in there, we have to protect *the name itself*. I don't want to be responsible for putting that name in the public domain.' She chews her lip as she thinks. 'Let's just sit on it for now. I'll tell the Super when I have a chance to do it in person.'

'Which one was he? A or B?'

'The *name on the envelope*,' Lee says pointedly, 'is B's.'

'Where's A these days? Could he have—'

'He took his own life in detention.'

'How come this dude—' Karl stops, starts again. 'How come the *name on the envelope* isn't still in there?'

'He got a lighter sentence. Got out when he turned eighteen.'

'I don't remember hearing anything about that.'

Lee shrugs. 'You weren't supposed to.'

'But that's a *nice* apartment,' Karl says, 'in a nice place. I mean, what are we talking, two grand a month? And he's an *architect*.'

'*Please* tell me you're not about to say he doesn't seem like a killer.'

'But he d—'

'Most people who do bad things do so because a confluence of events has manoeuvred them into that position and then pushed them to act, to do something out of character. How many times have we heard, "Oh, *my* Johnnie would never do that, he doesn't have it in him, you must have the wrong house" or, "I've been best friends with this guy for years, I know he's not a killer"? Yeah, he didn't have it in him and he wasn't a killer – until he *did* and he *was*. None of us know what we're capable of, if the circumstances were right. Or wrong.'

Karl raises an eyebrow. 'Are you telling me you think you could murder someone?'

'Well, I'm not *planning* to—'

'Reassuring.'

'—but I don't know what's going to happen to me. Like, imagine: one day you're outside your house, getting into your car, and – say – your mother is walking around to get into the passenger side.'

'I can't,' Karl says. 'You know Nora would insist on driving.'

'But before she can, a drunk, joyriding teenager ploughs into her, head-on, right in front of you, pinning her to the side of the car. And then starts laughing about it. Thinks it's the funniest thing ever, doesn't care. You can see him, pissing himself laughing, through the windscreen. Imagine it. Really. The anger. The rage. The *laughing*. And you happen to have your sidearm, and there's no one around and you know you can make it look like you fired on approach to try to prevent what happened from happening. What would you do? I mean, maybe you wouldn't want to *kill him*, but wouldn't you rapid fire a couple straight into his balls? Wouldn't you love to see the pain on his face that he's just caused you? Wouldn't you want to stop that goddamn *laughing*?'

Silence.

Then Karl says, 'That's fucking *dark*, Lee. Jesus Christ.'

'All I'm saying is child murderers can grow up to be architects who live in nice apartments.'

'What did Nora ever do to you?'

'Dividing people into good and evil is just lazy.'

'You *really* need to get a roommate.'

'Detective Inspector?' The new voice comes from outside the car. When Lee turns towards it, she sees Garda Claire O'Herlihy, one of the uniforms who's helping with the door-to-doors, standing a few feet away and bent at the waist so she can make eye contact. 'Have you got a sec?'

'Sure.' Lee gets out and then Karl does too, walking around the bonnet to join the women. 'What's up?'

'We've got a resident who'd like to talk to you,' Claire says. '*Only* to you. "The guard in charge." She might be a bit of a nut, but I don't get that vibe myself. She claims she has sensitive information about the resident in apartment number one and will only speak to the highest ranking member on scene about it. She seems a bit antsy. Nervous. She's in fourteen.'

Lee exchanges a glance with Karl.

'Have you talked to her already?' she asks Claire.

'She wouldn't answer any of the set questions. Says she needs to talk to you first.'

Normally in a situation like this Lee would send someone else in to *pretend* to be the ranking member on scene – this is, after all, the equivalent of asking to speak to a manager – but considering the name on that envelope ...

'All right,' she says to Claire. 'I'll go.' Then to Karl, 'Get that envelope into evidence for me and check on our Incident Room, will you? Once the pathologist has been and gone, I want to assemble everyone there and see what we have, so let's be ready to go. And watch out for our friend with the CCTV. And get someone in that bloody KB Studios place who actually knows something on the phone. We have a family to notify and we have no solid information about which family that might be yet.'

Karl nods. 'On it.'

'And don't say anything about—'

'I know, I know.'

Lee indicates then that Claire should lead the way, and together they head back inside the cordon, slipping on masks as they go.

Apartment fourteen is on the opposite side of the complex to the scene – they turn left off the lobby – and one floor up. They step into a lift that has a sign printed in bold type on a sheet of A4 paper warning that only one household can use it at a time.

When the doors open on to the first-floor corridor, Lee is relieved to find she can't detect any unpleasant smells. She asks Claire to wait by the elevators and then goes to knock on fourteen.

The door opens so fast that the woman who appears in its place must have been standing, waiting, directly on its other side.

She is blonde and lean in a way that suggests she knows exactly what her percentage body fat is and is actively working to make it a smaller number. Late thirties, ish. Wearing loose sweatpants and a well-worn T-shirt with tiny holes in the shoulder seams. Lee catches a glimpse of a thin, white scar just above the T-shirt's collar before the woman puts a hand there, pulling on the material absently while scanning the hall, right and then left, as if nervous that someone else might overhear them.

'Good morning, I'm Detective Inspector Leah Riordan.' She flashes her ID. 'My colleague tells me that you have some information you'd like to share with me.'

'Can you come inside? I don't really want to talk about it out here.' The woman steps back, opening the door all the way, revealing a hallway that looks identical to its counterpart in apartment one. 'It's just me. We can stand at opposite ends of the living room. And I'll open the windows.'

Lee hesitates. 'Do you have a balcony?'

The woman nods.

'Let's talk out there, then. We'll keep our voices low.'

The woman turns and starts down the hall. Lee follows her inside, letting the door swing closed behind her.

She notes that it doesn't lock — there's no *click* from the mechanism sliding into place — which suggests the door in apartment one could have suffered the same fate. It wasn't necessarily open on purpose. Someone could've thought they'd closed it, not realising it hadn't actually locked.

This apartment is a mirror image of the scene, with the living room to the right off the hall. As the woman hurries to the other end of it, to the balcony door, Lee does a quick scan of the space.

Everything is the same. Same glossy, clinical kitchen. Same brown leather couch. Even the abstract print on the wall is exactly the same.

What's weird is that something *else* is the same, too: the bare, impersonal vibe. Just like the scene, this looks like a show home someone is squatting in for a few days. There's almost nothing on the kitchen countertops, no personal items, no decoration outside of what came with the place.

This one doesn't even have the George Clooney coffee machine.

'Do you live here?' Lee asks as she steps outside.

The balcony is bare. It has a nice view of the courtyard and there's a frosted privacy screen between this and the next balcony over, to the left. A leafy tree almost obscures the view of apartment number one's terrace, but when Lee bends down a little, she finds clear air. If you were sitting down out here, you'd be able to see it perfectly.

'It's, ah, like a corporate let.' The blonde woman has gone to stand in the furthest corner of the balcony, maximising the distance between them. 'I'm just staying here, for a few weeks.'

Lee pulls down her mask. 'Where are you normally resident?'

'Well ...' The woman shifts her weight from one foot to the other. 'Dundrum.'

That's not even half an hour's drive from here.

'So why are you ...?'

'That's part of what I wanted to talk to you about.'

'All right then.' Lee takes out her notebook, flips it open, clicks the end of her pen. 'Why don't you start with your name?'

'Laura Mannix. Two "n"s and an "i-x" on the end.'

The woman reaches behind into her pocket and pulls out her phone, which has one of those credit-card-sized pouches stuck to its back. She slides a small, yellow card out of it and holds it up, stretching so Lee can read what's on it.

Bitten nails, Lee notes. Chipped red polish.

And then—

NUJ.

The National Union of Journalists.

It's a press card.

Lee flips her notebook closed.

'All press enquiries need to go through the Press Office,' she says, 'as you well know.'

She moves to go.

Fucking chancer.

'No, no, wait,' Laura protests. 'Please! It's not ... It's not that.' Her chin trembles; she looks as if she's about to cry. 'I didn't do anything, okay? I *swear*. But I think that whatever's happened in there ... I think it could be my fault.'

28 DAYS AGO

When Oliver wakes the next morning, he finds the other side of the bed empty and cold. This in itself isn't unusual; Ciara often gets up before him on weekdays. But then the events of the night before come back to him like a spray of bullets: one at a time but in rapid succession, each one compounding the pain of the previous hit. The fire alarm going off. Her possibly seeing the text message from Rich. Him trying to keep her inside. Her talking to the woman from The Westbury.

Her not talking to him at all when she came back in, except to say that she was going to sleep in the other bedroom.

The sound of the lock turning in its door a moment later had hurt him almost as much as the dragging of jagged glass across his skin had years earlier.

But he couldn't dwell on it, because he was consumed with the fact that the woman with whom he'd randomly spoken outside a hotel door a few weeks back just happened to be living in the same apartment complex in a city of half a million people, and the implications of it.

One problem at a time.

But now he worries that it was a mistake not to talk to Ciara last night, to try to explain himself.

She could have got up this morning and left, not just the apartment but *him* as well—

At the tinkle of steel against china, coming from the living room, Oliver's muscles sag with relief.

She's still here.

He finds her sitting on the couch, close to the patio door, which is standing open a few inches and letting in both a breeze of fresh, cool air and a soundtrack of chirping birds. Her legs are tucked underneath her and a cup of coffee rests in her lap. Her phone is on the arm of the chair, within easy reach.

'Morning,' he says.

She turns and looks at him, her face expressionless. 'Morning.'

He takes a seat at the opposite end of the couch.

'What time is it?' he asks.

'Just gone eight.'

'Look,' he starts, 'about last night—'

'Maybe this was a mistake.'

Her tone isn't angry or upset, just flat and tired.

But he thinks he can detect an invitation in it, as if this isn't a declarative statement but a proposal that he's being invited to discuss.

Or maybe that's just wishful thinking on his part.

'I don't know anything about you,' Ciara says, 'except what's in the present tense. What you like. What you're like.

What you're like with me, *to* me. Under normal circumstances, that amount of information might be a normal amount to have. I mean, we've known each other, what? A month now? But there's nothing normal about this. We're living together, *being* together, twenty-four-seven. But I haven't met a single other person who knows you. No family, no friends, no colleagues. I was just sitting here thinking, if I had to prove you are who you say you are—'

'Why would you need to do that?'

'—what evidence would I have? On the one hand, it's like you're this mystery man, but on the other, you're the closest person in the world to me right now. It's like we're on this road where there's two lanes going in the same direction, one accelerating everything, the other one slowing everything down, and I've got a wheel in each one and I'm stuck. And last night … You made me afraid, Oliver. You made me feel *afraid.*' She bites her lip. 'Of you.'

The words make his chest tight with pain.

'I didn't mean to,' he says. 'I just wasn't thinking … No, I *was* thinking, but only about how I'd told Kenneth you'd moved back to your own place, and what would happen if he found out I'd lied … And I was right, wasn't I? It *was* a false—'

'Don't,' she says in a tone that instantly silences him.

A beat passes.

'I'm sorry,' he says then. 'But I can't undo it. And I'm not trying to excuse it. I can only explain what was going through my head and promise that it won't happen again.'

Oliver pauses to take a deep breath. 'So where does that leave us?'

She looks away.

'You know, I could say the same about you,' he says tentatively. 'I only know what's in *your* present tense.'

'But the difference is I *want* to know more.' Ciara stretches to set the coffee cup on the table, then settles back into the couch and folds her arms: defensive pose. 'You don't seem to be at all interested in the rest of me. Not that there's anything particularly interesting or exciting there, it's just ... Sometimes I'd just wish you'd *ask*.'

He can't, of course, tell her the truth about why he doesn't, which is that he can't tell her the truth about himself. The more she shares, the more he'll owe it to her to do the same, and the more lies he'll have to tell to fulfil that bargain.

If she shares details about her family, he'll be forced to admit he's only in contact with one member of his. If she recalls adventures from her teenage years, he'll have to cover up the fact that he missed his entirely. If she lists her dreams, he'll have to come up with a good reason for why he doesn't dare to have any.

Lies are spindly, unwieldy things. Delicate filaments, like bundles of nerves in the body. Easy to twist, hard to control, impossible to keep hold of.

He tries not to tell any more of them than is absolutely necessary.

He says, 'What do you want me to ask?'

'Well ...' There's a hint of a smile on her face, which

relaxes something inside him, vents a little fear from the pressurised chambers of his chest. 'I suppose I've been waiting for an opportunity to rant about how my mother is the worst person in the world. Or about how my best friend upped and left for Australia – just abandoned me to go and have this absolutely *amazing* bloody time, and I kind of hold it against her that she didn't ask me to go with her, even though I know I would've said no. Or about how I'm not sure I like this job, or want it. I don't know *what* I want. I have no clue what my passion is and I worry that I don't have one.' A pause. 'Okay, so. I'm realising now that I'm just giving you excuses *not* to ask me questions.'

'No, no.' Oliver smiles. 'All good stuff. Very much looking forward to hearing all about it.'

'You're going to have to do a *much* better job of faking being interested than that.'

'I *am* interested.'

Her face falls serious again. 'Then why don't you *ask*?'

A version of the truth is always the safest bet.

'I just feel like I don't need to know all that right now,' he says. 'I kind of like our blank slates. No baggage. Nothing weighing us down. We have these stories we tell ourselves – and other people – *about* ourselves, based on what happened to us in the past, or what we did, or decisions we made, and then they become our future just by the telling. It's like a ...'

'Self-fulfilling prophecy?' she offers.

'Yeah. We want things to be different but we start by telling the other person how they were the last time, and that kind of, like, *limits* us to being that person again … I suppose what I'm saying is that, for once, I'd like to start something clean. Without any stories limiting where this can go, who we can be.'

'I'm not sure I understand,' she says, frowning.

'What if you'd told me you were shy? Just for example. I wouldn't have thought so otherwise, not based on your actions, but you said you are, so that's what I think now, and I treat you differently. Maybe we don't do things or go places we would've otherwise, because I'm worried it'll make you uncomfortable, because you've told me you're shy. But what if you're not really? What if it's something you mistakenly believe about yourself, or that someone else made you feel, or mistook you for? Wouldn't it have been better then that I didn't know, that you didn't tell me?'

I just want a chance to try to convince you of who I am before you find out what I did, before you find out what they say I am.

'When you're working out here,' Ciara says, indicating the living room, 'are you actually, or have you been watching old *Oprah* shows on repeat?'

He grins. 'Hours of it.'

'Thought so.'

'And Ciara …' He takes a deep breath. 'Look, the truth is there isn't really anyone for you to meet. Not here in Dublin, anyway. My family aren't here, and all the guys at work are older than me, and married with kids, and kinda boring, and I haven't really had the chance to meet anyone else yet. I've only been here a few weeks and, well, how do you meet

people except through work and college and stuff? I didn't
go to college here and I don't play sports and, well, we can't
go anywhere or do anything *now*, can we?'

She smiles. 'You're so lucky you met me.'

'I am.'

'And I'm in the same boat,' she says, 'in lots of ways. *You're*
the only person I know here. So I get all that. But … Well,
there are things I *do* want to know, that I want you to tell me.'

'Like what?'

He holds his breath.

'Like, who was texting you at four o'clock in the morning?'

'My brother,' he says. 'Richard. Rich.'

She nods, understanding. 'The one in Australia. The time
difference.'

'It was lunchtime there.'

'Okay, but why get up in the middle of the night for it? It
was just a text. And you were dressed; you didn't just hop
out of bed because you heard the notification.'

He has to give her *something*, he thinks.

'I didn't get up for it. I was already up. I usually am, at
that hour. I don't really sleep.' Admitting this reminds him of
one of those sequences from nature documentaries warning
of climate change: the cracking of ice, a cliff of it suddenly
breaking off from a gigantic glacier, the steady downwards
slide as it sinks and disappears into the sea. He feels lighter,
but what's just happened is a terrible thing – he's revealed a
secret. 'I'm an insomniac.'

Ciara raises her eyebrows. He thinks what's on her face

reads more like concern than suspicion, but he can't be sure.

'On a good night,' he says, 'I get about two hours. Three is great. Three is positively refreshing. I go to bed and fall asleep, like normal, but at some point, I wake up and that's it. I cannot get back to sleep. Doesn't matter what I do. Usually by five, six a.m. – it depends on the time of the year, it seems tied to when it gets light outside – I manage to doze off for another hour or two, if I'm lucky, but it's not proper sleep. Certainly not the restorative kind. Then I wake up, get up and feel like absolute shit all day. Repeat as required.'

'Do you get up every night?'

'Most nights, yeah. Before you were here, I might have turned on a light and tried to read a book or watch something on my phone, but I don't want to disturb you, so ...'

'But how do you function on so little sleep?'

He shrugs. 'You just get used to it.'

'Can't you take something? A sleeping pill?'

'I do take something, sometimes. Tranquillisers. But they're pretty strong. They knock you out, basically. I get a great night's sleep but then I'm groggy for the next two days. So I use them sparingly. I go as long as I can without them and then when I'm in danger of having, like, hallucinations, I take one. Usually on a Friday night, so I can just veg out for the weekend and be okay for work on Monday. That's the only thing that works for me. All the other stuff is like swallowing Tic Tacs.'

'When did you last take one of those tranquilliser things?'

'The weekend after we met. It'll be time to again, soon.'

'Why didn't you tell me about this?'

'I suppose I was embarrassed.'

'Why?'

'Because it's weird.'

'It's a medical condition.'

He sighs. 'Still.'

'Is there anything else I should know that you're too embarrassed to tell me?'

He considers the question.

And then he says, 'Well ... I don't want to get sick.'

She waits for him to say more and when nothing comes, laughs and says, 'Oliver, none of us *wants* to get sick.'

'I mean, I *really* don't want to. I hate hospitals. Rich had some health issues when he was younger' – a lie – 'and I don't know, something about the smell ... I wouldn't even want to go into one to take a test. So I will do anything at all to avoid them – including wiping down bottles of milk with anti-bac wipes and obeying arbitrary distance rules. It's not because I'm paranoid or a germaphobe, I just *really* don't want to have to go into hospital. So ... I don't want to be a complete dickhead, but what I've been too embarrassed to say is that, well, you live with me, so whatever you get I'll get too, so I need you to be just as careful.'

'I was being careful,' she says reassuringly. 'I am. What with the asthma ...'

He'd totally forgotten he's supposed to have asthma.

'Yeah.' He clears his throat. 'Yes, that too. I've mostly grown out of it, but this *is* a respiratory thing, so ...'

'Actually,' Ciara says, 'I was thinking: maybe we should be wearing masks when we come and go from here. Inside the complex, I mean. Until we're outside. That was my dastardly plan to avoid that guy from your firm seeing me, but it would also qualify as being more cautious, right?'

How absolutely perfect.

Even more so because she came up with it herself.

'Great idea,' he says.

'And speaking of wanting to avoid imminent death ...' She inhales. 'Oliver, last night, there could've really been a fire.'

'But—'

'*There could've really been a fire.* I don't care if it had gone off every night for the last fifty, you had no way of knowing for sure that there wasn't one. If you want to stay inside and risk your life, I won't stop you, but *you* tried to stop *me* from leaving.'

'I shouldn't have.'

'No shit.'

'I just thought if we went out there, he'd definitely be out there – the senior partner – and ... Well, I've just started there. And I was lucky to get the job in the first place. The director is my brother's best friend's dad. I don't want to let anyone down when they basically gave me the job as a favour.'

He wishes he'd used different words to make that point, but Ciara appears to take them at face value instead of wondering why he might have needed that favour in the first place.

'What does this guy look like?' she asks. 'The senior partner?'

Oliver mentally flips through the older guys in the office, picks one at random and then does his best to describe him physically.

'I didn't see anyone out there like that ...'

'Maybe he was in the courtyard?'

'Maybe.'

'Why did you go out on the street?'

'Why did you go back in?'

Good question, he thinks.

He says, 'I didn't want to disturb you.' It's lame and he knows it; time to change the subject. He picks up what must by now be a half-drunk cup of stone-cold coffee. 'Want a fresh one?'

'Sure.'

Oliver gets up and starts towards the kitchen, making sure to phrase his next question as a casual afterthought, not at all important, just *wondering* ...

'Who was that woman you were talking to?'

'Just one of your neighbours.'

'Which apartment?'

'Don't know.'

'What were you talking about?'

'How noisy it was,' she says. 'Why?'

'Just wondering.' He clears his throat. 'Did you get her name?'

He's in the kitchen now, at the fridge, his back turned

towards her. He wants to still be sitting in front of her, studying her, tracing her face for any glimmers of a reaction, but he also doesn't want to make it too obvious and settles for a glance as he flips the lid open on the coffee machine.

She's turned towards the window and he can't see her face.

'No,' she says. 'No, I didn't.'

When it comes time for her walk, Ciara slips on a disposable face mask before she leaves the apartment. Between Oliver's door and the main entrance of The Crossings, she walks with her head down, letting a half-curtain of hair fall in front of her face. She pockets the mask once she's reached the street and determined there's no one else around.

She doesn't want to risk meeting that Laura woman again.

Not until she's decided what she's going to do about her.

Ciara heads in the direction of the canal, following her usual route. If she crosses it and keeps going, she'll eventually emerge on to Stephen's Green, which she's taken to doing laps around while the gates remain closed.

But today, she doesn't cross the water.

Instead, she turns and follows the canal all the way back to her flat.

It's hot and stuffy inside, the space repeatedly warmed by the recent streak of sunny weather that feels like a cosmic joke considering the fact that everyone is trapped at home. There's a faintly sour smell in the air too, like she's left something in the bin or milk spilled in the fridge.

Ciara throws open the windows as far as they'll go and starts hunting for the source, eventually finding a rotting banana peel hidden under the plastic liner in the kitchen bin. She puts it inside the liner, ties a knot in the top and sprays the countertops with a floral cleaner to cover any lingering smells.

Then she takes her phone – her *other* phone – from a drawer, plugs in the charging cable and uses it to call her sister.

Siobhán picks up so quickly, the phone must have been in her hand.

'Ciara,' she says, exhaling. 'I was getting worried.'

'It's only been a few days.'

'Five, by my count.'

'I told you I'd call when I could. Things are hectic here and when I'm done for the day, I'm exhausted. I keep thinking I'll call Shiv when I have the energy to actually talk to her...'

A beat of silence blooms and Ciara knows why: her big sister is weighing up the pros and cons of pushing her, demanding some plausibility to go with that embarrassingly flimsy excuse, which would also risk potentially ending this conversation before it's even begun.

Siobhán ultimately opts for pretending to believe, for letting it go.

She always does.

'So what's going on up in the Big Smoke?' she asks.

'Not much. Working and falling asleep in front of Netflix. Like everyone else, I suppose.'

'What's Dublin like?'

'The opening scenes in something post-apocalyptic, at the moment. You know when Cillian Murphy wakes up in *28 Days Later* and everyone's left London except for him? That. How is it down there?'

'Beats me. We're barely leaving the house. Pat does all the food shops. There could actually *be* zombies out there for all I know.' A pause. 'What about your job? Do you like it?'

'It's fine.'

'What does it involve?'

'What does it *involve*?' Ciara frowns. 'Why would you ask me that?'

'Why wouldn't you answer?'

So now it's her turn to decide whether to push or pretend.

Ciara, too, goes for pretend.

'Right now it mostly involves making lists and looking at spreadsheets.'

'Sounds kinda boring,' Siobhán says.

Ciara knows her sister is just trying to get a rise out of her and she refuses to take the bait.

'It is,' she agrees, 'a bit.'

'Then why did you run away to Dublin to do it?'

'Aren't I lucky I did? I wouldn't even have a job to go to if I'd stayed at home. The hotel is closed.'

'You would have your emergency pandemic payment, or whatever it's called.'

'I'd rather be here.'

'Why do I feel like I'm not getting the whole story?'

'Because you always feel that way, because you're paranoid.' Ciara doesn't want to get into it with her sister, again. 'Anyway. How's Mam?'

'About the same. Or so I'm told, since we can't visit her now. They're trying to get iPads in, so we can FaceTime.'

'Does she know what's going on?'

There's a long pause before Siobhán answers.

'She has good days and bad.'

'What about ...' Ciara doesn't like to think about this bit; she has to force the word out. 'Pain?'

'They keep her comfortable. She sleeps a lot.'

'Do they know how much ...? How long?'

'No.'

There's another long silence.

'What are you not telling me?' Siobhán asks then.

That I might have got myself into something here.

'Nothing.'

'Is everything okay?'

Things might be the furthest from okay they've ever been, and you and I both know that that's saying something.

'Yeah, fine.'

'Are you sure?'

I've never been less sure about anything, about everything. Because I've met someone who's made a bonfire of everything I thought I knew and poured lighter fluid on it, and now I'm standing beside it, holding a lit match.

And the flame is almost at my fingers.

'You know,' Siobhán says, 'I really think there should be

one person in your life you don't lie to. It doesn't have to be me, but ...'

Ciara nods, forgetting that her sister can't see her do it.

'Shiv, can I ask you something?'

'You just did.'

She could hear a smile in her sister's voice as she said that.

It's an in-joke, born on Patrick Street in Cork many years before, when one of those God-awful charity workers – so-called – stepped in front of them, blocking their way on a dark, cold and rainy Christmas Eve, and said, 'Can I ask you ladies something?' and Siobhán, without missing a beat, quipped 'You just did', stumping the guy long enough for them to make their escape.

'Do you think people can change, Shiv? Like, *really* change? At their core?'

Her sister sighs so hard it sounds like a gale blowing down the line.

'What does that even mean, "at their core"? What does a person changing actually *look* like? How would you know if they did?'

'They'd act differently. Different to how you'd expect them to.'

'Based on what?'

'Based on how they'd acted in the past.'

'I think people can change their habits and behaviours,' Siobhán says carefully, as if she's on the stand in a courtroom, testifying for the defence, and the hot-shot prosecutor has just tried to trip her up with a cleverly worded question.

'And sometimes their mind and their beliefs. People get older and wiser and have more experiences, and that all updates their … Let's call it their central operating system. Because everything they do they learned in the first place, right? No one is born being X, Y or Z. And theoretically if you can learn how to be a certain way, you can *un*learn it, too. But at the same time, you can't erase the past. You can lock it in a box and put that box away, but you can't make it disappear.' She pauses. 'Is this about you? Because I think you absolutely can change. Your problem has always been that you don't *want* to.'

Ciara rolls her eyes.

It's the same old song.

That she's sick of hearing.

'I've got to go, Shiv. I have to work. I was just on a break.'

'Look after yourself, okay? And I can come up there, if you need me. Just give me a call and I'll get into the car.'

'You *can't*, actually.'

'Watch 'em try to stop me.'

Ciara smiles as she pictures Siobhán busting through a Garda checkpoint somewhere on the motorway, *Thelma and Louise* style.

'I'll call you again in a few days,' she tells her sister.

'Make sure you do.'

26 DAYS AGO

When Ciara suggests that they head to Merrion Square Park with a picnic, Oliver points out that according to Google Maps, it's technically *three* kilometres from The Crossings.

But he's only teasing her. The Gardaí would hardly bother with pedestrians, and he wants to go there too. It's a beautiful, blue-sky Sunday – and an increasingly warm one. The very last year you'd want it to happen, summer has decided to show up early, unexpectedly, in the middle of spring. The kind of weather that makes you want to sit on freshly cut grass in open space and lift your face to the sun.

The streets that connect The Crossings with Portobello Bridge are lifeless, but when they reach the canal it's as if they've slipped into another world. The waterside paths are thronged with people and pets strolling, and wherever there's a patch of grass or somewhere to sit and swing your legs out over the water, pale limbs and heads thrown back in laughter have already gathered around collections of supermarket bags filled with cans. Houses facing the water stand with their front doors flung open, letting the tinny sounds of Lyric FM drift out into the air. Next-door neighbours sit in deckchairs on the grass, having slightly shouted conversations with each other over walls and fences. Outside one house, two young children are having the time of their lives with a simple garden sprinkler, running repeatedly through its thin, upright stream with squealing, giggling abandon. In another, a disposable barbecue is cooking up a feast.

It's almost as if everyone saw the weather forecast and pre-arranged a socially distanced block-party.

An alien visitor would have to know what to look for to find evidence that anything is wrong, but it's there. Everyone milling about is doing so in small, confined pods; signs begging HELP STOP THE SPREAD OF COVID-19 are cable-tied to every second lamp-post; and whenever Ciara and Oliver come to pass another person or couple walking in the opposite direction, one or both parties steps aside, on to the grass verge or even down off the kerb and on to the road, flashing a friendly smile as they politely try to get as far away as they physically can.

When they turn on to Leeson Street, a stretch of city dominated by office buildings and schools that would've been quiet anyway on a Sunday, there's an unusual depth to its desertion. A solidness. At the opposite end, the gates of Stephen's Green remain locked. On the other side of the park, taxi ranks stand empty. The open-topped tour buses and horse-and-carts that tend to lie in wait on sunny spring weekends like this for foolish tourists on the north-west side are gone and The Shelbourne Hotel, normally a hive of activity with queues of blacked-out SUVs and uniformed doormen helping well-heeled guests to and from them, is shut, locked up, dark inside. Grafton Street, one of the busiest shopping streets in the world, a gauntlet of other people's swinging shopping bags, buskers and elbows during normal times, empty, is the most disconcerting sight of all. It's something that was never meant to be seen like this, like when the lights come on in the club at the end of the night.

But none of it is weirder than the fact that Oliver is seeing all this with Ciara by his side.

Every now and then he steals a glance at her, or squeezes her hand, or lifts the hand he holds to his lips to kiss it lightly, just to prove to himself that she really is there.

Still, despite everything.

But for how much longer?

There was nothing resembling a picnic blanket in Oliver's apartment – or hers even, if they'd been prepared to take a detour – so they lie flat on their backs in the park on a white bed sheet Ciara worries they'll never get the grass stains out of. She has no shades, so she rests her arm on her forehead, shielding her eyes from the glare of the sun. She's hoping her old bottle of off-brand body lotion isn't lying about being SPF30, because that's all she has on in the way of sunscreen. She didn't think she'd have to worry about sunbathing-in-the-park essentials when lockdown began, but here they are.

Apart from the occasional, distant belly-laugh or child's excited squeal, she can't hear anything except Oliver's gentle breathing as he dozes beside her after their lunch of sugary carbs and fizzy alcohol that they picked up in an almost deserted M&S food hall on Grafton Street. They found a spot right in the south-west corner of the park, near the railings and so near the road, but there's no traffic noise because there's no traffic to make it. They are right in the city centre but the soundtrack is Idyllic Countryside.

'Lockdown has its advantages,' she whispers.

Oliver stirs, hoisting himself up on to his elbows to look around the park. His forehead, she sees, is getting a little red. He searches among the plastic carton debris of their picnic lunch until he finds a water bottle and then sits up to take a long gulp.

She sits up too.

The expanse of grass around them seems, at first glance, to be densely packed with lounging bodies, but a closer inspection reveals dozens of groups gathered together but staying a fair distance apart. There's a few who are definitely breaking the one-household rule unless they live in a house where every single corner is chock-full of bunk beds, but it's hard to get worked up about it when they're all outside, and outside is looking as it does today: the sky a canopy of cornflower-blue and the sun shining from almost directly overhead.

'It's weird,' Oliver says, 'isn't it? It feels normal but also … *Not*. Like we're in a *Black Mirror* episode where some computer company has made a simulation of the world, but everything is just a little off.'

'I've never seen *Black Mirror*.'

'Oh, we're *so* adding that to the binge-watch list.'

'But isn't that all, like, dystopian stuff? The world is going in the wrong direction, etc., etc.? I'm not sure we really need to be watching that kinda thing right now.'

'Fair point. We'll stick it on the After list.'

The After list.

A promise of the future, dropped casually into the conversation. Ciara takes it and holds it and adds it to her collection, along with something he said about Ranelagh being a fun place for *them* to live and how she's going to love his brother's wife, Nicki, whenever it is they manage to travel home from Australia again.

Even though she shouldn't be collecting such things.

Even though she should destroy the ones she already has, because that's what's going to happen to them anyway, eventually, and why torture herself until then by pretending that there can be another way?

You can't erase the past. You can lock it in a box, yeah, but you can't make it go away.

The box is here now, sitting on the grass between them.

But Oliver doesn't know it exists and she's stubbornly pretending she doesn't see it.

'Do you ever think about what we'd be doing if all this wasn't happening?' he asks. 'If there was no pandemic?'

'No.'

This is true. This set of circumstances has proved so dangerously perfect in so many ways, she doesn't like thinking about what might have happened otherwise.

What might have had to happen.

'Really?'

'Nope.' She shakes her head. 'Why, do you?'

'All the time. In fact …' He takes out his phone, taps the screen a few times and then holds it out to her. 'I do more than that.'

She can't see through the glare of the sun on the screen, so she takes the phone from him and cups her hand around it until there's enough shadow to make out what it is. He's opened his Notes app to a list, it looks like.

'What's this?'

'Places I'm going to take you,' he says. 'After. Things we're going to do.' He pauses. 'Things I want to do with you.'

She only manages to read the first few items on the list before the words begin to blur.

Stella Cinema
Killiney Hill
Chapter One (chef's table)
National Gallery
Long Room
Sunrise @ Sandycove (swim?)

She doesn't even know what to say, much less feel.

She's stunned that he would admit to this, that he would show her such a thing. She's touched that he made this list. She finds it amusing that so many of the things on there are the same things that appear in tourists' schedules, that it's a list designed for two people new to Dublin, keen to explore the city but lacking any real knowledge of where to go. She's scared that she wants to do all this too, with him, that she can already picture them walking hand-in-hand around the streets, like they did earlier today but with normality having returned and there being nothing left to fear.

Apart from the thing that will never go away.

Ciara feels a sudden flare of heat on her cheeks. His face is inches from her own; there's nowhere to hide a reaction. She works to keep her expression neutral as she feels wave after wave of feeling rush up and crash over her, pulling her under and lifting her to the surface, leaving her dizzy and disorientated, her throat dry.

'And it's not on the list,' he says, 'but there's a hotel in Killarney where you wake up and you're just looking out at the lakes, and the mountains beyond, and you can't see anything except green and blue. When we can go places again, I thought we might go there. Just to not see city for a while.'

It was never supposed to go this far.

But now that it has, she doesn't want to turn back.

And really, what did she think was going to happen? Isn't there a part of her that wanted this all along, despite the cost of it? Hasn't she been lying to herself just as much as she's been lying to *him*?

'I want to do those things, too,' she says. 'With you.'

It's the truth.

He traces a finger along her forearm, connecting her freckles with an invisible line.

'Except for the swimming bit,' she adds. 'Because I would *definitely* drown.'

'I'd save you.'

She shakes her head. 'I'll save you the bother.'

'You don't swim?'

'I prefer to think of myself as a very good sinker.'

He laughs.

'I *do* miss the water, though,' she says. 'Looking at it, that is. I could see it from my apartment in Cork. The harbour. Well, estuary. I don't know, maybe they're the same thing. Anyway, I didn't realise how much I liked seeing it until I left. I feel a bit landlocked here.'

Another truth.

'I hate to break it to you, but we're on the coast.'

She slaps his arm playfully. 'We're near a *river*. I'm talking about seeing nothing but water all the way to the horizon. The beaches are well outside our 2K.'

'There might be somewhere else, somewhere closer. Come on.' Oliver moves to get up. 'Let's go.'

Less than fifteen minutes' walk from the bright greens of Merrion Square Park and the washed-out reds of the Georgian townhouses that surround it sits an industrial, futuristic feast of silver, grey and blue: Grand Canal Dock. Ciara has never been, and it's not at all what she was expecting from the name.

A shimmering square of water stretches towards the sea, overlooked by glass-fronted boxes: apartment blocks and office buildings. Everything is smooth and new, and stone, steel or glass. The open sea beyond the mouth of the Liffey is blocked from view by a row of buildings in the middle distance, but she can see the Poolbeg chimneys rising into the sky beyond, and there's more than enough water here to soothe her soul.

'Thank you,' she says to Oliver. 'This works.'

He grins. 'This isn't it.'

He leads her past the water and down a narrow street, a gap in the glass-and-steel boxes. They pass closed restaurants, a bank and a slew of dark office doors, but there are pockets of normality here too: teenage boys in wetsuits diving gleefully into the water, a couple of skateboarders criss-crossing the smooth pavement of the main square, a couple emerging from a grocery shop with takeaway coffees.

She has no idea where he's taking her until finally, they emerge at the other end and she follows him across the road—

He's brought her to the river, a stretch of it she's never seen.

On her left, the delicate white curve of the Samuel Beckett Bridge rises into the sky like a bird in flight. Through its tension cables, she can see more familiar Dublin landmarks in the distance: Custom House, the tip of the Spire piercing the sky. Feet away from them is a bright orange diving bell, according to its signage. She wouldn't have had a clue what it was otherwise.

She looks to Oliver, who is watching her look. 'This is—'

'*Still* not it. But if you'll just follow me ...'

He pulls gently on the hand he's holding and they both start to turn in the other direction, to the right, so they both see it at the same time.

A navy vessel is docked just feet away and on its deck, three people in full biohazard gear – overalls, gloves and boots, hoods fitted with plastic visors and respiratory masks – are using the spraying devices on their backs to hose down surfaces with what has to be disinfectant. Next to the ship is a large, long, sea-green tent surrounded by metal railings. Signs say it's a CLIENT REFERRAL TESTING CENTRE and point to the ENTRANCE THIS WAY and warn REFERRALS ONLY NO WALK-INS. The railings have black plastic tarps tied to the inside: makeshift privacy screens. A gangplank connecting the ship to the shore says it's the LÉ SAMUEL BECKETT.

They both stand, gaping at it, transfixed.

Since lockdown began, Ciara has been glued to the news. It's on for the hour that Oliver is out running, so she watches it alone. They usually start with the numbers, and those are never good. But the numbers are never the worst part, partly because that's all they are, because it's too much to take in to match them to the scope of human suffering that they represent. It's the details beyond the headlines, the sentences filled with words she knows but which, put together, don't make any sense, that catch in her throat.

Like how a convention centre in the middle of New York City had been turned into a 1,200-bed field hospital with a potted plant next to every bed because it was supposed to have been hosting the World Floral Expo. Or how, when someone dies of this thing in an Irish hospital, they have to be left in the clothes they've on, fitted with a mask even though they've stopped breathing and zipped inside not one but *two* body bags, neither of which will ever be opened again. And how a ship docked down in Cork is prepped to become a makeshift morgue if needs be.

But all of these things have been on the television, safely on the other side of the screen, at the start of evenings she and Oliver spend cuddled up on the couch watching TV shows that don't know this is coming, hermetically sealed time-capsules of Before, and being safe and well and kinda *liking this*. Walking out into the world and seeing them with her own eyes, right in front of her, is another thing entirely. She looks at the faceless bodies moving about in the biohazard gear and feels like what they're washing away with that chemical spray is every good thing about today.

'I didn't know this was here,' Oliver says. 'If it wasn't, you'd be able to see down as far as the port, to the mouth of the river, and a horizon of water, just like you said. Maybe if we walk down there a bit, we can—'

'I just want to go home.'

He doesn't argue. He squeezes her hand and they turn and walk back the way they came, mostly in silence, until they are back alongside the canal itself, back inside the mirage.

People are still lounging by the water, lit now by the late-afternoon sun. Music drifts out of open windows. The puffed-popcorn blooms of pink cherry-blossom trees sway gently in the breeze.

But it all looks like playing pretend now.

When they get back to The Crossings, Ciara's eyes go to the letterboxes. A slim, cream envelope is sticking out of the flap of the box for apartment one.

'Oliver,' she says, pointing. 'Look.'

He follows her direction, frowns.

'Junk, probably,' he says. 'Or a menu.'

He pulls the envelope out of the flap and looks at it for a second, blinking rapidly. Something is handwritten on the front – a name, it couldn't be anything more – but when Ciara takes a step closer to try to see it for herself, Oliver abruptly turns and slips the envelope into the letterbox beside his, the one for apartment number two.

'What did it say?'

Oliver's response is, 'It wasn't for me,' which, she'll think afterwards, doesn't at all answer her question.

TODAY

Lee stands on the kitchen side of the breakfast bar with her notebook open in front of her and a pen in her hand. Karl is in the doorway that connects the living room to the hall, leaning against the frame, arms folded. Laura Mannix is perched on the furthest seat of the couch, rocking back and forth a little, wringing hands in her lap, head down.

The balcony door is open all the way and both Lee and Karl are wearing masks. It isn't ideal, but they can't have this conversation anywhere anyone else might overhear.

'Right,' Lee says to Laura. 'Tell him what you told me.'

She has no idea how cooperative this woman is about to be. During the ten minutes they spent alone together, waiting for Garda Claire O'Herlihy to find Karl and bring him up here, Laura oscillated between bouts of cocky indignation and brittle nervousness.

When she speaks now, her tone hits somewhere in the middle.

'I'm a journalist. Currently the senior producer on *The Jason Dineen Show*. Previously features editor for ThePaper.ie.'

Karl greets this news with a shake of his head that Lee knows him well enough to know means he's not angry, just disappointed.

'Tell him why you're here,' Lee says. 'When you own a house in Dundrum.'

Laura looks down at her hands and mumbles something.

'Try telling us at an audible level.'

'I *said*' – she's flipped back to indignation – 'I'm here because of the Mill River case.'

Lee and Karl exchange a glance.

Karl says, 'Do elaborate.'

'It's a long story.'

'Oh, do you have somewhere you need to be? Apologies, but we have a guy putrefying downstairs so we'd really appreciate it if you could spare us just a few minutes of your time.'

Laura glares at him. 'I was at the *Tribune* back then. When it happened. We all knew their names, it was an open secret. A few months back, a group of us go out for pints and someone brings it up. One of the guys, a crime correspondent, says he heard that St Ledger was in London, living it up. Girlfriend, good job, the lot. And I thought, *Well, that's just the kind of injustice our listeners would want to know about*—'

Karl mutters, 'Be unnecessarily outraged about, you mean.'

'—so I started doing a little digging. Figured if I found anything tangible, I could use it for the show but also get a feature out of it too, maybe.' A pause. 'And I wouldn't call it *unnecessary*, Detective. He's a convicted murderer.'

'Who served his time. And it's Detective Sergeant.'

Karl correcting her on his rank, Lee knows, means Laura is definitely *not* on the Christmas card list.

'You can't report his name,' he continues. 'Or risk identifying him in any way. So what good is a feature to you?'

'I can change identifying details. And there's still plenty to write about. There was that case last year, with the two teenagers – they couldn't report their names but they still got column inches out of it, didn't they?'

Column inches, long-form articles, front-page headlines – for weeks. Lee had remarked at the time that calling the defendants – now convicted murderers – Boy A and Boy B only served to *increase* the public's appetite for information, because without their names and faces, without details about their home lives or their hobbies or their family backgrounds, without their *ordinariness*, they were untethered from normality from the get-go and ascended to the ranks of Evil Psycho Killers right away.

Just like how, last year, the faceless, two-decades-long terror of the serial killer known as The Nothing Man had been instantly vaporised by the reveal of his actual name: Jim.

'I got a tip,' Laura says, 'that actually, something had happened in London, something went wrong, and St Ledger was on his way to Dublin, to work at a company owned by a family friend. All I was given was the name of the company, but that was more than enough to find him.'

This is the point at which, when Laura talked about this the first time, out on the balcony, Lee had put a stop to it, and ever since the next question has been waiting patiently on her tongue.

'How?'

Laura shrugs. 'I have my ways.'

Lee and Karl say nothing; they just wait her out.

'*Fine*. I used the Wayback Machine.'

Karl says, 'The fucking what now?'

'*The Wayback Machine*.' Laura pronounces each syllable distinctly, as if she's talking to someone who's still learning English. 'It's an internet archive that takes snapshots of websites and stores them. You can put in any URL and find out what that page looked like on, say, twelfth January 1999 or sixteenth September 2012. If the archive took a snapshot of it, that is. The further back in time you go, the less you find, of course. And it's really only the major sites when you get *way* back. But it had a snapshot of the KB Studios "Meet Our Team" page from a couple of months ago, so I was able to compare that with the current one and identify the new hires. There were two. No pictures or much of a bio – they were clearly junior members of the team – but one of them had a Swedish name and had recently worked in Dubai, and the other was called Oliver Kennedy and had previously worked in London. It wasn't exactly rocket science.'

'But how did you know it was him? *The* Oliver you were looking for?'

'That was my next job. Like I said, there was no picture of him on the company website, and no social at all, nothing – which I took as further confirmation. I had to get a look at him in person. I tried a few different things but, in the end, what worked was patience. I sat in the window of the café directly opposite the building and watched everyone who came in and out. About three days in, I saw a guy who could be St Ledger – right age, right colouring – come outside with the managing director of KB Studios, who I knew from his photo on the website. And when I got a closer look, I knew. It was him. No doubt.'

'How could you possibly—'

'It's the ears,' Laura says. 'They don't change with age. You can always tell by comparing the ears. And he was going by Oliver Kennedy. Kennedy was St Ledger's mother's maiden name. I mean, come *on*. It's like he *wanted* me to find him.'

Karl swears under his breath.

'How did you know what the ears looked like in the first place?' Lee asks. 'What did you have to compare them to?'

'Photos. In the primary school's newsletter.'

'And where the hell did you get that?'

'Same place I got the tip, let's just say.'

'Which was where?'

'I can't reveal my sources. I won't.'

'Let's come back to that.' Lee is having to work to keep her voice even; her patience is wearing thin. 'So, you get a tip-off that Oliver St Ledger is coming back to Dublin to work at KB Studios. You figure out that a guy about the right age using the name Oliver Kennedy, his mother's maiden name, starts work at KB Studios shortly thereafter. You see a guy come out of the office that's a visual match for a photo you have of Oliver St Ledger, plus seventeen years. That about right?'

Laura nods. 'Yeah.'

'But how did you end up here? In his apartment building?'

'I just followed him. He doesn't drive, he walks everywhere. Um, walked. I looked the place up online, just to see if maybe there was a unit for sale or something so I could get inside, have a look around, and this listing came up. Short-term let.'

'I meant what were you planning on *doing*?'

'Collecting more information. Approaching him, maybe. Eventually.'

'*Did* you?'

Laura looks away. 'No. But I did speak to his girlfriend.'

For a moment, Lee thinks she's misheard. She looks to Karl, who says, 'His *girlfriend*?'

'Yes. His girlfriend. Her name's Ciara.'

Laura can't keep the triumph off her face; she's clearly enjoying telling them something they didn't already know.

'Did she come here with him from London?' Karl asks.

'Don't know. Her accent was Irish, though. Cork, I thought.'

'And what was the highlights reel from that conversation?'

'*Conversations*, plural. There were two.'

'Did you tell her who you were?'

'Hardly. There wouldn't have been a second conversation if I had.'

'What about a last name?'

'Didn't get it.'

'Did she know about his past?'

A beat passes.

'I don't know,' Laura says then. 'I thought if she didn't know, I should warn her. But I kept it vague. I told her I knew he'd done something bad and that his last name wasn't really Kennedy. And she said ...' Another shrug. 'Well, not much.'

Karl is getting a little red in the face.

'Right,' he says. 'So. To recap: you, a complete stranger, walk up to this woman and say, hey, I know your boyfriend's done some bad shit and his last name isn't really what he says it is, and *her* reaction was "not much"?'

'I figured she was protecting him.'

Lee considers this, lets it percolate. Either this mystery girl was in a relationship with a convicted murderer and was protecting him from Laura or ...

Lois Lane here had the wrong Oliver.

Karl asks Laura when she last saw this woman.

'Probably ... Three weeks ago?'

'Were they living together?'

'Could've been.'

'So,' Lee says, 'you never actually spoke to him, but presumably this Ciara woman relayed your conversations ...'

'I sent him a note. I dropped it in his letterbox. Explaining that I didn't want to *expose* him necessarily—'

Karl snorts.

'—but I did want to talk to him. Hear his side of things. I never heard back.' She folds her arms, lifts her chin. 'Look, I wasn't wrong. I *know* it was him. And I didn't do anything wrong here. I wasn't harassing them—'

'Yeah, *right*,' Karl mutters.

'—and by law I couldn't have revealed his name or where he was, but maybe the fact that he *thought* he was about to be exposed … Maybe that's why he did what he did.'

'You seem very cut up about it,' Karl deadpans.

Laura glares at him. 'I didn't do anything wrong. He did. It's not *my* fault he couldn't live with himself.'

'We found an envelope,' Lee says, 'in the letterbox for apartment one addressed to Oliver St Ledger. That from you?'

Laura nods.

'What are we going to find when we open it?'

'Just a letter explaining that I'm not trying to expose him, I'm only trying to talk to him.' Her eyes widen. 'Are you saying he never got that?'

'When you first spoke to me, before my colleague here came and joined us, you indicated that you'd never been inside apartment number one.'

'Why would I have been?'

'So you haven't?'

'No.'

Lee has been taking notes while Laura speaks; now, she makes a show of setting down her pen. She pinches the front of her mask and pulls it away from her face for a couple of seconds, letting some air in, *breathing* it in, and moistening her lips because every time she talks for too long with this thing on, she ends up feeling like she's been lying face-down in desert sand. Then she lets it go, fixes it back into position and picks up her pen again.

'Here's what we're going to do, Laura. That was all very interesting. Fascinating, even, at times. But I'm going to ask you to tell us it all again, right from the beginning, only with one little difference.'

Laura looks confused.

'*This* time,' Lee says, 'you're going to tell us the truth.'

26 DAYS AGO

His heart is beating so fast and hard he's worried that Ciara will see it pulsing through the skin on his neck. She must see *something* because once they get inside the apartment and she turns to look at him, she frowns and asks him if he's okay.

Her voice sounds oddly distant, muffled, as if they're underwater.

Or just that he is.

She tells him he's sweating. He mumbles something about the heat and the sun and walking so far after drinking at lunchtime, and Ciara disappears to find a moisturiser she says he should put on his face and two paracetamol for the headache he's lying about having.

In the half-minute she's gone, he does his best to collect himself, splashing his face with palmfuls of cold water over the sink and wondering what the hell he should do.

He needs to see what's *inside* that envelope, he decides.

That's the priority.

When Ciara comes back in, he blurts out, 'Let's get a

takeaway for dinner,' followed by a smile to smooth over the abruptness. 'I don't feel like cooking.'

She could offer to cook – or try to. She could say it's too hot for hot food, like his mother used to when he and his brother were small. But she does something *else* that doesn't work for his plan: she suggests they download a food-delivery app.

'Yeah,' he says noncommittally. Ciara hands him a tub of something and he slowly unscrews the lid and sniffs at the white cream inside while working furiously to come up with a reason why that's a bad idea. 'Problem with them, though,' he has to pause to lick his lips, his mouth is so dry, 'is that my Eircode never comes up on their system, so the drivers always get lost. The couple of times I've tried it, I just ended up having to direct them here on my phone before eating cold, soggy food. What about Georgie's?' A dine-in restaurant nearby that they went to once, by chance, the night before all restaurants were ordered to close to indoor diners. 'They're doing takeaway now. I can just go and collect it.'

Ciara looks doubtful. 'I thought you weren't feeling—'

'I'll be fine,' he says, cutting her off and then regretting it. He picks up the paracetamol tablets she's set on the counter for him. 'After these, I'll be grand.'

They look the menu up online and then Oliver calls them to place the order. When they ask for a telephone number he gives them his own but with the last two digits transposed, as per his habit; he doesn't provide any personal information unless it's strictly necessary.

It's only afterwards he worries that Ciara might have noticed, but she doesn't say anything.

Georgie's tells him the food will be ready for collection in forty-five minutes.

'Fifteen minutes,' he says to Ciara when he's ended the call. 'I might as well head there now.'

'Want me to come?'

'No.' He clears his throat. 'I mean, um, no need. No point in both of us going. Minimise contact and all that, right?'

'Shame we can't eat outside,' she says, looking wistfully towards the terrace. 'When it's still so warm.'

That envelope was hand-delivered to a secure building and it turns out a woman he thought he met randomly outside a hotel a few weeks back lives here too. They are *definitely* not going out on to that terrace, now or ever again.

'I think I've had enough heat for one day,' he says, pointing to his forehead. The skin there has started to feel hot and tight. He checks he has his keys and his wallet, and turns to leave. 'Back soon.'

He puts on a mask before he goes into the corridor.

Not long after he'd moved into The Crossings, Oliver realised he'd never been given a letterbox key. The next day in work, he'd asked Louise, the office manager, about it. She was tasked with overseeing the employee accommodation but had no idea where the key was. She had the keys for the *other* KB Studios apartment, though, which she said no one was using at the time. She'd slipped *its* letterbox key off its set and handed it to him, saying, 'Think they're all the same at that place,' with a shrug.

At the time he thought that was an easy way for people to get their property stolen, and made a mental note never to have anything delivered while he was staying there. Today, he hopes she was right – and that his next-door neighbour hasn't had a sudden urge to check for post this late on a Sunday.

Oliver finds the lobby empty but there're a few residents in the courtyard, making the most of the evening sun. None of them are looking his way.

Aware of the fish-eye lens of the CCTV camera hanging behind him, he angles his body into a position he hopes will hide the fact that he's opening the 'wrong' box.

He slips the small key into the lock in the box assigned to apartment number two, holding his breath—

Click.

It turns easily.

Oliver pulls down the flap.

The envelope lies face-down, on top of a postcard advertising meal deals at a local pizza place.

He allows himself one second of self-delusion, one moment of hoping that everything isn't about to come crashing down, that this might not be the beginning of yet another end.

Then he reaches into the box and takes it out, turns it over.

Oliver St Ledger.

Handwritten in blue ink. Cursive.

A woman's hand, he'd guess.

The envelope looks innocuous, its threat invisible – but the fallout from it could be potentially cataclysmic. It's a shard of graphite ejected from the reactor in a nuclear explosion.

Fear freezes him in place, standing in front of a letterbox that isn't his, holding an envelope with his real name on it, in a semi-public place.

His heart pounds in his chest.

The paper trembles in his hand.

And then the mental Geiger counter in his head starts to beep, loud and piercingly, once, twice, then several times in rapid succession, and when he *still* doesn't move it starts to scream in an unbroken, high-pitched beep—

Oliver shoves the envelope into a pocket of his jeans, locks up the box and leaves the building.

Even though April has barely begun, there's a lazy haze in the air that he associates with summer evenings.

He thinks of one in particular now, from back in London, from last July.

A group of them, crowded around a picnic table at a food-truck festival in Shoreditch, with a canopy of fairy lights strung above their heads. The bulbs grew a bit brighter for every inch the sun slipped lower in the sky.

He thinks of the exact moment he realised that Lucy, sitting beside him, had draped her arm casually across his thigh, and how he waited for her to realise and remove it, but she didn't, and instead she'd turned and met his eye and told him silently that she knew it was there, that she'd put it there on purpose and that she'd done it because she wanted him in a way that she didn't want the others.

He'd felt a heat start to spread across his chest then – and not the kind he was used to. Not the burning, dangerous, panicked kind that tightened his windpipe and made it difficult to breathe, but a warm glow of happiness, of belonging, of *safety*.

But unbeknownst to him, even then, at that moment, everything was already falling apart.

And now, it's happening again.

With Ciara, who makes him feel like that *all* the time.

And even more so.

Oliver walks in the direction of Georgie's with the envelope shoved in his back pocket, so acutely aware of its presence, it may as well have a pulse. Halfway there, he stops at an empty car park into which a neighbouring coffee shop has moved a couple of picnic tables. The coffee shop has been closed since the start of lockdown, and the entire spot is in shadow. Oliver goes to the table furthest from the street and sits with his back to it.

Pulls out the envelope, rips it open.

There's a single piece of paper inside: a white sheet of A4, folded horizontally into thirds.

He takes a deep breath and unfolds it—

And blinks in surprise, because the paper is completely blank.

He turns it over, checks the back. Nothing there either. He goes back to the envelope and looks inside, looks at the underside of the flap. Blank there too. Why on earth would someone send him—

To see if he really is him, he realises.

Which means he's just made a terrible mistake.

It would've been so easy to neutralise this threat. He sees it all the time: other residents receive mail in error, usually for former tenants, and they leave these envelopes and packages sitting on top of the letterboxes with things like NOT AT THIS ADDRESS and RETURN TO SENDER scribbled across them. All he had to do was the same, only he didn't even need to write anything. Just leaving the envelope there would've communicated that he wasn't him, that that wasn't his name, and without an apartment number he didn't know who it *was* intended for. Yes, other people might have seen the envelope as they collected their own post, but his name wasn't in the public domain. It was illegal to put it there. All he needed to do was let the person who'd thought they knew it know they were wrong.

But instead, he'd taken the bait.

And in taking the envelope, confirmed for whoever had sent it that their search had led them to the right door.

That he *is* Oliver St Ledger, Boy B from the Mill River case, notorious child murderer.

He crumples up the paper and lets it fall.

He puts his head in his hands and cries.

23 DAYS AGO

Yesterday morning, Oliver had been what he told her is called *doomscrolling* – mindlessly browsing bad news stories on his phone – when he'd come across an article that said movies like *Contagion* and *Outbreak,* virus thrillers that had come out years before, were rocketing to the top of streaming and rental charts all over the world. When Ciara said she'd never seen *Contagion*, Oliver had snapped his fingers and said, 'That's tonight sorted, so.' She's reminded of a scene from it now as she leaves the midday sunshine behind and enters the gaping entrance of Stephen's Green shopping centre. She'd been surprised to see it open; shopping centres, as far as she knows, are supposed to be closed.

The last time she was here, the entrance was a bustling meeting place with steady streams of shoppers going in and out; today, it's just her and the masked security guard making sure she avails of the hand-sanitiser station and follows the newly implemented one-way system once inside.

After passing through the dim of the entrance, Ciara emerges into an enormous atrium of glass, light and iron girders painted white. Storefronts line the balcony levels, which rise two storeys above her head. Even though she can't immediately see every corner, it's obvious the place is deserted, lights off, shutters rolled down. Her footsteps squeak on the linoleum floor and the background music, playing from unseen speakers, echoes around the space.

The shops on the ground floor are all closed too, it looks like, and access to the higher levels is forbidden, the stairways roped off and the elevator locked. A handwritten sign warns that the public toilets are closed, which immediately makes her feel like she needs to go. She's wondering why on earth the place is even open at all when she turns a corner and finds out: one of its tenants, Dunnes Stores, is too.

Ciara feels elated, almost giddy, at the thought of being able to walk around a department store, to potentially shop for things that aren't edible – or even just to *look* at them, since she can't really afford to buy. She makes a beeline for the door where two female staff members stand in plastic visors and latex gloves, wearing tense expressions. They point her to a small queue inside waiting patiently in front of a down escalator.

'Grocery,' one of the women says when they see Ciara's confusion.

She doesn't need to buy any food and she knows that Oliver wouldn't love to hear that she'd done an extra, unnecessary trip on her own. But she's here now, she thinks, and if she just goes down for a look, for a walk around, who's to know?

She joins the queue, making sure to stand right on the strip of yellow tape stuck to the floor. No one else in the queue is wearing a mask so she doesn't take hers out of her pocket. There is a little table by the door offering customers complimentary plastic gloves – the clear, cheap, baggy kind that are surely a total pain in the arse to wear – but no one seems to be taking up the offer.

From behind her, a woman calls out, 'Sir? *Sir?*'

When Ciara turns, she sees a tall man in a duffel coat striding into the store without stopping, leaving the two staff members glaring murderously at the back of his head.

He's wearing noise-cancelling headphones and the kind of rigid, ridged face mask that she's seen tradesmen on TV wear when they're stripping lead paint or working in plumes of dust. Every pore in his body is emitting a mix of self-importance and impatience. He's ignored the women, it seems, mustn't have heard them calling after him with those headphones on. But there's no excuse for his not seeing the queue waiting to descend to the basement, which he blithely strides past now.

As Ciara watches this masked-up man earn a look of pure disgust from everyone standing patiently, spaced two metres apart, on strips of yellow tape, she can't help but note the strangeness of the scene and what she would have made of it a month ago. Today is the eighth of April. On the eighth of March, she was still twenty-four hours from her first date with Oliver, the night they ended up in The Westbury.

She doesn't know what's more terrifying: how much has

277

changed in such a short space of time, or how little time it's taken for people to adapt to this situation.

How easily *she* has, to hers.

When it's her turn, Ciara steps on to the escalator, childishly excited about getting to walk around a grocery store by herself.

But the feeling quickly fades. Despite the store controlling the numbers of customers, enough of them have been allowed in to create a bustle and there seems to be no 'shop alone' rule in place here. Couples are ten a penny and there's even some full family units: pairs of parents with variously sized children attached to them with little hands, moving in convoy through the aisles. Trolleys choke open spaces and all of the checkout desks look swamped by queues. A member of staff is doing his best to spray and wipe the self-service checkout screens after each use, but the ratio of screens to customers is making it look like a losing game of Whack-a-Mole.

Ciara has just stepped off the elevator when she begins to feel the first wave of unease. It's nothing more than a faraway train on approach to begin with: a quickening pulse and a sudden, cold sweat in the small of her back.

But she knows exactly what it means, what's coming. It may have been a while, but the feeling is unmistakable.

She's going to have a panic attack.

Ciara takes a deep breath, tells herself that she's fine, repeats this. She drifts into the fresh produce section, unsure of what she's actually looking for or where she's heading to, forgetting now why she's even come in here at all. She can't really get anything to bring back home without revealing to Oliver that she's gone in somewhere, but at the same time she's paranoid she'll be pegged as a shoplifter if she comes in and goes out again without buying a thing.

Who would bother doing such a thing with things the way they are? *Only* shoplifters, she's sure the store security will think.

Which makes her heart beat faster.

She'll buy a bottle of wine, she decides. Something she can pretend she got in a local shop when she gets back to the apartment. She starts towards the off-licence section, or at least where she thinks it might be, pretending she doesn't feel the sped-up thumping in her chest.

A woman with a basket stops right in front of her, forcing Ciara to stop too, and reaches out to snatch something from the shelf beside Ciara. This movement releases a cloud of sickly floral perfume into the air and as Ciara turns her head away to avoid taking a breath in, she sees—

A flash of a familiar face at the end of the aisle, stepping out of sight.

'*Excuse* me,' Cheap Perfume says pointedly.

Ciara steps out of the way and absently collides with the front end of someone else's trolley.

Her balance is off, as if her head isn't quite connected to her body. The store seems even busier now, bodies and breath around her on all sides. She sees people touching things, calling to each other across the aisles, brushing each other as they pass.

And then all of a sudden there is not only a lack of air but no space, no space at all, only other people and their hot, germ-filled breath, and the danger that floats out of it and sticks to Ciara's skin, and she knows – she's *sure* – that in the next few moments, if she doesn't get out of here, she will faint.

She swings right, then left, desperately searching for a sign pointing to or sight of an escalator that will carry her out of here and back into the open air outside.

She can't find either.

A grey blur is encroaching on her vision from all sides and her chest is tightening.

Someone comes close, too close, right up to her. Ciara wants to push them away and almost does until she spots the black uniform of the store and, above it, the sheen of a plastic visor.

'Are you okay, love?' A woman with too-dark eyebrows and bright red, sticky lips is peering into her face through the plastic. 'Are you all right?'

People are looking, Ciara can feel it.

'How do I—' Her mouth is dry, her tongue uncooperative. She tries again. 'How do I get out?'

'Here.'

It's a new voice, a woman's, from her left side.

A familiar one.

An unwelcome one.

But Ciara doesn't have the strength to protest. All she wants to do is get out. Once she's done that, she'll worry about getting *away*. She yields to her unseen helper and focuses on the floor as it changes beneath her feet.

Marble-effect linoleum, scuffed with shoe marks.

The cold ridges of an escalator step.

A coarse floor mat with lettering she can't read because it's upside down.

She feels almost drunk, the kind when you know you're not walking straight but you walk as if you are, too heavy on each foot, as if the sheer will of your own belief will be enough to steady you but actually just makes everything worse.

Stone steps. Grey cement. Different light—

They're outside.

The fresh air is cool and welcoming and transformative. Ciara closes her eyes and gulps down lungfuls of it.

When she opens them again, she sees an almost deserted King Street. Her would-be Samaritan has led her to one of the benches outside the Gaiety Theatre and is now gently pulling on her, encouraging her to sit down.

'Give yourself a minute,' she says. 'Take a few deep breaths.'

Ciara is racing back to normal, to feeling perfectly fine, and chasing after it is a wave of hot, itchy embarrassment.

'Here.' A bottle of water appears in front of her face. 'I've already drunk some but if you don't mind, I don't mind … Actually, here. I have some anti-bac wipes. Let me clean the neck of it for you.'

When the bottle reappears, Ciara takes it and gulps it down.

'Thank you,' she says then.

'Has that happened to you before?'

Only now does Ciara turn and look directly at the other woman and finds her suspicions confirmed.

It's Laura who is sitting next to her.

What the hell is she doing here?

Was she *following* her?

'Oh,' Ciara says, pretending to only have recognised her now. 'Hello again.' And then, playing dumb, 'Is that what that was? A panic attack?'

'Came on suddenly, hyperventilating, feeling sick?' Laura nods when Ciara does. 'Sounds about right to me. What happened?'

'I don't know, I just felt ... claustrophobic.'

'Anywhere now that isn't practically empty feels that way to me. I'm totally paranoid about catching this thing. How was your headache, in the end?'

It takes Ciara a second to remember her physical reaction to the fire alarm.

'Oh. Fine.'

'Look, ah ...' Laura clears her throat. 'There's something I wanted to say to you. I was going to say it the other night but ...' She shifts her weight. 'I don't really know how to put this, so I'm just going to come out with it, okay?'

Ciara braces herself.

'I know it's Oliver you're staying with. And I know there's a good reason why you might not have wanted to confirm that for me the other night. I'd understand if you're trying to protect him. What I want to make sure, though, is that if you *don't* know what that good reason might be, if you're not trying to protect him, if you don't know who he is, then ...' Laura stops. 'Did he tell you about the envelope he found? The one with his real last name on it?'

Blood rushes in Ciara's ears as she does her best to look utterly confounded.

'It isn't Kennedy,' Laura continues. 'And I'm a journalist. I'm hoping—'

'I have to go,' Ciara blurts out.

She doesn't trust her knees to hold her, but she stands up anyway. She lets the bottle fall from her hand and is vaguely aware of the splash of cold water that soaks the lower right leg of her jeans.

She takes three steps away, then turns back to face Laura.

'I don't know what this is,' she says, 'or what's wrong with you, but Oliver and I have known each other since we were in primary school so whatever this is about or whoever it's about, it's got nothing to do with us.'

Then she turns and walks away, fast, almost running. Feeling like her heart might be about to burst out of her chest.

And thinking, *This bloody bitch is going to ruin everything.*

Oliver paces back and forth across the living-room floor, practising his opening line in his head.

There's something I really need to tell you.

He's made a decision.

Not just now but really, if he's honest with himself, back on Sunday night, just a few hours after opening the envelope.

He's going to tell Ciara the truth.

Not the whole of it. But *most* of it. There are some things he can never say out loud, things he can't bring himself to summon to the forefront of his *own* mind, let alone plant forever in someone else's.

What really matters are the broad strokes, and his plan is to tell her those as soon as she gets back from her walk.

He doesn't want to do it. Every hour he gets to be with Ciara, every minute she still thinks of him as the Oliver she thinks she knows, is too good of a drug to cut himself off from – but he must, because he also knows it's a drug that will kill him in the end.

He can't continue on like this, with all the secrets and the lies and the hiding.

He can't stand to *feel* like this, as if he's constantly holding his breath, waiting for the other shoe to drop, dreading the inevitable moment of reveal.

He has to tell her.

And then… Well, whatever happens happens.

He had thought the timing of their meeting was a gift from the universe to make up for all it had taken away from him in the past: days before a once-in-a-lifetime global pandemic that had changed the whole world in a matter of weeks, that forced people to make decisions without precedent, like what to do when lockdown loomed and the only way to keep seeing the man you've just met was to move in with him. And then there was the fact that Ciara didn't use social media, had only just moved to the city and agreed with him that this was a unique opportunity.

For her to grow something real in a protective environment, away from the scrutiny and influence of family and friends.

For him to show someone what was in his heart now, and would be, always, before they found out what he had done without any forethought seventeen years ago.

The first sign of trouble had come less than forty-eight hours after she'd moved in, on that first Monday morning, when Kenneth called to warn him that a friend of his wife's had moved into the other apartment KB Studios were renting in the complex. The woman was a nurse who lived with her elderly parents who needed to cocoon, and the apartment was empty, so … Problem was, Kenneth's wife – Alison – had always absolutely hated Oliver *and* the idea of her husband doing anything to help him. She didn't know that he was back in Dublin, much less that he was working in the family business and living in a place they were paying for, and Kenneth was adamant that she couldn't find out.

But this immediately got Oliver worried about something else: *Kenneth* finding out that Ciara was staying here.

Alison might well have told this family friend where the other KB Studios apartment was, and she could casually mention to Alison that she'd seen a couple out on its terrace, and Alison could say this to Kenneth, who might then think – and justifiably so – that Oliver was taking advantage of his kindness when he'd already done so much, and he might even have to admit to her who one half of the couple was, and then Oliver would be in real trouble, homeless *and* unemployed.

He'd been contemplating how to protect himself from that scenario when, just hours later, he found himself forced to explain something *else* away.

Since leaving London, he'd been having his monthly sessions with Dan, his therapist, by Zoom, and had had one scheduled for the Monday after Ciara moved in. He'd asked if it was possible to move it to noon, to match up with the hour Ciara said she was going to go for a walk. But she'd returned earlier than expected and overheard Dan admonishing Oliver for failing to tell him before now that he was in a relationship, which Dan was not pleased to hear coming so soon after the implosion in London.

In other circumstances, Oliver might have felt a little proud of the elegance of his solution. Dan became Kenneth, and avoiding the terrace killed two birds with one lie. But it just made him feel sick. That night, he lay in bed and wondered what it must be like to live your life with worrying that every little thing is forming the first link in a chain in a series of catastrophic events. He couldn't even imagine it.

And then there was the woman from The Westbury, the one who'd given him a cigarette, who it turned out was not only living here but *talking to Ciara* too, and since Sunday night he could add the envelope situation to the list.

It was all getting too much. He was maxed out on lies.

And he absolutely *hated* telling them to Ciara.

So he's going to stop now.

When he hears her keys clink out in the hallway, Oliver stops pacing and turns to face the doorway, ready to face *her*.

His rubs his clammy palms on his thighs, takes a deep breath. His right leg refuses to stop shaking.

He will kiss her, he thinks. And hold her. Just for one minute more.

And then he'll tell her everything.

Almost everything. The broad strokes. If he can manage to get any words out from behind the lump in his throat.

There's something I really need to tell you.

He'll start there, he thinks.

But when she walks into the living room, it's *her* who says those words to *him*.

She made her decision on the walk home: she has to tell Oliver about Laura.

She got away without telling him what Laura said the night of the fire alarm, but since the bloody woman seems intent on a confrontation, and since she could tell Oliver that she'd *already* confronted Ciara ...

He'll know then that Ciara's been lying to him, and that will be that.

But Ciara needs more time with him as the woman he *thinks* she is, so she needs to get in there first.

She lets herself into the apartment, setting her keys down on the hall table as the door swings shut behind her.

The place is quiet and the door to the second bedroom is closed; she assumes Oliver is in there, still working.

The safest option, she thinks, is to play dumb. Tell him what Laura just told her. Ask him what the hell it means.

And tell him what *she* just told *Laura*, making like her first instinct was to protect him, to lie for him even, and therefore – hopefully – reaffirm her trustworthiness.

The problem is that she has absolutely no idea how he'll react.

Her eyes flick to the keys. The front-door key could scratch someone, maybe, but—

What is she doing?

This is *Oliver*, for God's sake. He's not going to hurt her.

But then again, this *is* Oliver.

Ciara shuffles out of her jacket and hangs it from one of the hooks in the hall. She pauses for a moment to lean forward and rest her head against the soft, familiar material of the sleeve, closing her eyes and steeling herself for what she's about to do, for saying the things she knows she has to say to him.

It's only the truth. Considering how well she's been doing telling him lies, this should be easy.

Ciara goes to the living-room door—

Her breath catches in her throat.

Oliver is *right there*, standing in the middle of the room, apparently waiting for her, looking tense and ill at ease.

She wants to ask him what's wrong but she's afraid if she doesn't push these words out of her mouth right now, she'll never say them, so instead she says:

'Oliver, there's something I really need to tell you.'

One footstep off the ledge and now she's in freefall. Too late to change direction – or her mind. All she can do is try to ensure she doesn't hit anything on the way down, and has the best possible landing.

Even if the odds of surviving the impact are astronomically slim.

'Can we sit down?'

Oliver nods and moves to take a seat on the couch. She takes one beside him, and then one of his hands in hers.

It's cold and clammy.

She thinks maybe hers is, too.

'So,' she starts. 'I … I haven't been completely honest with you.'

He's rigid beside her, barely breathing, watching her with unblinking eyes. Looking at her in the same way she'd imagine he'd look at an apex predator he was worried was going to suddenly lunge at him and bite into his neck.

'Something happened today,' she says. 'Just now. In town, on my walk. And it makes me think that I should tell you about the *other* thing that happened because … Well, maybe you know what it all means and you can explain to me.' She squeezes his hand. 'The first thing was the night of the fire alarm. The woman I was talking to outside. She asked me something weird—'

He squeezes *her* hand the same way her sister does during take-off and landing because she's a terrible flyer and is always terrified.

'—and I didn't tell you at the time, because you were

paranoid about that guy from the firm knowing I was here, and there was a lot going on with us that night and I didn't want to add to it. I just didn't want to listen to you going on about it, to be honest, so—'

'What did she say?'

It's the first time he's spoken since she came in.

'Well …' Ciara swallows hard. 'She asked me if I'd recently moved in, and I said I didn't really live here, that I was staying with a friend, and then she said, "Is it Oliver?" I knew you didn't know anyone here, and then I was thinking, shit, maybe she's pretending to live by herself and actually she's the wife of this senior partner or whatever and she's trying to catch me out, so I didn't say anything. Then she says, "It is Ollie?", which made me even more confused because you never mentioned that anyone calls you that … And then she said something about how I could … I could go to her for help if I ever needed it?'

He's squeezing her hand so tight, it's started to hurt.

When he speaks, his voice is barely above a whisper.

'And what did *you* say?'

'Nothing, to that. I thought she was a headcase.'

'Did she tell you her name?'

'Not that night,' Ciara lies. 'But today she did. It's Laura.' She pauses, looks down at her hand in his. 'You're, ah, kind of hurting me. A little.'

He pulls away as if her hand is on fire.

'Sorry,' he says. 'So … You met her again today, this Laura woman?'

Ciara nods. 'I was in Stephen's Green' – let him assume it was the square – 'and she just walked right up to me. Said she knew it *was* you – Oliver – that I was staying with, and that she knew there was a good reason why I might not want to confirm it, and something about my wanting to protect you. She said she knows your last name isn't Kennedy. And that she's a journalist.'

His face is as pale as she's ever seen it.

'Who is she, Oliver?' She swallows hard. 'And who are *you*?'

TODAY

'She's lying,' Lee says.

She and Karl have stepped into the corridor, leaving Laura Mannix alone inside her apartment, still insisting that everything she'd told them was the truth – and furiously and fruitlessly deleting pictures of their crime scene from her phone, if Lee's instincts are correct.

'At least by omission,' she continues. 'Because why would she assume it's a suicide? We don't know what he did yet, but for all *she* knows he's lying downstairs in a pool of blood with a knife in his heart.'

'Or suspended from the ceiling in a gimp suit,' Karl offers.

'You know, I think I've had more than enough of your sex games for today—'

'—is a sentence *I've* never heard before,' he finishes, grinning.

'Karl,' she says warningly.

'All right, all right.' He folds his arms. 'So, what? You think she's been inside?'

'I know she has. I mean, does she really expect us to believe that she does this super-sleuthing, reconnaissance crap, tracks this guy like a bloodhound back to his apartment and then can't be arsed going from one side of the building to the other when there isn't sight nor sound of him for two weeks? *And* ignores the smell in the lobby that's coming from his side?' Lee scoffs. 'There's something she's not telling us. This puzzle is missing a big piece. She says she's doing this for the radio show, and that, yeah okay, she might get something out of it in the future, but who's funding this fishing expedition in the meantime? Who's paying to put her in a place like this, indefinitely, when she lives half an hour away? And why is she *still* here, when she hasn't seen him for two weeks?'

Karl frowns. 'Why *is* she still here?'

'For a front-row seat to this would be my guess. Which is why she talked to us. I bet we just secured ourselves two starring roles in her "definitive account", available soon from a bargain bin near you.'

'Suits me,' Karl says. 'One step closer to *Crimecall*.'

'They're never going to let you on there, Karly. Let it go.'

'But I've a face for it.'

'For narration, is it? Because that's all they let our lowly ranks do on there: talk the public through the CCTV images.'

'Well, a boy can dream, can't he?'

'The problem is—'

'I'm *too* good-looking so I'd just distract from it? Beauty *is* a curse.'

'—if she did go in there and take photos, what can we even do about it? You can't interfere with a crime scene before it's designated a crime scene, so we don't have her on that. It's not trespassing without intent, so we don't have her on burglary unless she took something of his when she left, which maybe she did, but ...' Lee sighs. 'Maybe obstruction. She didn't tell anybody about the body and she just lied to us.'

'What about impeding the apprehension of an offender?' Karl suggests. 'No warrant required. My favourite.'

'They're definitely never going to let you on *Crimecall* if you go around saying shit like that, Karl. And who's the offender? We don't have a crime yet, remember?'

'What if we *do*?'

'Then we haul her in. But until then ... Maybe I could convince the Super to get this place designated a secondary crime scene. Then we could search it, at least.'

'*And* annoy her.'

'Two good reasons.'

'In the meantime,' Karl says, 'I have some good news for you.'

'And you waited until *now* to bring it up?'

'I spoke with the managing director of KB Studios, Kenneth Balfe. You can see what he did there. But get this: his son, also Kenneth but goes by Ken, is BFFs with Richard St Ledger, Oliver's older brother. They've been friends since school; the families would've known each other. Richard lives in Australia now and Ken is in Toronto. Kenneth – stay with me here – knows the whole story, or *thinks* he does, because he was going on about what a good guy Oliver is and how he just made a mistake and he was only a child, yada, yada, yada. Said it was just "kids being kids". What kind of fucked-up kids does *he* know? Anyway—'

'So it *is* him, then?' Lee interrupts. '*The* Oliver St Ledger?'

'The guy who was living in that apartment was, yeah.'

'Did you get a—'

'Yes, I got a number for the brother.'

'And to think you started off the day butt-naked in handcuffs.'

'So you've been thinking about that, have you?'

'Is the elder Balfe here in Dublin? Could he identify the body for us?'

'Dalkey. And he's going to call the brother.' Lee's face must immediately convey her concern because Karl adds quickly, 'I made it clear we don't know who's in there yet, don't worry. Said I'd call him back when I knew.'

'I don't want the brother getting a call from anyone else first.'

'I don't think Balfe will be spreading the news. He seemed *very* concerned that his wife would find out about him not only employing a convicted child killer, but giving him a place to stay as well.'

'Did you ask Balfe why no one missed him?'

'He took unpaid leave a couple of weeks back. The firm was encouraging it to help with overheads while construction is stopped. He'd have been due back Tuesday.'

'He wouldn't have been in contact with him otherwise? Socially?'

'Apparently not. The guy was doing his son's friend a favour. Beyond that ... I don't think they were exactly bosom-buddies.'

The door leading to the stairwell opens then, directly opposite, and Garda Declan Casey steps out.

'The pathologist has finished his initial survey of the scene,' he says to Lee. 'Asked if you wanted a walk-through before they start on removing the body?'

'I do,' she says. Then, to Karl, 'Get Lois Lane's prints, would you? And whatever else you can get out of her. You never know, she might just admit she went in and took photos. Give them to you, even. Stranger things have happened.'

'Got it from the context,' he says, 'but am I supposed to know who Lois Lane is?'

'Really, Karl?' Lee pauses. 'She used to be the host of *Crimecall*.'

Declan frowns at this, and Lee indicates with a jerk of her head that he should set off back down the stairs before he corrects her and ruins it.

He turns and goes, and she follows him.

Tom Searson, deputy pathologist, is waiting for her in the lobby along with her old friend, the stench.

He's in a full forensics suit – white disposable coveralls, gloves, mask – and holding out another one to her, still folded and wrapped in plastic.

She takes it with one hand while pulling her face mask off with the other.

'Lee,' Tom says with a smile in his voice. 'Long time no see.'

He's a short man with a bit of a beer belly, so the suit is stretched across his middle but baggy and loose everywhere else.

'I know. How are things?'

'Oh, you know.' He rests his hands on his belly and rocks on his heels a little. 'Can't complain.'

Lee rips open the plastic pack and starts pulling out the contents.

'You got here in record time,' she says. 'Are you near?'

'Donnybrook. Could've cycled over.' Tom nods in the direction of apartment one. 'Have you been in?'

'Yes, unfortunately.'

'It's particularly unpleasant in there, I must say.'

'Definitely in my Top Ten. Maybe even Top Five, with the maggots.'

Tom turns to collect a little jar of Vicks VapoRub off the top of the letterboxes.

'There's no shame in it,' he says, holding up the jar. 'I prefer to stick it out myself but I'm used to it. I'd rather you be able to concentrate. Consider it a study aid.'

'Hey, if it was good enough for Clarice ...' Lee bends so she can step into the coverall. 'What have we got in there, do you think?'

'Do you like riddles, Lee?'

She raises an eyebrow. '*Riddles*?'

'There's one that goes like this,' Tom says. 'A man takes to his bed in his chateau in the French Alps in the dead of winter, leaving the window open. The next morning he's discovered dead of a stab wound to the heart, with a glass of bloody water on the bedside table next to him. How did he die?'

While he's speaking, Lee zips the coveralls all the way up to her neck, takes the Vicks from Tom and smears a generous glob across her upper lip. Then she dabs a dot just inside each of her nostrils for good measure.

It immediately starts to sting, making her eyes water. But even on a shallow breath, the menthol feels as if it's shooting its way straight into her brain.

She hopes it still feels that way when they get inside the apartment.

'I presume,' she says, 'that if there was a shotgun under his bed or a serial killer waiting outside ...?'

'Trust that you've been furnished with all the pertinent details.'

Lee pulls on the pair of gloves, puts on a bigger, more rigid face mask.

'An icicle,' she says. 'Grabbed it through the window, stuck himself with it, stuck it in the glass afterwards. It melted, The End.'

Tom's eyes crinkle above his mask; he's smiling.

'Very well done!'

'Why the hell are you asking me about riddles, Tom?'

'Because,' he says, pointing down the corridor, 'we've got a good one waiting for us in there.'

23 DAYS AGO

He doesn't want to scare her, or upset her, although both are surely unavoidable.

What's important now is that she lets him tell her the truth, that she stays long enough to hear it. He needs her to know that he's not a physical threat, that the things he'll speak about are so far in the past, so separate from the man he is now, that they may as well be on another planet. To increase the chances of her believing this, he gets up and moves towards the kitchen, standing near the breakfast bar, leaving a generous space between his body and where she is still sitting, on the couch.

'I am who you think I am, Ciara,' he says. 'I promise you that. But a long, long time ago, when I was very young, when I was just a child, I was involved in something that … That I deeply, *deeply* regret. That I should never have done. That I wish I hadn't every single moment since.'

He risks a look at her face. She's sitting perfectly still, blinking rapidly.

'The most important thing,' he continues, 'is that you know I would never hurt you.' Her eyebrows rise slightly, in surprise he thinks. 'I *couldn't*. That's not who I am. It's not who I *was* either, but getting people to understand that ...' He takes a deep breath. 'The other thing I need you to know is that this was real, you and me. It *is* real.' His hands are shaking worse than ever; he sticks them in his pockets to try to hide this fact. 'Look, I'm just going to come out with it, okay? There's no easy way to say this ...'

But he doesn't know where to start.

With what happened, or what people *say* did? With his role in it, or the outcome?

'Have you ...?' He has to stop here and lick his lips; his mouth is suddenly devoid of even a hint of moisture. 'Have you ever heard of the Mill River case?'

Total silence, as if they've both been transported to the airless vacuum of space.

Then she says, very softly and slowly, drawing out the vowel sound, 'No ...?'

Good, he thinks. *That's good. Blank slate.*

He can control the sequence in which he shares the pertinent information, build up to the big shock.

'It happened in 2003,' he says. Ciara would have been eight years old, already living in the Isle of Man. 'In Kildare. Mill River was this new housing estate – hundreds and hundreds of homes – that had been built just outside Ballymore. On the banks of the river. There was a ...'

Oliver stops. He has never had to say this out loud, never had to explain what happened to him to anyone else in his whole life. They always knew already. Either because that's why they were meeting, as in the case of Dan, or because they were demanding answers from him after someone *else* had already told them, as in the case of Lucy, in London, just a few months ago.

And now he finds that he's not sure he can.

'There was a murder,' he says. 'Of a boy. Aged ten.'

Ten.

The older he gets himself, the worse that fact becomes.

The more it drips with horror, the heavier the droplets become.

'And—' He takes another deep breath, feeling like his heart is about to break out of his chest cavity, wondering if this is what a heart attack feels like, if he is on the verge of having one. 'And two other boys, aged twelve, were convicted of it.'

He can't look at her.

He looks at the floor.

Tears he didn't know he was crying blur his vision, start to drip on to his cheeks.

When he finally says the words that matter, his voice is barely a whisper.

'And I ... I was one of them.'

78 DAYS AGO

They'd met on the street outside, Ciara having arrived first, hugging each other before pushing through the restaurant's revolving doors and joining the queue for the host's attention. He'd led them to a four-top just inside the window, offering both an uninterrupted view of Emmet Place and a close-up of the man talking animatedly on his phone while also picking his nose at one of the outside tables.

'Look at him,' Siobhán said, rapping a knuckle on the window to get his attention. 'Having a right old dig for himself. Just what you want to see with your lunch.' When she threw him a disgusted look he threw one back, but also – mercifully – stopped picking.

As they shuffled out of their winter coats and sat into their chairs, Ciara waited, literally biting her tongue until the first possible moment to ask about the only thing that's on either of their minds presented itself.

'So? What did the doctor say?'

When she sees her sister's eyes glisten, she wishes she'd waited a little bit longer.

'They're going to move her into hospice care.'

Even though that's what Ciara was expecting – what they've both been expecting, for months now – it still comes as a body-blow.

Ciara absorbs the impact in silence.

Then she says, 'What was Mam's reaction?'

'She wasn't there. It was just me and Dr Corrigan. He says they'll tell her she's going in for respite – and that's what *we'll* be telling her, too, even though we know she won't be coming back out.'

'Why?'

'Because that's how it's done. You've got to give people hope, even when there isn't any.'

They slip into a silence.

Ciara's heart hurts for Siobhán. She has always been much closer to their mother – being older, she could remember her from *before*, when by all accounts she was an entirely different person, loving and funny and full of beans – and even now, after she's gone, Ciara will still have her older sister, but Siobhán will have no one further up the generational chain. No older, wiser family member to turn to, to rely on, to ask for help. She'll be the full stop at the end of their family's sentence.

She'll also be the capital letter at the start of her own – her husband Pat, who Ciara secretly thinks is incredibly boring but who adores Siobhán, and their kids, Lily and David – but that won't do much to lessen the loss.

Ciara reaches across the table and takes her sister's hand. 'I'm sorry, Shiv.'

She sniffs, smiles a little, sadly. 'This is happening to you, too, you know.'

'I know, but … I never knew the same woman you did. Or at least, I can't remember her if I did.'

'That woman died seventeen years ago.' Siobhán wipes away a tear, keeping her eye make-up intact. 'This will be her second death. Or maybe even her third, after …'

She trails off.

She won't say his name. They never do.

'At least this time,' Siobhán says, 'we'll get to grieve.'

'Did they say how long?'

'Anywhere from one to six months was his best guess.'

'Shit.'

'Yeah. It *is* that.'

Ciara gives her sister's hand a squeeze before letting go.

Siobhán straightens up, collecting herself, and turns her attention to the menu – God knows why, because they meet here once a month and they always order the same thing: two club sandwiches with fries, two Cokes, a pot of tea for two after. When the waiter appears and starts reeling off the specials, another ritual is played out: Siobhán silences him with a hand and says, 'We know what we're having, thanks.'

After he's gone, Ciara asks, 'Do you ever think about it, Shiv?'

'What?'

Ciara is unsure of what to call it. She settles on, 'Back then. That day.'

'Why the fuck would I do that?'

Her sister picks up the water jug, pours two glasses. Ciara lets her take a sip, watches her swallow, makes sure she has so she doesn't start to choke when she says, 'I've been thinking, lately, about Oliver St Ledger.'

Siobhán freezes, then lifts her head to glare at Ciara, stone-cold.

'I don't want to hear that name,' she says.

'He's out there, somewhere—'

'I *said*, I don't—'

'—living his life, being normal, getting to do all the things—'

'*Acting* normal, Ciara. *Acting*.'

'And that doesn't *bother* you?'

'It doesn't do anything to me, because I refuse to let that cretin take up even a single molecule of oxygen in my life. Which is why I'm not having this conversation. Let's talk about something else.'

'Did they ever tell you what actually happened?'

'Something *else* else.' But then Siobhán frowns. 'Who's "they"?'

'Mam and Dad.'

'Seriously? The woman who hasn't even said his name for nearly twenty years and the man who was so traumatised by it all that he tied a rope around the banister outside my childhood bedroom? Why yes. We talked about it all the time. Cosy fireside chats, they were, as I recall.'

'I could do without the sarcasm, Shiv.'

'And I could do without this whole conversation.' Her

sister sits back, folds her arms. 'What's this about? What's going on?'

'It's just that … I only know what's on the internet. Which is what was reported, back then.'

'So?'

'So that's what the public were told,' Ciara says. 'But he was my *brother*. If you only know what was reported too, and Mam didn't tell you anything, well then … Time is running out to ask questions, isn't it?'

'To ask *Mam* questions? Don't you fucking dare do that.'

'I wasn't going t—'

'We *know* what happened.'

'In general, yeah, but I mean, like …' Ciara searches for the right words. 'The ins and outs.'

'The *ins* and *outs*?' Siobhán repeats in a loud enough voice to attract a couple of head-turns from surrounding tables. 'He's dead, Ciara. Nothing's going to change that. We can't bring him back. Why would you even …? What is *wrong* with you?'

Over her sister's shoulder, Ciara sees the hostess turn towards their table with a frown on her face.

'People are looking, Shiv.'

'So what's new?' Siobhán twists around to throw their nearest audience members – a middle-aged couple two tables away – a filthy look.

'I do remember one thing,' Ciara says. 'From back then.'

'Just the one? Aren't you lucky?'

'I remember Mam saying, over and over, that it couldn't have happened the way they said.'

All this earns is an eye-roll from Siobhán.

'Look, I'm not trying to upset anyone here, Shiv. Quite the opposite. What if we could get something for Mam, some information, that would make her feel better? That would give her some peace before she goes?'

Siobhán scoffs at this. 'Like what?'

'What actually happened.'

'We *know* what—'

'Maybe we do,' Ciara says. 'But maybe we don't. The woman has been tortured, for years, by that one afternoon. Even all these years later, she can't understand what happened to her son. The official story, what that detective said in court – it never answered her questions. And what the newspapers wrote, they say what happened before and what was found afterwards, and that the two— That the boys had conflicting stories about what went on in between. But that's it.'

'Because no one wanted the gory details of what two children did to another *child*. Because they were *normal*. Unlike you, apparently. And you're wrong about it not answering Mam's questions. The problem was she never got answers she *liked*.'

A beat passes.

'I know what you're doing,' Siobhán says then, her tone gentle now. 'Trust me. I've done it myself. But you're looking for something that isn't there. Yes, their stories contradicted each other. But they were *twelve*. They were in more trouble than they even knew. And the ending of both stories was exactly the same: murder. That's what matters. Not the gruesome details.'

'That wasn't what—'

'You can't bring him back from the dead, Ciara. And do me a favour: stop pretending that this is about Mam.'

A waiter arrives with their Cokes, his eyebrows rising slightly as he seems to catch the end of what Siobhan said. After he leaves, she announces that since she's spent the morning inspecting biohazard waste facilities at the Bon Secours hospital – Siobhán works in medical waste management – it's probably no harm for her to wash her hands one more time before the food arrives.

'And when I come back,' she says, 'we talk about something else.'

As Siobhán walks off towards the bathrooms, Ciara turns to look out of the window.

The nose-picker is counting out coins for a tip with the same hand he'd been picking with.

Anywhere from one to six months.

It's hardly any time at all. Almost certainly not enough to get to the truth of what happened that day at Mill River – those five, ten minutes seventeen years ago that would rob her of a brother, her father of his will to live and, according to Siobhán, the mother Ciara would have had otherwise.

But she has to try.

Siobhán is right: Ciara wants to be able to set their mother's mind at some semblance of ease before she goes, but *she* needs the truth too, for herself.

The question is … How to get it?

23 DAYS AGO

He dares look at her, wanting to find her eyes, to meet them with his and use them to show her that he is still *him*, still Oliver, the man she knows, the one who feels like his heart is too big for his chest every time he looks at her, who thinks he could be falling in love with her, who wants nothing more than for her to stay because she is the only thing that has ever truly made the pain go away.

But Ciara's eyes are in her lap. She's as still as a marble statue. With the blood having drained from her face, she's the colour of one too.

'It was just a normal day ...' There's nothing else to do now but keep going, to rush it all out before she leaves, to try to explain before what might be his only chance to comes to an abrupt end. 'I was walking home from school with this other boy from my class, Shane, and ... It was all over something *so* stupid. And *we* were stupid. But in just a matter of minutes, everything got completely out of hand.'

He blinks back tears, thinking of it.

He's spent the last seventeen years trying not to.

'There was this boy,' he says, 'in Fourth Class. A couple of years younger than us – we were in Sixth. He lived next door to Shane – we all lived in Mill River – and he would sometimes follow us home, asking us questions and trying to tag along. He was annoying but ... I think he just wanted to hang around with us. He was the only boy in his family and I never saw him out around the place with any other kids from the estate.'

He's going to have to say his name. He can't very well tell the story without it, so he takes a deep breath and pushes it out even though the words feel like sharp, pointy objects that slice open the inside of his cheeks.

'Paul Kelleher. He was ... He was ten.'

Ciara's head is still down, but he sees her shoulders start to shake – with shock, or maybe even fear. The idea that she would be physically afraid of him makes his chest constrict.

But it's too late to stop now.

He has no choice but to keep going.

'So on this particular day, Paul is following us home like he usually does, but he's being more annoying than he usually is, calling out our names, over and over and over. And then he ... Well, for some reason, probably because we were totally ignoring him, he starts throwing things at us. Pebbles. Most of them miss, but a couple hit our schoolbags and then Shane gets one square in the back of his head. And he like, reels around on Paul, and I think he's going to roar at him or something, but instead he says, "Okay, *fine*. You can come with us. We're going down to the water to skim stones." And then he gives me this look, like ... *Follow my lead*. And he takes off running. Paul follows him. I do, too.'

Oliver tries to take another deep breath, even though it feels fruitless, even though it feels like his airways have permanently closed for business and all he has is what's in his lungs and however many minutes it will take him to exhaust it.

'The estate was built on the bank of the river,' he continues, 'that's where it got its name. The houses kind of sloped down to the water, and then in order to actually get to it, you had to climb through some trees ... So once the three of us were down there, we were pretty much hidden from view. And that's when ...' He swallows. 'That's when ...'

Now, finally, Ciara lifts her head.

'That's when Shane just starts, like, pummelling Paul. That's the only word I could use to describe it. Shane had been kept back a year, he was nearly thirteen by then, and Paul was small for his age ... I don't remember everything but I remember Shane towering over Paul, and Paul looking up at him' – his voice cracks – 'like—like—'

He can see him now, as if they're all here, in this room.

Paul's eyes, not pleading, but questioning.

Why are you doing this to me?

Oliver is struggling around sobs now, but there's no point trying to stop it, he just has to get the rest out and then he can talk to Ciara, try to assess the damage, try to start fixing things.

He will do anything to fix this.

To keep her.

To keep *them*.

'At first, I didn't intervene. I just stood there. But then Shane was like, come on, and Paul was kind of squirming, trying to get away, and he'd started to cry by then, so I went and I' – his voice cracks again here, goes up a pitch – 'I didn't intervene. I joined in. I held him. By the arms. In place. So that Shane could keep … So that Shane could—'

Ciara looks away; she can't look at him any more and he can't blame her.

He swallows hard, twice, trying to force the lump in his throat out of the way so he can get the last bit of horror out.

The worst bit.

78 DAYS AGO

How do you find someone who doesn't want to be found?

Having exhausted the search bar of every social media network, news site and internet search engine she can think of, all to no avail, Ciara resorts to typing this very question into Google.

How do you find someone who doesn't want to be found?

A list appears at the top of the first page of results, a preview of an article that's been linked below.

1. Full name, nicknames, family names.
2. Day/city/state of birth.
3. Hometown/last known/current city/state.
4. High school and/or college names.

It's clearly aimed at people who are looking to find *Americans* who don't want to be found and who have access to things like census information and government databases.

And so, for her, it's absolutely useless.

Ciara goes to close down the window – she's at her desk

at work, the club sandwich she had with Siobhán sitting heavy in her stomach – but then she sees the next two items on the list and stops.

> 5. Former and recent employers.
> 6. Friends and family members.

Friends and family members.

Oliver had had an older brother, didn't he? He'd have been Siobhán's age ... But what was his name?

Ciara drums her fingers on the desk, trying to remember.

Oliver and ... Oliver and ... Oliver and ...

Richard.

Richard St Ledger. She types this name and 'Ireland' into the Google search bar and hits ENTER.

The top result is an Instagram account.

Ciara checks the coast is clear before picking her phone up from the desk and opening the app. It'll be easier to navigate there than on a computer screen.

She starts scrolling through his posts.

She only has the faintest memory of what Oliver looked like, let alone his brother, so she can't tell just by looking at him if this is the right one.

This Richard St Ledger is living in Australia, with his wife and two small kids. He seems to spend a lot of time at the beach and standing in front of mirrors at the gym. But there's a recent photo of a thirty-first birthday cake (right age) and a tricolour in his bio (so he's Irish) and the only time she's ever encountered a St Ledger was seventeen years ago, so it could be him.

She wonders why he didn't change his name, but then why would he? He didn't do anything and his brother's name is protected by law.

Still …

She keeps scrolling down, careful not to double-tap any of the photos – if this is the right Richard, then he'd know *her* name for sure – until she comes to one taken much closer to home. It's of Richard with his back against a waist-high glass railing, his head turned away from the lens as he looks out over the bird's-eye view of London behind him. The location tag says, 'Sky Garden', which Ciara knows sits atop the skyscraper known as the Walkie Talkie.

The photographer's legs are reflected in the glass and Ciara stares at them for several seconds, wondering if she's looking at Oliver St Ledger's chino shorts, muscular calves and white Vans. But then she touches a finger to the image and finds the legs tagged as *@balfeyboi91*.

She follows it to the corresponding account: Ken Balfe, whose bio is also sporting a tricolour.

Ken Balfe.

Ciara puts down the phone and goes back to her computer, opening up Facebook. She's already logged in. She types *Ken Balfe* into the search bar – and finds the corresponding profile easily.

There's no evidence that he's been active on the site recently; the top post on his page is from nearly a year ago.

But the 'About' section has lots of useful information, most notably that he went to secondary school at St Columba's Community in Naas, Co. Kildare.

She silently thanks him for filling it in.

The primary schools in the area were segregated by gender, but the secondary was mixed. St Columba's is where Siobhán went for a couple of years, and where Ciara had been supposed to go until they'd left the area a month after her father's death, when their mother announced she just couldn't stand to be there, suffocating in memories, for a single moment more. So it's entirely plausible that Ken Balfe and Richard St Ledger have been friends since school, since *before* everything happened.

Which would mean that Ken would know about Oliver.

Which *might* mean he'd know where he is now.

But what good is this information to her? What's she supposed to do with it? Send him a message asking if he would kindly provide contact information for his friend's younger brother, the convicted child murderer?

She couldn't do that any more than she could send Richard St Ledger a message on Instagram and ask him a version of the same thing.

How do you find someone who doesn't want to be found?

But that's not really the right question, Ciara thinks now. What she should really be asking herself is *how do you find a child who was convicted of murder now that he's a grown man and his name is protected by law?*

Ciara only knows of one case where young children were

convicted of murder; it had happened in England before she was born. Those boys were now men who lived under assumed identities, guaranteed lifelong anonymity – because their names were made public, they had to shed them immediately after the trial.

As she scans the case summary on Wikipedia, looking for any details that may help her in her search, she studiously ignores the shards of horror that jump out of her like glinting knife blades.

... blown his cover several times by sharing his true identity ...

... in possession of child abuse images ...

... returned to prison ...

Maybe this is a mistake.

Maybe she shouldn't be looking for Oliver St Ledger.

What if she finds him, and somehow gets him to talk, and what he says only makes everything *worse*?

Ciara takes the half of the British pair who hasn't reoffended and puts his original name into Facebook's search box, just to see what comes up. There's a handful of profiles with exact-name matches, but of course none of them can be him. She feels a pang of sympathy for those men and wonders why on earth they don't go by nicknames or something. She scrolls down the page until she sees that a group has been returned in the results.

JUSTICE, NOT PROTECTION! has almost eight thousand members.

Ciara feels compelled to turn around and make sure no one is standing silently behind her, looking over her shoulder.

She's in a small, open-plan office, but the only other occupied desk right now is on the far side of the room. She should be safe.

She moves the mouse, clicks.

Ciara only needs a few seconds on JUSTICE, NOT PROTECTION! to ascertain what it is – or more specifically, who it's for: keyboard vigilantes. The aim of the game, it seems, is to expose the protected identities of convicted criminals who the group, playing both judge and jury, have decided should be exposed.

Each post is, supposedly, a tip, and there are hundreds of them. They seem to follow a standardised format: a bad photo of someone either blurred by the movement of the camera or taken from too far away to capture any detail, paired with a caption that makes claims like *this is so-and-so (1ˢᵗ degree murder, Preston, 2004) in the Waitrose on Chatham Way* and *my wife and I made so-and-so at Cinema World, Belfast, last night – 100% him and he knew I was looking but I just stared him down,* authored by people hiding behind blank profile pics and gobbledegook usernames. Underneath each one is a trail of dozens of comments, most of which seem to be either fantasists outlining what injuries they'd inflict on the criminal given the chance or fully paid-up members of the Outrage Brigade spouting ill-informed nonsense about the law of the land.

It's a cesspool and Ciara feels ill just looking at it. Plus it seems very much UK-centric and so unlikely to be of any use to her.

But at the top of the page is an empty box and an invitation to *Search this group*.

She types in *Oliver St Ledger* and hits the ENTER, holds her breath—

There's a match.

23 DAYS AGO

'It went on for a while,' Oliver continues. 'I don't know how long. And then Shane stops, and sort of sees Paul for the first time, properly, like he hasn't even realised what he's been doing, like he's been in some kind of fugue state, and Paul has got blood all over him and he's got this cut.' Oliver traces a line through his right eyebrow with a finger. 'There's a *lot* of blood. I remember, one of his eyes was filled with it. He looked ... It was terrifying. But what we didn't realise was that it was just a small cut that bled a lot and that it looked much, much worse than it actually was. We panicked. We'd had PE that morning, I had my clothes in my bag – I got out a T-shirt, my NASA one, and gave it to Paul to hold against his forehead, to try to stop the blood, but it just kept ... It kept coming. And then Shane and me, we look at each other, and that's when ... That's when—'

The rest comes quickly, in a rush.

Almost there, he thinks.

'—Shane says to Paul, we're going to wash the blood off in the river. And I just *knew* what was going to happen, what he'd decided to do, but it was like— It was like there was one half of me that felt like, yeah, good idea, that's what we have to do, what *I* have do now, to help Shane, to protect him, to stop him from getting in trouble. But at the same time, the other half of me was looking at Paul, all covered in blood, saying okay and obediently following Shane down to the water, and that part wanted to scream, "What the hell are you *doing*? *Run*. Run *away*." But I didn't. I didn't say anything. Instead, I … I just followed them to the water and I helped Shane push Paul into it and then I helped hold him down.'

One last breath, three more words, and then it'll all be out.

He inhales; it makes his chest hurt.

'Until … Until he drowned.'

Silence.

Ciara says nothing, remains staring blankly out through the glass of the patio doors.

Oliver can't stand to let the words he's just said hang in the air any longer, so he carries on.

'The guards came that night. To our homes. Shane had come up with a story that he said we both needed to stick to, that was basically yeah, we saw Paul on the way home, but he ran off towards the river and we just carried on. But we'd been spotted with him, by several people – he'd had on this distinctive jacket, a bright red one – and the sightings didn't match up with what we'd said, and when they found him … They found the T-shirt, too.'

He pauses here, remembering the moment that realisation dawned, when he knew with absolute certainty that there was no way out of this, that they had committed an act so horrible that it had literally ended one life and, figuratively, two more: the ones he and Shane were supposed to have.

'Everything happened really quickly after that. We were charged and sent to Oberstown – it's a juvenile detention centre. There was a trial. Our identities had to remain a secret so we became Boy A and Boy B. We were both found guilty of murder, but got different sentences based on our level of … involvement. I got out on my eighteenth birthday and Shane … Well, Shane took his own life on his. He still had another fifteen years to go at that point.'

Now, finally, Ciara raises her head.

Oliver doesn't hesitate, doesn't risk losing his chance, doesn't even wait to interpret the look on her face, the way her features are crumbling—

'I'm not some evil seed, Ciara. I'm no psycho monster. I was just a child who, for five minutes, completely lost his fucking mind. A kid who, on the way home from school one afternoon, made a stupid, *terrible* mistake because he didn't want to look like a coward in front of his older, bigger friend. I was *twelve*. I couldn't undo it so I did the next best thing: from that moment on, ever since, I have tried to make up for it. I have done every *single* thing I was supposed to. I took my punishment. I was a model detainee. Did all the therapy, obeyed all the rules. Whatever they asked of me, I did it and then more besides. And since the day I was released I haven't as much as *littered*. But it doesn't matter what I do because all anyone thinks about, all anyone cares about, is what I *did*.'

He moves closer to her.

One step, two.

'And then I meet you. And you like me. And when I'm with you, it's like … I feel like *me*. The me I should've been. The me I really *was*. Am. And even though I knew it couldn't last, knew you'd find me out eventually, I kept wanting to feel that way, so I kept seeing you. And then, unbelievably, a bloody *global pandemic* comes along, and we hear there's going to be a lockdown, and you're living in this tiny apartment, working from home, just moved to Dublin, not knowing anybody and' – he shakes his head in disbelief – 'you don't even *use social media*, so I think to myself, *I'll just take these two weeks. I won't tell her for two more weeks.* And I hoped, I desperately hoped, that by the time the truth came out, you'd have seen enough of me to know that *this* is me. Now. Here.'

Oliver stops, holds his breath. So long as she's still here, so long as she's willing to listen to him—

But then Ciara gets up and runs out of the room, into the bathroom.

And starts retching.

78 DAYS AGO

FYI Oliver (Ollie) St Ledger back in Ireland – KB Studios Dublin.

A 'Jane Smith' with no profile picture posted that in JUSTICE, NOT PROTECTION! one week ago.

The comments on it are either advising her to repost it following the established format or expressing confusion because no one knows who Oliver St Ledger is. A few members ask for the victim's name or other details so they can identify the case, but 'Jane' never returns to answer their questions. When Ciara searches within the group, she can't find any other posts from this user.

On a hunch, she searches for *Oliver (Ollie) St Ledger Dublin* across all of Facebook, but filters the results so that they're confined to mentions in Groups. It turns out that 'Jane Smith' posted the exact same thing in at least eight other places, including a victims' rights organisation and a group obsessed with Irish true crime.

Her profile is set to private, but the lack of a profile picture suggests there wouldn't be much useful information there anyway. Whoever she is, she *really* wanted someone to do something about Oliver St Ledger's supposed return to Dublin, even though, a few anonymous Facebook posts aside, she seemingly wasn't prepared to do much about it herself.

KB Studios.

When Ciara Googles this, she finds a website for a firm of architects based on Upper Baggot Street, Dublin 4 – and then on their MEET OUR TEAM page, a brief bio for an Oliver Kennedy – with no headshot.

OLIVER KENNEDY

BSc (Hons) Arch Tech

Oliver graduated from Newcastle University with a 1.1 BSc (Hons) in Architectural Technology in 2013 and joined us in 2020 from MPQ Engineering in London. He brings with him a passion for sustainable design, a flair for innovation and a wealth of experience in projects large and small.

Ciara's blood runs cold. Intellectually, she knows none of this adds up to much. There's a guy named Oliver who could be the same age as Oliver St Ledger, and he used to work in the same city Richard St Ledger visited a few months ago – so what?

But *instinctively* ...

She just has a feeling that this is him.

The Oliver.

Ciara glances at the other window she has open on her screen, the one that shows she has seventeen unopened emails and only a couple of hours left in the workday to resolve whatever crises they contain.

That's what she should be doing, because this is ridiculous. What does she think it's going to achieve, this online wild-goose chase? She's letting her imagination run away with her. She's distracting herself from the reality of the situation, which is that her mother is dying and soon it'll just be Siobhán and her, and no 'truth' is going to change that.

This isn't him.

But if it *was*, how might she confirm that?

Another email *pings* into her inbox.

Ciara glances at the time-stamp. It's five minutes to the hour.

She'll give herself those five minutes, she thinks, just five minutes more, and then she'll stop.

She goes back to Facebook to search for *Oliver Kennedy*, but the profiles she finds don't look like they're for the same person. The scant few details she has – Newcastle, London, Dublin – don't match up. She goes back to Instagram on her phone and does the same thing, also to no avail.

Then she has an idea. She brings back up Richard St Ledger's Instagram and starts scrolling through the list of people he's following.

There's no Oliver Kennedy, but there *are* Kennedys.

Several of them, in fact.

She picks one at random – Maurice – and scans his pictures, stopping at a picture of Sydney Harbour from back in November. It has no caption or hashtag, but there is one comment.

> **K Meara**: Lucky you! Holiday?
> **Maurice Kennedy**: Visiting family!

Family.

Adrenalin starts to fizz in Ciara's veins.

She opens Richard's Instagram on her computer screen, scrolls back to November and starts systematically comparing the two accounts. She has no idea what Maurice looks like, but going by his social media skills and his amateur, unfiltered photographs, she's guessing he's an older man. No one like that appears in Richard's photos, and Maurice doesn't post pictures of people at all, only badly framed landscapes and random objects sitting in low light.

The best she can hope to find is a commonality, something that shows both men were in the same place at the same time.

And she does.

On 7 November last, Maurice Kennedy posted a picture of a line of vintage cars with a wide, sandy beach and cloudy skies visible in the background.

On 8 November, Richard St Ledger posted a picture of himself posing next to one of those cars.

Richard was the family Maurice was visiting. The St Ledgers are related to Kennedys. Kennedy could even be

Oliver St Ledger's mother's maiden name, which would make him choosing it as his new name entirely plausible.

Ciara goes back to the bio on KB Studios and stares at the text in Oliver Kennedy's bio until it blurs.

This could actually be him. The only person left who really knows what happened on that day in 2003.

The person who could, potentially, provide her with the answers she seeks.

But how is she supposed to ask him her questions?

TODAY

'Just try not to think about,' Tom says, his voice muffled by his mask and the papery layer of forensic coveralls over Lee's ears. 'Take shallow breaths. Focus on the scene. We won't be in there long. You ready?'

Lee nods.

'Then let's go.'

Tom turns and steps over the threshold of apartment one, and she follows him.

A series of metal step-plates have been placed in the hall; they move carefully from one to the other, as if navigating stones set across a fast-moving river.

Voices and rustling noises from the living room tell Lee that the scenes-of-crime officers are still at work in the other rooms. Just as they reach the bathroom, the next open doorway – the smaller of the two bedrooms – flares with a bright camera flash.

'After you,' Tom says, waving a hand. 'Step into the far corner for me, to your right.'

When she enters the bathroom, she sees their reflections in

the mirrored wall above the sink: two earthbound astronauts in ill-fitting spacesuits, their true selves only visible for the two inches of skin between the top of their face masks and the hood of the coveralls.

There's no danger of catching anything while walking a crime scene, that's for sure.

She goes to the step-plate Tom has directed her to and then carefully rotates on the spot, shuffling her covered feet until she's facing the body.

It's in the same position as it was on her previous visit, but the surfaces around it – tiled wall, sink, mirror, what remains of the glass – are now dirty with smudges of black fingerprint dust. A portable scene-light has been erected in the opposite corner to where Lee stands, on a diagonal from the body, its harsh white bulbs pointed down at it. Someone has collected the safety glass pebbles.

Tom takes up a position a couple of feet away, closer to the deceased. Between them, the portable light and the bathroom fittings, there is no room left for anyone else to enter the room without disturbing the body or the area immediately around it.

It's also starting to feel like some kind of terrible sauna where not only do you have to wear your own clothes, but layers of them. Lee feels a warm bead of sweat slide down her spine and settle in the small of her back.

'You okay?' Tom asks.

'Yes. No.' She waves a gloved hand. 'Let's just get this over with.'

He turns towards the body. 'All preliminary at this stage, as you know. Caucasian male, late twenties, about six foot. Dead, at my best guess for now, for round about two weeks. No flies because the apartment was as good as sealed to the elements, which I think you'll agree we're all very grateful for today. The deceased is lying face-down in the remnants of the shower door with some shards of it on his clothing and in his hair, suggesting that it was his fall through the glass that caused it to break. He has a wound to his left temple' — Tom points at the head, then at the brown-ish smudge on the bathroom wall, which has gained a small piece of yellow tape with a number written on it stuck just alongside it since she saw it last — 'which corresponds with this bloodstain here, indicating that that is the point at which he hit his head immediately after he went through the shower door.'

The stench feels like it's got so thick that it's taken on a solid shape, and that shape is coiling around Lee's neck like a deadly python, slithering and tightening, making her windpipe dangerously small.

'Accident?' she asks, being economic with her words so as to avoid letting the python inside.

'The fall was possibly, yes, but I don't think that's what killed him. The scalp tears easily and bleeds a lot, so lacerations can look a lot worse than they actually are. Their impact is mostly aesthetic. Of course, I'll have to wait until we do the PM to prove it, but I'd be surprised to find a skull fracture. He'd really have to have walloped himself off the wall there with some mighty force in order to sustain a fatal head injury and' – Tom holds out his arms – 'you can't swing a cat in here. You wouldn't have the space to build up to it and going through a pane of glass would slow you down.' He pauses. 'Let's talk about *why* he fell. Did you look in the medicine cabinet when you were in here before?'

Lee nods. 'There's Rohypnol in there.'

'He has a prescription for it, I'd say. We know it for its more nefarious uses, but it's primarily a tranquilliser used to treat things like chronic insomnia. But I'm confused as to why, if he'd taken it – and we have to wait for toxicology to confirm that – he was in here in the first place, still mostly dressed, walking around. There are more pills missing from the pack in the cabinet, so presumably he'd taken them before. He must have known it'd be a wise idea to already be in bed when he swallows them.'

'The blankets,' Lee says. 'They were pulled back on one side. So he was probably *in* bed ...'

'I think so, yes. And then he got up for some reason. Although he's not dressed for bed, but that's neither here nor there. Anyway' – Tom winks at her – 'are you ready for the riddle?'

I'm about ready to projectile vomit, Lee thinks, *so I'd rather just skip to the bit where we leave this stench-fest.*

But she says, 'Go on.'

'Where's the blood? Can you see any? Apart from our little smudge there on the wall.'

Lee hasn't been looking. She's been pretending that the entire area to the right of Tom is pixelated, that she can't see what's there, that she can't see the discolouration, the bloated face, the skin slipping and—

She swallows hard and breathes in deep, trying to capture every last molecule of the VapoRub's remaining menthol scent.

'Why don't you just tell me whether or not there is,' she says, 'and I'll believe you?'

'There's no blood, Lee. And even the smallest, shallowest wound to the scalp bleeds profusely. The scalp is chock-full of blood vessels. And yet, no blood, except for our impact on the wall there. None on the floor—'

'How can you tell? There's that … sludgy stuff.'

'That's not blood and that came after. It's like there's a halo of cleanliness all around the head and upper part of the body. But there *was* blood, with a scalp laceration like that. So, where did it go?'

Lee tries to think, but almost immediately her thoughts are back on the smell, and how it's so incredibly overpowering that she could have shoved an open jar of Vicks up each nostril and she'd still be smelling the damn thing. She can *feel* it. It's not just hanging in the air, it's clinging to it. And everything else as well. The second she gets home tonight she's burning everything she's wearing. She'll have to wash—

'Water,' she says. 'The blood got washed away.'

'Yes!' Tom seems excessively pleased about this. 'Because …?'

'The shower was on.'

'I think' – Tom indulges in a dramatic pause here – 'he might have died by drowning.'

Lee looks down at the body, immediately regrets it, looks away again.

'He *what* now?'

'Death by drowning doesn't require submersion, you see. There just needs to be enough liquid to inhale, to get into the lungs. So, hypothetically, if our friend here had taken a tranquilliser and then got back out of bed, stumbled in here – perhaps he needed to use the toilet – and fell through the shower door, and he landed as he is now with his mouth and nose on the tile – and right, I may add, in the little depression formed by the drain where water would tend to pool – and the shower was on … Well, he might have been a little stunned by the blow to the head, or the Rohypnol was kicking in, or both, and he falls unconscious in that position, which of course means he keeps breathing, and he drowns in a couple of inches of water in his own shower.' Tom pauses. 'This is why I truly will never understand why people go skydiving and bungee-jumping and all that malarkey. It's so *easy* to die. Why try to make it happen?'

'Why was the shower on in the first place?'

'Good question. He could've simply hit the lever during the fall or in his attempts to get back up. Those things' – he points at the shower handle – 'all it takes is a little force and the water would start to flow. He could've been *planning* to have a shower and just misjudged how quickly the tranquilliser would kick in. But that's not your million-dollar question, Lee.'

She raises her eyebrows. 'It isn't?'

'The million-dollar question is: who turned the water *off*?'

Her stomach sinks.

'We might have a problem with that,' she says.

'Oh? How so?'

'There's a woman here who's been annoying the hell out of us since lockdown began. Noise complaints, ratting on her neighbours, etc. When she rang this morning, the station thought it was more of the same. They sent out two new recruits. One of them said he turned off the tap, that it was dripping.'

Tom nods a couple of times, considering this. 'I can't rule out that he didn't turn off the water himself, in the last throws of consciousness. But either way, I doubt there was anything of evidentiary value on the lever anyway.'

'What makes you say that?'

Tom clasps his hands together and rests them on his stomach. Lee likes the guy, but she wishes he'd tone down the Golden Age-detective routine.

'The whole place is wiped clean,' he says, 'according to your scenes-of-crime fellas. Every single surface wiped down throughout the apartment. Thorough job. They haven't found a single print yet. So that's your *real* riddle. Why would someone wipe down an apartment after an accident? And why on earth didn't they call for help?'

23 DAYS AGO

She doesn't close the door to the bathroom, and Oliver doesn't want to go in there and loom over her while she's being sick, so he waits in the doorway of the living room while she retches.

'I'm so sorry, Ciara,' he says. 'I know those are just words but I am. I'm so sorry I did this to you.'

After a while she climbs to her feet, splashes some water on her face and meets his eyes in the reflection in the mirror over the sink.

When she turns around to face him, she looks pale and broken.

'So who's Laura?' she says.

'I don't know. I don't know her. But presumably she's found out where I am and is trying to get to me. To write about me, I suppose.'

'But you said you were Boy A and Boy B. She can't report your name.'

'No, but ... She could still cause trouble.' He pauses. 'She already has.'

There's a silence then that he doesn't dare break, because he isn't quite sure what is happening here.

Ciara is still here. That's not what he was expecting.

And she's asking questions, which ... He doesn't know what to make of that. But he'll let her dictate these next few minutes. They can go at her pace.

He knows this must be a lot to take in.

'How did you get your scar?' she asks. 'Really?'

'In the rec room at Oberstown.'

'What happened?'

She's wrapped her arms around herself now; she looks likes she's literally holding herself together. He wants to reach for her, wants to do the holding-together for her, wants to tell her everything will be all right.

But he can't. He doesn't know if it will be.

'Shane did it to me,' he says.

She blinks at him. 'What?'

'We'd been in a few years by then. He'd grown pretty disturbed. He just fell apart when we were in that place. Couldn't cope at all. And he ... He blamed me. For not sticking to the story, I suppose.'

Ciara is looking paler still.

'What happened in London?'

'I met someone,' Oliver says. 'Lucy. And she was careless. I mean, I didn't tell her the truth so she didn't know *not* to be, but ... Reporters can't print my name or show my face, but that doesn't mean there aren't people who wouldn't know me, who wouldn't recognise me, and go running off to Facebook or Twitter to tell everyone what I look like now and who I am. Guys I went to primary school with, old neighbours – relatives, even. No one apart from my brother really even speaks to me now. So I have to be careful. I don't put anything online. But Lucy did. Instagram stories, with me in the background. I didn't realise. And there's all these forums, you see, where these nutjobs, these vigilante idiots who think it's up to them to be judge and jury *and* the prison system while they're at it ...' He shakes his head, angry at some long-ago memory. 'A picture from Lucy's Instagram somehow made its way on there. Onto one of these forums. They couldn't confirm it was me, of course. How would they know? There's nothing to compare it to. But that didn't stop them trying. They had Lucy's name – from the account – and started messaging her, asking her questions, and then *she* started asking *me* questions ...' He exhales. 'I had to leave, to stop things from really blowing up.'

Ciara starts to cry.

'I have to, too,' she says, her voice wavering. 'Now. I can't stay.'

Oliver takes a step towards her, then another when she doesn't react to the first.

He holds up his hands as if to signal that he comes in peace. She holds up hers to tell him not to come any closer.

He stops. 'Can I hold your hand?'

She shakes her head but doesn't move, doesn't resist when he reaches out and takes it. He presses it to his chest, to his heart.

'This is me,' he says. 'Here, now. Not that boy, that *child*, who was stupid and cruel and made a terrible, *terrible* mistake that he can never undo and never be sorry enough for and never take back but—'

'Why did you do it?'

'Ciara, you *know me*. I am who you think I am, who I've been these last few weeks. *This* is me. The real me. And I wanted you to see that, to know that, before all this—'

She jerks her hand away, takes a step back.

'Why did you do *it*? Back then? Why didn't you put a stop to it? Why didn't you *save him*?'

She's crying harder now, cheeks glistening with tears.

'I don't know,' Oliver says. 'I really don't know. I've thought about it so many times … For years it was *all* the time. But I can't explain it. It just happened, I wasn't thinking … A therapist told me once that when you're that age, you have no sense of permanence. It's hard for you to intellectualise forever. You understand the difference between right and wrong, and you *sort* of understand that your actions have consequences, but you don't really accept that those consequences can't be undone. It's not an excuse, but … That made sense to me. And things like this, Ciara, they're not about good and evil. I wasn't some psychopath-in-training. Things happened, a series of things, that created this moment in time when Shane and I made a decision we shouldn't have and, you know what? That happens all the time. But in our case, the stupid thing we did had the worst consequence imaginable.'

Ciara starts moving towards the bedroom door. 'I have to go.'

'Please don't, just stay, for—'

'You don't get to ask me for *anything*,' she spits at him.

She goes into the bedroom, pulls her suitcase up on to the bed and starts throwing her things into it.

He watches, helpless, hanging back at the door.

'Where will you go?'

'Back to my place,' she says.

'For how long?'

'I don't fucking *know*, Oliver.'

'I'm just trying to figure out—'

She reels on him. 'You've just told me you *killed a child*.' It comes out as a scream whose volume seems to surprise even her.

He nods, acknowledging this.

'When I *was* a child,' he says quietly.

This freezes her in place for a second, and hope rises in his heart.

But then she turns back to the bed and zips up the case. Lifts it by its handle and plonks its wheels on the floor. Turns around and waits for him to step aside so she can get out of the room without having to touch him.

'I'm sorry,' he says again. 'I don't know—'

She pushes past him and leaves.

64 DAYS AGO

The man Ciara thought could be Oliver St Ledger worked on the fourth floor of a glossy new office building that loomed over all the other, older, smaller ones on Baggot Street Upper – according to what she could glean from Google Street View. The firm of estate agents who'd been tasked with finding tenants for it had made a slick video showcasing the building's interior and posted it to their website. Inside were four floors' worth of glass-box offices, a reception desk large enough to accommodate three gatekeepers in the lobby and electronic turnstiles protecting access to the stairs and elevator.

You couldn't just walk in and wander around.

She'd need a reason to be there.

Pretending to be a client, she figured, would be the quickest way to get found out; she would have no idea what to say or who to ask for – and what were the chances that, even if she managed to keep up some kind of pretence for a while, the firm would choose Oliver Kennedy to meet with her? Going by the website, he seemed like a junior member of staff.

She'd thought about impersonating a courier who was delivering something that had to be signed for, but almost immediately that plan revealed itself to have two flaws. One of those three receptionists would probably insist on taking it off her hands and, even if they allowed her upstairs to deliver the package in person, what could it possibly contain that wouldn't immediately set alarm bells ringing for the recipient? If Oliver Kennedy *was* Oliver St Ledger, he'd spent his whole adult life protecting his real identify. Someone else might dismiss it as a mix-up or mistake, but *he* wouldn't. And then he'd be on high alert.

Which just left one option, as far as Ciara could see: apply to work there.

Get inside under the guise of a job interview.

On the KB Studios website, the JOIN OUR TEAM link had led to two listings for current vacancies, one of which was a junior office manager. Ciara set up a new Gmail account under a fake name and sent in a CV with it. A week had passed, draining her nerve away a little more each day. What the hell was she doing? How did she think this was going to end? What was her plan: walk up to this guy and say, *Hey. Are you Oliver St Ledger? Great. Would you mind telling me exactly what happened on the afternoon that you murdered Paul Kelleher?* But when a message arrived in her inbox calling her for an interview, she found she had just enough nerve left to say yes.

So now she's sitting on a cushioned bench in the lobby, looking at the enormous reception desk in real life, rubbing clammy palms off her polyester trousers.

Thinking there's absolutely no way she can go through with this.

Can she?

She'd arrived ten minutes early and has been instructed to take a seat and wait. *Someone will come and get you*, the receptionist had said. For one wild, fleeting moment, Ciara had pictured that someone being Oliver St Ledger – but it was difficult to. Besides the astronomical odds, she couldn't quite build a mental image of his face.

Up until the murder, her mother had kept *everything*: every school report, every crayon drawing, every souvenir. Afterwards, she'd stopped not only adding to her collection, but looking at it, too. There were dozens of dusty shoeboxes and dented biscuit tins piled up in the attic, and in the last week Ciara had spent a day going through them. She thought the chances were good that her mother had accidentally archived a picture of a future killer, and she was right.

The Mill River Boys' National School published a glossy newsletter at the end of every academic year and her mother had saved them all. The class photos they included weren't captioned, so they were of no use, but the newsletters also included collages of action shots from the school's various sports teams, and they *were*. Twelve-year-old Oliver St Ledger had played rugby. There were two full-colour photos of him in the newsletter sent home in June 2003. One of them showed him running with the ball, his features blurred by motion, but in the other he was standing with his hands on his hips, in full-colour and looking perfectly clear.

Ciara had stared at the photo for hours, studying every detail – and then cut it out and slipped it into a discreet pocket of her wallet, which was now in her bag by her feet.

But she has no idea if she'll be able to match it to the adult now.

Or what she'll do if she can.

'Ciara Murphy?' A young, slim, blonde woman in a tight-fitting black dress has appeared in front of her.

Not knowing how good of a liar she could really be, Ciara had hedged her bets. She'd kept her own first name but adopted a fake second one: Murphy, the last name of every other person on this island, seemed like a safe choice. She'd taken the same approach with her CV, listing her real jobs up until her last one – Customer Experience Specialist at Blue Wave, which roughly translated into Call Centre Minion for a cruise company – but pretended that she was still there, that that was her current role when, in reality, she'd been working in events for a hotel chain for nearly six months. She hadn't bothered making up any college education.

'We're almost ready for you,' the blonde says. 'If you come with me, I'll bring you upstairs.'

Ciara stands, collects her things and starts to follow the blonde towards the bank of elevators, trying to ignore the thunderous beating of her heart in her chest. It's so hard it's loud, and it's so loud she's worried that when they get into the elevator and the doors close behind them, the other woman will be able to hear its pounding too.

'Don't be nervous,' the woman says. 'He's very nice.'

'"He"?'

The elevator doors open and they step inside.

'Kenneth Balfe.' The blonde punches the button for the fourth floor. 'He's the managing director. He likes to do all the interviews himself, even for the admin staff.'

Kenneth Balfe.

KB Studios.

The strength goes out of Ciara's knees and her body slumps against the side of the elevator.

Why the hell didn't she put two and two together before?

Because she was too busy focusing on Oliver St Ledger. Who definitely works here, because his brother's friend apparently owns the joint.

The blonde is frowning at her. 'Are you all right?'

'Yes, fine, thanks.' Ciara smiles weakly. 'I'm just not great with elevators.'

'Oh, you should've said.'

'No, no. It's fine.'

'We're almost there, anyway.'

A *ding* signals that they've arrived.

The doors slide open to reveal another reception area, this one outside a pair of double-glass door with KB STUDIOS stencilled on them in gold. Two grey sofas form an L-shape around a coffee table strewn with glossy brochures while, in the corner, a water dispenser gurgles next to a scale model of an office block. Its miniature trees look like wispy cotton balls that have been spray-painted green.

'Take a seat,' the blonde says. 'I'll let him know you're here.'

Ciara obeys and watches her disappear through the glass doors. Beyond them, she can see the promise of an open-plan office space, people milling about. She's too far to properly search their faces, but—

Her eyes land on a framed picture hanging on the wall next to the doors.

It's of a smiling, slightly red-faced man in his late fifties, early sixties, accepting a chunk of blown-glass from a woman in a glitzy evening dress. And he looks exactly like what the Ken Balfe she found on Instagram might in a few decades' time.

The man who's about to interview her must be Kenneth Balfe *senior*. Not a teenager at the time of the murder, but a grown man. An adult whose teenage son was friends with the brother of one of the killers.

Which makes him, she thinks, far more likely to remember things from back then. Including peripheral figures. Like the other family members, for instance.

Her, possibly.

She can't chance meeting him. She has to get out of here.

Ciara grabs her bag and starts to walk away, just as she becomes aware of the glass doors to the office swinging opening behind her. She holds her breath, thinking it's the blonde woman coming to collect her, waiting for the call of her name.

But it doesn't come.

She can't risk waiting for the elevator, so she starts hurrying down the stairs instead. Blood rushes in her ears.

She winces at the conspicuous clacking of her heels on the marble. She reaches the first landing and turns to start down the next flight—

And that's when she sees him.

Standing at the top of the stairs. Looking at his phone in his hand. Tall. About her age. Neither muscular nor soft, but solid. Broad-shouldered. Dark hair, thick and messy, but in a way that suggests it was carefully teased to look so.

Oliver St Ledger.

It's him.

It's him it's him it's him it's him it's him.

She knows this for sure, even if, at the same time, she can't quite believe it.

Out of sight, she hears the double doors to the office swing open again and a female voice say, 'Ciara—? Oh,' and then, after a pause, 'Oliver, did you happen to see a woman here when you came out? Brown hair, black suit?'

Oliver's head begins to rise, his gaze lifting from his phone.

Ciara hurtles herself forward, nearly missing the first step, awkwardly regaining her balance and then dashing out of sight, heels clacking loudly, all the way down the stairs.

22 DAYS AGO

Oliver awakes on the couch, immediately feeling the pinched pain of a tight muscle in his neck. His tongue feels thick and bristly, his insides gnawing and empty. A cluster of dented, empty beer cans sit on the coffee table. The light in the room suggests it's early morning.

Then he hears the sound that woke him up: his phone, ringing.

He thinks *Ciara* and whips about, desperately looking for it, chasing the sound before it stops, knocking cushions and—

Sending the phone flying on to the floor.

He just wants to hear her voice, he thinks. It doesn't even matter to him what she's saying with it.

But it's KEN B that's calling him.

'Kenneth,' he says, his voice thick with sleep.

'So you *are* alive, then. This is my third time trying you.'

Oliver pulls the phone from his ear to check the screen; it's crowded with Missed Call notifications and unread texts.

'Are you all right?' Kenneth asks.

'Yeah, I ah … I think I just overdid it last night.'

'At home alone?'

'One too many beers,' Oliver says. 'Should've quit while I was ahead. That's all.'

Silence.

Then Kenneth asks, 'You holding up okay over there?'

Oliver forces himself to smile, so the other man will hear it in his voice. 'Yes. Fine. Thanks.'

'Did you see the email we sent around yesterday? It looks like this lockdown thing is going to be extended for another three weeks, and I'm hearing it could go on all summer. We've got projects teetering on the brink left and right. There's even a rumour Google are going to pull out of the Sorting Office, the new-build down by the docks, and if they do, that could trigger a mass exodus. We're all right for now, in the short term, but just to plug a few holes in the immediate future, we're offering everyone two weeks' unpaid leave, if they want it—'

'I'll take it,' Oliver says. He can't possibly focus on work right now, and he's in no fit state to do it.

'You sure?' Kenneth asks. 'I said *un*paid. You heard that bit, right?'

'Yeah, it's fine. When does it start?'

Kenneth laughs. 'All right, Mr Eager Beaver. Monday is a Bank Holiday so how about we say Tuesday?'

'Great.'

'Just do me a favour and email Louise, will you? Keep her in the loop.'

'I will.'

One less problem to deal with.

'And let me know if you need anything. I know you're on your own over—'

'It's fine,' Oliver says again. And then, in case he sounds ungrateful for Kenneth's concern, he adds a, 'Thanks.'

'Look after yourself, Ollie.'

Ollie.

Oliver just about manages to hang up the phone before something in his chest breaks apart.

The only people who ever call him that are the ones who've known him since then, since *before*.

These days, that's just Kenneth and Rich.

It used to be comforting. It used to make him feel safe, that people could know the whole truth of who he is and still want him in their lives, still love him, still *like* him. But now it just makes him feel trapped, a man forever imprisoned by the actions of his own self as a child.

Things he did without thinking, in the moment.

Things he's been wishing every single second since he could take back.

Oliver lets the phone drop on to the floor, curls up on the couch and starts to cry.

His body racks with sobs; he loses track for how long. He cries until he feels empty, until a pain in his chest begs him to stop.

Until it gets dark outside.

TODAY

There's a tiny, shed-sized coffee shop in the little park opposite The Crossings. As per restrictions, it's only offering a takeaway service from a little open hatch at the side, but Lee flashes her ID to gain access to the interior and thus, their cupboard-sized customer toilet. When the young barista hands over the key, Lee finds she can pinpoint the exact moment he smells the death on her: his smile falters, is replaced by a flash of confusion, and then is followed swiftly by a wrinkling of the nose and the clamping shut of the mouth.

'I'll just be a minute,' Lee tells him, smiling sweetly.

In the bathroom, she pulls the toilet lid down and unloads her wares. After her walk-through of the scene, she went scrounging for donations. She's managed to rustle up a clean Garda-issue T-shirt – size 3XL, but she'd rather wear that as a muumuu than keep her own shirt on. She swaps them over now, typing a knot in the hem of the T-shirt and then stuffing the knot inside her trousers because detective inspectors shouldn't really be seen to be dressing like teenage girls wearing their boyfriend's clothes. She's swiped a thick elastic band from the Tech Bureau van; she uses it now to gather her hair into a knot on top of her head, off her face and out of reach of her nostrils. Finally, to what will be her saving grace: a care-pack that Garda O'Herlihy produced from the glove compartment of her patrol car.

It's a little zip-lock bag, the size they give you at the airport, containing a travel-sized shampoo, shower gel and women's spray-deodorant; a mini toothpaste and toothbrush; two sanitary pads; a pocket-sized pack of antibacterial wipes; and a bar of chocolate wrapped in gold foil. Garda O'Herlihy explained that she makes these up herself, that she always keeps a few in the car, especially when she's on nights, because that's when you tend to meet the most vulnerable.

Today, it just so happens to be saving the arse of a detective inspector who smells like she's been slow-dancing with a rotting corpse.

Lee makes a mental note to buy O'Herlihy a pint.

And/or donate a Boots voucher.

She brushes her teeth — it can't hurt — and sprays the deodorant everywhere, including over her hair. She squirts half the bottle of shower gel into a cupped hand, adds water to make a foam and then slathers it all over her face, neck and forearms. She regrets putting on the T-shirt, which now has a dark rim of damp around the collar — she should've done this bit first, really. She dries herself with fistfuls of toilet paper that quickly clump and stick, and eats half the chocolate because she hasn't eaten yet today.

When she's done, the little mirror above the sink informs Lee that she looks absolutely terrible, but at least she doesn't smell any more.

Well, no, actually, she smells of many things – Fresh Cotton, Eucalyptus Revive, Zesty Blast – but at least none of them are Advanced Decomposition.

She stuffs her shirt in the bin by the toilet, goes to leave, then feels bad and goes back to tie a knot in the top of the liner so the shirt doesn't stink out the bathroom.

She tries not to think about how bad things might have been if she hadn't been in full protective gear in there. Tom said he didn't smell anything off her when they climbed out of their suits, but she wouldn't trust that man's nose. Whatever's up there has probably been long cauterised.

When she hands the key back to the barista, she studiously ignores the way his eyes widen as he takes in the state of her. She buys two cappuccinos to take back with her across the street, out of guilt more than anything.

Karl is waiting for her by the car, holding a laptop that he lifts when he sees her approach. She thinks for a second it might belong to Laura Mannix, and is about to congratulate him on working wonders in apartment fourteen while she was in apartment one, but when she reaches him he says, 'CCTV is in.' And then, 'What the fuck happened to you?'

'I think it started twenty years ago when I thought, *You know what? I think I'll apply for the Guards.*' Lee holds up the coffees. 'You ready for another round?'

'What I really want is some food.'

'I've half a bar of chocolate in my pocket.'

'Since when? Because if it's been on a tour of the crime scene, nah, you're grand.'

'Any luck with herself upstairs?'

'None at all,' Karl says. 'She clammed up after you left. Refused to say any more. But I did Google Lois Lane. Former host of *Crimecall*, my arse.'

'So you've had a productive half-hour, is what you're telling me?'

'How was the scene?'

'Worse than before. But get this: Tom Searson thinks the guy might have drowned.'

'*Drowned?* I thought you said he was on the floor of the shower?'

'He is. Tom thinks the shower was on and a couple of inches of water collected in the depression around the drain. Guy's unconscious but breathing, face-down, and he inhales enough of it to drown.'

'Jesus,' Karl says. 'What a way to go.'

'And there's more: someone turned off the water. It could've been him, but it might not have been. But here's the real kicker: the entire apartment has been wiped clean.'

'Shit. Do you think that could've been …?'

'I think,' Lee says, 'let's watch that CCTV.'

They settle into the car in the same positions as earlier: doors open, Karl in the passenger seat and Lee behind the wheel, coffee cups resting on the dash.

Karl balances the laptop on his knees, opens the lid and

powers it up. 'Mr Instasham said the icon should be right here on the desktop …' He tracks a forefinger across the pad.

'Mr who?'

'And you're giving *me* shit because I didn't get Lois Lane? The guy from the property management company. Crap Instagram Account Man. So, how are we doing this?'

'The quickest way possible. What have we got?'

'Ah … Nine different feeds, it looks like.'

'I think the lobby is our best bet,' Lee says. 'Let's start there and work our way backwards from this morning.'

'I've got facing out and facing in.'

'In, please.'

'That's what she s—'

'*Don't* you even *dare*.'

After a few clicks and taps, Karl angles the laptop so they can both watch together.

A high-resolution, colour video is now playing at high speed and full screen. It's the feed from the camera in the lobby that's positioned over the front doors, showing the doors leading out to the courtyard and the letterboxes.

They sip their coffee and watch residents coming and going, the progress of the sunshine on the floor – as well as the clock in the bottom right corner of the screen – tracking the days as the video plays.

It's a slow process and the coffees are gone before they see anything of interest, from five days before.

'There,' Lee says, pointing. 'Play that forward at normal speed.'

They watch as a familiar figure enters the frame.

'Well, well, well,' Karl says. 'What have we here?'

It's Laura Mannix, standing in the lobby of The Crossings, looking out through the main doors.

She does this for a while, as if waiting for someone who never comes. Then she turns around and, very quickly, slips something into the letterbox for apartment one.

When she moves out of shot, it's to go back towards the elevators and so, presumably, back upstairs.

'There's our envelope,' Lee says. 'What time was that?'

'Ah ... Five fifteen, ish. On Monday last. She didn't do a very good job of hiding her face from the CCTV, did she? She stood in front of the camera to make sure we saw it.'

Lee shrugs. 'Maybe she didn't know it was there.'

'There's a big camera on the ceiling.'

'There's a *standard fish-eye lens* on the ceiling,' Lee corrects, 'in the corner, and so what? People don't really think of CCTV in places like this, lobbies and lifts. And if you're not doing anything wrong, you wouldn't be thinking about it all, would you?' She nods at the laptop. 'Play on.'

Karl taps a key.

'Remember,' he says, 'we've only forty-eight more hours to go.'

But they only have to speed through another five of them before they see Laura Mannix again: coming out of the corridor from the direction of apartment one and, moments later, going down it.

'Well, well—' Karl starts.

'Once was enough. Pause there and let's watch it at normal speed.'

When they watch the events in chronological order, Laura Mannix goes down the corridor towards apartment one and doesn't return for nearly fifteen minutes. She doesn't appear to be holding anything, but she has a little clutch bag on a chain slung diagonally across her chest, as if she's on her way somewhere.

Like before, when she moves out of shot, it's not to go out of the front doors or head into the courtyard, but to move back towards the lift that will take her upstairs to her side of the building.

'So that's what,' Lee asks, 'Monday morning? Ten or so?'

'Nine fifty-two, to be exact. When she returns to the lobby. Our friend was definitely dead by then, right?'

'Is there another angle? Where we can see the door for number one?'

Karl presses a few keys and traces a forefinger across the trackpad.

'Here we go. Fire exit at the end of the hall.'

The camera this time is positioned in the corner of the ceiling above the fire exit that leads outside, and only a few feet from apartment one. The door itself is hidden from view below the camera's line of sight, but anyone coming or going from the apartment would be clearly visible.

'Shame about the seven days,' Lee says. 'When we've such a good shot of it.'

'There she is.'

They both watch as Laura Mannix goes to the door of apartment one, hesitates for a moment or two and then slips inside.

'That lying little bitch,' Karl says.

Lee sighs heavily. She's starting to feel the strain of the day – and this case – even if she's only a few hours into each of them.

'She didn't kill him, though,' she says. 'He was already dead by then.'

'How do you know this wasn't her second visit? Don't serial killers always go back to the scene of crime?'

'How many serial killer cases have you worked, Karly? They must have been on my days off.'

'Zero-point-zero-zero,' he says, tapping his temple, 'because they never get to the serial bit with me.'

Lee snorts.

'I don't think Laura Mannix is a serial killer,' she says then. 'And did you see how she just pushed open the door? Like I said, unless she took something ... We don't even have her on burglary. I doubt that's enough time for her to wipe down surfaces, either – and she's nothing with her that could do that. And if she did that on a previous visit, why go back and risk leaving some trace now?'

'And why put the envelope in the letterbox if she's just seen his dead body in there?'

Lee turns to Karl, eyebrows raised. 'Yes,' she says. '*Excellent* question, Karl.'

'I'm choosing to ignore your tone of surprise.'

'Why *did* she do that?'

'Well,' he says, 'she told us that what's inside is a love letter about how she's not going to do anything bad, she won't name him, yada, yada, yada – but what if she had left previous letters that weren't so nice? He doesn't respond, she goes to check the apartment, she finds him dead, she's like, 'Uh oh, I've fucked up here,' so she writes a nice letter she knows he'll never get, but that we'll find, and we'll rule her out then as being a source of any angst in his life because, hey, her message to him was so nice.'

When he finishes, he turns up his palms with a flourish.

'Proud of yourself, Karl?'

'Indeed I am,' he says. 'Very.'

'You know, I think you could be right.'

They watch the remainder of the CCTV, but find nothing else of interest. Aside from Laura Mannix, no one seemed to enter or leave apartment one at any time throughout the previous seven days.

Karl closes the laptop and they sit in companionable silence for half a minute, digesting everything.

'How did she find him?' Lee asks then. 'Who was her secret tipster? That's what I want to know. Oh.' She's remembered the chocolate. She pulls it from her pocket now, grimacing at the soft substance she can feel give way to her fingers through the foil. She holds it out to Karl. 'Sorry. You might want to—'

'Give it to me. It'll taste the same going down.'

They lapse back into silence – or near silence, since Karl is a noisy chewer even when there isn't that much to chew.

Then something occurs to Lee.

'Which one is the *other* KB Studios apartment?'

Karl says something that sounds like, 'What?' distorted by a mouthful of food.

'Which one is the other KB Studios apartment?' Lee repeats. 'They rent two, remember? Which one is the other one? What number?'

'Dunno. Why?'

'Because it's owned by Oliver St Ledger's brother's friend's neighbour's dog or whatever it was. A connection going back years, potentially. Maybe even ...?' She waits for the penny to drop with Karl.

'All the way to 2003,' he finishes. 'Clever girl.'

'Was there anything in the door-to-doors?'

'I can check.'

'Why don't you call back your buddy? Kenneth Balfe. Ask him, it'll be quicker.'

Karl wipes his sticky fingers on his trousers – 'Next, we solve the case of why you're still single,' Lee says wryly, to which Karl snaps back, 'And then after that, why you are, too,' – before taking his phone from a pocket, tapping the screen and putting it to his ear.

The device's volume is loud enough for Lee to hear without the speaker-call option.

'Hello? Yes?' a voice says.

'Mr Balfe, it's Detective Sergeant Karl Connolly again. No further news, just a question for you, if you wouldn't mind.'

'Oh. All right.'

'We were told that KB Studios rents two apartments in The Crossings. Obviously, we know one of them is apartment one. Would you happen to know the number of the second?'

Kenneth Balfe answers right away.

'Number fourteen,' he says. 'Although it's not one of our employees that's in there at the minute, it's a friend of the family's. Well, my wife's friend, really. She's a nurse, but she lives with her elderly parents who are supposed to be cocooning, so we offered to let her stay there since it was empty anyway. Well, my wife offered and I do what I'm told. Happy wife, happy life, you know yourself.'

Karl is grinning at Lee.

She mouths *name* at him.

'Would you happen to have her name?' Karl asks.

There's a rustling noise on the other end of the line.

'Let me just ask my wife, she's in the other room. But I think she said it was Laura something ...'

61 DAYS AGO

Ciara is dreaming of Mill River. She doesn't have many clear memories of the place but her subconscious fills in the details, making the river more of a trickling stream, lining its bed with tiny pebbles and clearing its banks of trees, so you can see the water from the estate, and you can see right through the water to the pale limbs that lie—

Her phone is ringing.

Through the fog of half-sleep, Ciara reaches for her bedside table where it's always plugged in overnight, but there's no phone *or* bedside table.

When she opens her eyes, she finds an unfamiliar scene: a small living room filled with mismatched furniture, grubby white walls that could do with a fresh coat of paint, sunshine streaming through paper-thin curtains. And she appears to be lying in a bed in sheets she doesn't recognise right in the middle of it, which doesn't make any sense until ... The last dregs of sleep leave her like clouds parting in the sky, and she remembers.

She couldn't afford to stay in the hotel *and* keep paying her rent back home, so she'd found a cheaper alternative via

Airbnb. The owner was surprisingly agreeable, happy to take cash payments and to let the place out week to week; it was the off-season, she figured, and he was probably happy with any level of occupancy. But then she'd collected the key, let herself in and discovered the truth: the photos online had been taken at extremely generous angles and the guy was *lucky* to have anyone paying any amount of money to stay there at all.

The ringing is coming from the tiny kitchen, tucked away on the other side of the room. Ciara throws back the sheets and hurries towards the sound, finding her phone vibrating angrily on the Formica countertop.

SHIV, the screen says.

Shit.

Ciara knew that, sooner or later, she'd have to explain herself to her sister, but she was hoping for more of the *later* bit.

'Hello?' Her voice comes out croaky and dry. She tries again, does marginally better. 'Hello?'

'Oh, so you *are* alive,' Siobhán snaps. She's outdoors: Ciara can hear the sound of passing traffic and whipping wind. 'Get up and let me in. I'm downstairs. Is your buzzer broken or something? I've been pressing it for ages.'

Ciara can't think of a single other Sunday when her sister randomly showed up at her front door, but of *course* she would do it today. The woman must have a sixth sense.

'I'm not there,' Ciara says. 'Am I supposed to be?'

'Where the hell are you?'

'In Dublin.'

'In *Dublin*?'

'I have a job interview.'

'A *job interview*?'

'Are you just going to repeat everything I say, Shiv?'

'Yes, until you tell me what the hell is going on.'

'An opportunity came up,' Ciara says carefully. She has practised this but needs to avoid making it sound that way. 'We have a new property opening up here in the summer and they were looking for someone from Events to be on the opening team. I applied for it months ago. I'd forgotten about it, to be honest, until they sent me an email last week. I can't see myself taking it, especially not now, with Mam. But I figured I may as well go along. For the experience. It's first thing tomorrow morning but I came up yesterday to, you know …'

'Abuse your employee discount?'

That doesn't kick in until she's worked for the company for twelve months, but since it's an easy explanation, Ciara says, 'Exactly. Yeah.'

A beat passes.

'Are you sure about the not-taking-it bit?' Siobhán asks. 'Because with Mam and everything …'

'I'm sure,' Ciara says. 'Why were you calling over?'

'Because I made the mistake of drinking a litre of coffee before I left for my walk.'

'Go buy another one at the café on the corner. Millie's. You can use the bathroom in there.'

'I think I'll have to. It's Situation Critical.'

Ciara ends the call and immediately feels terrible about lying to her sister. She wishes she could tell her the truth, which is that the truth is what she's chasing.

But Siobhán doesn't even want to hear Oliver St Ledger's *name*, let alone that Ciara has been playing internet detective and has now temporarily moved to another city to see if she can accidentally on purpose cross paths with him and ask him questions about that day, the one that cracked open a fault-line through the heart of their family.

To discover the full horror of it, whatever it may be.

So that their family – what's left of it – can maybe find some peace.

But lying, it turns out, is *hard*. She's told her boss at work that she needs to take a few personal days because of her mother's worsening health situation, and now Siobhán that she's come to Dublin to interview for a job that doesn't exist. She hasn't even approached Oliver St Ledger yet and already it feels like there are multiple threads to keep hold of, to keep straight in her head.

She won't be able to do this. She's just not cut out for this sort of thing.

Ciara goes back into the main room and to the assortment of items laid out on the couch. She'd only packed a bag for an overnight stay but returning to Cork to collect more things is out of the question; there is the expense of another train ticket, but mostly it is Ciara's absolute certainty that if she left Dublin now, she would never come back.

She's just about got the nerve to stay.

She knows she doesn't have enough to travel all the way back here, again.

So she had to go shopping, on an extremely tight budget. The huge Penneys on O'Connell Street had provided extra clothes and underwear, toiletries, a notebook. She takes the notebook now, opens it to a fresh page and scribbles down in bullet points what she told Siobhán.

Just in case.

She'd had to go elsewhere to find the other things she needed. Eason's for the blue lanyard and compact laminating machine. The Three store on Grafton Street for her pay-as-you-go phone. The stationers next to Oliver's office for printing her new ID.

There'd been a guy of about eighteen or nineteen working the counter at the time, and he'd handed over the envelope very slowly, staring at her with a weird look on his face. 'It's for a costume party,' Ciara had said to him, at which point he'd tried – and failed – to act like he'd no idea what she was referring to.

And then to one of the charity shops on South Great George's Street for the thing she didn't know she'd needed.

She'd just happened to be passing by on her roundabout way back from O'Connell Street when she'd seen it in the window, artfully arranged as part of a themed display. There must have been a rash of space-themed donations lately, and the shop was taking advantage. There was a LEGO Saturn V rocket, already built but standing next to its pristine box;

a stack of astronaut biographies; and a blanket, mug and T-shirt sporting NASA logos.

And a little tote bag, showing the Space Shuttle flying over skyscrapers.

It was stamped with a logo that said, 'Intrepid', which, when Ciara Googled it on her phone, turned out to be a museum on an aircraft carrier in New York.

Ciara knew absolutely nothing about who Oliver St Ledger was now, and only very little about who he'd once been. If she had to make a list of things that interested him she'd have to guess, and she could only really do it twice. *Rugby*, based on a photo from nearly two decades ago in a school newsletter – which, she'd have to presume, they didn't offer the opportunity to do much of in Oberstown, the juvenile detention centre. And *space*, based on the T-shirt he was wearing the day of the murder, the one that had ended up covered in someone else's blood.

It wasn't much, and it wasn't likely that either of those things still played any kind of role in Oliver St Ledger's life. But it was all she had, and she knew absolutely nothing about rugby. She could at least fake the space thing a bit. Read a few Wikipedia pages, re-watch *Apollo 13*.

And just because you were interested in it didn't necessarily mean you knew every last detail about it. You didn't have to be obsessive. You could just be the kind of person who was interested enough to have bought yourself a souvenir after a visit to a museum.

Something practical, easily carried around, put on display without looking obvious.

A conversation starter, maybe. Hopefully.

Ciara makes herself a cup of tea and picks up another one of her purchases: the newspaper she bought yesterday that she ended up feeling too sleepy to read when she got back. She spreads it open now, across the piles of things on the couch, and scans the front-page headline.

FIRST IRISH CORONAVIRUS CASE CONFIRMED.

21 DAYS AGO

Oliver wills himself to get up from the couch and go into the kitchen, where he stands at the sink and gulps down several glasses of water without turning on any lights. His stomach is growling and upset, but he has no appetite. He can't imagine eating. He fills his water glass again and goes into the bathroom to get a pill.

There is a moment then, in the bathroom. In front of the cabinet, holding the blister pack in his hand.

The pills are lethal, deadly if you don't follow the dose. They're what you do when you've exhausted all other options, because they're so damn strong. It's why he only takes them, at the very most, once a month, and never *ever* exceeds the dose.

He counts the pills now: seventeen between the two blister packs.

He doesn't know how much time passes, but—

Oliver shoves them back in the medicine cabinet and firmly closes the door. It's not an option. He'd tried it once, not very hard, and was glad when it didn't work. *A permanent solution to a temporary problem*, is what Dan says. Usually right before he says, *This too shall pass.*

But will *this*?

He goes into the bedroom and sees the bed is made, which at first he can't figure out. But then he remembers: he hasn't been in it since Wednesday morning, and Wednesday morning Ciara was still here. She must have made it. He spreads his hands across the sheets, trying to detect some trace of her decaying presence, but there's nothing there.

He climbs on to the bed, folds himself in under the blanket, imagining that it's her arms he can feel, holding him tight, keeping him safe, and dreams of a cold river and a young boy's eyes looking up at him, asking the same question over and over.

Why are you doing this to me?

Now, as then, Oliver doesn't know.

At some point on Saturday he forces himself out of bed and wanders into the kitchen to get something to eat, not because he's hungry but because he can't stand to listen to the incessant gurgling of his stomach juices any more. He finds an open box of breakfast cereal and starts eating it dry and by the fistful, standing up. As each blast of sugar hits his bloodstream, more and more of his surroundings emerge from the fog of exhaustion and take on a solid shape.

The curtains are closed, even though it's the middle of the afternoon. The kitchen is littered with half-drunk glasses of water, the remnants of an uneaten lunch from – Wednesday?

Has that been sitting there since *Wednesday*? – and the air is stale and smells odd, like sour milk. He should clean up, but his limbs feel heavy. All he wants to do is go back to bed.

Well, what he *really* wants to do is talk to Ciara, but that's not an option.

Unless he can persuade her to come back, to listen to him just for a few minutes. To let him explain himself now that the shock may have subsided somewhat. Of course she reacted that way, he wouldn't have expected anything else. But maybe now, with a few days' distance, with the revelation having had a bit of time to lose its electrified edges …

His phone. Where is it?

He pushes aside the kitchen countertop's detritus, searching, until he finds it under a government-issued COVID-19 advice booklet, dark and dead. Another search eventually turns up the charger; he goes back into the bedroom and plugs it in next to the bed.

What is he supposed to say to her? What words could possibly convince her to come back and speak to him?

At the *buzz-buzz* sound that signals the phone is charged enough to have powered itself back on, he picks it up and starts typing Ciara a text message. It goes through several drafts and deletions, but eventually he settles on: *I know it's over but I don't want it to end this way. Can we talk? We can meet somewhere public if you prefer.*

He waits for the notification that it's been delivered, but it doesn't come.

One minute passes.

Two.

Has she blocked him, he wonders, or is her phone just turned off? He chances calling her and gets his answer: it goes straight to voicemail.

He doesn't leave a message. Instead, he rolls over, burrows beneath the blankets, and closes his eyes, desperate for sleep to come and save him from the torture of his own thoughts, the reality of this situation, what it might mean for his future, his regrets.

Eventually he dozes.

It gets dark again.

A ringing sound, aggressive and electronic and out of place.

Oliver jerks awake, sits up in the dark and thinks, *My phone*. But it's not his phone, it's the buzzer, pulsing out of the intercom in the hall.

Someone is here.

He's confused by the light. What time is it? What *day*? He feels groggy and disorientated, yanked out of one time and dumped in another.

Would Kenneth have come over? He doubts it. Which means that really, it could only be—

Oliver jumps out of bed but his body isn't ready for it, and he stumbles and falls hard against the wardrobe door, sending a shooting pain emanating out from his left elbow in all directions.

The buzzer goes again.

He scrambles to his feet, hurries out into the hall.

It's her.

He can see her on the little square video display.

'Ciara,' he says, pressing the OPEN button, not caring that her name has come out of his mouth sounding pathetically grateful and desperately hopeful.

Her voice, tinny from the speaker: 'Can I come in?'

'Of course. Of course. Of course.'

On the video screen, she disappears from view and there's a clicking sound as the outside door opens.

Oliver goes to open his own front door and stands on its threshold, one hand holding it open, facing down the corridor. He tries to rub alertness into his face with his free hand while he waits.

What is he going to say to her? What is *she* going to say to *him*? When she rounds the curve in the corridor, her face offers no hints – at least until she reaches him, when her brow furrows with concern.

'Are you okay?' she asks.

This is promising, he thinks. That she cares.

'I just haven't slept properly,' he says, his tongue feeling thick.

'Since I last saw you, by the look of things.'

'Yeah, well.' He swallows hard. 'Are you coming in?'

'I was going to. We need to talk, but ...' She hesitates. 'I don't think you're in any fit state to, right now.'

'I'm fine,' he protests.

'I can see that you're not. You look like shit and your pupils are the size of saucers.' A pause. 'Have you been drinking?'

He shakes his head, *no*. 'I just need to sleep. But I'm okay for now. Come in—'

'Like hell you are.'

'*Please.*'

A beat passes.

'Look,' she says then, 'why don't you just go to bed, get a good night's sleep and I'll come back tomorrow. We can talk then.'

The kindness in her voice cuts through him. He doesn't deserve it. He doesn't deserve *her*.

'Okay,' he says, 'but will you stay?'

It takes what feels forever for her to decide.

'All right, but only to make sure you rest. And I'll be on the couch.'

They go inside, and he closes the door behind them.

'What's that smell?' she says, wrinkling her nose.

All he can smell is her, the stuff she puts in her hair that smells of the sea and sunny days. He thinks of the day in the park, her lying beside him, nothing else on the earth but blue sky and their heartbeats.

She gently guides him towards the bedroom, motions for him to get into bed.

'Are you back?' he says. 'Can you love me anyway?'

She doesn't speak and he closes his eyes before he can see the answer on her face.

He hears the blind coming down, the heels of her boots crossing the floor, the soft *click* of the bedroom door as she closes it gently, saying, 'We'll talk in the morning, okay?'

56 DAYS AGO

'Go ahead,' are the first words he ever says to her.

It's Friday lunchtime and her fifth time following Oliver into the Tesco opposite his office building, swinging the Space Shuttle tote bag on her arm, pretending to be just another office worker buying yet another unimaginative meal deal. Today, though, she lost him somewhere inside and then, distracted, had picked up a bottle of water of the kind with a sickly sweet fruit flavour added. She can't afford to spend money on props; this will actually be her lunch. So she's paused by a stack of Easter eggs (*Easter? Already?*), wondering if she can be bothered to go back and change it. That's when she looks up and sees him, standing less than two feet away, leaving a space for her to join the queue ahead of him.

She's never got this close, never been able to look directly at him. Never *felt his presence* before now.

She can't do this, she thinks. She's not able to.

He's got a strange look on his face. Expectant, almost. Like he's ... *challenging* her? Does he know who she is? Know what she's planning on doing? She feels like her real motivation is on naked display, written all over her face. If she could just get a hold of herself, take a minute to prepare ...

She'll come again, she thinks. On Monday.

She'll be more ready then.

'It's okay,' she says, starting to turn. 'I've just realised I've got the wrong one.'

Ciara turns and heads back towards the fridges, feeling his eyes on her as she moves away.

And the beat of her own heart, pulsing with promise.

She takes her time swapping the water and then walks to the very back of the store, making a show of searching for something, before going to the tills and joining the queue there again.

He's long gone.

She finally feels like she can breathe again.

But then, when she gets outside, she hears a voice say, 'Nice bag.'

It's him. Standing in the next doorway, looking right at her. The sandwich he's just bought is tucked under his arm, getting squished by the pressure. There's the hint of a grin on his face, tinged with something else she can't readily identify.

She stops. 'My ...?'

'Your bag,' he says, pointing to the NASA tote.

And she takes this as a sign.

Due to the reporting restrictions, the details in the articles she'd found were scant, but they'd all spared a column inch to mention the fact that Boy B had hidden a bloodstained

T-shirt with a NASA logo in a rubbish bag inside a holdall under his bed. His grandmother had bought it for him. It proved, his legal team argued, that he didn't want to hurt Paul Kelleher, that he had never intended to, but that after *Shane* had, Oliver had gone to the boy's assistance, tried to help.

'Thanks,' she says. 'It's from the Intrepid. It's a museum in—'

'New York,' he finishes. 'The one on the aircraft carrier, right? Have you been?'

It was seventeen years ago, he was a child, and maybe he didn't even *like* space things. Maybe his grandmother was playing a guessing game. But it was all she had, and then, when she'd seen the bag in the window of the charity shop ...

But it turns out he did.

And still does.

'Yeah,' she says. 'Once.'

He can't have been there. He wouldn't have been. She'd checked: the Space Shuttle on display there was only added in 2012, and she presumes he can't have travelled to the United States since he got out of Oberstown because he'd have had to declare his conviction at immigration. For direct flights from Ireland, that happened at the airport on this end; America had Homeland Security controls at Dublin and Shannon. He wouldn't even have made it on to the plane.

And memories of one visit a while back should be easy enough for her to flub.

He asks, 'Was it good?'

Ciara hesitates, because this is it. This is where she makes her choice.

People think the decisions you make that change the course of your life are the big ones. Marriage proposals. House moves. Job applications. But she knows it's the little ones, the tiny moments, that really plot the course.

Moments like *this*.

She wants the truth of what happened that day for her mother, before the woman's time runs out. She was never the same after that fateful day, after the knock on the door that revealed two strange men outside, one in a Garda uniform, one in a dark suit, both of them looking apologetic and solemn.

I'm afraid we need to ask your son some questions.

It had broken something in her mother's soul that could never be repaired, that had somehow only grown more broken since.

It's about the local boy who went missing, Paul Kelleher.

But Ciara also needs the truth for herself.

It may not bother Siobhán – or her sister might do a good job of pretending it doesn't – but for Ciara, the not knowing is a torment. Both boys had different stories; in each, the other was the ringleader, the real killer, the bad seed that started it all. The Gardaí had a third: who started it didn't matter, because they'd both contributed to the boy's death.

Is Shane in? Could you ask him to come down?

The jury considered everything – how quickly Oliver had let go of his lies, his tortured tears in interviews, the bloodstained NASA T-shirt – and decided that whatever had happened had happened because Shane took the lead. Perhaps this was helped by the fact that their family lived in a house in Mill River set aside for social housing, that her father was one of the long-term unemployed and that, before any of this had happened, Shane had struggled to concentrate at school and been held back a year. Meanwhile, Oliver's family occupied one of only six detached, corner houses on the estate that came with an extra acre, he had two doctors for parents and one of his character references was the parish priest. He even *looked* better – clean, neat and handsome compared to Shane's pale pudginess and spray of angry red acne. The judge punished Shane with a sentence of no less than twenty years and promised Oliver he'd be out at eighteen, which by then was less than five.

Ciara could remember the foreign stillness hanging over the house hours after the sentencing, her lying on the camp-bed in Siobhán's room because for months she'd been unable to sleep in a room alone, knowing they were both wide awake, staring into the dark.

'What happened?' she'd asked her sister.

'Your brother murdered someone,' came the flat reply.

Ever since, whenever anyone got close, Ciara felt something clamp down inside her, something sharp and dangerous, like a bear-trap. Fearing that there's something in her soul that lies in wait, a part of her unknown even to herself, a dark, barbed-wire thread through her DNA that could make awful things happen if the opportunity arose.

How can she be sure she isn't like him?

She keeps a screenshot on her phone of a quote by, supposedly, Abraham Lincoln: *Discipline is choosing between what you want now and what you want the most*. Maybe that's true, but discipline has never been her problem. It's *fear* she struggles with. She thinks *courage* might be choosing between what you want now and what you want the most, because what she wants now is to walk away, to shut this down, to close the doors. To retreat. To stay in the place where she feels safe and secure. In this moment, that's nowhere near Dublin, or KB Studios, or Oliver St Ledger.

But she needs to know what happened that day.

Exactly what happened.

Who or what Shane was then. Who or what he might be now, if he had lived.

And here is her chance.

'Yeah,' she says. 'But not as good as Kennedy Space Center.'

18 DAYS AGO

When Oliver awakes, the bedroom is bright with early-morning sun and something is different about it. He pulls himself up on to his elbows, looks around. It was messier last night, he thinks; there's no clothes strewn about the floor now. The air is odourless and the window has been opened – he can hear the chirping of birds outside. He's grateful for the glass of water he finds on his bedside table and gulps it down greedily, trying to banish the layers of acrid dryness that coat his throat.

Noises, in the kitchen: running water, the pump of the coffee machine, the tinkling of a spoon inside a cup.

She stayed here last night then. All night.

He hopes that's a good sign.

Oliver puts on fresh clothes, acutely aware that this would be his fourth day in a row wearing the same ones otherwise, wincing at the pain in his elbow and then vaguely recalling walloping it off something last night.

He quickly brushes his teeth and splashes his face with water in the bathroom before he goes into the main room to meet her.

'Good morning,' she says.

'Good morning.'

She's sitting on the couch, drinking coffee. Perched on it, really, back ramrod straight. She looks tense. *Braced.*

He's unsure whether or not it's okay for him to sit down beside her so he hedges his bets, sitting on the couch but at the opposite end, leaving plenty of space between them.

'How are you feeling?' she asks.

'Okay.'

'Did you sleep?'

Not really, he thinks. He tossed and turned, and he lay awake in the dark, and even though every limb was heavy with exhaustion and his eyes were stinging and his temples throbbed – even though all he wanted to *do* was go to sleep – his body, for whatever reason, wouldn't let him.

'I got a little,' he says. 'I dozed. Where did you go? Over the weekend?'

'Home. Where else could I go? There's a lockdown, remember.'

With everything that's going on, he's not sure he did.

'What time is it?' he asks.

She leans forward to tap her phone, illuminating the screen.

'Seven thirty-five,' she says. 'On Easter Monday.'

He'd forgotten about that, too.

There's a part of him that would like to keep going like this, talking as they are, suspended in limbo.

But a larger part of him has to ask the question, has to know:

'Are you back?'

She doesn't answer immediately. Instead, she leans back, sighs. 'I don't know what I am, Oliver, to be honest.'

He risks moving a little closer.

'I can't say this enough, I know, but I *am* sorry. I didn't want to lie to you, but I just didn't see another way. If I told you that up front, if you knew—'

'Would you ever hurt me?'

He recoils as if she's slapped him. 'What?'

'You can't blame me for asking.'

'Ciara, I would never—'

'But how do I know? I don't know what you're capable of now, do I? And I was living with you and absolutely no one knew I was here. Well, except for a *journalist*, as it turns out. What about her, by the way? What are we going to do about that?'

The *we* sends a balloon of hope rising in his heart, but remembering Laura pierces it instantly.

'She can't legally print my name,' he says.

'What about your picture?'

He shakes his head, *no*. 'It's my identity that's protected; so anything that might lead to the discovery of that ...'

Ciara nods slowly, as if considering this.

'I know this is all a lot to take in,' Oliver says. 'I just want you to know – and I'm probably the only person in the entire country who can say this – but these last couple of weeks ... They were the happiest of my life.'

Silence.

Oliver holds his breath.

'Mine too,' Ciara says softly, eventually. 'But now ... Now I don't know what to do. Or think.'

'You don't have to forgive me,' he says. 'Know that. And being with me isn't condoning what I did either. I won't take it as that. You know *I* don't condone it. Far from it. But it was a long time ago. And I take responsibility for it – I *did* take responsibility, I served my time. I live with the regret of that one afternoon every single day and I will until the day I die. But that doesn't change what we have, what we've had these last few weeks. When you were here, that first night you came over, I felt ...' The lump in his throat is back. He tries and fails to swallow it away. 'I just want to feel that *again*, Ciara. I wish we could. So tell me what I need to do. Tell me what you need to hear from me to make you want to stay.'

She looks at him then in a way that reminds him of that first day by the canal, that first night here in this room, all the mornings since—

He reaches for her.

He pulls her into his arms, presses his cheek against hers, puts his head on her shoulder.

And, miraculously, she lets him.

Slowly but surely, he feels her relax her body into his, feels her arms reach around him, feels the squeeze of her hand on his back.

He's too scared to move, in case it stops, goes away.

When she speaks, her voice is muffled against his chest.

'I don't know what to do.'

'Can't we just feel our way through this?' he whispers.

The nod of her head is practically imperceptible.

He dares find her lips with his. She hesitates at first but then responds, pulling him in, kissing him back.

It's a weird day for both of them, stepping around each other as if on eggshells, not sure what the other one is feeling in any given moment, anxious that it's not the same.

He's too afraid to ask her if she's going to stay that night, afraid that that will open up an opportunity for her to realise that coming back was a mistake, that she can't be with him, that she can't even stand to look at him. There's already been a few times when she turns to him and inhales as if she's about to say something, but then changes her mind and doesn't.

And all the while, Oliver is trying to ignore his most pressing problem: he hasn't had a proper night's sleep in going on five days.

It's taking its toll. He can feel himself shifting into the most dangerous stage, the one he usually tries to avoid: when the fabric of reality starts getting unpicked by unseen forces, when he starts to hear and see things that actually aren't there. And then there are the moments of what he's been told is called *microsleep* – when he *does* fall asleep, but uncontrollably, and only for a few moments at a time – which usually signals that he's reaching the end of the line, that he's testing his limits, and that if he doesn't take action soon things could get really, really bad.

He doesn't want to have to check out now, on the day that

Ciara came back, when things between them are so delicate and tenuous, but if he *doesn't* sleep, he could ruin everything inadvertently. So, as the sun starts its retreat from the sky, he admits to her that he's going to have to take one of his pills.

'Oh,' she says. She sounds disappointed. 'Should I leave? I can come back—'

'No, no. You can stay. If you want to, I mean.'

'What happens when you take one?'

'I conk out.' He smiles. 'That's about it.'

'And you'll be, like, all right tomorrow, then?'

'A bit groggy,' he says. 'But feeling one hundred per cent less zombie-like.'

She smiles at *him* now, for the first time since The Truth, and it's like a radiator inserted into his chest.

He takes her hand. 'Thank you. For coming back. For still being here.' He leans over and kisses her, light but lingering, on the cheek.

When he pulls back, he sees that her eyes are filled with tears.

'Ciara—' he starts.

'Sorry,' she says, wiping at them. 'I haven't really slept either the last few days. I think I could probably do with a good night's sleep too.'

He waves a hand, indicating the bedroom. 'I don't mind if you take the bed, I could sleep here.'

'No, no. It's fine.' She reaches for his hand, squeezes it. 'Do you want to eat first or …?'

'Better if I don't.'

'I might order something. Or run over to Georgie's.'

'Your keys are still on the hall table,' he says.

'Thanks. I'll try to be quiet.'

'There's really no need. You could have a rave in here and I wouldn't hear it. Those things completely knock me out.'

Oliver goes into the kitchen to pour a glass of water from the sink, and then into the bathroom to get a tablet. In his experience they take a few minutes – maybe as many as ten – to start to kick in, at which point you'd better get yourself into bed because the next stage falls like a curtain, like a heavy object from a great height.

If he's standing he will fall down, wherever he is.

And God, he's ready for it, this blissful unconsciousness. He wants to stop feeling as awful as he does. He wants to wake up tomorrow feeling rested and energised and ready to start building a life with Ciara, for the rest of his life – his After – to finally begin.

He swallows a tablet.

He goes back into bedroom, takes off his shoes and socks and then, too exhausted to bother with the rest, pulls back the blankets and climbs into bed. He hears the living-room door close with a soft *click* and then the muffled sound of the TV on at low volume.

He closes his eyes.

He opens them again.

From this angle, he has a line of sight out into the hallway. Ciara's bag is sitting on the floor there, her large black leather one with the handles that doesn't close at the top. She would normally drop it on the floor of the bedroom, but she hasn't set foot in here since she returned.

What has got his attention is what he can see sticking out of it: a large black Moleskine notebook, with the corner of a paper napkin sticking out of *that*.

The napkin has the logo of the Sidecar Bar printed on it.

That's the bar at The Westbury, where they had their first date. Did she take it from the bar the night they went there, to keep as a souvenir?

The thought that all the way back then – only a few weeks in reality, but what feels like years in lockdown time – she was thinking that *this*, him and her, was going to be something fills him with a sleepy warmth.

He raises his head, holds his breath, listens.

The fridge door opening and closing; Ciara is in the kitchen.

Oliver throws back the covers, gets up and goes to the bag. He already feels a little woozy, so he keeps his hands held out for emergency wall contact, should the need arise. He's not planning on snooping, he just wants to know for sure. He wants to be able to take the promise of Ciara's love with him to bed, to infuse it into his dreams. If she still has that, even after Wednesday, and if she's carrying it around with her …

That *has* to be a good sign, right?

He bends to reach for the napkin, pulls it out.

Something is written on it. Notes, it looks like, in blue pen.

French 75
NYC bar – no sign/secret door
Only child

He blinks at it, confused. It looks like a list of things they talked about on the night but …

Why would she write these things down?

Maybe she keeps a diary, he thinks, and she was just making notes to help her remember things until she got a chance to write about them, later.

His eyes stray from the napkin in his hand to the notebook in the bag.

And then to the closed door of the living room.

He reaches for the notebook.

It has the bloated, crinkled look of heavy use. He opens it, flicks through. Each page is filled with Ciara's handwriting.

He stops randomly at one.

Space Shuttles
Challenger – 28/1/86, O-ring failure (cold), explosion at 'throttle up'
Columbia – 1/2/03, foam strike/tiles damaged, burned up on re-entry
Atlantis – KSC Florida
Discovery – Smithsonian, Virginia
Endeavour – California Science Centre
Enterprise – Intrepid, NYC (test vehicle)

If the TV is still on next door he can't tell any more, because he can't hear anything over the thunderous rush of blood in his ears.

He turns the page and finds a square of printed text, glued on to it. The paper is glossy and smooth, as if from a magazine. It looks like it's been cropped from an interview; there's a question printed in bold at the top and then the corresponding answer underneath.

What's your top tip for visiting Kennedy Space Center?

Don't miss Atlantis! I love the way it's revealed to you, unexpectedly — like a surprise. You go into this big, dark room to watch a movie about the Shuttle programme and you think after that you'll move into another room to see the Shuttle but then, right at the end, the screen itself disappears into the ceiling and you find yourself looking right at the Atlantis — with the cargo bay doors open and at an angle, so it actually looks like it's flying through space! After I'd explored all the exhibits in the main hall, I went back and watched the next group of people get surprised by the Shuttle.

He turns another page.

2020 — left Apple (Cork)
2017 — graduated Swansea
2002 — moved to Isle of Man (7)

He flips to the back cover, where an A4 page has been folded in half and taped in place along one short edge. He unfolds it, turns the notebook so he can read what's on it. It looks like a screenshot of a LinkedIn profile for a woman named Ciara Wyse who lives in Dublin and works for Cirrus, but the accompanying profile picture is of someone else.

There's a fog rolling in now from all edges of his brain, making everything cloudy, blocking all pathways out, cutting off the trails of his thoughts before they can even establish themselves.

It's a familiar feeling and, he knows, a chemical one.

It can't be stopped.

He knows this, and yet he wants to push it back, to keep a little space clear in the middle, so he can think straight, so he can figure out …

This notebook.

Things she told him, but written down.

With dates like …

Like she needed to remember them.

Not a diary, but a …

Through the fog, he sees three words emerge clearly.

A cover story.

Ciara needed a cover story.

He looks again at the living-room door and wonders who – *what* – is actually in there.

But the fog is growing thick, swirling, taking over. He stumbles a little, and has to reach out and place both palms on the wall to steady himself.

She's a journalist after all. That's what Ciara is. What she has to be. It's the only explanation.

Which means he can't let himself fall asleep.

He *cannot*.

No.

Oliver turns and stumbles into the bathroom, feeling woozy, drunk. When he looks down, the ground seems very far beyond his own bare feet. And it's moving, the streaks of pale marble in the tiles morphing and swirling—

He falls to his knees, holds his head over the toilet bowl and sticks his fingers down his throat. It's too late to stop it, but maybe he can delay it a bit. Long enough to think.

Long enough to figure out what he needs to do.

With *her*.

But the fog is swirling, clouding his mind, pulling his eyelids down. He can see it coming towards him on a black tide.

Cold water. He can keep himself awake with cold water.

Oliver hoists himself up and steps into the shower – his elbow burns with a fresh pain; he must have hit it – and smacks the lever until a monsoon shower of droplets starts hitting his skin. But the temperature is set to its usual one – warm, getting warmer – and it just makes him want to go to sleep even more. He twists the dial he thinks will make it cold, but it doesn't get cold. No change.

His hands are starting to feel as if they're detached from his body, as if he's watching someone else's hands at work, and they don't seem to have any grip.

The sink, he thinks. There's cold water in the sink.

He stumbles back out of the shower, hitting the porcelain basin with his body and narrowly missing hitting his head on the mirror hanging above it.

He turns on the tap. Ice cold.

He tries to fill his cupped hands with enough to throw at his face.

'Oliver?'

She's standing in the doorway, staring at him. He doesn't even remember turning around.

'What's wrong?' she says. 'What are you doing?'

Her words sound distorted, like some unseen editor has slowed down the audio.

'Who are you?' he spits through his teeth.

He looks around for the notebook, the napkin, but he can't see them.

He can't remember what he did with them.

'Oliver, did you already take your pill? Because I think you should be in—'

He feels himself sway and tries to take a step to steady himself, reaching out for the shower door he hopes is where he thinks it is, but he stumbles and then he's falling and there's an impact and pain and a wall rushing towards him and the sound of breaking, falling, shattered glass—

And then Ciara screams.

23 DAYS AGO

'It was just a normal day. I was walking home from school with this other boy from my class, Shane, and …'

Ciara puts her head down so Oliver can't see her face, can't judge her reaction. She holds her body as still as she can, tries not to shake, tries not to cry.

How is she supposed to do this?

How is she supposed to listen to this and not react, not reveal that she knows this already, that he's describing not only what *he* did, but what her *own brother* did, too?

'It was all over something *so* stupid,' he says. 'And *we* were stupid. But in just a matter of minutes, everything got completely out of hand.'

She's encouraged to see that his eyes are filling with tears.

He talks about Paul Kelleher, about how he used to follow them home, and how on this day he did it while throwing stones.

'Most of them miss, but a couple hit our schoolbags and then Shane gets one square in the back of his head. And he like, reels around on Paul, and I think he's going to roar at him or something, but instead he says, "Okay, *fine*. You can come with us. We're going down to the water to skim stones." And then he gives me this look, like … *Follow my lead*. And he takes off running. Paul follows him. I do, too.'

She tries to imagine her brother behaving this way, attempts to play the scene out in her head like a film reel. But she was only eight at the time, and her memories from then feel fake and edited, as if contaminated by family photographs and stories she's heard since. She doesn't feel at all confident that she could say who Shane really was, what he was like, how he tended to behave.

'The estate was built on the bank of the river,' Oliver says, 'that's where it got its name.'

I know.

'The houses kind of sloped down to the water, and then in order to actually get to it, you had to climb through some trees.'

I remember.

'So once the three of us were down there, we were pretty much hidden from view. And that's when …' He swallows. 'That's when … That's when Shane just starts, like, pummelling Paul. That's the only word I could use to describe it. Shane had been kept back a year, he was nearly thirteen by then, and Paul was small for his age … I don't remember everything but I remember Shane towering over Paul, and Paul looking at up at him' – his voice cracks – 'like—like—' He pauses, tries to regain his composure. 'At first, I didn't intervene. I just stood there. But then Shane was like, come on, and Paul was kind of squirming, trying to get away, and he'd started to cry by then, so I went and I' – his voice cracks again here, goes up a pitch – 'I didn't intervene. I joined in. I held him. By the arms. In place. So that Shane could keep ... So that Shane could—'

He stops, swallows hard.

Ciara's heart feels like it's breaking in two, ripping down an invisible seam, bursting open like stitches. One half is heartsick about what Shane did, about what he was capable of doing ...

But the other is filling with warmth, with feeling, with *love* maybe, even, for how much regret Oliver feels about it now, how much it hurts him just to tell the story.

He's a good man, she thinks. Now. He turned out to be.

Maybe Shane would've too, if he'd got this far.

They made a terrible, *terrible* mistake – something that the word *mistake* doesn't even begin to cover. That's not in dispute. But they were *children*, ones who'd never done anything like it before, who'd been perfectly average, everyday kids up until this awful afternoon.

And now Oliver wouldn't even *break the travel limit*.

Shane might have been all right.

Everything might have been.

Ciara desperately wishes he was here to prove that himself. And to show it to their mother, to take away the pain she'd felt for so many years, the blame she'd inflicted on herself, the responsibility she'd taken for his actions.

She'd always blamed herself.

'I was his *mother*,' she'd used to mutter, its implication lost on nine- or ten-year-old Ciara at the time.

Soon after, her mother had stopped talking about it altogether.

'Shane says to Paul, we're going to wash the blood off in the river. And I just *knew* what was going to happen, what he'd decided to do, but it was like— It was like there was one half of me that felt like, yeah, good idea, that's what we have to do, what *I* have do now, to help Shane, to protect him, to stop him from getting in trouble. But at the same time, the other half of me was looking at Paul, all covered in blood, saying okay and obediently following Shane down to the water, and that part wanted to scream, "What the hell are you *doing*? *Run*. Run *away*." But I didn't. I didn't say anything. Instead, I … I just followed them to the water and I helped Shane push Paul into it and then I helped hold him down. Until … Until he drowned.'

Silence.

Ciara feels sick. For so many years, she had wanted the details and now that she has them, she'd give anything to give them back.

'The guards came that night,' Oliver says. 'To our homes.'

I was there when they arrived.

'Everything happened really quickly after that.'

The way I remember it everything happened in quick succession, one long horrific blur of tears and whispered arguments and a house as quiet and sad and empty as a funeral home.

'We were charged and sent to Oberstown – it's a juvenile detention centre. There was a trial. Our identities had to remain a secret so we became Boy A and Boy B. We were both found guilty of murder, but got different sentences based on our level of ... involvement. I got out on my eighteenth birthday and Shane ... Well, Shane took his own life on his. He still had another fifteen years to go at that point.'

She looks up at the mention of Shane's suicide, hoping that, somehow, Oliver has more information about it, that he can tell her more about why her brother did such a thing, what it was that had, evidently, pushed him to his absolute limit. She'd never seen him again after his arrest and what little she knew about his time in Oberstown she'd picked up from eavesdropping on whispered conversations.

'I'm not some evil seed, Ciara. I'm no psycho monster. I was just a child who, for five minutes, completely lost his fucking mind. A kid who, on the way home from school one afternoon, made a stupid, *terrible* mistake because he didn't want to look like a coward in front of his older, bigger friend. I was *twelve*. I couldn't undo it so I did the next best thing: from that moment on, ever since, I have tried to make up for it. I have done every *single* thing I was supposed to. I took my punishment. I was a model detainee. Did all the therapy, obeyed all the rules. Whatever they asked of me, I did it and then more besides. And since the day I was released I haven't as much as *littered*. But it doesn't matter what I do because all anyone thinks about, all anyone cares about, is what I *did*.'

He moves closer to her.

One step, two.

'And then I meet you. And you like me. And when I'm with you, it's like ... I feel like *me*. The me I should've been. The me I really *was*. Am. And even though I knew it couldn't last, knew you'd find me out eventually, I kept wanting to feel that way, so I kept seeing you. And then, unbelievably, a bloody *global pandemic* comes along, and we hear there's going to be a lockdown, and you're living in this tiny apartment, working from home, just moved to Dublin, not knowing anybody and' – he shakes his head as if in disbelief – 'you don't even *use social media*, so I think to myself, I'll just take these two weeks. I won't tell her for two more weeks. And I hoped, I desperately hoped, that by the time the truth came out, you'd have seen enough of me to know that *this* is me. Now. Here.'

She is *desperate* to tell him that she knows.

And what she feels. Which is that she knows *this*, here, now, is who Oliver really is. These last few weeks.

The night she stood here, in this room, in his embrace and saw the scar. The evening on the terrace, when he surprised her. The sunny day in the park.

Every little good thing, she collected them all and kept them safe in her heart, because every one was proof that *Shane* wasn't evil, that he was good, that he could've lived a good life and been a good man if he'd just been able to hang on long enough to come back out into the world, like Oliver had.

And somewhere along the way, she'd started to *love* Oliver, too.

And now, she wants to stay. To be with him.

To turn this into something real.

But first, she has to tell him *her* truth, reveal who she really is, how she found him, *why* she did.

So they can forgive each other, and start afresh.

But now is not the time. Let the dust from the demolition of these lies, the ruins of the past, settle. Let the shock absorb.

Until then, for now, she has to act like anyone else would, hearing all this for the first time. So she gets up and runs out of the room, into the bathroom, and does her best to sound like she's being sick into the toilet bowl.

18 DAYS AGO

Oliver is on the floor and his head is filling with pain and there's shattered glass everywhere and the water is warm and Ciara is shouting something at him, the same words over and over, sounding like she's very far away.

He tries to clear a patch in the fog, to catch the words, to *hear* them.

'I'm Shane's sister! Ciara Hogan. And I *know*. I knew it all, from the start. And it's okay, Oliver. It's okay, it's okay, it's okay …'

He thinks he says, 'What?' but he doesn't hear it; it might have only been inside his head.

'I'm sorry,' she says. 'I just wanted to know what had happened that day. And what Shane might be now. What he might be *like*. And if the answer is like you, then that's a good thing. Because *you're* good. You're a good man. I believe that. I've seen it.'

Oliver starts to cry.

If he really *was* a good man, he'd tell her the truth.

All of it.

'No,' he says. 'I'm not.'

And those words *do* come out.

Ciara says something about calling an ambulance.

Everything he has left, everything the rolling tide of dark hasn't yet reached, he uses to roar out, '*No!*'

'But you've hurt your head—'

The water stops. Ciara must have turned it off.

Oliver tries to turn and look up at her face, but everything feels so heavy. How did he ever carry his head on his shoulders when it feels like this? It's pulling him down, towards the ground.

And he realises he's on his knees, inside the shower, with little pebbles of …

Is that *glass*?

'You need help, Oliver. Here, let me—'

But when she reaches for him, he grabs her legs.

'No,' he says through clenched teeth. '*No.*'

'Oliver, for God—'

'I don't … deserve …'

'Oliver—'

'*It was me.* It was me. All … me. Not Shane.'

Her hands release him and he falls away, drops his head back to the ground.

For what feels like forever, there is no noise at all except the *drip-drip-drip* of the tap above his head. Oliver is dimly aware of the corresponding droplets hitting the back of his neck.

'Not Shane,' he says again.

Then Ciara says, very quietly, 'What are you talking about?'

He turns his head until his cheek is on the cold, wet tile and his mouth isn't obstructed. 'When I told you …' His lips feel loose, his tongue thick. He needs to sleep. He can't outrun it any more. Everything is too warm, too heavy … 'What I told you … happened. What was me … was Shane.' One last push, with all the force he can manage, clearer words, louder voice. 'Swap us over. Swap me with Shane. That's … that's the truth.'

He starts drifting off, feels the dark tide lapping at his feet, swirling around his ankles.

'You're saying …' Ciara sounds so far away. 'You're saying that *you* started it? That you beat up Paul? That it was *your* idea to drown him?'

He opens his eyes.

All he can see are Ciara's trainers, inches from his face, but they're red.

No, wait – *everything* is red. Like a filter.

Something is bleeding. *He* is.

'Yes,' he says. 'Yes. That's why … he attacked me … I wouldn't tell the truth … He couldn't go on … No one believing him.'

He hears Ciara crying, but he can't console her.

He can't do anything.

He tries to lift his head, but only manages to move it slightly, so that now he's looking at tile.

And then he hears something else.

Feels something else.

Water.

Not just in his mind but here, in reality. And not a *drip-drip-drip* like before. This is a thundering downpour, splashing all around him, filling his head with its gushing sound.

And Ciara crying, still.

And then no more.

The tide is in.

TONIGHT

'We're meeting the Super in twenty minutes,' Lee says. 'So for the love of God, find me the crime.'

Karl shrugs. 'I'm not sure we have one.'

They're at the station, sitting opposite each other at one of the desks in the back. Lee is slumped in a swivel chair, absently swinging it a couple of inches from left to right and then back again, her eyes red from rubbing them in frustration a few moments ago. Karl is on a hard plastic chair that he's pulled up to the end of the desk. He's leaning an elbow on it, and leaning his chin on his hand. The grease-stained, brown-bag remnants of a McDonald's dinner lie strewn between them. Lee is still picking half-heartedly at a box of cold, limp McNuggets.

It's approaching nine o'clock and almost completely dark outside, and they're both absolutely exhausted. But *at* nine o'clock, they have to meet with their Chief Superintendent to bring him up to speed, brief him on their investigations and give some indication of where they plan on taking things next.

And despite everything, they still don't have a crime.

———

To Kenneth Balfe's credit, after they'd suggested to him that the tenant in one of his apartments might have had a role to play in the death of the one in the other, he'd got both Laura Mannix and his wife Alison to come down to the station for voluntary chats.

Alison Balfe had quickly admitted that her husband wasn't as discreet as he liked to think he was, and that she'd known full well who it was in apartment one *and* working in her husband's office. She hated Oliver St Ledger, didn't want anything to do with him and thought he shouldn't be anywhere near the family's business, and she saw an opportunity to make the problem go away by whispering about it to her old college friend, Laura, who these days happened to be working for a radio shock-jock. But since the court order protecting Oliver's identity only covered the *reporting* of it, there was nothing Lee or Karl could do to Alison Balfe. She hadn't broken any laws.

Laura's tales of Wayback Machines and ears not ageing and fortuitously convenient corporate lets made a great story, but that's all it was. She'd been trying to keep Alison out of it, she told them. Karl had told her she should write a crime novel.

But she had admitted entering apartment one, taking photos of Oliver's body and leaving again without alerting anyone to his death. She hadn't even told *Alison*, which might have contributed to the current state of affairs: the two women were refusing to talk to each other. Laura insisted that she hadn't touched anything while she was inside, and so had no reason to wipe anything down before she left again, but she *did* admit to deliberately setting off the fire alarm at the complex at least twice. These were attempts to flush the residents outside, including Oliver St Ledger and his mysterious girlfriend, to create opportunities for her to see and maybe even approach them.

The post-mortem had concluded a couple of hours ago: Oliver St Ledger had officially died by drowning. Toxicology would take longer to come back, but the working theory was he'd taken a Rohypnol, which he had a prescription for, and fallen in the shower. Right about now, Kenneth Balfe was formally identifying the body.

Whoever *had* wiped down the surfaces in apartment one had done a bloody good job. Of the prints they did find, only two sets were not a match to the deceased, and they were in low-traffic areas: the back of the TV unit, the bottom of a wardrobe door. They could plausibly belong to previous occupants. They didn't match anything on file.

The only item of interest recovered was Oliver's phone, which showed text messages exchanged with a user he'd entered as 'Ciara', the last of which was from nearly two weeks before.

Twenty days ago, Oliver had sent a text to this woman saying:

I know it's over but I don't want it to end this way. Can we talk? We can meet somewhere public if you prefer.

Eighteen days ago, he'd received a response from her.

Maybe we can have a drink after lockdown ends. Stay safe x

The content of their historical messages suggested that Oliver and this Ciara woman had been seeing each other, but had evidently broken up before his death. No one was answering at the other number now; ringing it got you an automated message saying the user could not be reached at this time. The text messages contained no useful detail that might help identify the sender. They were awaiting registration information from the service provider, but in the meantime they'd been informed that it was a pay-as-you-go number. The user could have potentially registered any name and address they liked because none of it was subject to verification.

Also on Oliver's phone were a string of text messages and missed calls from his brother, Richard, wondering why he wasn't answering. One of them apologised for an earlier conversation in which Richard had apparently told Oliver that he shouldn't be staying in that apartment, that he knew Alison Balfe 'hated his guts' and couldn't be trusted, and that Oliver needed to get out of there for his own safety. The last one, sent last night Irish time, had said if Oliver didn't check in within the next twenty-four hours, Richard was going to send Kenneth to his door.

When Lee spoke to Richard this afternoon, just before he boarded the first of three flights that would eventually land him back in Dublin – and facing a two-week self-isolation – he'd explained that he was the only member of the family still in contact with Oliver. After a threat of exposure in London a couple of months earlier, Oliver had cut all contact with the friends and colleagues he'd had there. He'd had a therapist, Dan, but they were only speaking once a month at the moment.

Richard had asked that the court order continue to be observed and no information about his brother's true identity be released to the press. Lee assured him that would be case. The Garda Press Office, as a rule, released as little detail as possible, and the story that appeared on ThePaper.ie this afternoon had contained about as much information as the press were ever going to get.

Gardaí investigating after body of man (29) discovered in Dublin 6

Gardaí in Dublin are investigating the death of a 29-year-old man whose body was found at an apartment block in Harold's Cross, Dublin 6, early this morning. The grim discovery was made following reports by neighbours of an odour. Gardaí are now probing the circumstances surrounding the man's death, although sources say foul play is not suspected. The body has been removed to St James's Hospital, where a post-mortem will be carried out. Anyone with information can contact the Garda Confidential Line on 1800-666-111.

Thankfully today was Reopening Plan Day, and all available column inches and airtime were saturated with the government's five-phase plan to slowly reopen the country beginning on 18 May, as well as the heady news that as of Tuesday, everyone could venture as far as *five* kilometres from their home after five weeks of being confined to just two.

No one cared about a nameless body being found in an apartment, especially when it wasn't even because of a crime.

'Something's not right about this,' Lee says, absently wiping drops of condensation off the side of her McDonald's Coke with a forefinger.

'Unless I missed the news about the pathologist finding a seven-inch blade in the dude's back,' Karl says, 'it's an accidental death. The end.'

'Let's talk it through.'

'What have we *been* doing?'

'Okay. So.' Lee sits up. She takes a few sips of the Coke, even though she knows the sheer amount of ice in there will have diluted any caffeine benefit. 'Okay. So. Okay.'

'Off to a great start there,' Karl mutters.

'How do you still have energy for sarcasm? You didn't even sleep last night.'

'It's because I am a – how do you say? – *young person*.'

'There's seven years between us, Karl.'

'You tick a different box on the form, that's what matters.'

'Who turned off the water?'

'*He* did,' Karl says. 'Tom Searson said that was a possibility. St Ledger had enough left in him to reach up and slap the lever down, but not enough to not sink to the floor and drown in whatever water had already collected there.'

'What about the text messages? His says he doesn't want it to end this way and offers to meet somewhere public if she prefers. That sounds like there was some big blow-up, that she might feel unsafe meeting him behind closed doors.'

'But it could also refer to lockdown,' Karl says. 'They're two households, they're not *supposed* to be meeting behind closed doors. And her response doesn't suggest anything is wrong. Lee, can I ask you a question? Do you *not* have enough work to do? Are you bored? Is that it?'

'Why isn't she answering that number now?'

'She changed it.'

'Why?'

'Because people *do*. Sometimes, people change their phone numbers.'

'How long have you had yours? I think I've mine going on twenty years.'

'Lee, come on. We both know there's always something that refuses to fit the jigsaw. That doesn't mean we can't still see what the picture is. And you have to admit, the only reason you're still even looking at this jigsaw at all is because of who he is. Take away Mill River, take away Laura Mannix – what have you got? A guy who drugged himself and fell in the shower. The end.'

'You do know that you saying "The end" doesn't constitute a legal judgment?'

'It should,' Karl says. 'It's much more efficient.'

'We'll have to look for this Ciara girl.'

'How do you suggest we do that? Unless something comes back on that phone registration – and I'm not holding my breath there – all we have to go on is a first name.'

'And a Cork accent. And Laura's physical description.'

Karl rolls his eyes. 'You're right. I'm sure we'll find her in no time.'

Lee drums her fingers on the desktop, thinking.

'Why are you so determined to find a crime here?' Karl asks. 'We're not going to get any blowback. There's one relative who lives on the other side of the world and he wants all this kept hush-hush. Laura Mannix knows she's dodged a bullet and will be on her best behaviour from here on out with this – she's not going to be a problem either. So let's just tell the Super our thinking is that it was an accident but we'll have a look for this Ciara woman, sure, and we're waiting for toxicology to confirm, but beyond that ...' He turns up his palms. 'What else is there to do?'

'I just feel like we're getting swindled somehow,' Lee says. 'Like someone is offering us a brand-new car for a bargain price and assuring us everything is above board. We *know* it can't be true, but the car seems fine, so we can't quite put our finger on where the lie is.' She sighs. 'Let's say he did turn off the water by himself. Fine. But why was his girlfriend using a pay-as-you-go phone? When did you last meet a twenty-something who wasn't on bill-pay? They need unlimited data for all their, I don't know, tick-tocking and stuff.'

Karl snorts at this.

'And isn't it a bit convenient,' she continues, 'that not only is the phone disconnected now, but that their communications stopped, what? At most three or four days before he died? And then you have the fact that the entire apartment was wiped clean, the door was unlocked and … What was that other thing? Oh yes, he was a *convicted child killer* whose identity was protected, with a journalist on his tail.'

'But he wasn't murdered,' Karl says.

They both sit in silence for a moment.

Then Karl says, 'Can I throw something crazy out there?'

'You've never asked my permission before.'

'What if there *is* no Keyser Söze?'

Lee looks at him blankly. 'What's that?'

'Seriously? Lee, your pop-culture references are all *over* the show. You give out to me for not knowing that Louise Lane woman—'

'Lois.'

'—but *you* don't know *Keyser Söze*?'

'I know we're meeting the Super in fifteen minutes, Karl. That's what *I* know.'

'What if there *is* no Ciara?'

'But there was. He was texting her. And Laura met her.'

'He was texting *someone* and Laura *says* she met her. Look, I'm not saying there wasn't a girlfriend. I'm not saying Oliver didn't think her name was Ciara. But what if that was – drumroll please – actually our friend Ms Laura Mannix?'

Lee tries to push aside her brain-melting exhaustion to consider this.

'It fits,' Karl continues. 'And it would explain the convenient timing of the end of their relationship and why she's not answering the phone now. Laura poses as Ciara to get close to St Ledger. St Ledger roofies himself and drowns in a puddle of shower water. Laura goes to the apartment, discovers this, freaks out because she thinks he did it on purpose because he found out who she really was or whatever, and she'll get the blame, so instead of reporting it, she cleans the place down and leaves. Sends that text message to make the' – Karl makes air quotes – '*girlfriend* go away. Waits for him to get whiffy enough for someone else to call it in and then worms her way into our investigation because getting some juice on that is the next best thing. Tells us she didn't speak to him – again, convenient – but that she *did* talk to his girlfriend. I mean, come on. You have to admit it all fits.'

'Maybe *you* should write a crime novel,' Lee says. She chews on her lip, thinking. 'It's not a *completely* crazy idea, but … She must be ten years older than him.'

'So? Guys in their twenties love that shit. And she's hot.'

'Oh, she *is*, is she? Good to know your mind was on the case, Karly boy.'

Karl grins. 'My *mind* was.'

'Why do I always feel like I need a shower after I talk to you? Can you stop sexualising our witnesses, please?'

'I mean, she definitely has that I-might-wake-up-tomorrow-morning-to-find-her-standing-over-me-with-a-knife energy, but yeah. And, hey.' He holds up his hands. 'Ciar*a*. Laur*a*. They both end in "a".'

'I'm just going to forget you said that last bit.'

'I'd appreciate it.' Karl nods solemnly. 'Not my best work.'

'Laura as Ciara. Ciara as Laura …' Lee leans back in her chair and resumes her absent-minded swivelling. 'It's not the *worst* theory you've ever had, but that's not saying much now, is it?'

'Think about it: none of the other residents reported seeing this Ciara woman.'

'They didn't remember seeing Oliver either. Not since lockdown began.'

'There were no pictures of her on his phone.'

'There were no pictures of *anybody* on his phone.'

'And all the text messages conveniently contain no identifying information that might lead us to Miss Mysterious. I rest my case.' He winks. 'The end.'

'We'll have to get the cell-tower data for the Ciara phone. Track its location. Maybe that would lead us to CCTV or something. A traffic cam. Something on a city street. We might find her that way.'

'Or we might waste hours of manpower investigating a non-crime to get a grainy picture of Laura Mannix.'

'So what do *you* suggest we do, Karl?'

'I think if we're going to do anything, it's get Laura on obstruction of justice. She should've called us two weeks ago and she's been fibbing to us today. She still *is* fibbing, if my theory is correct. Which, of course, I think it is.'

'Of course,' Lee says, rolling her eyes.

'I think there's a far greater chance of that than there is of anything else going on here. I mean, consider the alternative. Someone force-fed this dude one of his own roofies and pushed him through the shower door, and left absolutely no definitive proof of their existence save for a phone that no doubt will be registered to some made-up name and useless address. Wiped the apartment clean. Managed to be going in and out of it for however long they were together without being seen except by one woman who can't be trusted. Knew to leave before the seven-day CCTV loop kicked in. And made the whole thing look like it was just a tragic accident. We both know that master criminals are nowhere near as common as Netflix would have us believe.'

'Hmm,' is all Lee says to this. She looks at the clock on the wall. 'Better make a move.' She gets up with a groan.

Karl gets up too, stretches. 'So what are we saying here?'

'Let's go with accidental death pending toxicology and further enquiries. Low chance of blowback. We'll tell the Super we're going to try to find this mysterious Ciara woman and bring Laura Mannix in for a more formal chat.' She sighs. 'And here was I, thinking I'd have a nice quiet, relaxing weekend ... I was even going to get my shit together, you know?'

'Do you ever think,' Karl says, 'that maybe you *have* your shit together, it's just that your shit doesn't look like everybody else's?'

'Did you just come up with that?'

'I'm not just a pretty face, you know,' he says with a wink.

'Right now, you're not even that.'

'It's hard to hear you through the glass house you're standing in.'

'Oh – and after we do this, you're going to give Eddie Moynihan his cuffs back.'

'*What?*' Karl makes a face. 'Why?'

'Because it's the right thing to do.'

They start making their way around the desks, heading in the direction of the Superintendent's office.

'Where am I going to say I got them?'

'I don't know,' Lee says. 'But whatever you do, don't tell him where they've been.'

3 DAYS FROM NOW

On Tuesday the two-kilometre restriction becomes five, and Ciara is up with the dawn. She knocks back a coffee – she's kept that habit, even investing in a knock-off Nespresso machine she saw on sale in Aldi – before sticking her feet into her trainers and heading outside. The sun is weak and chilly, but pushing its way up into a cloudless sky. She walks along the canal, then cuts down Haddington Road past St John's College, turning right onto Bath Avenue. When the expanse of Sandymount Strand comes into view – and, beyond it, the gentle steel-blue waves of the Irish Sea stretching all the way to the horizon – she feels a physical release, a lead weight disappearing from her shoulders, a lightness shooting through her heart. And then the assault of the sea breeze, whipping her hair in every direction and sandblasting the skin on her face.

She likes it.

It's waking her up, bringing her back.

For more than two weeks now, she's been mostly hiding out in the studio apartment, scurrying out after dark to buy groceries and newspapers, scouring them and the internet for news on Oliver St Ledger. It finally came on Friday online, Saturday morning in print: *Gardaí in Dublin are investigating the death of a 29-year-old man whose body was found at an apartment block in Harold's Cross, Dublin 6, early this morning. The grim discovery was made following reports by neighbours of an odour emanating from the man's apartment ... foul play is not suspected.*

She had thought she would've spent those two weeks with Oliver. She was going to tell him the truth, all of it: who she was, why she'd felt compelled to find him, and that she had, in little ways, started to love him.

That she wanted to stay with him, to see if that love could grow.

But his admission had changed everything. Now she grieves for two people: the Oliver who never was, and the Shane who never got to be.

The pain in her heart is acute, mixed and confusing. She catches herself thinking of Oliver, of being with him, of believing in him, and finds herself wishing things had turned out a different way. But then she remembers what he said, that he had been the ringleader, that what had happened all those years ago had happened because of *him*, and with a cold, steely certainty she knows things couldn't have gone another way.

She's not worried they'll come for her. She had set out to build a lie that would protect her, a kind of shark-cage that would keep a distance between her real self and Oliver, and she'd inadvertently created a phantom. She'd realised this standing feet from his unconscious body, watching a puddle of water build in the bottom of shower, knowing what could happen when a person's nose and mouth were resting against the tiles.

Knowing she could just walk away.

She had borrowed the job and last name of a real Cirrus employee she'd found on LinkedIn and made her own profile in the hope that if he looked, he'd find the fake one first and go no further. She had only ever communicated with Oliver via a pay-as-you-go-phone, which she'd registered to Oliver's name and the KB Studios address, and before she'd left his apartment for the last time, she'd used it to send a text message that suggested she and Oliver had broken up. She'd watched the text message light up Oliver's phone's screen and found another layer of protection: that day by the canal he'd asked her for her last name, but he'd never actually entered it. She was just 'Ciara' in his contacts. Her real phone had never left the studio flat back at Sussex Court.

She'd stayed in his apartment that night, while Oliver's body grew pale and cooled, scrubbing every trace of herself away. The only person other than Oliver who ever even knew she was there is the journalist, Laura, and what information does she have, really? Not much more than the Gardaí. Laura knows what Ciara looks like, yes, but Ciara is already making an effort to change that.

And why would anyone be looking for her? Oliver fell and died. He had a tragic accident.

He had got himself into that shower, in that position, and was slipping into unconsciousness. She had turned off the water when she'd first entered the bathroom, when his head was in the sink. All she'd done was reset the scene. Put the shower back on, like it was when she'd found him. Back to first positions.

There was no responsibility to shoulder.

As far as she was concerned, Oliver had done it to himself – and apparently, the Gardaí agreed.

Foul play is not suspected.

In the dark, though, late at night, when she's on the cusp of sleep and doesn't have the energy to tell herself any more stories, she has to accept that she has done the very thing she's spent her life terrified that her brother had, that in the pursuit of *that* truth, she's found another one: there *is* a killer in her family.

But it's her.

The only solace she's been able to find is that she understands now there might be a difference between *killing* and *being a killer*.

She hopes, for her sake, that there is.

Even though it's early, the beach is dotted with dozens of people, but with the tide halfway out there's more than enough room for everyone. Ciara can walk along the water's edge without even coming close to any other early-morning beachgoers.

She watches the ripples of the waves for a while, the sun splintering into shards on the surface, shifting and disappearing, breaking over it again.

Then she feels, rather than hears, her phone ring in her pocket.

Siobhán.

As far as her sister is concerned, Ciara came to Dublin for a job interview at a phantom hotel, owned by the chain she already works for, for a position on their opening team, the staff who ready everything in the months leading up to the day they open their doors and welcome their first arrivals. When things with Oliver began to look promising, Ciara had called her sister and told her she was taking the job but that it was temporary, just for a few weeks. Her *real* job, in the meantime, had been decimated by the coronavirus restrictions; there were no events going on at all during lockdown, and eventually most hotels closed. Her boss in Cork had instructed Ciara to apply for the Pandemic Unemployment Payment, which she did, and she passed her 'workdays' in Oliver's apartment reading and playing Solitaire. Eventually she'd made her continued stay in Dublin more plausible by telling Siobhán that, under the circumstances, the hotel had offered her a room to stay in for the duration, free of charge.

Now the government has announced the reopening plan, she can't expect to actually return to work until July at the earliest. She can't afford to stay in Dublin that long *and* keep paying rent in Cork, so she's going to chance taking the train home at some stage this week. She's not worried about meeting a Garda checkpoint along the way; it turns out, she's pretty damn good at lying.

She'll tell Siobhán now that she'll be home soon, she thinks, as she answers the call. First order of business when she gets there is to visit her mother. She's not sure what the likelihood of that is at the moment, but surely when a patient is in hospice care, allowances can be made.

She needs to tell her what she's found out, about Shane.

'Hello?'

Siobhán said there was nothing Ciara could do to bring him back, but she was wrong. She's brought Shane back to himself, to who he was before, in their memories. She's been able to correct them, to clean them, to make them accurate and true.

'Ciara?' Her sister's voice is faint, barely audible above the whipping wind. 'Can you hear me? Are you there?'

'I can barely hear y—'

'Ciara, it's Mam. She's about to go.'

Running.

Ciara is doing it before she even forms the intention to, holding the phone to her ear, shouting, 'Hang on, hang on, hang on …'

She's saying it to her sister, but willing her mother to, too.

As she runs back up the beach, up to the steps to the path and around the corner of some cement structure that she hopes, if she stands in its shadow, might block the wind.

'Siobhán?'

'You sound much better now.'

'Is she lucid?'

'I think she can hear me. She can't talk, but …'

'Is it just you there? Are you alone with her?'

'Yeah?'

'Put me on speaker.'

There's a rustling noise and then, when Siobhán speaks again, it has the amplified, echoey quality that assures Ciara that her mother is now listening too.

She takes a deep breath.

She bites back her tears.

'Mam,' she says, 'it's me. Ciara. There's something I need to tell you. It's … It's about Shane.'

Author Note

The first case of COVID-19 was reported in Ireland on 29 February 2020: a male who had travelled to an affected area of Italy returned here with the virus. On 9 March, all upcoming St Patrick's Day events were cancelled and on 12 March, it was announced that schools, childcare facilities and cultural institutions would close. These were followed by pubs three days later.

The first 'lockdown' was announced on 27 March. At the time, we didn't know it would only be the first or that it would stretch well into the summer. Initially we were told it would last for two weeks. All non-essential journeys were banned. All non-essential workers had to remain at home. There was to be no mixing with people who didn't live with you and vulnerable people had to 'cocoon' in their homes. In essence, the message was: stay at home except to purchase food or to take brief, individual exercise within a 2km radius of your residence. On 8 April, with Easter weekend looming, An Garda Síochána launched Operation *Fanacht* (Stay) to ensure compliance with a new law under the Health Act

1947: Section 31A – Temporary Restrictions (COVID 19) Regulations 2020. Breaches could incur a fine of up to €2,500 or even a jail sentence. Two days later, on 10 April, lockdown was extended for a further three weeks.

I spent this time alone in a tiny studio apartment in Dublin city centre that had a bed that came down from the wall. (Yes, just like Ciara's. My apartment was much, much nicer though!) I rewatched *Lost* and built LEGO and baked banana bread and had Zoom cocktails and posted Instagram stories and got the idea for this book. (You can still watch those Instagram stories in a 'Lockdown' highlight on my account, @cathryanhoward.) I didn't have to worry about home-schooling or losing my job or vulnerable relatives, and I was grateful for that every single day. Also, as a card-carrying introvert, there was a part of me that *liked* having to cancel everything and stay at home. But still, as time went on, I started to go more than a little stir-crazy.

On 1 May, our government announced a phased plan for reopening the country that would see schools remain closed until September and restrictions gradually lifting, beginning on 18 May. For now, the 'lockdown' would remain in place, except for one concession: from 5 May, the 2km-radius exercise limit would increase to 5km. I had steadfastly followed the rules from day one and so had not been to the beach (4km from my door) since restrictions began. Come Tuesday morning, I set an early alarm and was at the water's edge on a very cold and windy Sandymount Strand by eight a.m. – yes, just like Ciara.

In the early days of this pandemic, many writers took to social media and elsewhere to vow that they would *never* write about this in their books, that once this was over no one, including them, would ever want to think about it again. But back then, we had no idea that this event would change the world. And while I was locked down in Dublin, I had an idea for a story about a couple locked down in Dublin, for whom the strange, isolating circumstances of this new and uncertain world was just the opportunity they were waiting for – and I wanted to write it, so I did.

Across what turned out to be three lockdowns, these characters kept me company. My hope is that in a brighter, more hopeful world, their story has entertained you.

Dublin, Ireland

January 2021

Acknowledgements

Thank you to my agent Jane Gregory; my editors Sarah Hodgson and Stephanie Glencross; Penelope Killick, for sending life-changing emails; Casey King, Garda consultant extraordinaire; Andrea Carter, for answering random legal questions early on a Saturday morning; and everyone at David Higham, Blackstone Publishing, Corvus/Atlantic Books and Gill Hess. Thanks to Hazel Gaynor and Carmel Harrington for Nespresso-requiring WhatsApp audios, Quarantini boxes and Zoom chats (I probably *could* do this without you, but I wouldn't want to) and, as ever, thanks to Mum, Dad, John and Claire. Iain Harris, I hope you enjoy your dedication as much as you do flight-tracker apps, casual blazers and people messaging you to tell you they've seen your name in my books.

And finally: thank you to *you*, the reader. I thank you most of all.